Praise for *The*

M000030931

"A twisty, fast-paced novel--intrigue of the highest order. Highly recommended!"—*Ward Larsen, USA Today bestselling author of Assassin's Strike*

"Justin Lee is a must-read new talent."—*Mike Lawson, Edgar Award Nominated author of the Joe DeMarco series.*

"... packs a powerful punch with a looming terrorist threat, multiple kidnappings, unexpected killings and some high level political infighting. Lee keeps the reader guessing {until} the very end with a twist I never saw coming."—*Drew Yanno, bestselling author of In the Matter of Michael Vogel and The Smart One.*

"THE SILENT CARDINAL is a taut, complex thriller that grabs the reader on the opening page and refuses to let go until the last."—*James L. Thane, Author of South of the Deuce*

"Millions of lives hang in the balance in this fast-paced nail-biter. J. Lee delivers a thriller with constant twists and turns, taking readers on a thrill ride that is hard to put down."—*Steve Brigman, author of The Orphan Train*

"... Ben Siebert is back in action. *The Silent Cardinal* is a standalone novel, though, and it's a standout. ... Seibert fights a lethal enemy to unravel a deadly mystery."—*Pamela Wight, author of The Right Wrong Man and Twin Desires*

Fans of *The Hubley Case*, J. Lee's debut novel, will not be disappointed with his follow up thriller, *The Silent Cardinal.* Readers will cheer the return of former marine Ben Seibert, while enjoying the wild ride of espionage and murder in this taunt page-tuner."—*Alfred C. Martino, author of Pinned, Over The End Line, and Perfected By Girls*

✳✳✳

Praise for *The Hubley Case,* winner of the New York City Big Book Award And "Best Book" Award for Thrillers

"**A terrific debut...**"—Kyle Mills, #1 New York Times Bestselling Author

"*The Hubley Case* **is an enjoyable popular thriller helmed by a clear hero.**" — Foreword Review

"**For fans of this genre, this is still a worthwhile read. The writing is crisp and easy to read... the action portions of the book—where there is actual violence or the threat of violence—are particularly well-written and create real suspense.**" — Windy City Reviews

"*The Hubley Case* **is an entertaining, action packed thriller that I thoroughly enjoyed reading. Ben Siebert is another of today's superhuman characters. He is good at everything but still presents as a vulnerable and honorable human being – albeit one who is good at killing. I imagine we will be hearing more of Ben.**" — Promoting Crime Fiction

The Hubley Case **is an intriguing mystery thriller, and I was engaged throughout trying to unmask the man directing the deadly, mysterious, masterfully planned game. All in all, an enjoyable, manipulative, cunning tale of greed and murder. A Must Read!**" — Cross My Heart Writings & Reviews

The Silent Cardinal

J. Lee

Moonshine Cove Publishing, LLC

Abbeville, South Carolina U.S.A.

First Moonshine Cove edition 2021

ISBN: 9781952439063

Library of Congress LCCN: 2021902700

Book cover design by Scribe Freelance Book Design
Interior design by Moonshine Cove Staff

To Dad, the invincible hero of my childhood and beloved friend of my manhood. I can't put into words how much you mean to me.

Acknowledgments

Writing and publishing a book takes help from others, and there are a few authors with deadlines of their own who took the time to help me. Though it doesn't give them the thanks they deserve, I wanted to show my appreciation for: Mike Lawson, a real mentor; Kyle Mills, who taught me lessons eleven years ago that still prove true today; Ward Larsen, for his incredible support; Drew Yanno, for giving beyond what I could ask; Pam Wight, for her keen eye and candor; James Thane and Steve Brigman, for their support and efforts. And Alfred Martino, for both reviewing this book and calling a college kid almost twenty years ago to offer some valuable advice.

Getting this book here was very trying at times, in part because of things no one can control such as the pandemic. As such, I leaned on the encouragement a few fine gentlemen provided, probably more than they know. Steve Boswell, Rob Lee, Josh Heidelman, Brad Haar, Dave Olverson and Dave Pohlman...thanks for caring, guys.

I'd also like to thank, in no particular order, a few people who helped make this book what it is today:

Andy Lane, for being an awesome early reader and even better person.

Adrienne Sparks and Kristen Weber, for their edits and assistance.

Gene Robinson and the Moonshine Cove staff, for its partnership and assistance.

Steve Boswell, for being my biggest fan, giving so much of his time and energy, and accepting me into the family from day one.

My most beautiful bride: Kristen: for being the mind-blowingly fantastic mom I knew she'd be, ten wonderful years of marriage, shrewd editorial feedback, and bearing with a husband who has a tendency to pack ten pounds in a five-pound bag and then ask her to carry it. Love you, Prin.

Last but certainly not least, to all the readers and supporters out there who take the time to check out my books, contact me, spread the word, and be a source of inspiration. I know I can't list you all, but from close family members to those I haven't yet had the pleasure of meeting, I'm truly grateful for your support.

THE SILENT CARDINAL

cardinal : (kahr-dn-l): of prime importance; chief; principal

"Knowing what you want, and how to get it, this is the central power of the Cardinal bird."

—Universe of Symbolism

Prologue

"If you tell me, the twins will not be harmed."

"I swear," he choked out, "I don't know."

"Poor Lydia and Jessica…"

He sank into the chair's supple leather as perspiration oozed from his pores. His left hand clutched the cell phone and his right fist was balled, upturned next to the empty bottle of Voss.

Despite how crowded the trendy restaurant had become since he arrived ninety minutes earlier, he felt utterly alone. A solitary, helpless figure surrounded by throngs of boisterous Wednesday night diners.

"This is your final warning."

The voice was so formal. All business.

"Before your nine-year-old nieces suffer more than you can imagine."

And stoic. Cold. It finally dawned on him…this was going to happen.

"Don't you think I'd tell you if I knew anything?"

"Is Ben Siebert really worth it?" the voice asked.

It was the question he couldn't stop thinking about. He waved the waiter away and fought back an overwhelming urge to jump from his seat and bolt for the door. Call the deal off and run like hell. Sprint past the hostess stand and dash through the shiny metal door that stood a mere ten feet from the table.

But the rules were clear.

"This was your decision," the voice whispered.

When the line went dead he pressed the phone to his ear, hoping for a callback he knew wouldn't come. The time to change course had long ago come and gone. There was but one way now, and the voice was right: it was the one he chose.

But how could the right choice feel so wrong?

At 7:58 he tugged at his navy blazer, twisting his torso ninety degrees towards the floor-to-ceiling windows on his left. He grabbed the wooden pepper mill and gripped it tightly in front of the window. Then he searched for her face.

When he spotted her walking up Wacker Drive, fifty feet away, his mind overpowered his body. Anticipation of the future replaced concerns of the present. His nagging cough ceased, perpetual migraine subsided, and the brick wedged into his chest disappeared.

She was truly beautiful. So young. So innocent-looking. Her face was smooth, her long brown hair billowing in the breeze. She approached the restaurant with the same pep the Millennials in it had and could've easily passed for an innocuous bystander.

Yet her presence spelled ruin.

The three loud bangs emerged from nowhere. They were rapid, and the bullets shattered the elegant windows and penetrated his body before anyone around knew what happened. But soon after, fraternization turned to frenzy as horrified patrons ducked under tables and sprinted towards exits. They bumbled over one another, wailing for help and taking cover. Glass shattered as the stampede bumped into tables scurrying to safety. The unbridled joy so pervasive seconds earlier had vanished.

Yet he remained seated. Motionless and silent. Again per the instructions, but now by choice as well. He actually felt peaceful, for the first time in many years. He offered his final prayers to God and waited for his last breath. At first he felt warm all over, like a hot bath penetrating every pore. Chills followed as blood exited him like a river flowing from a lake. He looked up one more time at her soft, gorgeous face of doom.

Her eyes were filled with tears.

Part I

1

The voice in his ear sounded scrambled, or at least heavily muffled. Maybe he heard wrong. Or maybe the rain dancing on the roof of his car wasn't as gentle as it seemed and it made him hear things. Or maybe this was some sick joke from an old college buddy and the punchline was coming.

Robert Stevens, FBI Special Agent in Charge of the Chicago Field Office, jerked the gray Ford Fusion across two gridlocked lanes to the shoulder just before his exit at Western Avenue, evoking a series of honks and hand gestures from tense Chicago commuters stuck in the brutal morning rush. He turned the wipers off, cut the Bluetooth and jacked up the volume on his iPhone, but he soon learned it wasn't a bad connection.

Or the rain.

Or a joke.

"Who is this?"

"That is irrelevant."

"How did you get this number?"

"Another impertinent question."

Yes, it was definitely a scrambler of some sort. Over twenty years in the Bureau told Robert it was a good one at that. Very hi-tech. The voice sounded deep, heavy like a man's, but he couldn't be sure with the distortion. Regardless, it certainly didn't explain how this person had gotten his personal cell phone number. Or knew that he was driving to Chicago's FBI Field Office on Roosevelt Road.

Or that his daughter had called from Phoenix six minutes earlier...

Caller ID said UNKNOWN in classic unhelpful fashion. The remote trace he'd activated via text from his business phone was in process at the office right now. He checked his watch's second hand; it would be about twenty more seconds until a pinpoint location was established. Until then, he needed to stay calm and keep the voice on the phone.

"It is 7:56 right now, Mr. Stevens. I strongly suggest you stay on the Eisenhower to get to the destination no later than nine o'clock. Go alone. Do not call for backup. Do not alert onsite security. Upon arrival, precisely follow the instructions I've given to you."

"You can't tell me this and then say no backup."

"Yet that's exactly what I did."

"What's this all about?"

"Disobey in any way and there will be consequences."

"I won't disobey."

"And stop checking that Samsung on the seat next to you. You'll learn soon enough that your office's triangulation metrics were ineffective. Stick it back in your pocket and get moving, Mr. Stevens. There are too many lives at stake."

Robert's head snapped up and his eyes scanned the periphery. Cars crawled along I-290 in the heavy traffic and wet conditions, no helicopters or small planes were in the adjacent air space, commuters seemed to take no more interest of his car pulled over than what would be typical. But if they weren't watching from the outside, did that mean there was a camera on the inside? Nothing unusual came up on the morning security scan of his vehicle, but that felt less than reassuring.

He perused the interior of the vehicle. Attempting to conceal his search from whomever was watching him, he kept his head straight but slowly moved his eyes from one side of the car to the other. But he didn't notice anything unusual. There were dozens of places to conceal a small camera, and he didn't have enough time to look. Or to ponder how a camera could get past the scan. Or how someone could've gotten access to his FBI-issued vehicle in the first place.

"This is simply a warning, Mr. Stevens. Don't make it a tragedy."

Just like that, the voice was gone. As he expected, *69 was ineffective and there was no useful information in his phone's call history. Uncertain but believing he was in fact being watched, he tried to refrain from revealing too much emotion when the beep from the other phone went off. He read the text:

Trace unsuccessful. Multiple locations falsely identified.

There was nothing else to do.

Robert Stevens reached behind his passenger seat as directed by the voice, grabbed his portable siren and flung it atop the Fusion's roof with a magnetic clunk. The siren screamed as he sped eastbound towards Chicago's Ogilvie Transportation Center.

2

Chicago's Ogilvie Transportation Center served three of Metra's Union Pacific commuter rail lines and occupied two full lower levels of the Citigroup Center near the heart of downtown. Its main entrance on Madison Street boasted an elaborate dark-green metal frame and ten-story glass doors that stretched from the sidewalk at their base to the innermost of four stratified Ω-shaped window cutouts one hundred feet off the ground at their top. Every day, more than one hundred thousand commuters used its sixteen different tracks and eight island platforms to catch a train ride between Chicago and its suburbs.

Robert zipped past a line of taxis lurking like vultures at Canal and Madison as much as an overweight, out-of-shape sixty-two year old could and left the car running, siren off, in the Drop Off zone at the front of the building. Despite the surgery he had a few years back to repair a ruptured patellar tendon after a nasty spill off the diving board, his knee still throbbed as he ran to push through the revolving door. Flashing his FBI credentials to the Metra security guard at the desk who looked fully prepared to call Lincoln Towing, he wiped the sweat off his brow and limped through the pain.

Crowds were thinning, but Ogilvie was never empty during the day. At eight forty-five exactly, convenience store lines had dwindled and uneven stacks of rummaged-through newspapers lay outside the Hudson News to his right. Burrito Beach, home to his favorite chicken enchilada, was straight ahead past the escalators and part of a food court that offered a cacophony of aromas.

As instructed, Robert didn't sprint or lollygag, but found a pace somewhere in between. From the outside, he wanted to look like any other anxious traveler running late for his train. All the tracks were on the second floor, so he weaved between two young women to board the escalator, fruitlessly scanning the first floor below to see if he could find anything that would help him piece together where the scrambled voice he'd heard earlier was coming from. Peering over the railing, he noted a handful of teenage girls walking into Claire's and a middle-aged couple hand-in-hand coming out of Arts & Artisans. Because of the hour it wasn't terribly noisy, but there were still echoes of chatter coming from every direction.

When the TRACK 9 and TRACK 10 revolving doors came into view, he turned his attention to the east end of the second floor. Past Fannie May and next to GNC, he saw the dreaded sign as he stepped off the escalator and briskly walked towards the storefront.

The large, navy letters spelling out "Bath & Body Works" were mounted to wooden paneling and illuminated by nine overhead white spotlights. Display boards in the window advertised "Buy 3, Get 3 FREE" three-wick candles and "3 for $12" hand soap promotions next to the glass door entryway. Behind those displays were the cabinets.

The white storage cabinets just off the ground stood about two-and-a-half feet tall, serving as the base for large chiffoniers used to display product. Candles were featured on the dresser-like pieces of furniture. He hurried to the display and reached for the shiny metal knob to open the leftmost cabinet. Locked.

"Can I help you?" asked a twenty-something-year-old black woman in a blue-checkered apron and tan pants.

"Please open this," he replied, pointing to the cabinet and flashing his credentials.

The surprised woman fumbled for the right key for nearly thirty seconds as he watched her, adding to the pressure she must've felt. When the white door finally swung open, he squatted down in spite of his patellar tendon's objection.

"Give me some space," Robert said with a quick wave of his arm.

"May I ask what you are doing?"

"Ma'am, please," he implored with widened eyes and a forward thrust of his head.

She didn't object and he was left alone to remove fourteen different lotion dispensers of varying scents. He tossed them on the floor one at a time until he saw the large wad of brown packing paper covering the height of the internal storage space. Instinctively holding his breath, he slowly removed it from the surprisingly deep cabinet.

The backpack was exactly as described: Wenger brand, Swiss Army Gear model, black and red with several shiny zippers. Metal carabineer connected to the front flap with adjustable straps along either side. Six compartments of varying sizes, including a laptop holder, two side pockets with vent holes and an elastic mesh chamber designed for a water bottle.

It looked like a standard Nalgene. Hard plastic. Royal blue with a black top. Thirty-two ounce capacity. Made in the USA.

It was the clear liquid that filled it, which he knew wasn't water, that concerned him. An opaque black rubber tube ran from the bottom of the water bottle up through a hand-drilled hole in its cap, leading to the backpack's laptop compartment. He gently held the roughly quarter-inch hose-like tube between his thumb and index finger and felt nothing but standard, room temperature rubber as he traced it up to the zipper.

He opened it slowly and peeked inside.

Oh my God.

As if on cue, his personal cell phone began to ring.

UNKNOWN was making good on his assurances.

"Stevens."

"Get moving," the scrambled voice directed him in a way that reminded him of an angry Darth Vader.

He muted the phone, grabbed the backpack and quickly exited, adding to the bewilderment — or maybe the relief — of the poor sales associate. Truth was, he never looked back to see. Hanging a left out of the store, he booked it to the end of the hallway. Another left and he saw the walkway bridge.

It stood fourteen-and-a-half feet off the ground and connected Ogilvie to Two North Riverside Plaza, marked by a gold sign with stenciled lettering above its east end. No one was using it, and he motored past a Pret a Manger eatery to his right and Citibank ATMs to his left, scurrying towards the middle of the glass wall side. A series of intricate, white metal frames lined the top of the bridge and grey, black and white tile overlaid its floor. Standing in front of the window and looking towards Union Station, he gently placed the backpack on the ground and unmuted the phone.

"As you can see, we are very serious."

"Why are you doing this?"

"The device by your foot is twice as powerful as the bombs used at the Boston Marathon. Its magnitude and proximity to load bearing walls would most certainly cause the building to collapse minutes after detonation."

Before he could speak, his thoughts were trampled by more deeply-spoken instructions. Talking with UNKNOWN felt like being in an Aaron Sorkin film: rapid-fire dialogue where no one ever gets to finish a sentence.

"It's not on an automatic timer and the bomb squad will find it straightforward to deactivate. Instructions are located in the backpack's electrical cord storage compartment in case they run into issues."

"Why are you telling me this?"

"As I said earlier, this is a warning. We could have detonated it during the thick of rush hour and there's nothing anyone could have done to stop us."

Robert merely stared out the walkway window, silently acknowledging that the voice was right.

"When we hang up, cross the street and walk to Union Station. Head down the stairs and go in through the Madison

18

Street Entrance you're staring at right now. On Track 9, you'll find a train waiting for its 9:35 departure to Grayslake, scheduled to arrive at 10:56 and currently on time. Passengers began boarding nineteen minutes ago. Locate the lavatory nearest the locomotive cab. In its service compartment beneath the sink, you'll find a similar backpack and device. Its deactivation protocol is identical."

"This is nuts," Stevens murmured, almost more to himself than to the voice.

"You are to keep this quiet, Mr. Stevens. Our intent isn't to alarm the public or kill innocent people." The voice intensified. "If we read about this in the papers, we'll really give the reporters something to write about."

"It's not your intent to alarm the public or kill innocent people? You're planting bombs in public places!" Stevens exclaimed in a whisper, pressing the phone even harder to his ear as if that accomplished anything.

The voice returned to stoicism. "Obviously we did not intend to harm anyone today."

"What if an employee had unknowingly stumbled upon the bomb? What if malfunctioned and prematurely detonated?"

"They didn't find the device you're holding and they won't find the one on that train. Any public outcry that ensues will be your fault. And you will suffer the consequences."

"What do you want?"

"You know exactly what you have to do. If you don't, a similar contraption will detonate in another very public place."

"So much for not killing innocent people."

"Your deadline is clear. Twenty-three hundred hours next Wednesday night, Mr. Stevens."

"I'm not the right person to talk to about this."

"Of course you are. We'll be watching."

3

Wednesday, May 5

The subject's name was Benjamin Nicholas Siebert. But FBI GS-7 junior agent Roy Dietrich and his partner had been told he probably wouldn't be using a name at all tonight.

The dossier provided on Siebert was extremely thick, yet gapingly porous. Roy read it for the third time from the Chevy Traverse's front seat and still couldn't find anything straightforward about the man. Thirty-seven, widower, and single dad to a twenty-two-year old son. Honorably discharged from the Marines a decade ago with no known service since, yet labeled an active anti-terrorism subject matter expert and combat specialist. No stated occupation or estimated household income, yet assumed to be independently wealthy based upon spending activity and known assets. Identified as an ongoing Person of Interest on the national level. Family history left blank altogether. Religion identified merely as Christian. The only recreational activities identified, golf and racquetball, were blatantly generic. No formal aliases listed but confirmed to have used over thirty pseudonyms. No documented connection to the Bureau, yet requested by name by the Special Agent in Charge.

It was very atypical for SAIC Stevens to be involved in a citizen pickup much less give the order directly, and Roy could tell that the file had been stripped of several details before being given to them. He wasn't permitted to ask why, but it was clear to him that it contained only the information deemed necessary to find Benjamin Siebert. Not a damned thing else.

"What's this place again?" his partner asked, furrowing his brow.

"It's a non-profit organization that partners with local churches to give homeless people a warm meal and place to sleep."

"Screening process can't be too rigorous."

"Affirmative. And security is lax. Most sites don't even have a guard."

"And they think this guy is here?" his partner asked with unmasked incredulousness.

"So I was told," Roy replied, though he'd had the same thought.

"Why?"

"Apparently he volunteers a lot. At least twice a month."

"But doesn't use his name?" His partner again displayed his skepticism.

"I don't know. Anyway, let's go."

"Should we bring our weapons?"

"Chief said Siebert wouldn't be hostile."

"If he's so agreeable, why don't they just ask him to come in? Why do they need us?"

His partner's questions remained unanswered as they walked up salt-damaged crack-filled concrete steps so old they'd pulled away from the walkway. Roy had been instructed not to make a scene, and that made the brief conversation with the grandmotherly-looking woman taking names at the folding table in the First Presbyterian Church fairly straightforward. At first she was alarmed when she saw their FBI badges, but then she just wanted to help. They scanned the volunteer list and confirmed there was no Benjamin Siebert. Then they were given full "access" to roam the grounds freely, as if they really needed her permission.

At five past nine, dinner had already been served and a few volunteers were finishing up the dishes in the kitchen, adjacent to the cafeteria. They walked through the hallway past an empty sanctuary and up the stairs to the school's gymnasium, where the cots were arranged in even rows. Over 50 people had sought shelter in May. Roy wondered how many came in February.

Lights out started at seven but several "guests" — as the organization referred to them — were sitting in folding chairs in the adjacent hallway, talking to one another and the volunteers. It surprised him how much the guests looked like average Joes, a stark reminder that most everyone is just one bad break away from being homeless. Peeking their heads inside the quiet gym, his eyes had just acclimated to the darkness when he saw him.

The man stood about six foot four, fit and toned but not the physique of a bodybuilder. He wore light brown khakis and a plain black T-shirt with gym shoes. Tucked in a corner under a basketball hoop, he was setting up another cot, turning the metal frame over to place the mattress on top with impressive silence.

His nametag said Kurt Hayton but his face matched the picture in the dossier. Clean-shaven, light brown hair, almost buzzed, not styled. Fairly light skinned, no tattoos or piercings. This was their man.

"Excuse me, sir. Can we have a word?"

"Who are you?" Siebert whispered, wiping his hands with a towel before shoving it into his pocket, its end draping over his pants. Siebert looked him straight in the eye, benign yet laser-focused. He motioned for Siebert to follow and exited the side door leading to a stairwell.

"You are Mr. Siebert, correct?"

"Who's asking?" Siebert said flatly.

"We know you use pseudonyms for just about everything. Don't know why you'd do it for charity work, but that's not my business," Roy said with a shrug of his bony shoulders.

"Since you brought it up…what exactly is your business?" Siebert inquired, a bit more impatiently.

"We're with the FBI," he replied, flashing his credentials.

"And?"

"And Robert Stevens would like your assistance."

"Then let him ask for it."

"He's tried to contact you several times."

"I've been busy."

"Can you please accompany us?" The request came out more like a child asking a parent to attend a sleepover, and Roy mentally chided himself.

"Now?"

"Yes, sir," he answered, secretly hoping the conversation didn't escalate. What did escalation even look like with this guy?

"I haven't talked to Robert in a year. What's this about?"

"I honestly don't know," Roy shrugged. Man, he was awful at this fieldwork crap.

"Then I'm not going anywhere."

"Sir, my orders are to ask you nicely first," he replied, concealing his right hand tremor.

"And then?" Siebert replied, stepping towards him fearlessly.

"Mr. Siebert, please."

Please what, Roy wondered. Please don't punch me in the face and knock me unconscious with one hit? Please don't tell SAIC Stevens I'm no good at this? Please don't make me look like a Nancy in front of my partner? Who, by the way, may as well have stayed in the car.

"Let me get this straight. You were sent to find me at nine o'clock on Tuesday night and you don't know why? You're not a field agent, are you?" Siebert said more like a statement.

"No, sir."

"Administrative specialist?" Siebert asked, as the left corner of his mouth upturned ever so slightly.

"Yes sir."

"GS-7?"

"Yes sir, but I'm up for GS-9 next week if I play my cards right."

"What statue does Robert have in his office?"

"Sir?"

"Don't sir me. If you've been to Robert's office, you know there's a certain item next to his desk that's impossible to forget. I strongly suggest you tell me about it right now. If you don't, this conversation is going to take a drastic turn."

Siebert's piercing glare sent shivers down his spine. Roy was supposed to be the authority here. He was the one who represented the law. And yet Siebert had this formidable quality about him. Like he was more capable than his opponents, or had nothing to lose. Or maybe just never lost. Maybe it was the way his unblinking gaze made it feel like Siebert was moving on him, even when he was standing still.

"It's a full-size kegerator."

"Pressurized CO2 tank and everything. What does the sign say?"

"Pour a proper Guinness or get out." Man was he glad he'd read that sign.

Siebert didn't respond, just returned to setting up the cot frame. As the seconds dragged on Roy wanted nothing more than to just leave this man be, to get the hell out of there. Maybe his boss was right; maybe he really wasn't cut out for fieldwork after all.

"I guess I'd better go see Robert," Siebert finally said. "I wouldn't want to get in the way of your promotion."

"Thank you, sir." He didn't try to hide his relief.

"Is there anything else you can tell me?"

"Only that Mr. Stevens made it clear we had to find you ASAP."

"How'd he do that?"

"Told us we couldn't sleep until we did," Roy replied.

Siebert chuckled as he returned to his task, laying a thin white pillow on a neatly folded navy blanket atop the assembled cot.

"I drove here. I'll meet you at the office."

"I'm sorry sir…" his voice trailed off.

"He's offsite, isn't he?" Siebert knew the drill.

"Yes sir."

It should have been comforting that Siebert was familiar with the protocol, that he seemed compliant enough, and that the assignment to bring him in was going to be successful. Overall it was a win. And yet the whole thing felt terribly unnerving.

"You're not permitted to tell me where, right?" Siebert said with a punctuated nod.

"I'm afraid not, Mr. Siebert."

Afraid indeed.

4

The thirty-two-minute drive to a nondescript business park just outside Elk Grove Village was both uneventful and uninformative. The GS-7 behind the wheel either really didn't know anything or was impressively good at pretending he didn't. He must be a good kid, since Robert evidently trusted him, and being up for General Schedule 9 meant he had a Master's Degree or equivalent, so the intelligence was supposedly there too. The only evidence to the contrary — he'd learned on the car ride — was that the junior agent had joined the FBI hoping to one day work in Washington politics. Despite that fact, Ben was convinced the kid meant no harm and was just following orders. That didn't change the reality, however, that at just before nine o'clock he still had no idea why he was here instead of at home in his microfiber La-Z-Boy.

A habit as regular as breathing to him, Ben studied his surroundings. The office building off Touhy Avenue looked like any other. Aged red brick, white roof stained with dirt, seventies-era build, single story, front and back exits. He surveyed the adjacent area and noted a parked Dodge Charger he could hotwire in twenty seconds if need be. Should he need to alert someone to call for help, there was a Holiday Inn a quarter mile north near Landmeier Road and some open fast food restaurants roughly the same distance south by Estes Avenue. The business park was right off Highway 83, a major north-south thoroughfare that would give him plenty of runway if he needed to jet, with both directional entry ramps accessible from Touhy. Its un-gated front and back entrances, accessibility and proximity to public establishments certainly suggested that its value tonight was for secrecy rather than ambush.

But he would be ready just in case.

They walked through an unlocked front door and darkened lobby into a tiny conference room. The windowless space was dimly lit with dusty overhead incandescent bulbs covered in dirt and dried dead bugs. An unused projector screen hung down at the front.

Robert Stevens sat alone at the ten-person conference table half-covered with papers and folders, scribbling something on a bright yellow legal pad. He looked much as Ben remembered him — mid-sixties, six feet tall, two hundred fifty pounds, certainly not obese but a bit of a larger gut, white work shirtsleeves rolled up, tie removed, glasses on, eyes down. Robert didn't even notice they were there until the GS-7 politely interrupted his focus.

"Sir..."

"Ben...thanks for coming," Robert said softly, wiping heavy, baggy eyes and getting up to shake his hand.

"Not sure I had much choice. Roy here made it very clear I was coming one way or the other."

Robert chuckled at what they both knew was sarcasm. The junior agent didn't follow.

"How did you know my name?" the bewildered Roy asked, certain that when he provided Siebert his credentials at the church his name was unexposed.

"Good work, son," Robert replied with a hint of a smile. "That'll do for now. You go ahead and head on home. I'll call you."

"Thank you, sir," Roy answered before high-tailing it out of there.

"Robert, what's with this place?" Ben asked, collapsing into a ripped leather chair that leaned to the left like Pisa when he tried to get comfortable.

"This place?"

"Isn't it a little dumpy for the Special Agent in Charge of the FBI Chicago Field Office? I wouldn't be surprised if this dinosaur had asbestos in the walls."

"Since when are you concerned with appearances?" Robert responded while leaning back in his own chair to feel Pisa for himself.

"Generally speaking, I'd say to each his own. But when you have some whippersnapper drag me here in the middle of the night without telling me why…"

"It's been a while, Ben. How are you?"

Seeing Robert Stevens face-to-face, Ben couldn't help but think of Special Agent Nikki Benton and the events that had transpired a few years earlier. He'd first spoken with Robert over the phone after learning he was Nikki's old boss at the Phoenix FBI office. At the time, Nikki was heading up the investigation of his best friend's murder and making a series of questionable decisions. As a result, Ben needed feedback from someone who knew her well. A Marine buddy vouched for Robert's character and put them in touch, and the rest was history. Robert had proven reliable from day one. So much so that when the case finally ended and Benton's boss was identified as a traitor and killed in a warehouse explosion, Ben pulled some strings and got Robert transferred to Chicago to take over as Special Agent in Charge.

Of course, that all transpired before Ben and Nikki became a romantic couple following the case, totally changing the dynamic between the three of them. When their engagement abruptly ended, two things happened: Ben's heart got broken and Robert, understandably, sided with Nikki. They hadn't spoken since.

"I've been OK. How about you? How's Chi-Town treating you?"

"I miss Arizona winters."

"Wimp."

"Don't you mean old man?" Robert asked with a chuckle, easing the tension and giving Ben a sense of relief they could pick up where they left off. But then he continued with, "Talk to Nikki lately?"

Ben paused.

"Why am I here, Robert?"

"I don't mean to pry. I just —"

"Robert…why am I here?"

"This morning I got a phone call on my personal cell…"

Robert proceeded to tell Ben about his initial conversation in the car on I-290 and the events that followed. The SAIC tried to make it clear that not a detail was being spared as he recapped everything from the drive to Ogilvie up to the successful dismantling of both bombs. Ben knew Robert did it in order to hammer home the point that if he was to be brought into something, he had to be brought in all the way. But there was an obvious gap…Ben could tell Robert was holding something back.

"Any idea how they ditched the trace?" Ben asked.

"Probably false directional antennas or some other intermediary transmission layers. We weren't on the line long and cell phones aren't attached to a switch, so it takes the remote trace program longer to nail down a signal."

"How do you know they called from a cell?"

"I don't…not for sure, anyway." Robert then looked up, his eyes pointing towards the ceiling, as if trying to remember something. "But they were definitely watching me, live, and the car's been scrubbed clean at the lab. No cameras or any other surveillance devices were located. So while it's possible they were in a building parallel to me on the interstate using binoculars, the far more likely bet is they were mobile."

"How confident are you that the car is clean?"

"The FBI's top Midwest anti-surveillance team did a comprehensive search and analysis of my car. Six people went through it inch-by-inch with the best technology on the planet, much of it unknown to the public, and concluded the car was clean. And you know they took it seriously. I'm their boss' boss."

"Plus, if these folks did somehow slip one past all that, we've got bigger problems."

"Let's not even go there," Robert held up his hand.

"Did you find the other bomb?"

"In the exact location on the exact train they specified. Identical design and build. Same backpack."

"Both explosives were deactivated?"

"Precisely the way the voice said they could be. The bomb squad neutralized the devices and Forensics has them now. I don't expect to learn much. These guys don't strike me as the kind that leave their DNA on the trigger."

"Anything traceable?"

"Nada," Robert answered, shaking his head. "The explosive was a composition of very common products."

"So they're technically proficient and well-financed."

"It would appear so," Robert flung his reading glasses onto the table in frustration, sighing loudly as he tilted his head towards the ground.

"Any idea how they got past security?"

"What security?" Robert nearly shouted. "There aren't any metal detectors or 3D body scanners at either of Chicago's transportation centers, much less the suburban stations."

"What about cameras?"

"CCTV surveillance cameras at Ogilvie don't show anything worth seeing."

"I assume you're running facial recognition software on everyone who went into and out of the store?"

"Three hits so far. A guy who's been taking the train to work for fifteen years buying a gift for his wife, and a young couple playing hooky from work for a day in the city."

"Only three people?"

"Place opens at seven but not too many people buy lotion early in the morning. Four others went in but we're having a hard time positively identifying them because of crappy camera angles."

"What about surveillance inside the store?"

"There aren't any cameras."

"Say what?"

"You'd be surprised. Train station convenience stores are much more vulnerable than you think. There are 23,000 cameras on CTA buses in the city, but the security at Bath & Body works in Ogilvie is pretty lax."

"What about the train? Any eyes on that?"

"It was a rush hour train on a weekday."

"So…"

"So," Robert snapped, "it was already on its fourth run of the day, most recently coming from Fox Lake. Departed at six-thirty sharp and made eight stops en route to Union Station. Far too many opportunities for us to nail down when it happened."

Ben leaned back in Pisa and considered launching into even more questions, but the overarching one begged an answer first.

"Robert…I can appreciate the severity of this situation…"

"But you want to know what the hell this has to do with you."

He nodded.

Robert was about to respond when a voice Ben never expected to hear again emerged from the shadow.

"Because whoever did this assured Robert they'd detonate a bomb for real if we don't execute Bill Knoble by eleven o'clock next Wednesday night."

5

Susan Reynolds eyed Ben Siebert with very mixed emotions. As her brain recalled her previous interactions with him, her stomach shifted.

The former Marine looked much as she remembered when she first met him while working undercover on the Peter Hubley case two years ago. Hubley's widow had asked Ben to find out who killed her husband, and Ben's fierce loyalty had planted him right in the middle of the investigation, at one point even considered a suspect. She remembered how Ben's youthful, clean-shaven baby face gave off a boy scout like appearance even in his mid-forties. He spoke softly and smiled often. Her first impression of him back then was what it would still be today: gentle, quiet, and smart...the kind of man you hoped your daughter brought home one day.

And yet she'd learned over the course of the investigation that Ben Siebert was the most determined and driven person she'd encountered in over three decades of experience in the intelligence business. Once this man set his mind to something, it was going to happen. He tracked down criminals that not even the CIA could locate, and then administered justice in a way that Moses himself would say was too eye-for-an-eye.

She remembered how Dominick Riddle, the man responsible for Hubley's savage murder, had been found murdered in his Venice bungalow with over four hundred poisonous bullet ants still crawling on and through his rotting corpse. Best she could tell Seibert hadn't received any assistance from the CIA, NSA, FBI or any other government entity. He was operating as a lone vigilante of sorts, with a fraction of the resources that any one of those organizations had, yet somehow he found the fugitive responsible for murdering an entire

SWAT team when the entire intelligence community could not. Ben never admitted to it, of course.

Then again, she'd never asked.

To reconcile the fact Robert had pushed for voluntarily seeking such a dangerous man's help, she reminded herself that Ben had never — to the best of her knowledge — brought violence upon someone who didn't deserve it. His actions were sometimes severe, yet always justifiable. At heart he was a man who preferred peace despite having an uncanny knack for battle; a man who had endured great hardship after losing his wife and supporting his adopted son the only way he knew how; a man who desired more than anything to live quietly in the very small company of family and friends.

If she knew Ben would always be on her side, maybe he wouldn't scare her so much. Or maybe he would. Surveilling him had never worked; he was a ghost until he didn't want to be. He was also always a step ahead of everyone at obtaining information, and even she wasn't sure how he pulled it off.

But it was determination that was truly remarkable. Once his mind was made up, the train was out the station and there was no stopping it. Which would be great...if he worked for the CIA or the FBI. But as a loner, a wild card, a freelancer not for hire but willing to pick and choose his causes, he could be more of a liability than an asset. She still doubted Robert's decision to bring him in on this, but desperate times really did call for desperate measures.

"Susan Reynolds, it's been a long time," Ben finally responded. His eyes shifted towards her slowly, then halted with a piercing gaze like a searchlight suddenly finding its target.

"How are you, Ben?"

"I was doing better sixty minutes ago."

"I know the feeling," Susan said with a deep sigh.

"Still working undercover?"

"Those were the days. I was sorry to hear about Nikki."

"One thing at a time. Why is the CIA in the FBI's jurisdiction?"

"Terrorists able to obtain an FBI Special Agent in Charge's personal cell number and surveil him qualify as gray areas, don't you think?"

"Who said they were terrorists?"

"They threatened to detonate a bomb if we didn't meet their demands. That's terrorism in my book," she furrowed her brow.

"Fair point. But it still doesn't explain why you're here."

"I called her," Robert interjected, still seated at the ten-person table. Ben swiveled his head around slowly.

"The FBI and CIA working together...what's the world coming to?"

"It happens more than you think," she answered just before a truck horn blared from what felt like just outside the office building. She and Robert both jolted and snapped their necks. Ben didn't stir one iota.

"What does Bill Knoble have to do with these people?" Ben asked with a straight face, void of any expression whatsoever.

"Funny you ask. We were hoping you could tell us."

"Sorry to burst your bubble," Ben replied, just as deadpanned.

"William T. Knoble, Attorney at Law," she read from the dossier resting on her black bi-fold writing pad. "Fifty-four years old, practicing law since his early twenties. Stated concentration is personal injury, but he's done it all over his thirty-year career. Malpractice, health, international, real estate, family, bankruptcy and even a little civil rights. Sounds like a real ambulance chaser."

"Or a wealth of experience," Ben said.

"Undergrad at Western Illinois in Macomb. Majored in kegstanding, minored in Sociology. Went straight to law school at Southern Illinois University Carbondale after that, specialized in Litigation and Dispute Resolution."

"Is there a reason you're giving me his resume?"

"Was in the lower quadrant of his graduating class."

"You know what they call the guy who graduates last in his class from law school?"

"Took a job at Berger & Associates in St. Louis. One of the shadiest firms I've ever had the displeasure to read about. Over a dozen counter lawsuits filed against it in six years, didn't pay its bills or employees, filed for bankruptcy three years after Knoble joined. Closed up shop a few months later. Great place for him to cut his teeth."

"I'm sure he wanted his employer to go under," Ben replied with an exaggerated grin, exposing a dimple on his right cheek.

"Then he moves to Chicago and opens his practice. William T. Knoble Law Firm. Actually started out pretty prosperously, built up a decent client base and reputation focused on personal injury and small claims. Then he fell into the Berger mantra and started chasing ambulances… and anything in a skirt."

"He's not the first."

"The guy even looks like a shyster. Greasy hair, permanent squint. Yet it always looks like he's staring right at you. Lots of facial creases in all the wrong places. Gaunt-like six feet tall, one hundred seventy pounds soaking wet. Down from two hundred a few years ago."

"What's your point?"

"Just providing some context."

"You obviously already know I'm a…business partner of his, otherwise I wouldn't be here. But if you dragged me here to defend him or rationalize his behavior, you're barking up the wrong tree."

"That's just it, Ben," she softened her tone, closing the bi-fold. "We know. We know because of what you did two years ago…and how you did it."

"I'm not following."

"We know Knoble was at his peak of moral deficiency when you first met him. That he was representing a client named

Barry Lee Richard, and that coincidentally enough Barry Lee hasn't been seen since his acquittal. We know back then Knoble spent his days getting wife beaters like Barry Lee off with a slap on the wrist and sexually abusing his own staff, and his nights drunk as a skunk doing the same thing to bar patrons and servers."

"Get to the point, Susan."

"Right after he met you, somewhat miraculously, he turned everything around. New office, new clients, new creed. Sobered up, got religion, changed his ways, seemingly for the long haul. You call it being a business partner, others might call it giving the guy the hard kick in the ass he needed."

"People really can change, Susan."

"Spare me, Benjamin. Someone out there with the means to do so has promised to kill a lot of innocent folks unless we kill Bill Knoble first. No explanation as to why, no request as to how. They just want him dead. By a specific time, on a specific day."

"And what exactly do you want me to do about it?"

"We don't have time for games. Or to pretend you weren't the reason for his incredible transformation. Want to know why you're here? Robert, play the tape."

Robert retrieved the handheld black recorder from his shirt pocket and pressed PLAY. Susan watched Ben's face as he absorbed the words, quite certain he felt what she'd felt ten hours earlier, though Ben gave nothing away. His demeanor remained stoic, the blank expression on his face preventing a clear read.

"That's why you're here, Ben."

"You record all your phone calls?" Ben asked Robert.

"Standard bureau protocol when Caller ID is blank."

"Unreal."

"*Ben...*" she said.

"I heard. Twenty-three hundred hours next Wednesday night."

"We've got eight days and..." she tapped her watch, "...ninety minutes to figure out why these people want Bill Knoble dead. If we don't..."

"Think they're from Chicago?" Ben asked.

"What makes you ask that?"

"They called I-290 'the Eisenhower.'"

"It's a national designation," she replied, shrugging her shoulders.

Ben turned to Robert. "Did you know that before you moved here?"

"I can't say I did," Robert nearly whispered.

"Not enough," she replied, shaking her head. "It's not a secret outside of Chicago. It's on some of the road signs. I think even some GPS systems use it."

"Fair enough. Plus, they could be jerking our chain."

"So what do you think?"

"That it doesn't make any sense."

"Which part?"

"These people somehow snuck a forty-pound explosive into Ogilvie Transportation Center and simultaneously planted one on an active train. Yet they need your help killing a no-name civilian attorney?"

"What are you getting at?" she asked.

"I think it's pretty obvious. It would've been a lot easier for them to kill Knoble, yet they want you to do it. Why?"

"We're trying to figure that out."

"And why didn't they detonate one of the bombs?"

"Excuse me?" Robert interjected with a confused stare.

"Why go to the trouble of setting all this up just to warn you and call it off? I'm guessing it's not out of the goodness of their hearts. Can you pass me a water?"

"Scare tactics?" Robert answered as he handed Ben a bottle.

"They're not more-bark-than-bite kind of people. Why take the risk?"

"To get our attention," she said, rolling up her sleeves. Ben's request for water reminded her how hot it was in here.

"They could've done that with a sniper and one poor schmuck walking down the street. Yet for some reason they wanted you to know how capable they are, that they could pull this off right under your noses. Why?"

"Ego trip?"

"That doesn't fit with their insistence this not go public."

Neither she nor Robert offered a response, and Ben finally showed at least a hint of emotion.

"C'mon guys. You're supposed to be the experts, but instead you've got me worried that my hard-earned tax dollars are going to waste. Generally lunatics are egocentric and want the world scared of them. Power trips are very common with whack jobs. But these guys went out of their way to keep everything on the DL, even so far as to threaten you if word got out. Why would they want to prove they could do what they did and then be so intent on keeping it a secret?"

"I don't know," Robert answered, dropping one of the folders onto the table. "But frankly, the fact they want it that way is the one good piece of news in this pile of crap."

"That doesn't make it add up," Ben answered with a shrug.

"I didn't say it did."

"If all they're after is Knoble, none of this makes sense."

Susan began to answer, but Robert cut her off with a wave of his hand, his eyes squarely focused on Ben. As dismissive as it seemed, she didn't object as awkward silence lingered. Finally, Robert cleared his throat and answered with a louder voice, "The honest answer is we have no idea."

"Clearly."

"So will you help us?" Susan growled in frustration.

"Have you reached out to Bill?"

"Not yet," Robert replied. "We put a tail on him, two square blocks. But haven't made contact."

"And we don't plan to, either," she added. "We need to see what he does, where he goes, and who he sees…"

"When he doesn't think anyone's watching," Ben finished her sentence.

"That's right."

"That makes sense. What doesn't is why I need to know any of this."

"Knoble provides legal services to the under-privileged, correct?"

"Yes."

"Those too poor to pay for them?"

"Yes."

"Doesn't sound like this is an enemy of anyone, as of late."

"I wouldn't think so," Ben replied. "But like you said, he's got a long history."

"With baggage," Robert added.

"But why just now if it's someone from his past?" she asked.

"Why do women abused twenty years ago wait until today to press charges?"

"This is different, Ben."

"Yes and no. Point is, I gave up trying to understand why people do what they do a long time ago. Especially crazy people."

"So women who wait to press charges are crazy?"

"No, but maniacs who threaten to blow up train stations are."

"So that's what we're dealing with?" Susan challenged. "Lunatics? Seems pretty thin."

"Have you been listening? I just said they *don't* fit the profile."

"So who the hell are they?" she nearly yelled, jerking her arms in an exaggerated wave.

"Robert, I trust you have a team of research monkeys smarter than shit working around the clock to answer that question?"

"Of course."

"Every case Bill's ever had, every client he's ever served?"

"Yes."

"Every verdict that caused pain for someone? Every police incident, every report?"

"Yes."

"Every single interaction the guy's ever had?"

"As we speak."

"Excuse me," she snarled, "but can we put an end to this Socratic conversation and cut to the part where you tell us whether not you'll help us?"

"How exactly am I supposed to do that?"

Not sure she wanted the answer, Susan ignored the question.

"Ben, we know that even now you're the force behind the scenes for Knoble's non-profits, the bank behind his philanthropy. I don't want to know about Barry Lee Richard and I don't have to know how you scared Knoble straight...but we need to understand why these people would want him dead."

She paused for a moment before finishing: "We really need your help."

"Why me?"

"Aside from the fact that you know Knoble personally, you're a highly decorated former Major in the Marines with proven surveillance expertise and a demonstrated track record. What you did two years ago to save America from that cyber attack was nothing short of remarkable. Given your connection to Knoble, you can't be terribly surprised we're asking for your help."

"I don't understand what you're asking me to do. Obviously I don't want to see bombs detonated or Knoble killed. But I already told you, I don't have any idea who is behind this." Ben kept calm; not a hint of anger.

Susan flung her bi-fold. It landed with a thud on the mahogany tabletop. She leaned back in her chair with her arms outstretched, trying to convey urgency and exasperation.

"Well that's what I need."

"I guess you'd better keep looking."

"Ben," Robert said in a soft voice. "I realize the way we brought you into this wasn't very professional or fair. No phone call, no heads up, not even a request for your help. Instead, I sent a couple junior agents you could run circles around to ambush you at your nonprofit event. Kind of tacky in hindsight, and I'll take responsibility for that.

"It's fine."

"But I'm not apologizing either. I agree there are far more questions than answers right now. I know a lot of this doesn't make sense, and we're coming to you with a whole lot less than a full deck. But the reality is, we're up against a wall. We need all the help we can get.

"We've noticed that when you're the one up against a wall, stuff gets done. I've never understood how you do what you do, and frankly I don't want to know. But there's no getting around it. You're a doer, Ben. And lives are at stake here. You asked why you...*that's* why. That's what we need. We need that fire, that determination...we need you."

Susan admired Robert's ability to calmly and collectively get down to brass tacks. Her passion didn't allow her to do that, and she envied those who could. Even Ben had to appreciate Robert's approach. *Didn't he*, she wondered, as Ben showed no reaction whatsoever.

"I don't do government work."

"The train that bomb was on was scheduled to be at ninety-three percent capacity by the time it departed Ogilvie."

Ben looked at her without saying a word, stroking his chin to go with his piercing stare.

Robert continued, "It had eight trailer railcars attached to its locomotive. Every Metra railcar has eight single seats followed by fourteen doubles on the bottom level, twenty-five singles on top. The explosion and successive derailment would've killed four hundred people."

Still no reaction from Ben.

Susan interrupted the silence. "Imagine your son Joe riding one of those trains. Or Nikki..." she paused for a moment. "I need you to summon that fire. That drive I know is in you. Help us find out what the hell is going on. Use your never-ending list of contacts and sources, talk to Knoble, keep this between us but fish around and dig deep. Look for the missing pieces and help us fill in the gaps."

"I'm not sure I'll find anything."

"Partner with us, Ben. Do it in the name of saving lives. We're going to keep doing what we're doing, but I fear it won't be enough. We're running out of time as we speak."

Ben's creased brow and resolute stare softened and his head tilted sideways. She could see the wheels turning now, and she knew how much he didn't want tragedy to strike.

"What if we don't figure this out?" Ben whispered. "What happens if come next Wednesday night, we're still right here without a clue as to who these people are or what their true motives might be? Or why they want you to kill a typical attorney they could easily kill themselves?"

"I wish I knew."

6

He could tell something wasn't right with his employee, Timothy Rausch. He didn't know what it was, but he knew it was there. He sipped awful coffee from a cheap generic white porcelain cup and stroked his thick graying mustache, considering what it might be and how much effort it was worth to find out. On the one hand, he could care less what Rausch's feelings towards the job were. The man was former military and well aware one didn't get to pick and choose assignments. On the other, this wasn't the military, and apprehension very well could affect the mission. He had to deal with this now.

"What is it?" he asked, adjusting his glasses. "What's wrong, Tim?"

"Nothing," Tim Rausch answered after another bite of pancake. Life after the Army had done some damage to the man's body. His bald head was less impressive atop a three-hundred-pound forty-five year old than when on an in-shape twenty-five-year-old. It was pretty clear what'd happened — the short stack was nearly gone and Rausch was just getting started.

"Don't give me that. There's something on your mind. Spill it."

"Doesn't it surprise you how quickly they brought this Siebert guy in?" Rausch finished after swallowing the gargantuan bite.

"It was always Agricola's plan."

"But it happened so soon..."

Robert Stevens and Susan Reynolds certainly hadn't wasted time reaching out to the former Marine for help. It was apparent the bombs had done their job. The more he thought about the timing, the more sense it made. The clock was ticking, the FBI and CIA were desperate, and Siebert was that good.

"Everything is going according to plan," he lowered his voice and extended both arms out, palms down. He did a quick double pump of his wrists, reminding Rausch to keep his voice down as well. At just before one in the morning, there wasn't another person within twenty feet of their corner booth. But that didn't mean they should be careless.

"But this guy…he's not like anyone we've ever encountered before."

"Which is precisely why this operation is so important. You knew the risks when you accepted the job. Are you are certain your team understands how important it is?"

"Yes."

"There is to be no documentation."

"Of course not."

"No e-mails, voicemails, text messages. Zero paper trail, zero digital footprint."

"I heard you, Hector."

He pounded his fist on the table loud enough to startle the waitress across the room playing on her phone at the register. He wheezed air through his stuffy nose, sucking in as much as his lungs would allow. "What did I tell you?"

"We've known each other a long a long time. Do I really need to call you that?"

"Don't ever use another name. Arminius is it. We all have superiors. That's an order."

Rausch nodded before returning to the hash browns, his tail between his legs.

The truth was, he wasn't a big fan of the pseudonyms either, but such things weren't negotiable. His code name, Arminius, was based on the great German chieftain, but to him it still sounded like a pansy's name. At least compared to Agricola, the code name his partner had selected for himself. The Roman warrior reference carried a much more authoritative undertone than some German from two thousand years ago. But one thing was certain: only the call signs were to be used during this mission.

"And don't get sassy with me, Tim. I don't know the people on your team, so it's reasonable that I'd want to make sure they know the drill. Don't make me regret that I've given you so much leash."

"I understand, Arminius. You won't."

"When is the next operation planned?"

"Tonight. Twenty-three hundred hours give or take, depending on the target's movements."

"Traffic should not be a problem, but surveillance has to be superior. You never know where they might go. Catch a taxi, ride the L, duck in and out of a bar...your team has to be ready to adapt. No matter what. This cannot fail."

"We will be ready."

"You'd better be."

7

"Thanks a lot, Joe. This was a blast," she whispered, her narrow fingers gently curved around his rough right hand.

Abigail Merriweather couldn't have dreamt up a better way to spend her twentieth birthday. The improv show at Comedy Sportz Theatre was even funnier than she'd expected. She and Joe rarely indulged in Giordano's deep-dish pizza, and the double chocolate cake was to die for. The weather was perfect for a romantic hand-in-hand walk along Belmont Avenue towards Lake Michigan — seventy-three degrees, no wind, no humidity, no bugs. May didn't last long in Chicago but it was splendid while it did. She clutched the handwritten card from Joe as they moseyed along the unusually quiet and empty streets just before eleven.

But none of that was what made it great.

She'd been denying how deep her feelings were for a while now, but the truth had begun to engulf her rapidly and wildly, like a surfer's first pipeline. For the first time, she really wanted to experience an almost reckless kind of love. Her bustling heart had overtaken her trepidation.

"You know, you're not like any other guy I've dated."

"No?" a smiling Joe replied. His ear-to-ear grin suited his chiseled, clean-shaven face nicely. That right cheek dimple was so cute she stopped walking just to stick her finger in it, playfully twisting inward. Joe's six-foot stature was just right, about five inches taller than her.

"No. And I love it."

"What makes me so different?"

"Instead of Second City, you take me to a family-friendly comedy club. Instead of a motorcycle ride, we go for long walks. Instead bars or clubs, you take me fly fishing."

"That was an adventure in itself," Joe quipped in reference to the impromptu make out session in the river they'd had two weeks earlier.

She smiled shyly, feeling her upturned face take on a glow as their eyes met.

Feeling herself blush, she continued, "You're so attractive. And you made me a handwritten birthday card. Who does that?"

"This guy!" He briefly released her hand to point both thumbs towards his chest. She chuckled at the cliché reference and surveyed his tanned biceps beneath the tight-fitting white polo she'd given him. The best part was that he immediately grabbed her hand again, interlocking each finger between hers. She didn't care that her palms were moist…sandpaper and sweat were like peas and carrots tonight.

"I sure am glad we met," she whispered.

"I almost didn't go to Harper, or any other college. What a mistake that would've been," he said, winking, reciprocating the sentiment.

"Really?"

"Didn't apply until the day before the deadline. My dad bribed me with an extra thick Dairy Queen malt to turn in the paperwork. Then he convinced me to go when I got in."

"I've always liked your dad."

Joe stopped and looked straight at her, but not directly into her eyes. He focused above them, more towards her forehead. It was his tell. There was more running through his mind than he was letting on. She thought of probing him, but he quickly redirected.

"I'm glad you're having a fun birthday."

"The best ever," she answered, returning the gaze and sharing an unforgettable kiss a hundred feet west of the Clark Street intersection. Usually on the shy side and not one for PDA, in that moment she was oblivious to any potential onlookers and her surroundings. She could kiss this boy for an hour. But it lasted only a few seconds.

Squealing tires from the north seized the moment and they both turned towards the alley. When the high beams of the black SUV flipped on, it was as if it had emerged out of thin air, abruptly thrusting itself into their lives without explanation. In ten seconds the SUV was on the sidewalk, having deposited thick black skid marks on the grayish concrete. Three figures bolted out of its backseat.

They were all tall, at least taller than Joe. Abigail was in so much shock that the only thing she could tell was they were dressed in black from head to toe, wearing masks and gloves. She saw no other color. The driver stayed in the car as the three approached without a word. Before she knew it, one of them had lifted her up and walked her away from Joe, slinging her over his shoulder like a sack of potatoes. His rigid grip was like a vice around her waist. She screamed and kicked and beat on his back with both fists.

By the time her feet were back on the ground, she was twenty feet from Joe. The other two goons had grabbed him — one by the arms, the other the legs.

"Abbey, Abbey! Call for hel—"

Joe continued to squirm after they silenced his screams, but with seemingly minimal effort they swung the love of her life into an open trunk. Then they piled back in through the same door they'd come out of and the SUV was gone. The whole thing lasted thirty seconds.

8

"Got a minute," the voice from her office doorway interrupted Susan Reynolds's first bite of leftover kale salad, sure to be the highlight of her day at just past eleven on a Friday packed with afternoon meetings.

"Not really," she replied, a touch of food escaping from her mouth and landing on the previously pristine stack of white paper atop her desk.

"I'll be quick," Robert Stevens entered her office anyway, closing the door behind him. He wore a traditional navy suit and white dress shirt, and the wrinkles under his eyes indicated he'd already had a long day. She thought about how much older he looked just a year after meeting him. The SAIC job was taking its toll on the man. As he plopped himself into the black leather chair opposite her, he dropped a manila file folder on the desk.

Susan moved her salad to the side and reached for it. Just as she started reading, Robert started talking.

"CPD contacted me this morning. There was a kidnapping last night at Belmont and Clark. Just before eleven o'clock. Young couple out for a stroll, and an unmarked SUV pulled up on the sidewalk to snatch the boy. Left the girl crying in the street."

"I'm guessing the Chicago Police Department doesn't contact you after every crime is committed?"

"Check the name."

She scanned the police report's cover page and saw the reason Robert was there.

"Oh, damn…"

"Joseph Henry Leksa. Twenty-two years old, six-feet tall, short, light-brown hair. Blue eyes. Medium build. Student at Harper College in Palatine. Architecture major. And, oh wait, Ben Siebert's adopted son."

"Are they sure?" she asked frantically, flipping through the report only to find one useless picture of a sidewalk or empty storefront after another.

"Like I said, he was with his girlfriend. Abigail Louise Merriweather. Also twenty-two, from South Barrington, celebrating her birthday with her boyfriend of over a year. That pretty much confirms CPD got the name right."

"I see," she responded, dropping the folder onto the desk. She tried to drown out the ambient noise, but the ringing phones on the other side of the closed door, her secretary making travel arrangements for next week and the general noise of the CIA's Chicago Headquarters office wouldn't let her. Either that or she didn't want to really think about what it meant.

"This obviously isn't a coincidence," Robert broke the silence.

"We don't know that."

Robert didn't respond, opting instead for the absurdity of the comment to speak for itself. He wasn't tearing up, but the blank expression on his face and wide eyes didn't conceal what he was thinking either.

"This isn't your fault, Robert."

"I know," he answered, clearing his throat. "But I'm still responsible for the events that led to it, and I'm pretty sure Ben won't make the distinction."

"So you haven't talked to him?"

"Sent a unit to his house, but he wasn't there. Decided against an aggressive hunt or an APB right now."

"We don't know how he'll react."

"Cut the crap, Susan," Robert sneered before jumping out of the chair as if on a spring. Arms extended as he spoke, the passion in his voice was unmistakable. "One day, all is well in the Siebert household. Ben's playing golf and volunteering; his son's taking classes and seeing a beautiful young woman. Then I bring him into our little terrorist party, and now his son's been kidnapped."

He paused. She didn't respond.

"I'm the one who pushed to get him involved, Susan. I'm the one who brought him into this mess."

She remained silent. Robert paced the room and shook his head, looking down at the ground and away from her.

"How the hell did they know we talked to Ben?" Robert shook his fist in the air.

"We should bring him in, Robert. Right away."

"If we do that, there's no way he'll help us with Knoble."

"Robert," she lowered her voice, "the circumstances — not you — of Ben's involvement are what led to his son's kidnapping. We don't know how he'll react, but regardless we have to bring him in ASAP. We have to tell him before he finds out another way."

"You know better than I do," Robert slowly lowered himself back into the desk chair. "What's the story with the boy?"

"I only know the CliffsNotes. Ben and his late wife, Anna, caught Joe breaking into their house when he was twelve. He was neglected, and it was pretty clear he was abused as well. As I understand it, Anna and Joe developed a sort of bond over leftovers. Not sure how that happens, but suffice it to say they didn't turn him in and wound up adopting him in the end. She died about a year later."

Recalling Anna Siebert's death reminded Susan of how precious life really is. The poor woman had only wanted to make a deposit, but wound up losing her life the next day. Rather than robbing the bank of its money, the killer had deprived Ben of the love of his life.

"So Ben's been a single parent for the past ten years?"

"That's right. Supposedly it's what Anna would have wanted, but mainly because he didn't want to send the boy back into the foster system."

Robert sighed. "So much for Ben helping us with Knoble. Susan...I really screwed the pooch."

"You're being awfully hard on yourself, Robert." The white lie at least sounded genuine. The truth was, Robert had a valid point. She would've been just as pissed at herself if she were in his shoes. But there was no use crying over spilled milk.

"Not only did I bring an innocent boy into Harm's way, but I sabotaged the best shot we had at finding out who these people are."

Her intercom buzzed and she pushed DO NOT DISTURB, watching Robert shake his head and close his eyes.

"I'll do it personally," Robert continued. "It's my fault. I should be the one to tell him."

Do it quickly, she thought.

Her circumstances speech notwithstanding, Ben was going to ignite. She knew they wouldn't be able to control the explosion that followed, but they had better at least watch the fuse from the inside. The only way to do that was to control how he found out and support him.

The irony she couldn't help but note was that it was possible Joe's kidnapping would further motivate Ben to help them. Find the bad guys and he'd find his son. Problem was, Robert was right in that it was likely going to result in Ben getting pissed instead. And that was why they needed to bring him in right away.

"Robert, for Pete's sake," she snapped after watching him sulk. He looked up almost in surprise. "You didn't kidnap the boy. You're the Special Agent in Charge. Act like it."

"Ten four," he quickly nodded and shot out of the chair again. The vigor in his demeanor indicated he was back, but she silently judged his lack of professionalism.

"You have eyes on Knoble?"

"Nothing new there," Robert replied. "He hasn't broken routine once."

"You might want to increase surveillance."

"I don't want to alarm him. We're still trying to see if there's something to learn without telling him."

"Your call," she replied against her better judgment. "When you find Ben let me know if you want any help. I'd be happy to be there with you," she lied.

9

"Let me repeat the indisputable fact; a man will find no better companion in life than his dog. Wives, girlfriends, war buddies, brothers, pen pals...no one holds a candle to a man's best friend. End of discussion."

Ben Siebert watched Tom Fedorak proudly end his sermon and grip an eight iron the way only he could: fist over fist, hands misaligned, fingers not interlocked. He looked like a five-year-old ready to play baseball. Then Ben's best friend and mentor gave his backside a suggestive waggle and told Ben to keep it in his pants.

They'd stayed close after their service in the Marines. Tom was his best man and had always been there for him, especially when Anna died. Without Tom — and his smart-ass comments and jarring humor — Ben knew life would look very different. Tom had also saved Ben's life three times over the years. And he never passed up the chance to point that out.

Father Time had done its damage, adding plenty of wrinkles and grey hairs to Tom's lanky frame, but the man's personality hadn't changed at all over the course of their relationship. He simply redirected his energy to golf and hot dogs; his temperament and general disposition remained fully intact.

Tom dressed like a golfer — khaki pants, white polo, blue lightweight pullover, red Titleist hat with a yellow tee tucked behind his ear — yet he was anything but one. He swung through and sent the Pro V1 straight into the woods.

"You little son of a bitch!" Tom cried, tomahawking the tee box with the head of his Callaway driver.

"I guess using the ball the pros use doesn't make you better after all. You should save money and buy Top Flite," Ben quipped. "They come eighteen to the dozen."

He'd asked Tom to meet him for a round at Glen Eagle Club to fill him in on his conversation with Robert Stevens and Susan Reynolds. Walking and talking for two hours, they concluded Ben's only recourse was to reach out to Bill Knoble directly. Feel him out, without sharing everything that had transpired, and see if he knew anything. Or gave anything away. Ben was skeptical and didn't see it unraveling the mystery, but nothing else came to mind.

"Maybe if you wore a glove it would help your swing," Ben said as they began the walk down the fairway towards Ben's ball.

"Maybe if I shoved a glove up your ass it would help yours."

"Just trying to help. So you really think I should get involved with this?"

"Gloves are for women. And yes, you should to talk to Knoble."

"Why can't the FBI do that?"

"Grasshopper!" Tom yelled before stopping his slow trot to point his finger in Ben's chest. "There's a reason I still call you 'Grasshopper' you know. It's because you still need my *tutelage* the way an infant needs the tit. We've been through this. The FBI can't reach out directly because Knoble might freak and they could end up with nothing. You've got to find out if there's anything worth finding."

"You think Knoble's dirty?"

"No, but maybe he's into something over his head. What's the harm in finding out?" Tom shot back before restarting his trot.

"I could think of a few things."

Tom halted again and turned to face him, this time pointing both index fingers into Ben's chest. "You just pipe down and do your thing, Grasshopper." Tom hollered loud enough to draw a few nasty glares from the foursome on the par three seventh hole. "Don't you question my judgment either, you little shitter. There's too much at stake *not* to do this. Write that down. Don't have a pen? Remember it then."

The caddies couldn't take it. After thirteen holes of filthy jokes, nineteen lost Titleists, five Chicago-style hot dogs and two cigars, Tom had finally cracked them. Both twelve-year-olds erupted in laughter.

"That goes for you too, you little piss ants. Don't let me catch you laughing at Grasshopper again, or I'll send your sorry little asses into the woods to look for my ball on the next hole."

Just my luck, Ben thought as they approached his beat up Slazenger.

Middle of the fairway, clear shot, wind at his back, perfect six iron from a centered pin on a green with no break...as close to a birdie as he was going to get. And his ball was sitting in someone else's divot.

Just as he was about to hit, Tom's phone beeped.

"Is Mr. Tom Fedorak, self-proclaimed Golf Etiquette Grandmaster of the Universe, with a cell phone on a golf course? You're slipping, Tom," he joked.

"You know better than that, Grasshopper. You wouldn't catch me dead with a phone on a golf course."

"Well it's not mine. It came from your bag."

Tom's rail-thin, blonde-haired caddie nodded in agreement when Tom turned to him seeking corroboration. Tom moaned exaggeratedly, moseying towards the custom-labeled golf bag. Mumbling something about respect, Tom bent down to check the bag.

Ben hit his ball and in customary fashion pushed it right off the green. Waste of a perfectly good drive. Missed the sand trap, but par was now a stretch and birdie nearly impossible. He shook his head and went to hand his caddie the club when the look on Tom's face stopped him cold.

Tom was squinting at a small, grey and black Motorola flip phone. There was an intensity in his face that Ben rarely saw.

"Grasshopper, over here."

No jokes, no smiles. Tom kept his eyes on the phone.

Ben grabbed it and shielded the screen from the sun's glare. The text message read:

Mr. Siebert:

Be in the clubhouse at 18:44 to receive our call.

Do not alert anyone.

Do not be late.

We will be watching.

Beneath the message was a picture. It was very grainy and had poor resolution, but it was clear enough: a teenage boy, brown hair, baby-face, mouth duct-taped shut, black blindfold covering his eyes.

It was his son, Joe. And his neck was bleeding.

10

The clubhouse was a fifteen-minute walk from the fourteenth hole, so Ben commandeered the nearest golf cart and left the cadies to calm down the infuriated golfers in their wake. Tom hopped in the front seat and Ben floored it, cursing the governor that capped the vehicle's speed as he tightly gripped the steering wheel.

They cut through numerous confused foursomes, five different holes and several cart-restricted areas en route to the quarter-mile winding blacktop driveway that led to the main entrance. Tom yelled for people to get out of the way, but most got the hint when Ben didn't slow down as they approached, on the cart path or otherwise. The chaos was loud, but the air between them was silent. Ben couldn't stop wondering things. *What could anyone want with Joe? Where was he? Had they already harmed him? Who were they?* In the midst of so many unknowns, only one thing seemed certain: answers wouldn't come if he missed that call.

Ben was already into his third giant leap up the blue slate steps by the time Tom got out of the vehicle. He barged through the ornately carved wooden doors and made straight for the front desk. All the club's calls went through Reception before being redirected, and his watch said he was a minute early. Terri, the attractive, twenty-something-year-old college student working summers as a receptionist, was staring down at her phone, twirling her dark hair around a painted orange nail as she popped bubbles with her chewing gum. She startled so hard at Ben's abrupt entry that she spilled her Starbucks latte all over the desk. As the frothy foam trailed the tan liquid in a parade across her keyboard, she looked down in distain and then angrily up at him.

"Mr. Siebert, what can I do for you?" Teri asked with obvious annoyance.

"Has anyone called?" he blurted out, pointing to his watch as if that would mean something to Terri.

"I don't...think so."

"Terri, forget about the mess for a second. I need you to think. Has anyone called in the last five minutes?" Ben leaned in even closer for eye-to-eye contact.

"No," Terri replied, startled. "Not in the last five minutes."

He sighed and wiped his brow with the bottom of his now untucked green polo. Terri stared at him as the latte puddle grew, waiting for an explanation she wasn't going to get. Tom marched into the room shortly thereafter and put his hand on Ben's shoulder before tilting his head, then sighed in relief when Ben nodded in confirmation that no call had come.

"Can I help you, gentlemen?"

Glenn Susin, the pompous assistant clubhouse manager who didn't know his ass from a hole in the ground, possessed a unique brand of condescension that most members found displeasing. Many of them were surprised the overdressed stooge was still employed and a secret petition had been circulated to rectify that. On top of his patronizing tone, Glenn was easily four hundred pounds and his neck fat muffled his words, meaning members actually had to work to understand his disdain.

"You're still on probation, aren't you Glenny boy?" Tom sneered.

Glenn looked towards the ground and scratched his slightly balding head before ominously eyeing Ben and ignoring Tom.

Before Glenn could respond, the phone on Terri's desk started to ring.

"Don't answer that!" Ben snapped.

"Mr. Siebert, I demand to know what's going on here!" Glenn said as loud as a clubhouse whisper could afford. He started to approach the phone when all of a sudden Tom's not-so-gentle forearm pressed against his chest and he was moving backwards until he reached the wall with a thud. Terri jumped at first, but then remained motionless in shock, this no doubt a first for her. Glenn immediately lost his bravado and his lips started quivering. His flattened Adam's apple emerged when he swallowed hard, leaning his now glistening head backwards.

"Listen to me, you glorified hall monitor...it's time for you to relax. You understand? Ben has to take that call, and he has to do it without you squabbling like a little girl. I'll personally explain everything when it's done. But for right now, shut your damn mouth."

By this time the phone began its third ring, and Ben didn't have the luxury of waiting for Glenn's nod. He stepped in front of Terri and grabbed the receiver, pulling it over the desk as far as the cord would permit. He got about three feet before the line went taut.

"This is Ben Siebert."

"Mr. Siebert, we knew you would make it," a scrambled voice replied.

Aside from an educated guess that it belonged to a male, he knew there would be little information obtained from the voice itself. Scramblers were simple yet effective devices.

"Where's my son?"

"In the room next to ours, safe for the time being."

"Let me talk to him," Ben said, pacing as much as the three feet of slack would allow.

"You're not in a position to make demands."

"His neck was bleeding."

"To get your attention."

"You listen to me, you —"

"Spare me the threats, Mr. Siebert. We know you're a serious man and we know you love your son. That's precisely why we're confident you'll do whatever's necessary to get him back."

"Talk."

"That's the spirit, Mr. Siebert. Transfer this call to the Food and Beverage Manager's office in the dining room to your left. Mr. Collins doesn't begin his evening shift until nineteen hundred hours on Fridays, so we'll have the privacy we need. Say nothing to the bombshell behind the desk and come alone. Leave Mr. Fedorak to deal with Mr. Susin. Pick up the easternmost table's pitcher of ice water along your way and bring it into the office. Be on speakerphone with me in no more than twenty seconds."

11

Leaving behind a very confused Terri and Glenn, Ben silently transferred the call and motored straight into the dining room, grabbing the pitcher of water from the first table. He could hear Tom yelling at Glenn as he closed the door behind him, and then it was silent.

The club had a grillroom and small café to serve guests during the day, so the restaurant wasn't open for dinner until eight on summer Fridays. Ben saw only one staff member, Julio, setting the tables. The overhead lights still off, the room's only illumination came from the end of the sunset that peeked through the blinds. All the TVs were off as well and the mobile buffet had been moved to the bar downstairs connected to the men's locker room. It was empty and quiet. Once inside John Collins's office, he shut the door and answered the blinking red light via speakerphone.

"I'm here."

"Its admirable that you view the boy as your son, considering how you first met."

The personal reference caught Ben off guard, but he couldn't reveal that.

Don't give them anything. Less is more.

"What business of it is yours?"

"Truly, it's commendable. Especially since your wife died so soon after she made you take the boy in. Ten years as his only parent. The only thing the boy had in life after such a rough start. It shows just how much you love him."

Don't go there, he silently ordered himself.

"We don't want your son, Mr. Siebert. The quicker you listen and obey, the quicker you'll get him back. However, and consider this your only warning, if you try to cross us in any way we'll send him back to you in pieces."

He tried not to think of his boy, but the picture of Joe's bound hands and bleeding neck was planted firmly in his mind.

"Do you understand, Mr. Siebert?"

"Yes."

"Retrieve the Motorola cellular phone in your right pants pocket."

"I've got it."

"We can see that, Mr. Siebert."

He looked around the three hundred square foot room, scanning for anything out of the ordinary. He'd not been in John's office before, but it looked pretty typical. A few pictures of small children on the wall, an overstuffed bookshelf with hardcover texts and loose-leaf papers falling off every shelf, half-drawn blinds in front of a north-facing window, a relatively clean desk adorned with standard office equipment.

Plenty of places to hide a small camera.

"Use both your hands to disassemble the Motorola and retrieve its circuit board and SIM card. Then use the yellow Momentous swing trainer iron leaning against the western wall to smash both into multiple pieces. Once done, flatten them with your foot. Be sure both are completely destroyed, Mr. Siebert. Your son's life depends on it."

He did as instructed, knowing that the circuit board — which contained the microprocessor and firmware — was the only form of data storage on the rudimentary cell phone. And that the SIM card — which cellular providers used to store account data — was the only way to identify the phone's subscriber. He was destroying the two components that could give him additional information about the caller or allow him to see the picture of Joe again.

"Now," the voice said, "dump all the fragments into the pitcher of ice water. Push it all to the bottom with your hand and displace some of the water onto the desk."

"Done. Now what the hell do you want?"

"It is our understanding that Mr. Robert Stevens of the FBI and Mrs. Susan Reynolds of the CIA recently contacted you..."

His heart sank. Were these the same people that called Robert? He'd mentioned that the voice that called him was scrambled.

Knowing he was being watched, Ben continued to show no emotion, but inside he felt reality crushing him. If these were the same people, there was no doubt they had both the skill and ethos to kill his son.

"Mr. Siebert, pay attention."

"Yes."

"We assume that they explained our request to you?"

"Yes."

"Excellent. Now that we're all caught up, over the past fifteen months you have worked on and off again with Mr. Knoble, have you not?"

What the hell did Bill have to do with any of this?

"Mr. Siebert?" Ben kept his head straight but moved his eyes around the room still looking for the camera.

"Yes, I have."

"He hasn't always been such a generous nonprofit lawyer, has he?"

"What do you want, his life story?"

"Not the time to be sarcastic, Mr. Siebert."

"No, he hasn't."

"And is it accurate to say that you're at least partly, if not directly, responsible for his charitable transformation?"

"I suppose."

"And that you still financially support several of his outreach programs and nonprofit organizations, mostly via anonymous donations?"

"Yes."

"Very interesting, Mr. Siebert. I assume your connection to Mr. Knoble is the reason Mr. Stevens and Mrs. Reynolds consulted you?"

"You'd have to ask them."

"But we're asking you."

"I don't really know why they contacted me." Ben worried that he was giving too much away by even acknowledging his conversation with Robert and Susan, but there wasn't much choice in the manner. The real question was how did these people know about the conversation in the first place?

"What did they want?"

"To know if I was aware of any enemies he may have. Or if I had any idea what this was all about."

"And what did you tell them?"

"That whoever called Stevens was crazy."

"Always the tough guy."

"Just answering your question."

"It would be wise not to make enemies of us."

"You kidnapped my son. You're the one making enemies."

"Purely a means to an end, Mr. Siebert. As we said before, we have no interest in harming your son."

"How do I know that?"

"You don't."

"How do I know Joe's even still alive?"

"You don't."

"I need proof that he's okay."

"Don't confuse a want with a need."

"How comforting, asshole." His quick and sharp tone was intended to look like a accidental kneejerk response, as if emotion had momentarily gotten the better of him. But he'd planned it that way to try to evoke at some emotion from the other end of the line.

Stretching the tension without snapping it was a very fine line, and Ben knew these people would make his son pay the price if he crossed it. But he had to do something, and time was running out. If the conversation continued to go exactly the way they wanted, he'd learn nothing. His hope was that his refusal to obey right away would throw the guy off, just a little, and maybe give him something to go on.

"We did not invite you into our discussion with Mr. Stevens."

The scrambler couldn't conceal the voice's increased aggression. Ben knew this was as far as he could push it, and it wasn't much. But it did seem clear his involvement wasn't something the perps were happy about.

"And I didn't ask to be invited."

"Yet here you are right in the middle of it, perhaps hindering our objective."

The voice continued before he could respond.

"To get your son back, all you have to do is ensure Mr. Knoble's death prior to twenty-three hundred hours Wednesday night. That's five days from now. Given your background and qualifications, that should not pose a significant challenge to you."

"I'm not killing a man for no reason."

"The choice is yours, Mr. Siebert. But if you want to see your son alive again, Mr. Knoble had better be deceased by the deadline."

"How?"

"It makes no difference to us, so long as you accomplish the mission. Convince Knoble to take his own life for all we care. And do not concern yourself with how to prove his death. We will be watching closely."

"How do I know you'll honor your end of the deal?"

"You don't."

"No deal."

"Mr. Siebert, again, we did not invite you to our party with Mr. Stevens. But as you are now a guest nonetheless, we're going to take advantage of your skill set and personality."

"What's that supposed to mean?"

"It is our belief that you will be more effective at fulfilling the objective than Mr. Stevens. As that is our sole interest in this matter, it makes sense to motivate you to do so. Back to your question about proof we have your son..."

"No, proof that he's still alive."

"Locker 2482 downstairs contains but a taste of what there will be plenty more of should you fail to terminate Mr. Knoble by the deadline. Good day, Mr. Siebert."

When Ben heard the dial tone, he raced down the stairs and through the men's locker room backdoor entrance towards Locker 2482, ignoring greetings from Julio, Jerry the shoe shiner and a few members. Blind corners just made him go faster, pushing through a twosome and knocking over a stack of towels by the showers.

The beige locker with wooden trim stood centered in a row of ten. Its gold nameplate was labeled, but Woody had quit the club a year ago and the empty locker was now used for guests. Ben opened it inch-by-inch, nervously squinting his eyes until it was fully ajar.

Only one item was inside: a small, unmarked shoebox-sized container with an ordinary blue bow on top. Classic brown with no note, décor, or words. Inside the box was a gold locket, worn with years and stained with what looked like dried blood. He recognized it immediately but opened it to confirm.

On one side: a picture of Joe and his late wife Anna, Ben's two favorite people in the world. He remembered taking that photo in the family living room, in front of the family's nutcracker display, before Joe's birthday dinner at Ed Debevic's.

On the other side was the phrase Anna had insisted Ben have Things Remembered inscribe on the locket. At the time he thought it corny, but the words had become unforgettable and immeasurably cherished to both him and Joe. Especially since they lost Anna just a few weeks later:

You'll always have my heart.

Ben had given the locket to Anna during their first year as a family. That year was in many ways very trying for Ben, but Anna always said it was the best of her life. After her death, it instantly became Joe's most prized possession, a priceless memory of the wonderful wife and mother that Anna was. Joe wore it all the time, even in the shower. Everywhere he went, no matter what he was doing, the kid wore that locket.

And now it was covered in blood.

12

When Joe came to, it was hot — and dark.

He held his palm inches from his face. Nothing.

He widened his eyes until the sockets hurt. Nothing.

He got on all fours and pressed his forehead into the rank vinyl of the cot until it bumped the hard surface beneath. He stood up and reached for the ceiling, groping with his right hand and feeling nothing but air. Rotated his neck in panoramic desperation, seeking a trace of light, maybe in a corner or under a roof. Just one ray of hope.

Nothing.

He'd never been in a place so void of light. He felt blind. He was blind. Shivers overtook him despite the sweltering heat. It felt like a hundred degrees in this cage, yet he couldn't stop shaking. Was this some sort of oven? Was shaking his body's reaction to asphyxiation? Was this how he was going to die?

He tried to remember how he got here. They'd yanked a mask down over his face, and they were asking questions, questions about Dad. He kept saying he didn't know, because he didn't. Then...

He reached across his body and felt for his right hand. Some sort of bandage had been applied. It felt like gauze. Just like the bandage on his neck. His hand ached but didn't throb like before. His neck didn't hurt.

What happened next? His mind strained to recall the details.

The pinch.

That's right. He'd felt a sharp pinch, like a bee sting. In his neck. The other side of his neck.

Then...darkness. He couldn't remember anything after that.

He felt the rest of his person and confirmed he was in the same clothes — polo shirt, jeans, gym shoes. No belt, wallet, or cell phone, however. His ribs felt bruised, maybe cracked, but it could've been extreme shortness of breath. There was no air in this place. Aside from his hand and neck, he seemed physically uninjured. He felt around his heart. *What...*wait a second*...no.*

"Give me back my locket, you assholes!"

He meant it to be a loud and forceful roar, filled with every ounce of energy he could muster. Like a lion. A demonstration of his strength, to show these people they'd regret what they'd done. Instead, it came out like a pitiful whimper that even he could barely hear. And yet it was apparently all he had left because his knees failed him and he collapsed to the ground on all fours. Sobbing uncontrollably, snot running from his nose onto his chapped lips, he gasped for air in between jagged, uneven heaves of desperation.

What am I going to do? I'm not resourceful like Dad. I'm not tough like Tom. I'm not going to make it. I'll never see Dad again. I'll never see anyone again. Or anything. I'm going to die in the dark. In a pitch-black oven that smells like low tide. Alone.

The more his brain began working again, the more he wished he hadn't woken up. Each lucid thought was far more terrifying than the last. Even with all the different thoughts running through his mind and the broad variety of images that flashed in and out, there was one constant that kept reappearing:

Abigail.

The last he remembered, they had her. But they didn't keep her, at least they didn't throw her in the trunk. *Did they leave her? Or did they take her somewhere? Where?* He remembered asking them...they never answered, or at least he didn't remember.

What are they...doing...to her? Oh, God. Please...

Dejected, he extended his arms and legs outward until he was lying flat on his stomach, his shirt and skin undoubtedly atop multiple layers of concrete floor filth. He rested his head in his left hand, weeping indiscernible moans. As he exhaled, he felt the dirt — agitated by his own breath — kick back up and cling to his mucus-coated face.

His hot, putrid breath reminded him of the dense heat in the room, and the emptiness of his stomach. He'd die from heat exhaustion soon. Or he'd starve. Or maybe he'd die of thirst first, his arid throat complained. Maybe he'd go crazy in the darkness and find a way to kill himself.

At that moment God intervened, and Dad's words played in his mind:

Don't ever give up, Joe. No matter what happens in life, no matter how scared you get, don't ever stop fighting. Get back to basics. Close your eyes. Breathe. Pray. Remember your five senses. Do all you can with what you have. Never give up.

Dad had uttered those words to him right after Mom died — an event they'd never really spoken about — when Dad was the one hurting. Hurting even more than he let on. That was before they'd bonded as father and son. Before Joe knew Dad really wanted him. Before it finally hit him: "Mr. Siebert" really did love him as a son; he really was "Dad."

In this dark Hell, it gave Joe strength to remember that Dad had followed that very advice. That he'd used those very words to help get him through losing Mom.

Never give up.

He stood to his feet and followed the advice step-by-step, closing his eyes.

Remember your five senses.

He took a few more deep breaths despite the pain in his lungs, willing himself to focus. First, he walked the room's perimeter running his hand along the wall and counting the steps between each corner. Its surface felt as unyielding as the floor, but seemed rougher — like maybe jagged stone rather than uniform concrete. Best he could tell, the room was about twenty by twenty. He couldn't reach the ceiling, so it was at least eight feet tall. But even if the ceiling was ten feet tall, he was still only in four thousand cubic feet of space.

Next, he walked the entire area one body-width "row" at a time, his left arm extended in front of him. He wanted to cover every square inch, and then did it again to hopefully catch anything he'd missed. Aside from the smelly cot and a door latch that didn't budge, there was nothing. No freestanding objects, completely empty walls aside from cobwebs and dirt, and a ceiling he couldn't reach standing on the bed.

It smelled horrendous, like a toilet that needed flushing. There was a mustiness to it, like a basement but closer to a sewer. It was damp but not wet, aside from the humidity. He was sweating profusely and had shouted enough that it now hurt to swallow. He needed water.

"I don't knoooow," he howled, repeating the answer he'd recalled shouting before the sting in his neck.

He couldn't hear anything. In fact, it seemed the walls somehow absorbed his wails. Almost like a padded room, except the walls were hard. No voices, movement, or light came through from the outside, and he suspected that nothing escaped from within.

Nothing.

He had no sense of time, except that it felt like years since he'd seen sunlight. He felt his cheek. His facial hair was longer and pricklier than he'd ever remembered it being. The most he'd ever gone without shaving was three days. How long had he been in this horrifying armpit of darkness?

And how was he going to get out?

13

"How's your studying, kiddo?" Mr. Knoble asked after misjudging another sip of coffee, burning his upper lip and then unsuccessfully trying to conceal it.

"So-so," Genie answered, pretending not to notice for a second time. Five years as Mr. Knoble's assistant had taught that any answers to law school questions best be kept vague, otherwise he might try to help.

"Contracts is a son of a biscuit, isn't it?" He smiled.

She chuckled. Mr. Knoble seemed determined not to curse in her presence, despite having a mouth as filthy as a garbage truck when outside of it. She heard him on the phone every day, yet with her he replaced the offensive words with similar-sounding ones that made no sense. She didn't take offense. It didn't feel condescending. It was his odd way of complimenting her.

"Definitely my toughest class in 1L. *The Paper Chase* nails it, eh?"

"The what?" she asked.

"Wow, I'm getting old..."

Mr. Knoble smiled before another bite of English muffin. It was dimple-laden and ear-to-ear, filled with cosmetically whitened teeth, and it reminded her that he'd become a relatively handsome older man. Seeing someone as often as she saw Mr. Knoble — at least six days a week — could made it easy to miss the gradual changes, but with him they really stuck out.

Which was good, because image was important to him. He'd lost so much weight she'd nearly forgotten his earlier look.

73

Somewhere in the neighborhood of 170 pounds now, with thick dark hair parted to the right, which he colored but didn't need to, a good job and sense of humor, he'd be a fine catch. For a woman twice her age. He was six feet tall but must've felt that was insufficient because he wore elevator dress shoes to add two inches. She never saw him in anything but a black pinstriped suit, even for their Saturday morning breakfasts.

"Thanks, Cindy," Mr. Knoble smiled at the waitress as she topped off their waters.

They'd been coming to The Sloppy Pancake every Saturday morning for the past two years at six o'clock sharp, and Cynthia Ramirez was their waitress every time. Their first breakfast was impromptu, but a few days later Mr. Knoble asked if Genie could join him every week. He suggested the same time and place and offered an extra twenty-five grand for her troubles. Even without the bonus she wouldn't have said no, especially considering everything he'd done for her such as covering her night law school tuition.

But she wondered, *why this place?* The floors were sticky, it wasn't the closest diner and the food was nothing special. There was something she didn't know. She asked Mr. Knoble once. He said The Sloppy Pancake is a lucky place to eat breakfast. She never inquired again.

"Did her son ever thank you, Mr. Knoble?" she asked when Cindy was out of earshot.

"Thank me?"

"For the five thousand dollars you loaned him to fix his car?" she replied incredulously.

"I'm sure he will when he gets a chance. He's got two jobs plus the paper route and a baby girl to think about."

"But, sir, that check didn't go through any of the non-profits. It was from your personal account. I don't have any way to track repayment."

"It wasn't a loan," Mr. Knoble answered, keeping his eyes pointed at his plate.

"That's very nice, sir. I'll call the accountant and have it added to your deductions. We can route it through one of the Donor-Advised Fund."

"Forget it," he said before taking a massive bite of his veggie egg white omelet. Pointing to the white blob on his plate that looked like a sorry excuse for a folded taco with cheesed broccoli oozing out the sides, he said, "These aren't that bad once you get used to them."

"Sir, what do you mean?"

"I mean there's no need to report that one."

There were definitely times, such as this, when Mr. Knoble's charity was equally perplexing as it was benevolent. She couldn't put her finger on what she wondered about, but sometimes things just didn't add up. Mr. Knoble was a fierce bookkeeper with crazy attention to detail when it came to taxes, yet here he was leaving $5,000 worth of deductions on the table.

He spent $50,000 to renovate the office two years ago, and the contrast was night and day. Brand new interior, revitalized outside, and clients that weren't sleaze balls trying to get away with something but were also much less wealthy. It was around the time he stopped drinking and started eating better; totally out of character. She wasn't complaining. The new Mr. Knoble was much better. But, he was so fundamentally different from his former self that it struck her as mysterious. She didn't doubt his good intentions, but she questioned the circumstances from which they were born. Even with the piecemeal explanation she'd gotten over the last two years, she knew Mr. Knoble hadn't told her everything.

"What's on your mind, Genie?"

"Why wouldn't you report it? It's a good thing that you did. Why not save yourself some money? It doesn't take away from him at all."

He nodded, communicating silent agreement but clearly thinking through a verbal rebuttal. Law school had taught her the importance of reading people, how to study facial expressions, body language.

"You reap what you sow, Genie."

"Huh?"

"Our firm…the work we do…we don't do it to benefit ourselves. That's not our purpose, our motivation. But it does. Don't ever think otherwise. Trust me, helping others isn't nearly as altruistic as you think."

"I'm not sure I understand."

"You don't have to. Just remember it one day when you're running an international conglomerate. What goes around comes around, kiddo. Believe me…"

Was there something illegal going on? Dangerous? Was she somehow an unknowing accomplice to some evil deed shrouded in generosity? She didn't want to call BS on her boss and bite the hand that fed her, but…

After cutting a near-perfect rectangle out of the center, she dipped the butter-coated blueberry pancakes into the golden-brown lake of syrup that filled the void.

"So much syrup that your teeth hurt, right?" Mr. Knoble grinned, still able to crack her up despite her apprehension.

"You betchya."

"You think that's good," he replied, rubbing his hands together, "just wait until I introduce you to butter-dipped filet mignon."

She laughed out loud and normalcy returned. That's how it went with them. Mr. Knoble's bizarre behavior, followed by her questioning, followed by business as usual. After a run-through of the week's accounts' activities, they were finished eating and ready to go. At 6:50 Cindy dropped off the check and hugged them both as she did every week, telling them how much she looked forward to next week.

I'll bet you do, the skeptic in her couldn't help but think as Mr. Knoble dropped a crisp Benjamin on the table to cover the $19 tab.

The sun rising between Chicago skyscrapers temporarily blinded her as her eyes adjusted from The Sloppy Pancake's dimly lit dining room. When her vision returned, she laid eyes on the ruggedly handsome man she'd come to know through Mr. Knoble.

Ben Siebert leaned against the Ford Taurus's black passenger door, wearing a pair of pleated khakis and a light blue polo. His veiny, toned forearms always caught her attention, but his pallid and unshaven look today was uncharacteristic.

"Mr. Siebert, how nice to see you," she said.

He was by far the largest individual contributor to four out of the seven non-profits Mr. Knoble ran. And that didn't count the anonymous donations, which she was certain were most if not all his. She first met him two years ago, when Mr. Knoble was going through his transformative period, and she always suspected he was a part of it in some fashion. Every time they interacted, it seemed Mr. Siebert paid attention to her, that he truly listened to what she said and was genuinely interested. She always appreciated that.

At the moment, however, he looked intensely focused on Mr. Knoble. It seemed he was there for a specific reason, and that it had nothing to do with charity.

"Bill, I need a minute."

It wasn't a whisper, but it wasn't regular conversational volume either. Traffic was light but a passing vehicle would've muted his words.

"Ben, what can I do for you?" Mr. Knoble asked, extending his arm for a shake.

"Let's go," Ben replied, opening the backseat door instead.

"Can this wait? I've got an appointment."

"I'm afraid not."

"OK...um...Genie," he said to her, trying to conceal his obvious nerves. His fingers gave away that his hands were shaking, and it felt like he was avoiding eye contact altogether when he said, "I'll see you Monday. Have a nice weekend."

"Have a good day, Mr. Knoble," she answered as her boss climbed into the backseat.

A brief wave from Mr. Siebert and the Taurus pulled away from The Sloppy Pancake. And there she was again, left to wonder about Mr. Knoble and his mysterious affairs.

14

The voicemail replayed in FBI Special Agent Nikki Benton's head on an endless loop like cars speeding around a track.

"Sorry to bother you, but we need to talk. Ben's son is in trouble."

There were very few things that Tom Fedorak, or anyone for that matter, could say that could persuade her to ditch *The Big Bang Theory* reruns and a bowl of Boomchickapop popcorn. But that was one of them.

Café Salsa was a small, authentic Mexican restaurant just down the street from her apartment. It sold strong drinks, friendly smiles and traditional Mexican fare. Since her suburban migration four months ago, it'd become one of her favorites. The steak burritos were delicious and margaritas a delightfully loopy way to end the day.

But tonight, sitting alone in the four-person booth, restless and uninformed, she found even the homemade salsa unappealing. Dim lights and chintzy banjo music didn't relax her. She finger-combed her blond highlights as she waited for Tom.

Why am I letting Ben back into my life?

"How are you, Nikki?" the voice jolted her out of deep deliberation.

It came from behind, despite the fact that she was facing the restaurant's only entrance and didn't see anyone walk in.

"Tom," she answered, offering a forced hug before collapsing back into the padded red leather booth that wasn't so padded.

Tom Fedorak looked almost exactly the same, not that she expected much change in just a year. Rimmed glasses, lean but not thin, creases around the eyes and mouth, but overall little evidence of aging. Light brown hair combed straight back, no gel. He wore a midnight blue hoodie and navy T-shirt, jeans and white gym shoes. Classic Tom attire, minus the red checkered flannel jacket.

"I gotta know...do you still have that turtle? How is that little shitter?"

Even she was surprised to hear the feminine giggle escape from her mouth.

"Old man's still got it," Tom smirked. Cocky, but lacking the trademark ear-to-ear grin that would've made an appearance under normal conditions.

"You always could make me laugh. And yes, I still have Spot, thank you very much."

"You know, it's still not too late to change it to Shitter."

"He's doing well. Pretty much runs the place — eating, sleeping and, yes, filling my apartment with his tortoise funk." A broad grin spread across her face.

"I'm not sure how special that stank is, but if you're happy, I'm happy. Still playing Chris Hansen?"

"Yes, Tom," she replied, leaning in with a sneer. "Said another way, I'm using the advanced computer science degree and FBI position I worked my butt off for to catch pedophiles before they ruin children's lives."

"Bastards."

"Won't argue with you there."

"You ever need someone to teach those thugs a proper lesson, you let me know."

"I'll keep that in mind."

"Talk to Robert Stevens much? He still Special Agent in Charge at Chicago?"

"You know he is, Tom. And you know he got the job because of Ben. And you probably know that he still pesters me as to why we can't give the relationship another shot."

"Speaking of that..."

"What's going on with Joe?"

"That's what I like about you," Tom replied, accepting a humongous mug of dark beer he must've ordered before sitting down, "you're sharp as a katana."

"A what?"

"A sword. More specifically, a twenty-seven inch, hand-forged curved blade that cuts through bone like scissors through paper. Leave it to the Japs to have a weapon like that."

"Thank you for comparing me to a barbaric and archaic lethal weapon. Always the charmer."

They exchanged warm smiles after Tom's exaggerated wink, easing the tension but still doing nothing to explain why they were there.

"You haven't lost your sense of smart ass," Tom broke the silence. "I like that. It's no wonder Grasshopper fell so hard for you."

Memories of Benjamin Siebert rushed into her mind like they always did — gentle yet firm, nonexistent at first but swift thereafter. She remembered their first encounter, when she thought she was on a routine stakeout and Ben wound up holding her at gunpoint before she knew what was happening. His quick, strong move turned out to be a harbinger for their relationship afterwards.

Examples surged her brain like an inrush current. It wasn't the first time and it probably wouldn't be the last. Usually it happened when she was alone, before bed and ready for that bowl of popcorn. But there was no hiding it from Tom tonight. He was Ben's friend and mentor of over twenty years. He probably taught Ben most of what he knew about deciphering facial expressions and body language. She didn't even try a poker face.

"Tom...what's going on with Joe?"

If Tom's hesitation showed her it was serious, the way he barely choked out the words made it surreal.

"He's been kidnapped."

15

It didn't take Tom long to give the details, because he didn't have many to give.

He shared the conversation Ben had with the scrambled voice at the golf course, the request regarding Bill Knoble and what he'd learned about Joe's kidnapping from his contact in the Chicago Police Department, mainly that they had bupkiss and were getting nowhere fast. When he was finished, she sensed there was more. She couldn't put her finger on it, but it felt like there were a few pieces of the puzzle missing. She opted to focus on what was offered.

"I had the dried blood from the locket tested for DNA. It's Joe's."

"Do you know how old the blood is?" she asked.

"No."

"Why not?"

Tom shook his head before continuing, "You and Grasshopper even talk alike. He asked the same thing, said he's having a Raman spectroscopy performed, whatever the hell that is. I still don't see why."

"You don't think it'd help to know how old the blood is?"

"I'm pretty sure it's from between Thursday night when Joe disappeared and Friday afternoon when Ben got the locket. Ben said Joe wears that thing everywhere."

"But how do you know?"

"Nikki, I'd sequence the genome if I thought it'd tell me something useful. But unless the age of a person's blood somehow identifies who or where his captors are, I consider it a waste of time we don't have."

"Where was he abducted?" she asked.

"On the North side, near Belmont and Clark."

"Time?"

"A little past eleven."

"Anything to go on?"

"Unmarked black GMC Acadia, plates removed, four guys in black, crappy street-camera angles, no facials, average heights, maybe a little taller, medium builds except for one who was heavyset, never said a word."

"Did you talk to the girlfriend?" she asked before taking another swig of her margarita.

"Not yet."

That struck her as odd, but she moved on.

"Any other witnesses?"

"No."

"Was no one else was in Chicago that night? That's a busy intersection."

"It was past eleven on a Thursday. Not a lot of foot traffic at that hour. Plus, the night before was Cinco de Mayo, so the city was in hangover mode."

"What about businesses? Restaurants, coffee shops? Isn't there a Target around there? People don't stop buying groceries because of hangovers."

"There aren't many joints close enough. There's a Starbucks on the corner but it closed a few minutes before. The only people around didn't see anything, just heard the girlfriend screaming afterwards. On top of it you've got two construction sites a quarter-mile apart..."

"So traffic is down."

"Scaffolds and coverings all over the place. Takes up half the damn sidewalk. Looks like an asphalt jungle over there. Bars close early on weekdays to pay staff OT on the weekends when people actually show up."

"Can I get a copy of the phone call transcript from the golf course?"

"Golf clubs don't plan on hearing from terrorists."

"Translation," she snapped, not in an interpretative mood.

"They don't record phone calls."

"What about the cell phone? Anything salvageable?"

"Cell phones that old don't have water-resistant components. Even if they did, it sat in a pitcher of water for a long time. I took it to the best guy in the business and he said it was toast."

She bit her lower lip before continuing, "You said you thought these guys might be military...why do you assume they're men?"

"Ben said they sounded like men."

"They used a scrambler, no?"

"Yes."

"So how do they sound like men?" she sternly asked.

"They called the female receptionist a 'bombshell.'"

"Maybe they did that to throw you off," she flailed her arms in a suggestive manner.

"Could be. You asked what I thought."

"Why assume military?"

"I'm not assuming anything, Nikki. Some things they said suggested they might be. The text said Ben had to take the call at 'eighteen forty-four,' as opposed to a 'quarter 'til seven' or 'six forty-five.'"

"Maybe they're just precise."

"They said Knoble had to be dead by 'twenty-three hundred' Wednesday. Military hours on both occasions."

"Tom, most of the world uses a twenty-four hour clock system. North America, Australia, India, Saudi Arabia and a handful of countries most people have never heard of are the only ones that use a.m. and p.m."

"Even a scrambler can't completely conceal an accent. If they were foreign, Grasshopper would've picked up on it."

"Unless they're good at disguising it."

"Damn good. And I do mean *damn* good. He's been around the block a few times."

"What else? I know there's more. There always is."

The waiter reemerged and while she waved him away, Tom asked if they had hot dogs and shrugged in protest when the confused server said no. He ordered three beers, to be delivered at the same time, and a "pile of meat." No further description rendered.

Once the waiter was gone Tom continued with, "They kept referring to him as Mr. Siebert, very formal."

"That makes you think military?" she skeptically inflected her voice.

"Look Nikki, I wish I had more to go on. I wish I could tell you their names and addresses and shoe sizes. But then I wouldn't be talking to you, would I?"

"Why do you keep saying they? Ben spoke to one person."

"We know at least four people were involved in Sport's kidnapping. Plus, the voice on the phone used plural pronouns."

"That doesn't mean multiple people are holding him."

"I guess not. You're assuming he used *we* instead of *I* to throw us off the scent?"

"I'm not assuming anything."

"Touché, Nikki. Did I say you haven't lost your sense of smart ass? I meant that you've taken it to the next level. I suppose misdirection is possible. Hell, anything is possible at this point." Tom flicked both wrists outward in frustration.

"They...or...whatever...had everything planned out. From getting access to the locker beforehand to planting the phone in my bag to knowing about the staff and its schedules. This was well researched. Organized, professional."

"That doesn't mean it's military, but I see your point. Let's get back to what we know. We know they were close enough to see through binoculars."

"Or a small camera."

"Maybe, but the fact they were watching you the whole time and had visibility to several areas of the golf club means if they were using cameras, they'd need quite a few of them. I'm assuming you had the place combed for surveillance ten minutes after you found the locket?"

"Five."

"That didn't take long."

"You know Grasshopper. He's got a connection in every corner of every town. One phone call and surveillance was on its way."

She shrugged. That was Ben all right.

"Did they find any cameras?"

"Not a single one."

"So we're back to assuming binoculars."

"I'll buy that. So they were close and somehow got access to a club's locker room. Not that helpful considering they pulled off a public kidnapping without leaving any clues behind."

Tom's flared nostrils made her wonder if Tom was holding something back, but she again decided to move on.

"Security system?"

"ADT is hooked into every window and door on the property."

She shot him a curious glance.

"Members leave their valuables in the lockers when they play. And the display case has some goodies too."

"The voice said Joe was in the room next to theirs?"

"Whatever that means."

"None of that screams male or military to me."

"I didn't say I knew," Tom snapped. "I said they were hunches."

"What else do we actually know?"

Tom paused to drain what was left of his glass. Eyes still fixated on her, he cleared his throat in a level-set sort of fashion, leaning his elbows on the table and lowering his voice.

"We know the communication was concise but effective. Just like they taught us in the Marines, hammered it into our heads. The threat was strong, aimed right at what means most to Grasshopper, and the terms didn't change. That might not surprise you considering it was the first conversation, but it happens more often than you think. Especially with a guy like Ben. He knows how to talk people down, knows what people need to hear."

"He sure does."

"The tone in the voice was emotionless, stoic, business-like."

"They're definitely professional, regardless of the rest."

"Now you're the one using plural pronouns. Talk about an effective red herring. Maybe you're right. We could be looking for one douchebag after all."

"All we've got are uneducated guesses. There's no proof or even halfway decent leads to go on. It's pretty thin, Tom."

"No shit, *Nikki*. Everything about this is thin. But there's something we're missing. Over the last day and a half I've reached out to everyone I thought could help and come up with bupkis. If I had more time I might be able to track them down, but Wednesday is four days away. I need your help."

"What am I supposed to do?"

"I can appreciate the awkwardness of the situation from your perspective. I really can. But this kid saved my life a few years ago and I'll be damned if there's anything I won't do, including sacrifice my own, to save his. I can't risk him losing his future because you broke Grasshopper's heart. So get over it."

The soft glow from the yellow incandescent above the table illuminated Tom's face enough to reveal tear-filled eyes. He didn't blink and stopped talking.

"This has nothing to do with that. If I could help, I would. I just don't see how I can."

"I don't see either. But I need you to find a way and find it now. Access any official resources you have, on or off the record. Any favors you've got coming, people in high places you can ping, pull that trigger. Hook into your network, check the police file, do a whole bunch of other crap I haven't even though about."

"Tom, I can't drop everything I'm doing for a treasure hunt," she replied without thinking. She immediately regretted it and knew she deserved what was certain to come next.

"Don't give me that. The FBI has a shit ton more resources available to it than an out-of-practice former Marine in his sixties, and I need you to access them right now. The kid's got until Wednesday, Nikki. I barely have time to ask, much less wait for an answer. You were the closest thing to a mother the kid ever had outside of Anna. So as much as others may need you, I need you more. Are you going to help me or not?"

Help me. It finally dawned on her...

"Tom, why isn't Ben here asking for help?"

"I was wondering how long it'd take."

She felt a rush of panic; adrenaline surged through her body.

"I haven't seen Grasshopper since yesterday. I've called but it goes straight to voicemail."

"What else?"

"After Joe's kidnapping, I gave Bill a bullshit reason to contact me every day. It wasn't a great reason but he bought it. Today, I didn't hear from him."

"Did you call?"

"Six times. This afternoon he missed his Saturday volunteer duty at the soup kitchen on the south side. He hasn't missed one since..."

"Since he met Ben."

"Two years ago," Tom replied as he nodded her head. Finally it added up why Tom had reached out. It wasn't because she offered some incredible insight or access to the FBI. It was because she knew Ben, and Tom was desperate. He knew she wouldn't be able to say no.

The rush of fear returned. She remembered what happened when Ben Siebert set his mind to something. How enraged he became and skilled he was. How protective of his family, and unapologetic for what that meant.

"Ben's got Knoble," Tom softened his voice and looked into her watery eyes. "There's no telling what he'll do next."

16

Senior CIA Intelligence Officer Susan Reynolds sat at the seldom used family kitchen table in front of an iPad so worn the rose gold hue had rubbed away to reveal a color that could only be described as "metal." The kids were still at college for another few weeks and her husband Phil was snoring like a tuba on the couch nearby. Her vibrating cell phone made silent ripples in the glass of Kendall Jackson to her right. It was half past seven on a Saturday night and she was just getting started.

In a global world with a federal job, no hour was free from Outlook's ding. That sound always grabbed hold of her brain like a leech on bare skin; she was sure Pavlov was onto something. The OCD in her felt compelled to address each and every one of the e-mails, regardless of when it came in. Though she left the office every day with a clean INBOX, by the time she got home it was already well into the double digits. That's why when Phil, her teacher-husband, took his nightly catnap on the couch without a care in the world, she fired up her tablet and went back to work. Her gravestone would surely read "Death by a thousand e-mails."

The half-acre yard she never spent time in loomed outside their beautiful three-story colonial home. She preferred to keep the blinds open to at least look at the green grass and think of the fresh air, but that was the extent of her enjoyment. Sipping wine and contemplating irreversible past decisions, she rotated and pressed on her neck, stretching the facet joints until finally the negative pressure on the liquid inside created nitrogen gas bubbles and she heard three satisfying pops. Toggling between two Excel files and a forty-page briefing she'd be expected to know inside and out by seven-thirty Monday morning, just the thought of how long she'd be up made her yawn. There was never enough time.

Contrary to her inbox's incessant dings, people hardly ever called outside of work hours. E-mail offers folks a quick and easy way to dump their problems onto her and move on, whereas a phone call could and often did result in them getting more than they bargained for.

So when her cell rang, it actually startled her. She quickly silenced it and slid open the back patio door to step onto the brand new, $15,000 maintenance-free deck she never used. The weather was pleasant: a gentle breeze, sixty degrees with no clouds, and a moon almost fully waned. She could make out several of the constellations she remembered from her "easy A" astronomy class.

"Hi, Robert."

"Well, it's confirmed. Bill Knoble is officially missing."

"Nothing since this morning?"

"Nada. The last we saw of him was getting into Siebert's car right before we lost the vehicle in the city. No sightings since."

Disturbing as the news was, she wasn't surprised. She closed her eyes and recalled their phone conversation earlier that morning, when Robert had informed her of Knoble's abduction as well as the fact he'd been unable to track Ben down to tell him about Joe. It was a bad combination to say the least.

"I shouldn't have tried to reach Ben myself," Robert said. "I put Knoble at risk because I wanted to deliver the news personally, but I should've known better. You were right."

"Hindsight's twenty-twenty, Robert." She was letting him off easy yet again and they both knew it. They had a twenty-hour window from when they knew about Joe's kidnapping until Knoble disappeared, and they squandered it. But Robert wasn't the only one she was letting of the hook. She knew the right move and didn't push for it.

"You checked Knoble's apartment?" she blurted out, more to stop thinking about her mistake than anything else.

"Empty. Office too. No signs his disappearance was planned."

"Figures."

"I also reached out to our FBI field offices. All is normal in Boston and Portland."

"Because of Knoble's siblings?"

"His brother has twin daughters. His sister has a teenage son in high school. So if Siebert warned Knoble to get out of Dodge, my money would be on Boston."

"Robert, I think we both know Knoble didn't get out of town."

The silence on the other end of the phone confirmed he knew it, too. They were highly impressed by Siebert, but being impressed by a man didn't mean he was still the right person for the job after his son got kidnapped.

She lowered the phone and stared at the brilliant open sky and its dazzling half-moon. She thought back to her decision at college graduation to ditch outer space to pursue national intelligence. Her eyes grew moist when she recalled the photographs Robert had sent earlier of Siebert...leaning up against the Ford Taurus outside The Sloppy Pancake...waiting for Knoble.

Robert ended his silence. "I knew it. The second we learned about Siebert's son, we should've picked Knoble up."

She didn't remember it that way. In fact, she'd even suggested they increase surveillance on Knoble only to hear Robert object and say they wanted to keep tracking him undetected. But she opted not to call him out on it either. He was blaming himself enough, and it didn't make a difference now anyway.

"Now they're both gone, and God only knows what Siebert will do."

"Any ideas?" she asked.

"I can have an APB put out on Knoble."

"They said they wanted this quiet. That would not be quiet."

"I'm not sure we have much choice at this point."

"We don't know what Ben is going to do."

"So far every judgment we've made…correction, I've made…has been wrong. I don't want to assume the best four days before the deadline."

Just in the nick of time, she thought.

"Robert, you asked for my counsel and I'm providing it. If you put out an APB, you'll be telling the world to look for the one man these people want killed. And not only will they find out, but so will Ben. He'll assume we don't trust him."

"Do we trust him?"

"Trying to find them both is one thing. Throwing an advertisement on the city's bulletin board is another."

"So what do you suggest?"

She paused to rethink the idea through one more time. And to look for any other way, hoping it was possible another option would emerge in ten seconds that had eluded her for hours.

No such luck.

"Tom Fedorak reached out to Nikki Benton a few hours ago, correct?"

"How did you know that?"

"The intelligence isn't all gone from the C-I-A."

"You're tailing my employees?"

"I thought we were past jurisdictional horse manure at this point."

Robert suddenly got defensive and hissed, "you need to keep me in the loop. I don't like you surveilling my people behind my back."

"Robert…let's level set." she cleared her throat and sized up her prey. "Less than a week ago we invited Ben Siebert into a terrorist situation. A terrorist that contacted you directly; you, and no one else."

"What's that supposed to mean?"

"Exactly what it says — that you are the one they called. Presumably because they knew you would bring Ben Siebert, a renegade and expert at bending if not breaking the rules, into this fiasco. A few days later his son is kidnapped and the perps leave a pretty young blonde crying in the street, making it clear his son was the only target. Now a man who has proven to know no bounds, who will do whatever he feels is necessary to render justice, has gone AWOL. And he took Knoble, the subject of the original demand. This isn't a random series of coincidences."

"Thanks for the recap, but is there a point coming?"

"If I put a tail on Ben's ex-fiancé, who happens to be your employee, I expect some latitude. In a level playing field, Ben scares me more than the terrorists do. We know he doesn't want to kill innocent people. But he's incredibly capable of doing whatever it takes."

"And?"

She paused to hear the crickets chirruping away, and watch the moon-illuminated blades of grass dance in the gentle breeze.

"Back to my question. You had Tom Fedorak bring Benton into this?"

"Yes. I thought her insight into Ben's character might help, but I didn't want her to know the request came from me. Her value is in the personal, not the professional. Since we know Tom was in the loop on everything, given the fact she knows and to a degree trusts him, it seemed like a good choice."

"Did he tell her we sought Ben's help before Joe got kidnapped?"

"No," Robert replied with only a slightly less annoyed tone. "He just told her about his son and the ultimatum. Nothing about Ogilvie. I figured less was more."

"Make sure he doesn't. At least for now."

"Why?"

"Because we've got one shot at this. It's a long shot at best. But it'll only work if she doesn't know Ben was involved from the beginning."

17

Ben dialed the number from memory. It was an old habit, one he'd learned years ago. If information wasn't written down or stored in some device, there was no way to prove he knew it existed. For that reason, he'd trained himself to quickly memorize and retains all sorts of information, from phone numbers to addresses to code names and passwords. Often it was overkill, but there was little downside to the practice.

He tugged the Cubs cap over his head and surveyed the area on a pleasant seventy-eight-degree evening with no humidity. At 9:30 on Saturday night, the intersection of Dearborn and Division in Chicago's Near North Side neighborhood was bustling. Pedestrians crowded the sidewalk on both sides of the popular Division Street. En route to restaurants, bars, clubs and all other forms of city nightlife, some of the urbanites briskly motored along the east-west thoroughfare while others took their sweet inebriated time. A mile north of the heart of downtown, a one-minute walk to the Clark/Division Red Line train stop, an endless supply of twenty-somethings popped into and out of the plethora of apartment and condominium complexes along Division that capitalized on the stellar location. Taxis jammed the street intersection; horns beeped every few seconds to encourage the vehicle at the front of a long line to make the light. In the city of Chicago, yellow meant "floor it." The combined honks and conversational clatter was loud enough that Ben stepped inside the Walgreens on the northwest corner to conceal his location.

"Stevens here," Robert answered his cell phone, seemingly out of breath and also outside based on the rustling wind Ben heard through the receiver.

"I need to know right now if you trust me," he whispered as he reached the middle of the empty ninth aisle.

Robert hurried his answer. "Ben? Of course I trust you. I wouldn't have asked for your help if I didn't."

He withdrew the other cell phone from his blue windbreaker pocket and clicked the green "Start" circle, beginning the stopwatch count.

"Have the terrorists contacted you?"

"Ben, what are you doing?"

"We don't have time for that. Have they contacted you?"

"No." Robert sighed. "Where are you?"

"Don't ask questions unless you want answers."

"I need answers. Do you have Knoble? You should've called me after they called you."

"Bill will be fine…until the deadline."

"Does he know anything about all this?"

"There's something you need to know, Robert."

He paused.

"I'm listening."

"I'm not screwing with these people. They have my boy, and unless I can get some answers out of Bill, I'm giving them what they want."

Silence pierced the air like a warm knife through butter. Ben checked the stopwatch again as two girls turned the corner from the photo section and headed down his aisle.

"I have to go. I'll touch base before the deadline."

"Ben. Wait."

He hung up on the twenty-seventh second, a few seconds longer than the time required for the FBI to trace a one time use drop phone without GPS enabled. He walked towards the store exit casually, avoiding eye contact with the store employees and keeping the Cubs hat tucked over his eyes. He hung a left on the sidewalk to wrap around the building and stopped next to the Redbox kiosk. Leaning up against the wall, he looked across the street.

Katy-corner from the Walgreens, on the southeast corner of Dearborn and Division, sat The Lodge Tavern. Its jukebox music was loud enough to have a presence amidst the noisy foot traffic and street gridlock surrounding it. Green Christmas lights hung from The Lodge's roof year-round, and its cabin-like ambiance felt conspicuously quaint in its very modern location. Ben discovered that, founded in 1957, the vintage and rustic watering hole was a local favorite in large part because it hadn't changed much since. Folks crammed elbow-to-elbow nearly every night, and it was known for its friendly customer service. He watched a steady stream of young people mosey inside beneath its vertical wood paneling entryway and three American flags on display. The windows were open; Ben could see patrons enjoying their proper pours and food.

He checked the stopwatch. At 2:04 and counting, it would happen in the next two minutes or not at all. He leaned against the faint yellow brick wall and smiled as a young couple strolled by him. After scanning the area one more time, he withdrew the tiny binoculars from the windbreaker and perused the exterior. Making sure to expose the binoculars to the street cameras from at least two angles, he then shoved them back into his pocket.

The first police car approached The Lodge from the north on Dearborn. Lights off, sirens off. But an unmarked black Chevy Impala — the undercover car of choice for the Illinois State Police — followed close behind. It was clearly a package deal based on how closely the Impala tailgated the squad car. No civilian would ride a cop's ass like that. Then a second police cruiser turned onto westbound Division Street off State Parkway, slowly creeping along until it parked illegally in front of Butch McGuire's tavern across the street from The Lodge.

All three drivers exited their cars and walked into The Lodge. The tall, thin man in plain clothes from the Impala led the way, and Ben could see he was on a mission. The officers followed, all three more concerned with haste than concealment.

Ben watched a few more seconds before walking west past the Walgreens on Dearborn. At Clark, he hailed a cab and dropped the Cubs hat into the trashcan before climbing inside.

He had his answer. He'd needed to know if Robert Stevens trusted him, if Robert could give him an honest answer to an honest question, and if he could actually believe it. Robert brought him into this, but he needed to know if the SAIC was intent on bringing him out.

It wouldn't take long for authorities to find the cell phone he'd planted at The Lodge Tavern a few hours earlier. They'd be able to determine Ben had routed the trace signal to it instead of the phone he'd used to call Robert. Then they'd check the street cameras.

Robert was a smart man. He'd know that the trace the FBI ran — which had been triangulated off two cell phone towers to pinpoint the phone's location — was a setup. Data didn't lie, and the three vehicles that surrounded The Lodge two minutes later had made one thing clear:

The feds may've trusted Ben before, but they sure didn't now.

18

Sunday, May 9

"Don't you ever sleep," Sidarta Perdigao yawned into his cell phone. It was 2:43 a.m. in Curitiba, Brazil.

His fourth cup of Biohazard, the strongest coffee in the world, might as well been a warm cup of milk. With no sleep, shower, or shave the last two days, he felt dirty and itchy all over. His Curitiba Football Club shirt was stained with Vatapá sauce from two nights ago.

"Not when my family is in danger," Ben Siebert replied. "What do you have?"

He turned on the speaker and firmly stroked his stubble, widening his eyes to focus on three large computer screens. Their blue light in his darkened den seemed blinding yet didn't assuage the threat of his eyelids closing.

"Christopher J. Janosch. Fifty-one years old, just over six feet tall, about seventy kilos. Dark eyes, thin build. No noticeable limps, prosthetics, or easily recognizable birthmarks. Typical Midwestern American accent. I just sent his info to you."

"His hair's not dark enough."

"That's why God invented dye."

"Get someone else. This won't work."

"It'll have to. After 26 hours, fifteen calls, four time zones and three banks, this is the best I can do."

He knew the pause that followed wasn't meant to be passive aggressive. Ben was only processing what he said. And the match wasn't bad. Still, he hated disappointing Ben. Anything short of cartwheels would've felt like a letdown.

"You're right, I'm sorry," Ben whispered.

"No need to apologize."

"What's he got?"

"Chronic Obstructive Pulmonary Disease. Grade 4, end-stage."

"Emphysema?"

"And severe chronic bronchitis."

"Pretty typical for COPD. Smoker?"

"Social user, cigarettes and marijuana. But he got COPD from working in the mines for thirty years."

"When was he diagnosed?"

"Eight years ago."

"Prognosis?"

"Terminal."

"But...?" Ben inquired.

He knew Ben would pick up on his apprehension. The answers were coming too quickly, like a well-rehearsed script void of emotion. Ben was the best he'd ever met at identifying and exploiting a person's mental ambivalence. Depending on whether he benefited or suffered as a result, Sidarta always credited or blamed Princeton. Add a double major in psychology and civil engineering to Ben's brain, and this is what happens.

"C'mon," Ben snapped. "We're both tired and I don't have time. Spill it."

"He was supposed to die two years ago. Obviously that hasn't happened."

"Which means it could any day."

"Or that it won't. Doctors aren't always right."

"No," Ben said before sighing, "they're certainly not." Sidarta knew his friend was thinking of Anna — about how shocked the doctors were by her death just hours after her positive prognosis — but this was not the time.

"He's ready, Ben."

"Says who?"

"Says his brother, Larry."

"Larry's not Chris. I need to hear it from the horse's mouth."

"You Americans and your expressions."

"You know what I mean."

"At some point you have to trust someone. Larry and Chris are brothers; thick as thieves. They moved to Mexico eighteen months ago because Chris wanted to die in warm weather by the ocean, and Larry didn't want him to die alone. The poor guy has lost over thirty kilos in three years, half his bodyweight. He's shriveling away to nothing, day-by-day. He's ready."

"But you didn't hear that from Chris."

"I spoke to Larry, who spoke to Chris. So you either trust Larry wouldn't lie about this or we…how do you say…start from scratch."

"How bad is it?"

"It hurts Chris every time he takes a breath. But of course, I didn't hear that from a horse."

The pause that followed was critical. He knew Ben was finally seeing this play out, admitting he didn't want to do it. The horse was just an excuse to look for a way out.

"Is Larry really up for this?"

"He wouldn't do it by himself. He loves Chris more than anyone, and he's the one who'll suffer. But he also understands the way things are and that he can't change them. He knows the pain Chris feels, the chance this is for his brother. He trusts you, remembers that you saved his life twice. I think he's against it, but he wants to honor his brother's wishes."

"Chris is pushing for the money?"

"Wants to be very well compensated."

"You can handle the transactions?"

"Three different accounts on three different continents. All distinct procedures. Unique account owners, security profiles, everything. Airtight processes with plenty of checks and balances. Completely untraceable."

"And you have the technology?"

"As you said, we're both tired and you don't have the time. Either depend on me or don't."

"What else do you need?"

"Just the photographs and samples."

"You'll have both in an hour."

He didn't respond immediately. Doing so would imply he questioned Ben's resolve or motive, something he didn't want to do. He thought about letting it go altogether. They'd taken extreme approaches before.

But this was different.

"You're positive you want to do this, Ben?"

"There's no other way."

"Are you sure?"

Ben wasn't one to flip-flop, but he sensed a hint of trepidation in Ben's voice. It made him wonder if Ben was thinking the same thing he was.

"Prepare the transactions and forward me the account numbers. Be ready to move once you get the pictures and samples."

That would be a yes.

"Ten four."

"Thanks, Sidarta. I owe you one."

"Talk soon."

After Ben disconnected, Sidarta leaned back in his worn leather chair and stared towards heaven. His relationship with Ben ran deep, and it'd been more than fifteen years since they'd first met at their mutual friend's party in Houston. Those were easier times, some might say happier. They'd been through a lot together since. The best, and toughest, parts this life had to offer. But still…what Ben was asking could not only get him imprisoned, it went against his Catholicism. Ben would understand if he said no and had even said as much. He was a family man now. He had a little girl and a boy on the way. Times had changed.

The debate didn't last long. Asking for God's forgiveness beforehand seemed to negate the point, but he did so anyway. Looking at the desk photo of his wife and kids, thankful they were all safe at his sister-in-law's, he recalled what happened to Anna. And that reminded him why he had those responsibilities today, of who was responsible for his wife being alive, much less a mother of one and pregnant with another...

Really, there was no debate.

19

"It's six after two in the morning, Bill. Know what that means?"

Bill Knoble remained frozen. Sleep-deprived yet wide-awake in anguish. Unharmed but immobilized in what looked like a nonfunctioning electric chair affixed to a hydraulic lift. The seat was elevated such that his legs dangled two feet off the ground. His arms were bound to the wooden chair with thick straps that restricted movement. A chest harness and neck brace prevented him from leaning forward, and vice-like wire coiled around his thighs.

Suddenly a frigid and tasteless liquid was poured into his mouth — maybe water, maybe not. It felt like a bucket's worth. Every nerve in his face stung like frostbite.

"When I ask a question, answer it."

Ben Siebert, icier than the liquid, swiftly slapped his cheek. He wore tan pants and a black sweatshirt, sleeves rolled up. Bulging veins surrounded both ulnas as he crossed his arms, piercing Bill with a stare far more terrifying than the pseudo electric chair.

"It means today's Sunday. Because of you, I'm not going to get to bring Anna her lilies."

Bill had no idea where he was. The room reminded him of the back of an eighteen-wheeler. He didn't think he was moving, but the space was long and narrow — ten feet tall, fifty feet long, nine feet wide. It smelled like fish. Bondage prevented full range of motion, but every surface seemed comprised of metal, including the floor and roof. And either the undecorated walls were soundproof or he was in the middle of nowhere because he couldn't hear a thing when Ben's chilling voice ceased. The room was empty except for him, Ben and a small plastic table. He didn't have a great view, but he could see several shiny metal rods on it.

"Ben, I'm so sorry about Joe. But I told you, I have no idea what it's about."

"Enough lies."

"If there was anything I could do, you know I would."

"I don't *know* anything. Other than it's time for you to *think*…think like your life depended on it. Think of all the scumbag clients you've represented, the crooked business partners you had before we met. Anyone you screwed or thinks you did. Dig deep into that memory bank of shit, Bill. Somewhere inside is the reason my son's life is in danger. And you can bet your sorry ass I'm going to find it one way or the other."

"This is the second time I've feared for my life, Ben. And both were because of you. Once was enough. I'll tell you whatever you want to know. I'll give you my life story. I'll answer anything you ask. But as much as I want it to, none of it will explain who took Joe."

"I want to believe you, Bill. I really do. But I can't take chances. And talk is cheap."

Ben leaned in close, inches from his face, and he could feel Ben's warm breath on his cheek. "I'll do whatever's necessary to save Joe. Even with our partnership, the past few years and the good things you've done. I won't hesitate. Not for a second."

"I know you won't."

"No one will hear you scream," Ben said-matter-of-factly. "And no one knows you're here. After you passed out, I checked every square inch of your person for bugs and tracers. I changed cars and went through so many tunnels and garages that anyone who might've been following you is gone."

"No one was following me. I'm not hiding anything."

"We're all alone, Bill. In four days I'll do what I have to. For my son. You had your shot in life, you made your choices. Joe is going to get his. But not before I make certain you're not hiding something. Remember your scumbag client Barry Lee Richard...he got off easy compared to what you've got coming."

"I wish there was something I could do to prove I'm not lying."

"Don't try to talk your way out of this."

"I would never lie to you."

"You said you'd do anything to help Joe...now's your chance. Who's got my boy?" Ben wailed the question, jumping forward and grasping both of Bill's shoulders, his face even closer. He squeezed with ferocity. The intensity in his blue eyes...that unrelenting intensity. Bill couldn't help but piss his pants, closing his eyes in dread. The tears he felt falling down both sides of his face did do involuntarily.

Ben stepped back, keeping his eyes focused on him. The seriousness in his face was unparalleled. He grabbed one of the metal rods from the table, as long as a ruler, as thick as a chopstick. Point on one end, handle on the other. Then he lowered his voice to a whisper.

"This is going to hurt, Bill."

20

Nikki sat in the sprawling South Barrington residence an hour northwest of Chicago. It was just past three p.m. and she didn't know what to expect from Abigail Merriweather, Joe's girlfriend of two years and the last person to see him. The twenty-two-year old clutched her cup of tea with both hands, inhaling lemon and ginger as the steam enveloped and flushed her face. Her blue eyes were moist and her cheeks tear-stained, as if her piping hot drink had fogged her eyes and blinking caused condensation to run down her face.

"It happened so fast..." Abigail said, staring off into the distance.

"I know how hard this is. But anything you can remember might be helpful."

"Ms. Benton, we already talked to the police," said Abigail's impatient mother, protecting her daughter the way Nikki knew she would if it were her child.

Mother's Day was tough in general for Nikki. First, she lost her mom on 9/11. And second, she'd always wanted to be a mother herself. But having just turned forty-two with no husband, Nikki knew that day would never come. So every year when the country celebrated those women for whom it did, part of her couldn't help feeling jealous and unwanted. She grieved that she'd never be able to tell her little girl about the joys and struggles of being a stay-at-home mom. And the fact Abigail's mother reminded her of her own only made it harder.

Focus, she implored herself. *The day will be over soon.*

Mrs. Merriweather sat on the tan sofa next to her daughter, concern in her hazel, teary eyes, scribbling zigzags in the microfiber. Her short brown hair bore little resemblance to Abigail's long, flowing blonde locks, but their slender faces, high cheekbones and thin jaws were mirror images of one another.

"I understand your concern, ma'am. I'll be out of here as soon as possible. But I have to ask…even the tiniest detail might help us find Joe."

"Don't you have any more qualified leads than making my daughter relive the event?"

"Mom, please. If it can help find Joe, I want to."

"Thank you, Abigail," Nikki said, peripherally watching the mother's reaction as Abigail rested a hand on her thigh.

"We had…have…been dating for about a year. We met at Harper College, AGR75: Intro to Architecture. I couldn't decide on a college when I was a senior in high school, so I decided to get my generals out of the way. Joe sat in the back. He was smart, and a little reserved. He had this peaceful way about him, always sort of happy-looking, you know? I could tell right away he wasn't like most guys. He was gentle. For our first date I said I wanted coffee at a coffee shop; he took me to McDonalds. We liked each other right away."

"Did he have any enemies?"

"No. He wasn't a social bug, but everyone who knew him liked him."

"Was anyone upset with him lately?"

"Um," Abigail looked up, scanning her memory, "I don't think so. I never saw him get into it with anyone about anything."

Staring into Abigail's mopey eyes, Nikki knew what she had to do. It wasn't without its drawbacks. The last time she helped Ben, her world unraveled. Innocent people died, including an entire SWAT team. Her boss was killed after being revealed as a traitor. Running for her life and dodging death became regular activities.

But this wasn't about Ben. She once said she'd do anything for Joe. There was a time she was sure she'd be his stepmom. She recalled their relationship's turning point: that special embrace at the park and Joe's warm, accepting smile. She loved him then and knew she loved him now. And he needed her.

"Did you spend a lot of time at Joe's apartment?"

"How is that relevant?" interrupted Mrs. Merriweather.

"Ma'am," Nikki tensely replied, holding up her hand. "The more time she spent there, the more likely she'd noticed something unusual. To your earlier point, we don't have any better leads. Abigail is the last person to see Joe, and I'm trying to get him back to her. Let her talk. She doesn't have to answer anything she doesn't want to."

Nikki's sharp response quieted the anxious and shaken mother. Abigail remained unfettered, proving tougher than she'd originally thought.

"No, I didn't spend much time there. We didn't get serious until a few months ago and even then I never spent the night. We'd watch movies on Friday after class but that was about it."

"Any neighbor issues?"

"I don't think he knew any of them, and I never met any. He crashed at his dad's a lot, so he was in and out. Most of the day he was on campus."

"When did he move out of his father's house?"

"Six months ago."

The reference to Ben's place made her pause. She'd thought of telling them about her connection to the family. It may have increased Abigail's trust factor, but more likely it would've seemed odd and could've stirred up her emotions. She needed Abigail to stay focused on the facts. She needed to as well.

"Abigail, I'd like to talk about the night Joe was kidnapped. Is that okay with you?"

"Yes."

"Your report says the men were in black...did you see anything that might help you identify them?"

"Do you have someone who might've done it?" Abigail excitedly raised her eyebrows and leaned in, as if there was finally something worthwhile in this conversation.

"I'm afraid not. But often times it's an unusual — or I guess 'uncommon' would be a better word — physical characteristic that makes the difference. Something unique you'd be able to recognize if you saw it again. Tattoos, birth marks, noticeable scars, walking limp, high-pitched voice, things like that."

"They were completely covered up. Gloves, masks, long sleeves…I didn't see any skin."

"Did you notice any cleavage?"

"Cleavage? You think they were women?"

"Not necessarily, but right now we don't know much about them. Ruling women out narrows the field by fifty percent."

"I just assumed they were men. I didn't see cleavage, but their clothes weren't skintight. If they were women, they were beastly women. The one that picked me up was strong."

"What about accents?" Nikki asked.

"They didn't say a word. Almost like…" Abigail's voice tailed off. "I don't know what I'm talking about." She looked down at her light blue blouse, slightly shaking her head.

"You'd be surprised what can break open a case. Please, tell me what you meant."

"Well, there were four of them. Three got out of the SUV. One grabbed me, the other two Joe. Then they all got back in at the same time within seconds. With four people and so many moving parts, it would've been natural for someone to say something. It was like they went out of their way not to talk."

She considered Tom's military theory. Surveillance cameras revealed the captors wore the same outfit and drove an unmarked vehicle. In and out in less than a minute, and none of them said a word. They controlled both victims and kept a driver ready for a quick getaway. No weapons except effectively harnessed strength. They used surprise to their advantage skillfully. None of it screamed military by itself, but combined it made for a convincing theory.

But why would the military want Joe?

Then she froze.

Wait…

"Thank you, Abigail," she abruptly ended the conversation. You've been very helpful."

Abigail's face turned to doom on a dime. "Wait, what? That's it?" Abigail exclaimed, leaning forward on her toes. "How does that help you find Joe?"

"Every little bit helps," Nikki replied as she stood up. "Keep your head up." She offered a forced smile and turned towards the door.

"You've got to find him." Abigail grabbed Nikki's arm, clasping it with petite fingers with badly chipped nail polish. "What else can I do?"

The look of desperation in her eyes was heartbreaking, especially when Nikki had so little encouragement to offer. Even Abigail's mother was surprised by the sudden exit and encouraged her to stay, fearing her uninviting attitude had rushed Nikki out.

They offered from the front door to meet again as Nikki quickly backed her Chevy Malibu out of the driveway.

21

Clay Braun licked his lips thinking of the possibilities.

Olympic Drive ran through the center of a community that boasted massive, custom-built, three-car-garage homes on half-acre parcels. Residents were less than a quarter mile from two playgrounds, several well-kept ponds and a forest preserve with bike trails. Nestled between open prairies, with old-fashioned street lighting, it sat only two miles north of I-90 and adhered to strict property maintenance codes. Perfectly trimmed hedges, landscaped flowerbeds and uniformly manicured trees at the end of every freshly sealed driveway made it clear that these folks considered themselves winners.

Which meant that these hoity-toity South Barrington residents had busy, self-important lives. That they were certain their million-dollar homes would be perfectly secure with alarm systems and a guard dog sign; that they could otherwise go about their perfect little days, with their yoga classes and seven-dollar latte runs, without a care in the world. That was gold for him.

Accessing the Merriweather residence wasn't a problem.

He planted all the devices on Saturday in less than thirty minutes, while the parents took the "poor" girl out to help her cope with her "traumatic" experience. Standard surveillance was all that was necessary: nearly invisible audio bugs and hidden cameras that wirelessly transmitted signals to the mobile transceiver next him on the front seat. Nothing over the top, but plenty to get the job done. Reception was clear as his Chevy Tahoe crawled up and down the sixth-of-a-mile Olympic Drive to the cul-de-sac and back.

He made six loops over the course of the FBI agent's thirty-minute conversation with the girl and her mother. He probably could've just parked across the street, but with transmission devices that had a 6,500-foot range, why do that? Some little old lady across the street could be on neighborhood watch. And even on Mothers' Day, unfamiliar parked cars were the first thing people would notice.

Arminius would appreciate his thoroughness. Maybe as a reward he'd get some quality mother-daughter time with the Merriweather girls when this was over.

He was just north of Mesa Drive when the agent hurriedly exited the home and backed away in her blue Chevy Malibu. He aimed the tiny camera concealed in his sleeve and took rapid shots. He'd magnify the pictures later, but from a distance she looked about forty and fit. Good body. Another potential prize.

Nothing of substance came in their conversation, but the agent must have thought of something. Even the mother was surprised by how quickly it ended. Arminius would want him to find out what it was. He'd do some research on the agent before he called the boss with a report.

Might get me that reward after all.

22

The driver of the red Chevy Tahoe made three mistakes.

First, he looped around Olympic Drive six times. Probably to prevent the subdivision's residents from growing suspicious of a parked car, but to Ben it had the opposite effect. Next, just as Nikki exited the Merriweather residence, he continued south before hanging a right on Wood Oaks Drive to exit the community. Awfully coincidental timing. Finally, the driver then hung a right on Sutton Road towards Algonquin when he could've gotten to the same place simply by heading north on Olympic. The man was clearly going out of his way to avoid driving past the Merriweather residence.

Ben took his final pictures with the long-range Smart Scope and put it down to grab the 5,000-yard range binoculars. He focused the lens and followed it as long as he could. The Tahoe was still heading northeast on Dundee when it got out of range.

Ben remained on his stomach atop the Barbara B. Rose Elementary School roof, three-quarters of a mile northeast from the Merriweather residence. The front of the red brick, three-story building faced north, so Ben had positioned himself at its posterior to get a clear view of the house. His athletic pants and long-sleeved T-shirt matched the dark brown hue of the roof's standard asphalt shingles. If a bystander spotted him, his story would've been that he was a bird enthusiast who wanted to get some aerial shots of the Stillman Nature Center fowl a half-mile to the east. It wasn't the strongest explanation, but it would work given it wasn't a school day. Most folks would chalk it up to poor judgment and think Ben was weird if not a tad creepy, but they wouldn't be suspicious enough to report it.

While the precautions were in place, they were unnecessary. On an overcast Mother's Day there wasn't any foot traffic, and his view was good enough that he would've spotted any pedestrians before they spotted him. In addition, the back of the building was shielded from cars travelling on Penny Road, the east-west street running in front of the school that served as the closet thing to a thoroughfare. He'd verified beforehand the school didn't have cameras, so he was confident his reconnaissance went unnoticed. Nonetheless, he didn't make a single movement that could've been visible from a distance the entire time.

Assured the Tahoe driver was gone for good, he moved the Vortex binoculars to follow the Malibu as it drove away from the house. He bit his lower lip when the lens came into focus, hoping for one clear glimpse of the most beautiful woman in the world.

Even a year later, it amazed him how gorgeous Nikki was. When she arrived he stayed focused on the Tahoe, knowing that her conversation with Abigail the long-range parabolic microphone had recorded could be played back later. He'd wanted to watch her, to see that beautiful brown hair and captivating smile, but the Tahoe's driver had taken a keen enough interest in Nikki that Ben kept his focus there. But now that the Tahoe was out of the picture, he hoped for just a glimpse of her from behind as she drove south towards I-90. When she merged onto the interstate eastbound towards Chicago, he dropped the binoculars into the duffle bag next to the parabolic microphone.

He didn't run, which would attract attention, but he needed to get this information to his contact ASAP. The burly Tahoe driver didn't look familiar to him. He was about six-three, strong build, roughly two hundred pounds with a large torso. He had scruffy brown facial hair and wore a plain black ball cap with barbed wire tattoos on both arms. Ben wasn't surprised he didn't recognize the man, but with nothing other than a handful of still images to go on, he needed to get answers fast.

Though it probably wouldn't amount to much, he was also eager to listen to the conversation between Nikki and the Merriweather ladies with undivided attention. The sound waves' transmission through the transducer wasn't crystal clear at that range, but Nikki's voice still made him smile. Despite being muffled, her sweet and feminine intonation felt soothing to him.

And now she was a target.

23

"Nicole Angela Benton; goes by Nikki. Forty-two, single, parents deceased, sister she doesn't see much. Smart but not brilliant, capable but not innovative."

Timothy Rausch rambled on, providing Arminius information he already knew through the Silent Circle cell phone he required Clay Braun to use. Rausch, and informants like Rausch's contract employee Braun, were never sure what he did and didn't know. That was why he gave Braun the orders to stakeout the Merriweather residence, but then got the output summary from Rausch. That way, Rausch didn't hear what he told Braun, and Braun didn't hear what Rausch told him. It kept him a step ahead of everyone and his identity protected along the way. The details were theirs, and he paid for their services. But the big picture was his and Agricola's and no one else's.

Rausch was right; there was much more work to be done. It was almost midnight and he'd be up for hours. Flipping through a stack of photos showing Nikki Benton walking into and out of Merriweather's house, he carefully studied each page before asking questions, most of which he already knew answers to.

"How long has she been in Chicago?" he spoke into the phone.

"A little less than three years. Phoenix before that. All told she's been in the FBI for twelve."

"And before Phoenix?"

"Civilian job. Computer programmer."

"Did she learn anything from the Merriweather girl?"

"No, sir," Rausch quickly replied.

"How can you be sure?"

"We bugged every room of the house and surveilled their entire conversation. No breaks in the dialogue, nothing that wasn't recorded and photographed. She got nothing. Plus, there wasn't anything to get. The girl doesn't know anything. She spent half the time crying, still in shock. It was a waste of time. Benton left with more questions than answers."

"Keep someone there, someone other than Braun. Benton might be back and I don't want her noticing that creep."

"Will do."

"You mentioned Benton's visit not making sense before..." he segued, careful not to reveal more curiosity than was necessary.

"Yes, sir," Rausch replied. "Nineteen months ago she resigned from the FBI after spending her entire tenure in Domestic Terrorism. When she came back two months later, she moved into the Online Predator Division."

"Violent Crimes Against Children?"

"Pretty drastic shift after twelve years."

"And an unusual one for the FBI."

"My thoughts exactly, so I looked into it. It looks like her boss pulled some strings to make it happen."

"Who's that?"

"Robert Stevens. Career Bureau man. Stellar reputation, very sharp. He was Benton's SAIC in Phoenix for eight years."

"Career man, eh?" He chucked.

"What's so funny, sir?"

"Why'd she quit to come back two months later?"

"Because of her old SAIC in Chicago."

This time, Arminius didn't respond at all.

"Marcus Redmond," Rausch continued. "He was implicated in a scandal and killed in a warehouse fire before she resigned."

It was an explosion, you imbecile.

"So Stevens took over and brought Benton back?" He steered away from Redmond. The name itself was innocuous, but it would lead to questions.

119

"That's right," Rausch replied.

"She wanted a change and only agreed to come back if she could switch divisions. Doesn't seem all that bizarre, considering the reason she left."

"That's not the fishy part."

"You're questioning why Benton visited the girl?"

"In her new role, she shouldn't be talking to Abigail Merriweather. It's completely outside her jurisdiction. The entire conversation was outside FBI protocol."

"Maybe Stevens gave her a side job."

"There are four special agents in the Chicago office, each with over twenty years. Any one of them could run circles around Benton."

"Maybe they're too busy," he snapped.

"Actually their workload is relatively light. And this case is smack dab in the middle of their wheelhouse."

"What's that tell you?"

"That Benton's doing whatever she's doing on the side, outside of formal responsibility. It explains why she went there on Mothers' Day. What it doesn't answer is why she talked to the girl in the first place. It must be personal."

Maybe you're not such an imbecile after all.

Arminius flipped through Benton's personnel file, provided by another source, and stopped on page thirty-six. Her connection to Ben Siebert highlighted in yellow, he stared at the background Rausch didn't possess.

The impressive former Marine shed his tail late Friday afternoon, and then did the same to Knoble's FBI surveillance on Saturday morning. Arminius wasn't surprised. He'd learned long ago that you couldn't follow some men in secret. But Siebert was a loner, a specialist who thrived in the solitary. He wouldn't rely on an ex-girlfriend to help him find what was most precious to him, FBI or not.

Of course, the real threat Benton posed had nothing to do with Siebert.

He thought through the implications of doing nothing. Benton got zilch from the girl and should be off the case soon, so why stir the pot? It just wasn't *his* MO. He didn't play the odds, he bet on sure winners. Agricola didn't want surprises, and he needed Agricola to know he was in control. He couldn't let Benton jeopardize that. Not with who Siebert's next target was.

"What are your orders?" Rausch asked.

"Stay on her. Report back what she does, where she goes, who she talks to. Leave the why to me."

"Yes, sir."

"And keep your distance. She might not be a top investigator, but she's still FBI. I don't want her catching the scent."

"Understood."

"Touch base daily. Same number. I'll send a new descrambler code every morning."

He hung up and checked his watch. Agricola would be stepping off his Learjet 60 in eighteen minutes. Best not to bother him with this. Things were going according to plan and there was no reason to sound the alarm. He didn't need Agricola getting worried.

He'd take care of Benton himself.

Part II

24

Monday, May 10

At precisely ten a.m., FBI GS-7 Junior Agent Roy Dietrich knocked on the double-door entrance to Robert Stevens's corner office with as much confidence as he could muster; yet it still felt grossly insufficient.

He did what was asked of him last week. He found and delivered the mysterious Ben Siebert to the offsite location in Elk Grove Village. But since getting dismissed afterward by the SAIC, he hadn't so much as been asked for a debrief. Left to assume no news was good news, Roy went back to his administrative duties.

The unexpected phone call yesterday — on a Sunday afternoon — had presented him with yet another urgent request involving the former Marine. Since once again SAIC Stevens gave him neither the background nor the reason for the assignment, he could only assume it was because of how sensitive it was.

In his hand he held a red folder, the contents of which had both surprised and bemused him. He rechecked his watch for the third time in the past ten minutes. It was just after ten, meaning he'd turned the assignment around in less than eighteen hours and that included a Sunday evening full of calls. That had to count for something. But the lack of feedback on his last assignment left him wondering. And this was Robert Stevens. The man wasn't accustomed to waiting for things.

"Come in, Roy," the response came from the other side of the double doors.

He tugged at his navy blazer one last time and ran his hand through his short and perfectly combed black hair before entering.

"Good morning, Mr. Stevens."

"Stick with Robert, son. I hear 'Mr. Stevens' and I look for my father."

Stevens rose from behind the mahogany desk and walked past the kegerator and Guinness sign to shake his hand. The blinds were drawn and only Stevens's small desk light was on, making for a very darkened room. The large American flag mural was impossible to miss, and he noticed a half-smoked cigar burned into an ashtray atop the desk. Stevens's crackly voiced sounded old and worn. His jacket was nowhere to be seen; his navy tie had been loosened at the neck. The red suspenders looked too tight across Stevens's torso, like they were squeezing his lungs, and a potbelly protruded from around the taught polypropylene.

"Can I get you anything?" Stevens asked, motioning for him to take a seat at the four-person table.

"No thank you, sir," he answered, uneasily lowering himself into the leather chair.

"So," the SAIC replied while flicking on the overhead lights, "Do you have what I asked for?"

"Yes sir," he responded, laying the red folder on the table. "I checked the street cameras, and I did indeed identify a high-probable match. Right here," he said, pointing to the first photo of a 6'4" male in a Cubs hat, jeans and a blue windbreaker.

"Walgreens," Stevens replied, not necessarily to him but more as a general statement.

"Yes sir. Right across the street from The Lodge Tavern. The suspect entered the pharmacy at just before nine-thirty and stayed inside for thirty-seven seconds. Afterwards, he walked outdoors and hooked around to the side of the building. While there, he was clearly on the lookout."

Roy flipped the page to a close-up of Benjamin Nicholas Siebert. Siebert looked just as Roy remembered him last week. He held a small pair of binoculars pointed strait towards The Lodge, and his face was void of expression. The photo left little doubt what Siebert was doing, or that it was in fact Siebert. He was surprised when he compared the shot side-by-side with the FBI file photo. Aside from the cap, Siebert looked identical.

"Any surveillance inside the store?" Stevens asked, adjusting his reading glasses as he pulled the photograph to within inches of his face.

"Yes sir. Visual. He was on the phone the whole time." Roy pointed to the next page, showing Siebert standing alone in an aisle on a cell phone.

"Audio?"

"Unfortunately, he was talking too low for the store's system to pick anything up. They don't have microphones in every aisle."

Roy could've sworn he saw an ever-so-slight smirk creep across Stevens's face, but he was too busy trying to not screw up his report to think about it. Stevens could react however he wanted. All Roy had on his mind was the GS-9 promotion that lately felt within reach.

When the director didn't respond, flipping back and forth between photographs in the stack, Roy continued. "One thing that's clear is Siebert took interest in the CPD squad cars."

"Yeah?" Stevens raised his eyebrow.

"You can see it in the next close-ups..." he pointed to the photographs. "See how he turns his neck to follow the officers from their vehicles into the bar?"

"Indeed I do. And then he left..." Stevens replied.

"That's correct, sir. Just over three minutes after he walked outside."

"Interesting," Stevens answered, stroking his chin. Roy could hear the stubble pressing up against Stevens's fingers. "Where did he go?"

"Walked to Clark Street and hailed a cab. I tracked it to Park West, a multimedia facility in Lincoln Park on Armitage that also does live theater. There was a performance Saturday night. Siebert went in just before ten, but no surveillance shows him coming out."

Stevens leaned back in the chair and rested his foot on his knee, shaking his head and mumbling to himself under his breath. Roy wasn't trying to eavesdrop on the boss's conversation with himself, but he couldn't make out what he was saying nonetheless. Stevens appeared burdened by this news — his open face, his fingernail nibbling, the dialogue with himself — Roy kept quiet, but he knew something was wrong.

"Good work, son. That's twice you've delivered for me in the past week. I'll make sure your GS-9 advancement happens soon."

"Thank you, sir!" he replied, then worried he'd revealed too much excitement.

"You earned it," Steven's said without looking at him, his eyes focused on the pictures.

"Much appreciated, sir. I'll get this logged right away."

"No, leave it."

"Sir?"

"It's part of another investigation that I need to keep a lid on. I'll enter it."

"Sir," he continued. "I can do that for you and then restrict access to your level and above—"

"Roy, leave it," Stevens interrupted him with a dismissive wave. "And keep this confidential. Not a soul."

He wasn't about to remind SAIC Stevens that not logging evidence was both against bureau protocol and a little bizarre...not with his promotion coming sooner rather than later. Instead, he nodded his head and left the office with Stevens still fixated on the photos he'd provided, wondering what it all meant.

25

Susan Reynolds felt like an exasperated zombie. She hadn't slept thirty consecutive minutes the past three days and everywhere she turned, she found more frustrating dead ends.

The deadline for Knoble's execution was tomorrow. Yet she and Robert had no leads as to where he was, hadn't heard from the terrorists since the original call to Robert, and hadn't made any headway locating Ben. The FBI and CIA analysts confirmed the explosives in Ogilvie and on the train at Union Station were made of components readily available enough that they couldn't trace a rare material purchase. Furthermore, no fingerprints, DNA or other distinguishing marks had been found on either device.

The lack of results unsettled her. Robert had remained composed, but she felt like a basket case. Did she honestly think Ben was going to kill Knoble? No, she didn't. But neither did she like the idea of sitting back and waiting to see if it happened. Time running out, it felt like they were standing on the tracks, watching the freight train approach. She'd spent the better part of a week looking for any intelligence whatsoever on the terrorists and hadn't come up with one solid lead.

"Anything?" she answered her desk line on the first ring.

"No dice, Susan," Robert answered. "We've gone through a long list of former clients, landlords, ex-girlfriends, classmates and former business associates that may've had a bone to pick with Knoble. Over three hundred people in total. Every one of them checked out."

"What exactly does that mean?"

"They're either dead, had confirmed alibis during the time the terrorists called me last week or haven't spoken with Knoble in years. In most cases, decades. Knoble wasn't the kind of guy folks kept in touch with."

"The people who made the call don't have to be the ones who want him dead. Maybe they're hired help."

"I can't interrogate eight billion people on that basis, Susan."

"I know, it's just…"

"We're running out of time."

She stared at the large photo of the earth taken from outer space on her wall, her inspiration to think big picture. She closed her eyes and retraced the steps they'd taken, looking for the miss. Something had to be there. It always was.

"Ben's house has been empty the whole time," Robert continued. "I've got a unit there and all his other known locations. We checked the properties we know Ben has access to and got the same. But you and I both know the guy's got a Rolodex of people and places to choose from, and there's not enough time to run every one to ground."

"Robert, how can we not have *anything*?"

"You've been in the intelligence business longer than I have. Most fugitives, foreign and domestic, even the ones on the Most Wanted lists, last longer than seven days before we nail 'em. Let's face it, most anyone can hide for a week and have a decent chance at not being found. The typical fugitive is smart enough to not use credit cards and stay off his phone.

"And this is Ben Siebert, a guy who's trained in countersurveillance, comes from the military and has connections and a stockpile of cash. He finds some motel or hideaway, locks himself in for seven days and has food delivered, we're gonna have a hard time finding him in a week."

"What about the tape recording?"

"Nothing's changed since last week, Susan. We got the same results your analysts did. Linguist experts confirmed the tone of the terrorist's voice was relaxed and undistinguished. No surprise. Also like your analysts, they didn't feel there was enough evidence to indicate they were local to Chicago.

"We checked every building and street camera adjacent to Ogilvie, assuming they were watching me on the walkway bridge. Nothing. But let's be honest, that's an even smaller needle in a bigger haystack than Ben's Rolodex. Depending on what kind of equipment they had, they could've been in hundreds of places and probably weren't wearing a sign on their back. I've got the entire office turned upside down looking for anything, but the pickings are beyond slim."

"How are you so calm, Robert?" she barked. "This thing is gonna explode on our faces if something doesn't change quick. Pun intended."

"Make no mistake," Robert spoke softly, "I'm very worried. But panicking won't help us find Knoble or Ben."

She sighed, as loud as she could, directly into the receiver; the equivalent of throwing her hands up in person. Robert didn't respond, but she pictured him equally frustrated. But he was right; panic never helped.

Still…

"Robert, what are we going to do? We're no further along finding these people than we were a week ago."

After she said it, there was a pause. She hoped that meant Robert had an idea. Off the wall, long shot, whatever it was…she'd take it. Even the slightest possibility could open the door to a breakthrough. In her experience, it usually worked that way.

But instead of breathing more life into that snowball's chance, Robert killed it by saying, "Susan, I honestly don't know."

26

Wednesday, May 12

Ben's mouth was sticky-dry after the salty pizza last night, and his eyes felt crusty in the corners and bloodshot after a week of no sleep. It hurt like hell to swallow, like an awful case of strep. The phone vibrated loudly, unanswered, as he plunged his head into a sink of cold water.

It's Wednesday.

Groggy despite the plunge, he patted his dripping face with a towel, cleared his throat with a violent cough, and replaced his red polo with a purple one. As "freshened up" as he'd get, he checked the alarm clock. Three in the morning.

The baby monitor verified Bill was still asleep in the adjoining makeshift room, a custom-designed Ahern vault typically used in banks. The lawyer lay curled in the fetal position on the floor, his tattoo-covered bare feet inching out past the blue afghan next to a half-eaten plate of pizza and open two-liter of Diet Coke.

He answered the phone. "What do you think you're doing?"

"Nice to know you're alive, Grasshopper. What kind of a greeting is that?"

"Are you calling from your place?"

"Who in the hell do you think you're talking to? I'm not some limp dick hippie who doesn't understand proper surveillance. I've forgotten more about it than you'll ever know."

"You tell me."

"Not sure what that's supposed to mean, but I'm not getting any younger taking your shit. You didn't mention taking Knoble with you on your little journey off the grid," Tom replied loudly with deep inflection. "You realize that's a crime in this country, right?"

"I didn't have to tell you, Tom. You knew I would." He softened his tone and felt the tension on the other end of the line lessen.

"I'm not sure who the ass was that answered the phone," Tom replied, "but tell him if he shows again, he and I are gonna have words."

"Why'd you bring Nikki into this?"

Tom let the question sit for a moment.

"So that's why you're acting like a pissy little schoolgirl."

"Why, Tom?"

"Desperate times call for desperate measures."

"I don't want her involved."

"And I don't want an innocent man to die. It ain't a perfect world."

Ben looked again at the monitor, silently agreeing with Tom that the world was far from perfect.

"This is dangerous. She's not qualified."

"We need any help we can get."

"The FBI was involved before I was."

"Involved with finding terrorists, not finding Joe," Tom shouted into the receiver. The valid point danced in front of Ben like a puppet on a string. He paused a few seconds.

"Okay, let me say this out loud. Just so I have it clear in my head. You think straight-laced Nikki Benton, who's only gone out on a limb once in her life, hated every minute of it then and has regretted it since, is going to find Joe when the FBI and CIA can't?"

"We need eyes on everything, Grasshopper. Her personal connection to the kid could help make sure Joe's kidnapping gets the attention it deserves."

"You shouldn't have done that."

"You want to get Joe back? I've got feelers out to everyone I trust, and I'm not getting anywhere. The perps haven't

131

contacted you since Friday; Stevens in over a week. Tonight's the deadline. So when Stevens threw the idea out there, I didn't see much of a choice."

"It was Robert's idea to bring Nikki in?" he snapped, outrage in his voice.

"You're missing the point, Grasshopper. It doesn't matter whose idea it was. We need every bit of help we can muster."

"So when in doubt, put two people I love in jeopardy instead of one?"

"Have you gotten anything from Knoble?"

"I'm not finished."

"You won't…because we both know there's nothing to get."

"We'll see."

"Have I taught you nothing?" Tom sighed. "If there was something there, you would've gotten it already. Do you want Knoble to make crap up just to appease you?"

Tom paused before continuing. "Look…maybe it wasn't my place to call her. But I did, so get over it."

"Yet you didn't tell her the whole story?"

"How did you…never mind. No, I told her what was necessary."

"Nothing about their first call to Stevens or the bombs?"

"As you've pointed out, the FBI is already all over that."

"She's going to find out."

"Maybe so. But I didn't want her focus on anything but Joe."

"Tom, did you tell her, or anyone, about…" he stopped short of saying it.

"Against my better judgment, no I did not. But I think we should."

"Not now. Talk to your NSA contacts, run a parallel investigation. Crosscheck everything you can about Knoble. But keep Mexico City need-to-know basis."

"What's really on your mind, Grasshopper?"

He hesitated. Even Tom had his limits. Oversharing now would only put his mentor further into Harm's way.

"I should've recorded that call. What's wrong with me?"

"Grasshopper, they were watching you like a hawk. All that would've happened if you'd tried anything is you would've wound up smashing two phones instead of one. Are you holding something back from me?"

"What makes you ask that?"

"It's your turn to answer my question," Tom persisted.

Ben could hear Tom's heavy breathing. He didn't blame Tom for being frustrated if not outright upset. He thought about telling him about his phone call to Robert and The Lounge Tavern raid, but quickly decided against it. There were still far too many unknowns for that right now. Tom already had more than enough on his plate.

"We need to be careful about whom we trust," he answered.

"Are you referring to Nikki or me?"

"It's not that. She's out of her league, Tom. She'll try to help, but this is more dangerous than she knows. And she could really screw things up."

"More than they already are?"

"You know what I mean, Tom."

"She's got an interesting theory. She thinks they took Joe because of you."

"They made that pretty clear."

"You don't follow me. She thinks killing Knoble is a smokescreen. That this is all about you and he's just a lynchpin."

"Pretty presumptuous considering she doesn't know Knoble and hasn't talked to them."

"Be that as it may, do you think she's onto something?"

While devouring day-old pizza with nothing to wash it down, Ben again considered what Nikki might contribute. She was fastidious, detail-oriented and legally on the good guys' team…all things he wasn't. By that logic, she could be a great complement. But the risk was too great.

"They could've just gone after Joe. Why the train station fiasco?"

"You got me there, Grasshopper. But still…do you think she's onto something?"

"I suppose it's possible. What they're telling me sure doesn't make sense by itself. And these guys could've just as easily killed Knoble as kidnapped Joe, not to mention the bombs. So why take the risk? It just adds another failure point. Trust me, I'll find out if Knoble knows anything."

"What are you going to do?"

"Stick to the plan."

"Even if Nikki's right?"

"Tonight's the deadline. Don't have much choice."

"Just remember you can't take this one back, Grasshopper. You're a good man. You've always done what needed to be done, and at times that can paint a nasty picture of someone in the wrong light. But you've been principled. Much as I hate to admit it, your Brazilian amigo has a point. This one's different. A real life, an innocent life, is at stake."

"I know."

"Ben," Tom paused, almost as if hesitating, "I know you're keeping your cards close to the vest, even from me. And I trust there's good reason. Just make sure this is all necessary. Remember what I told you in the Marines."

"Aim twice, shoot once. There are no do-overs in war."

"This is war, Grasshopper."

27

The building lacked air-conditioning despite the stifling Mexico City heat. There was no running water for bathrooms or drinking, and a rotting four-person wooden picnic table next to the outhouse served as the lunchroom. It teemed with ants, desperate for a crumb.

The shop floor was 200 square meters and every centimeter was covered in tannish grit. Dust particles swirled as fans recirculated grimy, stale air. On top of that, the building lacked a confined paint booth for its spray operation. The first time Sidarta Perdigao stepped inside, fumes engulfed his face with such vigor that his nostrils stung.

How could people get used to this?

But they did. Forty-eight employees worked two twelve-hour shifts to earn an average of 150 pesos, about eight US dollars, per day. Mexican music rattled from a decrepit boom box and a shrine of Mary stood elevated in the corner, a small spotlight angled towards the Savior's mother's face. Such was the standard layout of a small manufacturing company near Mexico City, of which there was no shortage thanks to cheap labor and access to the US.

The "office" — a twenty square meter converted storage room devoid of light and hemmed in by cinderblock — sat thirty meters from the manufacturing floor. Three stray, emaciated Labrador Retrievers walked freely between the two buildings, but everyone knew not to pet or feed them. There were no pictures or trinkets in the makeshift office, just a stack of paper and one manila folder. Sidarta ran an extension cord to his laptop, three boxes of paper serving as a desk. Sucking down another bottle of Bonafont El Agua Ligera, he ran his hand through his wet hair and wiped his sweat-covered fingers on his Dungarees.

When the phone rang, he was torn. On one hand, he was close to going home, where glorious air conditioning would save him from mid-afternoon heat exhaustion. On the other, his last chance to back out was upon him. After this, he was a spectator.

"Any changes with Knoble?" he answered.

"None," Ben replied.

"Merda." *Shit*.

"Is everything ready?"

"I've been here for two days to make sure it is."

"And?"

He couldn't find it in himself to answer right away. The proverbial point of no return was here, and the guilt of the operation was putting up a stronger fuss than he expected.

"And?" Ben repeated. His voice was so calm, monotone. How was Ben not having the struggle he was?

"Friend," he whispered into the receiver, "this operation...it reminds me of the streets I had to drive on to get here. Uncontrolled intersections all over the place, bumps and potholes everywhere, crazy drivers that won't stop until it's too late."

"Your point...friend?"

"There's going to be an accident."

"I agree. Ready to go?"

He paused for a final time: *There is no debate.*

"All is good in Mexico, amigo."

Without hesitation, Ben replied, "Talk to Larry again?"

"Everything is prepared," he replied, smacking a mosquito on his neck before digging his filthy fingernails into his itchy skin.

"What did he say?"

"I said everything is prepared. Trust me or don't, but make up your mind."

"Ten four."

"Ben...if you decide to abort for any reason, make the call as soon as possible. He's there now, waiting for Larry."

"Waiting for what?"

"Confirmation from his brother the transfers are complete. Don't take it personally."

"I don't blame him."

"It buys you time."

"How much?"

"Until about six-thirty Chicago time. No later, friend. You wouldn't want to find a way out of this and not be able to take advantage."

"I'll call before then if anything changes."

"I'll be here. So will Larry."

"Sidarta..."

"Yes?"

"Nothing will change."

28

Genie was starting to worry.

It'd been four days since Mr. Knoble awkwardly climbed into Ben Siebert's Taurus and he hadn't been to the office, left a message, called, or e-mailed since. Clients showed up for scheduled meetings only to be turned away with an apology and promise to reschedule. She'd tried to reach him via phone, e-mail and text. A drive to his house revealed drawn blinds and an unanswered door. The cancellations piling up, she pulled the plug that morning and cleared the calendar for the balance of the week.

Mr. Knoble's disappearance would've been less mysterious years ago before he'd stopped drinking, when ripped jeans and T-shirts was the office dress code and absenteeism its theme. In those days she'd look forward to his unannounced vanishings, but at the very least she would've gotten a drunken text. For there to be nothing, it felt like something was wrong.

Her knee-jerk conjecture was that he'd had fallen off the wagon and was lying drunk on some bar floor. But after failing to reach Mr. Siebert as well, she considered the possibility of an accident. The thought of him comatose, clinging to life in some hospital bed made her feel guilty for her initial theory and intensified her concern. Her stomach suddenly felt queasy; she slammed her At-A-Glance shut and bolted to the bathroom. After a round of dry-heaves at the sink, she looked into the mirror.

She looked old. The long brown hair that symbolized her youth seemed stringy and in need of a trip to the salon. Her furrowed brow shouted that it was due for another round of Botox. She grabbed hold of either side of the sink with trembling fingers, trying to steady herself. She unsuccessfully tried to blink back tears, the individual droplets beading up and slipping down her fake lashes like some amusement park log flume.

She didn't want to overreact, but she didn't know what to do. Should she call Mr. Knoble's sister in Boston? As his emergency contact, Caitlyn might help her rule out an accident. Should she report him missing? Surely someone closer to him would have noticed his disappearance...right? Or was this on her?

She made her way back to Reception pondering such unappealing options and began surfing the web for missing person statistics. The phone call came 3:06.

"Genie, it's Bill."

"Mr. Knoble! Where have you been?"

"I can't explain right now. Can you meet me at eight?"

"Tonight? Mr. Knoble, what's going on? You've missed appointments."

"Everything's fine, but I need your help. I can't talk about it over the phone. Meet me at Townhouse at eight. If you're coming from Ogilvie, make sure you take Adams Street. Construction on Monroe is awful."

"Mr. Knoble, you're kind of freaking me out."

"Sorry, kiddo. Not my intention. See you tonight. I want to hear all about the exams and introduce you to butter-dipped steak. You deserve it."

To say she was relieved was an understatement. But when Mr. Knoble sent both a follow up e-mail and text confirming the time and place, she grew curious. He wasn't particularly good at remembering scheduled meetings, much less verifying one twice in advance. The earlier hand tremors returned.

29

Adrenaline and eagerness fueled Genie's walk east on Madison towards Townhouse Restaurant and Wine Bar near downtown Chicago. At first she was exhilarated just to know Mr. Knoble was safe, but his mysterious phone call and confirmations grabbed her the way a snake takes hold of its prey.

Townhouse was in the River West neighborhood, a few blocks north of Willis Tower and less than a half-mile from Ogilvie. She'd taken Mr. Knoble's advice to avoid construction by slightly overshooting on Canal to cross the river via Adams Street, just past the Charles Schwab building. Under different circumstances it would've been a pleasant walk on a pleasant evening.

Dusk upon Chicago at just before eight, she walked north up Wacker Drive under the light of a crescent moon. It didn't take long to spot Townhouse's prominent sweeping glass wall and shiny metal doors. Opposite the frou-frou wet bar, the southern wall's enormous floor-to-ceiling windows emitted a light-blue glint, the perfect atmosphere for the two-person tables that lined it. It offered an elegant setting for either a romantic dinner or business powwow.

She'd been there a few times before and it was always loud. This added to the location's mystique, since Mr. Knoble hated crowds. An hour before closing, people were packed in like sardines. She spotted Mr. Knoble sitting at the end of that southern wall of large windows, near the hostess stand next to the door. The ceiling's faint track lighting danced on his navy jacket and open-collared white shirt. His upper body twisted towards the window, his left arm lay flat against the table. His right held a brown pepper mill. Hair combed to the side instead of straight back, he must not have noticed her because he didn't wave, though he seemed to be looking straight at her. She continued walking past Au Bon Pain café bakery.

She knew right away they were gunshots, despite the fact she'd never fired a gun or heard one up close. Her rural Missouri background told her fireworks were wishful thinking. The three loud pops seemed to have come from behind, but with the echo there was no certainty.

Except the target. Mr. Knoble sat there, motionless, staring at her. His shirt was turning crimson before her eyes; his mouth hung open.

She hit the concrete sidewalk and assumed the fetal position, shielding her head with both arms as if that could prevent her death. Her cheeks were instantly flooded with tears. Her body shook like a maraca.

Full panic ensued, people running by her on either side, screaming and yelling. She nervously peeked between her fingers on each hand, peering through the tiny gap as if she were somehow protected.

Then she forced her hands down for an unobstructed view of her mentor, and dry heaved at the sight. Mr. Knoble's shirt was more red than white. He hadn't left the table and appeared slightly hunched over, staring at her. The glass window lay in pieces all over him. His mouth remained open, as did his eyes. He looked vegetated, like he'd had a lobotomy.

His stare continued…still seemingly straight at her…for thirty seconds. Then suddenly he hunched all the way over, plummeting facedown onto the table, arms dangling on either side. The impact sent shards of broken glass jumping off the table and when they landed in his hair, he remained motionless.

Her survival instincts took over and all she could think to do was run.

30

Susan Reynolds was hogging air after only five hundred feet. Her car still idling on Randolph — a sure tow candidate three blocks north of Townhouse Restaurant and Wine Bar — she forced her way against the crowds in sandals, jeans and a T-shirt. She figured running there would be faster than fighting traffic, police barricades and road closures, but her aching lungs were already regretting the decision.

When her cell phone rang, she stopped her sprint in the Franklin Street Parking Lot. The 115-space lot was about half-full and with a small sushi takeout joint on the corner. When she saw it was Robert — whom she'd called when she got the text about a sniper shooting — she pressed the phone hard into her ear to counter the sirens that were getting louder.

"Robert," she answered, gasping for oxygen.

"Susan…it *is* Knoble. He's dead."

She didn't immediately respond. The phone still glued to her ear, she looked up towards the bright moon and closed her eyes, feeding her deprived lungs air and feeling the sweat drip down her face. Then she shook her head.

"Are you absolutely positive?"

"Where are you?"

"Randolph and Franklin. In a parking lot."

"I'll send a car to pick you up."

"Robert…"

"Knoble was on the phone when it happened, Susan. We're getting the transcript as we speak. Three sniper shots. We don't have a clue where from yet."

She absorbed the information still too shocked to believe it. Even with the approaching deadline…with his son's kidnapping...with the threat of a massive explosion in a public place if he didn't...

Even with all that...she never actually thought Ben would do it.

31

"Is this really necessary?" Nikki said.

"If you want to see Grasshopper."

"Are you driving? You're breaking up. I can barely hear you."

"I've only got a few minutes. Are you game or not?" Tom's voiced echoed in and out of cellular service.

Exasperated, Nikki collapsed into her loveseat and sank deeply into its leather padding, pulling her knees into her chest. Still in Cuddl Duds pajama shorts and a cozy T-shirt at nine p.m., a big part of her wanted to hang up the phone and simply drift off. Maybe she'd wake up with no memory of the past twenty-four hours.

The death of William T. Knoble, Attorney at Law, had spread through the media like a cancer. Reporters were having a field day recapping the play-by-play of the nonprofit lawyer's shocking assassination. The flywheel of mystery, opinion, and conspiracy hit social media less than thirty minutes after paramedics called time of death. Over a dozen theories had been generated before Knoble's body made it to the morgue.

Crazy as many of those theories were, Knoble's death definitely had a resounding impact throughout the community. Social media tirades spawned real-life marches and protests — mostly peaceful, others more violent. Chicago became a scaled down, modern-day Haight-Ashbury within eighteen hours and didn't appear to be slowing down.

Thankfully no one got hurt, but hundreds of broken windows later, arrests were made, stances taken. African Americans and Latinos had taken to the streets to show support for a man who'd done work for their respective minority communities. Protestors reminded the CPD and DA's Office via rhyming chants that justice needed to be done. Analogies were made to the lack of control over gang violence on the South Side, an interesting comparison considering the vast difference in settings. Women's groups joined the effort to support a lawyer who'd represented abused wives and girlfriends pro bono. The same was true for members of the LGBTQ community. College students from the University of Chicago, UIC and DePaul joined as well, mostly because that's what college students did.

Reporters seized the day by sucking up the murder's energy like a new Hoover on a dirty carpet. Stories — mostly conjecture — told the world what a wonderful man Bill Knoble was and how shocking his death should make everyone feel.

The headline that, to her, best encapsulated the drama came from *USA Today*. Its giant words were printed in thick, bold ink, centered above a picture of Knoble's lifeless body lying on the broken-glass-filled table, his arm hanging down the side:

IS ANYONE SAFE IN CHICAGO?

Yet she felt more dejection than anything else. How could Ben do that? Even to save Joe, the thought of him taking Knoble's life had made her lose her lunch.

"Hey!" Tom interrupted her mental lapse, "I'm not getting any younger."

The reception was getting worse.

"No, I won't play his stupid game. I want to know where he is. I need to see him."

She probably came across as desperate, but the shoe fit. Twenty four hours had passed since Knoble's murder and three things were clear: progress on the police investigation was non-existent, Knoble's last known whereabouts and Ben's motive made him the prime suspect, and she was pissed. So much so that confronting him had become her obsession.

"When you're ready, you know what you need to do."

"Not this time, Tom. I won't get caught up in his bravado bullshit. Not after what I saw on the news last night."

"Let's not replay it."

"And another thing. As far as I'm concerned, you're a likely accomplice to murder. My guess is you knew something about it. I can't find Ben right now, but I can find you."

"Think so, eh? In that case, Ms. big time FBI Agent, I'd better be going. You're probably tracing this call. So if I don't see you, have a good life."

"Fine...you win!" she shouted, clenching her fist. "He wins."

"I wouldn't call this a win for Grasshopper."

"He's going to get what he wants, just like he always does."

"He didn't with you..."

She knew the moment required her to be factual, stoic. Stick to the data; react to the evidence. Leave emotion at the door. But what she knew and what she was capable of were often different things. Calling in sick earlier to play "what if" and second-guess her decision to dump Ben last year hadn't helped. Who could possibly say if this would've happened had they'd stayed together? Only one thing was clear: seeing Ben in her mind — reliving memories they'd made and recalling that she'd pinned him as the one — really did a number on her.

"Nikki?"

"I'm here," she said after a quick nose blow on mute.

"Follow his instructions precisely. You deviate even once, he won't be there."

"Why does it have to be this way?"

"Partly because he's wanted for Knoble's murder, by you and the cops."

"And the other part?"

"No clue. I'm sure he'll explain it to you."

"I don't know if I can do this, Tom. Ben kidnapped Knoble, and now Knoble is dead. What if they told him he has to kill me next? I'm not sure I can take the risk. I feel like I don't know him now," she replied, knowing that this conversation would make it back to Ben.

"That's a decision only you can make."

"Have they called him back?"

"Can't go there, Nikki. But listen, Ben trusted you by agreeing to meet at all. Maybe you could trust him not to harm one of the only two women he's ever loved."

"He killed an innocent man to save his son. He's a barbarian." She didn't believe it, but boy the words felt right. "I doubt he ever loved me."

"Listen, honey. You're not going to get a rise out of me. Or Ben. You don't want to play his games, don't. Don't want to expose yourself, don't. But don't think for a second that man didn't love you and doesn't still."

She didn't have a canned response for that.

"Regardless of what you think, his son is in danger. He's fighting for his boy. Damn it, I would've done the same thing."

"That doesn't make me feel sorry for him."

"Not my intent," Tom replied.

"What was your intent?"

"To prove your you can't be sure. His back's against the wall and when the rubber meets the road, Grasshopper's resolve knows no bounds. You don't want to screw with him on this. Believe me. If you can't face him on these terms, just say no."

Not this time. She wasn't going to let fear get in the way. She'd risk it. She'd play Ben's game, on his terms.

Then she'd bring him down.

32

The loud buzz jerked David Keene out of a numb state.

At a few minutes after ten he was the only one in the office, so he got the honor of retrieving the UPS package. Another late night at the third-floor *Chicago Sun-Times* Corporate Headquarters devouring chicken fried rice and sucking down Red Bull reminded him that every newspaper reporter — no matter how talented, no matter how lucky — had to pay dues.

And that those dues were a bitch.

He trudged towards the glass door with his shoes still off and wrinkled dress shirt half-unbuttoned, expecting another mundane delivery for another mundane day. He'd seen this movie and tonight's funk like any other's. He was half asleep, half bored out of his mind. But when he got to the door, he stopped on a dime and was suddenly alert. Adrenaline shot through his body like a steroid, and he stared at the seemingly innocuous package without moving.

It looked exactly like the package he'd received two years ago from Ben Siebert, while working at *The Chicago Tribune*. He tried to convince himself it was a coincidence, but the details argued otherwise. Cracking his knuckles, David approached the package on tiptoes.

The standard brown box was roughly one square foot and a plain white envelope had been taped across its top. The envelope had no address window and was roughly three by eight inches. "DAVID KEENE" was written in large, block capital letters.

He recalled the box that had changed his life two years ago. And he could swear he was looking at the same box now, right down to the thick black marker and duct tape used to affix the envelope to it. There were no other markings. Just like last time.

Could it really be him?

He hurried back to his office and shut the door behind him. Dropping it on the desk, he stood back and stared a moment, telling himself he wasn't sure he wanted to see inside. When he finally confronted reality there was no way he could leave it unopened, he discovered there was nothing in the envelope and only a single sheet of paper in the box.

David:

Don't quit your job yet. I know Kraft needs an answer tomorrow, but pass on the marketing position for now. You need to be a reporter a little while longer. I will contact you later as to why.

Sincerely,

You Know Who

David fell back into his chair, blurring the events of today with those from two years ago.

He'd been working late that night too. He didn't know why the package was sent to him, but it turned out to be a gift: a tip to the most coveted story of the year, as well as step-by-step instructions on how to position the article no one else had the data to write. The request went against company policy, but the story was big enough to take the chance. It paid off. Following Siebert's directions put him on the fast track.

His reveal of former FBI SAIC Marcus Redmond dying in an explosion in the Ukrainian village — and the follow up story about Redmond's corruption and treachery — started off with a bang. How Siebert knew the explosion was going to happen and what made him choose David were of little consequence. He hammered out the article and went over his boss's head to get it printed in the Sunday paper.

Shortly after, he accepted a new job at *Chicago Sun-Times* for twice the salary. In a closed-door office with an assistant, he relished working for the oldest newspaper publisher in the city. He got a staff, expense account and was awarded the freedom to choose his stories. He felt alive, full of vigor and purpose.

But his front-page masterpiece didn't translate to $300K, eight weeks off and no more weekends in the office. And the buzz wore off as all buzzes do. His article still made for a good icebreaker, but publishing was a what-have-you-done-for-me-lately business and folks have short-term memories. As the publisher consolidated to reduce headcount, he was forced to write what needed to be written. He learned that managing people was a pain, and that his fancy title only meant he had to make presentations for the real bosses. Six months after he started, the honeymoon was over.

But tonight, he was forced to consider if his lack of passion was really that bad...

He made good coin compared to his buds. He liked his boss, and had respect in the office. Things with his fiancé Julie were great, and the new house was swell. Even the mutt was growing on him when it wasn't chewing up his sneakers. But now — just as he was preparing for a new career — the note's vague promise of change, and its author, was working its magic.

How does he know about Kraft?

He could disregard it all. Just take the job and not look back. He didn't owe Siebert anything. He did what he did back then because he wanted to, and both parties benefited. That could be it. Why pass on Kraft for an unknown? It could backfire, and he could be stuck with nothing. He could ignore it. Just pretend he never saw the package.

Or could he?

33

Friday, May 14

The itinerary left little to the imagination.

It was attached to an e-mail she would've normally pinged as spam. But with Ben, everything was cryptic. The thing you needed was always disguised as junk. What appeared useful, a red herring. Since she knew it was coming, the e-mail's subject line gave it away:

MS. NICOLE ANGELA BENTON LUXURY TRAVEL SUITES

At 7:05 p.m. American Taxi would take her from her apartment to O'Hare to catch United Flight 5940 to Richmond, Virginia, departing at 9:20 p.m. out of Terminal One. After a night at the Courtyard by Marriot Richmond Airport, Delta Flight 2625 would get her to Atlanta at 5:44 a.m. the next day. Following twelve hours of layover at the world's busiest airport, she was to take Spirit Airlines Flight 146 to Dallas Fort Worth, arriving at 7:24 p.m. local time. *SuperShuttle* had been arranged to bring her to Dealey Plaza, where she would be met. All bookings, boarding passes and confirmations were included, and both the airline and hotel reservations were tied to rewards accounts in her name that she'd never set up or used before. She was to check a bag for a week's stay and have no carry-on.

It didn't make sense to fly east halfway across the country only to head twice the distance west the next morning. Nor did it compute to take three one-way flights, each on a different airline, when a quick search on the web would reveal there were plenty of direct flights from Chicago to Fort Worth for a lot less money. Why anyone would pay over $2,000 for such a hellish itinerary was beyond her.

Except that she wasn't flying anywhere.

After checking her bag curbside, it took forty minutes to make it through security. She jealously eyed TSA pre-check travelers as they whisked through their special bypass lines. Then she made the quarter-mile, neon light-adorned walk underground to Concourse C that any O'Hare traveler knew was a pain in the ass, emerging from the escalator with her purse slung over her shoulder and a thirst begging to be quenched.

Her instructions were to head to Billy Goat Tavern and Grill at Gate C19. She grabbed a high top against the wall and ordered a water and Chicago-brewed Goose Island IPA. The water glass was half empty before the waiter left and graciously refilled it. She glanced at her watch. Eight-thirty. Twenty minutes until boarding. Nursing her beer, trying to act normal, she scanned the immediate area for a tail.

People watching was only fun when she wasn't looking for something specific. When she was, it felt taxing. She worried that what she was seeking was right in front of her but she didn't see it, like a real-life game of "Where's Waldo." With real-life repercussions.

Of course, tonight nothing felt out of the ordinary. Everyone seemed like typical travelers: busy, self-focused, passing the time, waiting for a flight. But then again, what was she looking for? Her only guide was a bogus itinerary and set of instructions created by the man she was trying to outsmart and locate.

Her glass of beer essentially untouched, 8:50 arrived quicker than she wanted. Paying with a credit card — another of Ben's unexplained yet explicit instructions — she headed towards her departure gate. Along the way, she ducked into the bathroom and found the nearest stall. Removing her orange pullover, she exposed a buttoned blue blouse. She also unwrinkled and threw on the pink Cubs jersey that had been stuffed into the pullover's pocket, and stripped off her blue jeans to reveal black yoga pants. She grabbed the slim wallet and dropped her purse in the trashcan, then checked herself over in the mirror. All that remained of her original outfit were the Asics sneakers and socks. A few deep breaths later, she exited the bathroom and headed the opposite direction of her departure gate.

She repeated Ben's oxymoronic instructions in her head, which were as stressful as they were ambivalent:

Don't run but walk fast.

Don't put your head down like a robot but don't look around.

Don't walk alone but don't crowd others.

She made her way back through the underground tunnel exiting Concourse C, this time using the moving walkway. She briefly looked behind when she stopped to kneel down, pretending to tie her shoe. A few people staring at their phones, a couple holding hands, a few speed walkers to the right of the walkway. Traffic was light at the late hour and nothing seemed unusual. But what did she expect? The danger wouldn't be a loud, crazy-looking ogre running at her with a gun. It would look mundane until the last second and be over before it began. Wondering about it only made her feel anxious. She decided the hell with Ben's instructions, beelining it out the exit door with little care for revealing her haste.

All three curb front pickup lanes were busy. It seemed beeping car horns and traffic cop whistles came from every direction. She walked south as if in a trance along the innermost curb, which was reserved for rental car and hotel shuttles. Tugging her hat down over her forehead, she climbed onto the National/Alamo bus and grabbed a seat by the rear entrance.

Aside from the heavyset black woman driver in her thirties, there were only two people on board. A middle-aged Indian man dressed in a navy suit with a small black suitcase, and a blonde-haired woman in her early twenties sporting a "Pretty in Pink" T-shirt, yapping on a cell phone and giggling like a thirteen-year-old. She'd never been so happy to hear immaturity. It echoed innocuous in a situation that felt ripe with danger.

When the shuttle started moving she let out a sigh of relief. It was impossible to be certain, but it appeared she'd made it out of the airport unseen. She sank down into the hard blue plastic seat and closed her eyes. When the shuttle arrived a few minutes later at the National Car Rental facility on Bessie Coleman Drive, she was the first one off. Bypassing the counter en route to the Emerald Club aisle, she located the first row of cars and counted three down from the front. The four-door, light-grey Acura MDX crossover was shiny and new yet felt uninviting. As she approached the backseat's tinted windows, she knew he was there.

Sitting quietly. Watching her.

She swallowed down the lump in her throat and climbed into the driver's seat, then turned around to see Ben Siebert for the first time in a year. His weight and firm muscle tone was similar, but everything else about his appearance felt different. The clean-shaven baby face she remembered was grizzly with short, dark stubble. His short blondish hair was neither gelled nor combed. She'd never seen him wear blue jeans before. His eyes were heavy and red, her favorite smile absent.

His first words were probably supposed to ease the tension. Instead, they stirred up memories and made it worse.

"This reminds me of when we met."

34

She was just as beautiful as he remembered.

That alluring shade of chestnut hair that seemed to flow endlessly from beneath her Cubs hat. Those lean and toned runner's legs on display in yoga pants. Her athletic physique and flat stomach highlighted by a snug light-blue T-shirt. Nikki was downright gorgeous. And he'd never stopped loving her.

"What now?" Nikki asked.

Even when she meant it to be stern, her voice sounded sweet and soothing. It had an intrinsic gentleness that couldn't be concealed. Her trying only made it more endearing.

"You'll find a license and rental agreement in the glove compartment. Grab them and follow the exit signs."

Nikki kept herself turned from him, barely acknowledging his presence. He knew her game. She was trying her hand at poker, going over the top to attempt withholding emotion. He knew that deep down she was foaming at the mouth, but didn't want to give him the satisfaction.

You can't bluff a bluffer, Nikki.

She probably knew it wasn't working, but that didn't matter to Ben. What did was that she didn't want to reveal anything. She didn't want him to know how she felt. She didn't want him.

The Acura's passenger window was slightly cracked so he could hear approaching cars. The mellow whistling wind did little to soften the tension inside. Nikki turned right out of the garage, stubbornly refusing to acknowledge her passenger, hands at ten and two, eyes straight ahead. She handed the papers to the middle-aged woman at the gate and waited in silence. The clerk was quick, eager to get back to her magazine. She accepted the paperwork and wished them a safe trip before raising the gate.

Look back at me. Just once.

"Hop on I-190 east and take the Tri-State southbound," Ben said.

After Nikki closed both windows, the pleasant aroma that filled the car reminded him of how great she always smelled. It was one of the many little things he found so attractive. Tonight it was some sort of fruit-based perfume that, while new to him, summoned memories of happier times.

He knew the question on her mind, and he knew he had to wait for her to ask it. Forcing conversation beforehand would be a waste of time. They'd only been on I-294 for a mile when she did. Just as they drove past The Fashion Outlets of Chicago and its annoyingly bright neon lights, she yanked the crossover to the shoulder and brought it to an abrupt halt. The Irving Park Road toll booth was a quarter-mile ahead, traffic was light due to the hour, and cars whizzed past them on Chicago's most travelled interstate. She snapped her head as if on a swivel and blurted out what she'd been thinking for two days.

"How could you?" she screamed, a touch of saliva spraying from her mouth.

Her face muscles tightened to form an angry glare, pointed straight at him. Those astonishing hazel eyes revealed anger and disappointment, the latter much more difficult to witness. Their rapid blinking didn't thwart her tears, and Nikki waited in painful silence for him to answer.

He wanted to hold her hand, to tell her that everything would be okay. That she'd understand one day, maybe even think better of him when it was over. But such a fairy tale ending had no place in this real-life nightmare.

"Nikki, it's complicated."

"After everything we've been through, that's your answer?"

"We've got to keep moving."

"How could you kill that man?"

She screamed with harshness and volume that, even considering the circumstances, he didn't expect. She was

156

gritting her teeth so hard the skin on her cheeks reverberated like a muscle spasm. A look of disdain filled her eyes as she stared at his and refused to blink.

"Get back on the road and set the cruise to sixty-five."

"Ben!" she exclaimed. Then the waterworks erupted and she loudly sniffled her nose. She forced her lips together to prevent their quivering and frowned. "What you put me through tonight is enough. Having me pretend to fly all over the country, making me change my clothes in a dingy airport bathroom…"

"I did that for your benefit as much as mine."

"But for you to sit there and not give me an honest answer after all we've been through."

"Nikki, it's time for you to listen. I'll answer your questions, but I need you to park your disgust for me and start driving."

He hoped she would jump at the word "disgust" and quickly correct him, assuring him that wasn't the right word. But she simply put the car in drive and merged back into traffic.

"Nikki, I'm not here because I want to be," he said after a long sigh. "As much as I've wanted to see you, I didn't want it to be like this."

She started to respond but he held up his hand and shook his head, saying "No. Now you get to listen for a minute and let me explain."

"Then get to it," she replied coldly.

"I'm here because of Joe. Everything I've done the past week is because of him. My boy's life is in danger, and I'm not about to trust anyone else to save him."

He would sit in the awkward, strained silence that followed as long as it took. He could tell he'd touched a nerve, and he needed to squeeze as much out of that as possible. She didn't respond, but he saw in her face for the first time she was empathizing. That wouldn't make her suddenly accept what he'd done, but it was a start.

"You were brought into this without my knowledge, Nikki. And I need you to get yourself out. You have to remove any connection you have to it."

"You need something from me, do you?" she sneered.

"If you withdraw, I'll turn myself in."

"What?" she snapped her head back to look at him. He slowly twirled his index finger, instructing her to keep her eyes on the road.

"You heard me. You're here because you want to help render justice, right? Here's your chance. You back off, I turn myself in. No questions asked."

"What the hell, Benjamin?"

"I need you to do this, Nikki. I'd ask you to do it for me, but I know that's not much incentive. So I'm offering my surrender instead."

As he looked into her moist hazel eyes through the rearview mirror, he thought of telling her straight up to stop unearthing Hubley case files and interviewing witnesses; that she wasn't being as clandestine as she thought, and it was far more dangerous than she knew. But that would only encourage her to keep going.

"So I'm just supposed to back off just because you say so?"

"You'd be backing off to get what you seek. Go back to catching child predators. It's an important job, and you're good at it. Stop asking questions and snooping around. Stop exposing yourself."

"The 'Mr. Protector' facade has lost its appeal."

"Cut the sarcasm. You don't know who these people are. I don't even know who they are. But I know enough."

"I've never heard you scared before."

"They have my son, Nikki. I'm not scared. I'm terrified."

It was obvious she didn't expect such candor, and this time she didn't try to conceal her surprise. Her empathy momentarily increased, but he could tell that right after she was mentally switching gears. She was afraid of being played by a player.

"I'm sorry about Joe," she offered in a soft voice. "But why do I need to stay away?"

"Please just listen to me."

"No, Ben. I can't just take you at your word. Not after Wednesday night."

"My offer stands nonetheless. If you fully disassociate yourself from this case and everything in it, *right now*, I swear to you that I'll turn myself in the minute my son is safe." He paused for a moment. "I promise."

That got her to stare at him through the mirror, with no intention of looking away. He knew it would. She would want to study his face right after he said it.

"What did you just say to me?"

Her eyes were at an angle but he could see they were full of tears. She kept driving, but held that look for what felt like hours.

"Please, Nikki. Promise me back."

35

"Promise" wasn't a word either of them used lightly.

Not in their forced "partnership" during the Hubley investigation, the friendship that followed or their relationship after that. Even on the first day they met, when Ben was her suspect, they respected what a promise was. Pinkie swears were for teenagers. Promises were real. They meant something.

It was a vow she knew Ben would keep.

She also knew she was vulnerable, especially with Ben, and she had to guard against that. She couldn't allow her gullibility to be talked into anything. But this felt different; sincere. She'd seen that look from Ben before, and she was confident she knew what it meant.

Ben's intensity and determination ensured there would be no backing down. Even in the midst of regret, beating herself up for falling in love with a man who could do what he'd done, she knew his promise was rock solid.

She kept her eyes on the road, unwilling to look at him. "I hate myself for how much I misjudged you."

"Maybe you weren't as off as you think."

"It happened once already. I won't let it happen again."

"Nikki..."

"I believe you. I believe you'd keep your promise. That I could agree to your deal and this horrible conversation would be over."

"Is talking to me that bad?" Ben asked. The softness of his tone and inflection of his voice...it wasn't pitiful, but it begged for pity.

"I believe you really would surrender."

"You have my word."

"And I doubt they could catch you. Plus, I never even wanted to be involved in the first place. You're right, I'm better at catching child predators."

"And you should go back to doing it."

"I know all of that..."

"But...?"

"I can't accept. Ben, you killed a man. You may have your justifications, but Bill Knoble is dead and you're the reason why. You broke the law. And now you want to make a deal? I won't stoop to your level."

"Deals happen everyday under much worse circumstances."

"This isn't a plea bargain."

"Same principal. The good guys strike a deal with the bad guys to get more justice than they could without it."

"So you admit you're a bad guy?"

"It's your label, I just have to live with it."

"You're breaking my heart." She rolled her eyes.

"You're right about one thing, Nikki."

"What's that?"

"They won't catch me otherwise. Not soon enough. Eventually, sure. I won't hide forever. But not before I finish what I started."

"Which is what, exactly?"

"Getting my son back and rendering my own justice."

"And you had to kill an innocent man to do it?"

"Neither of us has time to debate decisions already made, so let's focus on the future."

She wasn't sure if it was intentional, but those were the exact words Ben used when he first brought up the idea of getting married. She tried to conceal it, but the image of him sitting on that Navy Pier bench, uttering those words under a fireworks-filled sky, flashed into her mind.

"If you take my deal," Ben continued, "I'll leave the rendering justice part to the police."

"And you're so sure they won't get you otherwise?"

"Your words, not mine."

"Maybe I underestimated the power of the FBI, CIA and second largest police department in the country. One of those 12,000 cops might surprise you."

"Why do you think that cell phone you're trying to send text messages with isn't working?" Ben casually replied from the backseat, like he was talking about the weather.

She sheepishly pushed the Android under her leg further down the seat, as if it wasn't already too late.

"It's the same reason I made you change clothes at the airport. I knew you'd try to alert the authorities."

"I *am* the authorities."

He held up a small, black rectangular device that looked like a bulky walkie-talkie. A small knob was on the top right, an inch-long antenna on the left.

"You're jamming my signal?"

"You've been trying to message for backup from the moment you saw me."

She glanced in the mirror only to see Ben's dreamy blue eyes staring back. They didn't look angry or betrayed. Rather, soft and understanding. She tried to hide how embarrassed and exposed she felt, but she was pretty sure it was a failed attempt.

"I'm proud of you, Nikki."

"You're what?"

"I'm proud of you for doing the right thing. For doing what you're supposed to do. That's one of the things I've always loved most about you."

Always…as in still does?

"All I'm asking is that you do it again," Ben continued. "You don't belong on this case and you know it. It's not for your department or you. Hand it off and go back to your real job."

She didn't respond for a few seconds. And of course, Ben waited.

He always knew when to speak and when to wait.

"How can I walk away knowing what I know?"

"First of all, you don't know anything. You only think you do. And I could ask how you could try to arrest me without even hearing me out first."

"Pretty simple. You killed a man."

"I'm surprised I have to convince you to do the right thing. I never would've thought you'd be so resistant to following the rules."

"I won't be manipulated, Benjamin."

"Don't be manipulated. Be pragmatic. You're not the right person for this case."

"Why do you keep saying that?"

"Other than the fact it's outside your department's purview, you don't have the skill set or temperament. You know I'm right. If I were the real bad guy, you'd be dead. They'll see your moves coming a mile away."

"You don't know," she quickly defended herself, trying to project confidence. "And you actually are the real bad guy. Remember?"

"Your personal history — you know, the only reason you're involved — it isn't an asset. It's a liability."

"How do you figure?"

"In addition to the conflict of interest?"

"You don't know that."

"Nice try, but I know you. I know your ticks and tocks, your yin and yang."

There wasn't an ounce of trepidation in his voice. His face was laser-focused as he simultaneously egged her on and further convinced her of what she already knew in her heart.

"Yes or no, did you kill that man?"

"Isn't it strange how people's recollection of someone changes after he dies?"

She snapped her neck around. His arms were crossed, and his right ankle was resting on his left knee. Gym shoes, no seat belt. Those intense eyes pointed right at her.

"What are you talking about?"

"When I first met Bill two years ago, he was defending a man named Barry Lee Richard. Barry Lee was a chronic wife-abuser who bought his way out of so many times you'd lose count. Who was the only attorney he ever had? That's right, the prick Bill Knoble. He orchestrated the quick release of a man who beat his helpless wife within an inch of her life."

"You don't have the right to kill him, no matter how big of a prick he was."

"And then there's his old treatment of his employees. Sexist is a generous word."

"What's your point? That you were justified?"

"My point is that now that Knoble is gone, all I read about are these women's groups. They march in the streets like a bunch of unorganized adolescents, protesting in his honor because he provided legal services to battered women. All of a sudden he's Mother Theresa's long lost brother, the last true advocate of women's rights."

"What does any of this have to do with your crime?"

"The guy went from a career's worth of charging $800 an hour to get wife-beaters exonerated and looking for the next ambulance to chase to running non-profits and being honest in a single heartbeat. It was only two years ago, yet everyone wants to know how such a horrible thing could happen to such a wonderful man. If there's one person responsible for that heartbeat, for Knoble being the humanitarian everyone is so sure he was, it sure wasn't him."

"What's your point? Want a medal for transforming Knoble before a life sentence for killing him?"

"Things aren't always as they seem, Nikki. You should be careful." He uttered the words without the slightest inflection, yet somehow they felt severe.

"What's that supposed to mean? Are you going kill me too?"

"While we're being so direct with each other, why did you drop me like a bad habit?"

"This isn't the right time to talk about that."

"Right time is a matter of perspective, isn't it? I've waited over a year. Now is as right as it's going to be for me."

As they passed the I-88 interchange, she could feel the tears making their way from her eyes to her cheeks yet again. All day long she'd dreaded this moment. This specific conversation, that specific question. Even after what happened with Knoble, it was her decision a year ago that she feared the most. Pathetic on one hand, inevitable on the other.

"I never meant to hurt you, Ben."

"Isn't that nice?" his sarcastic tone accompanied his shrugging shoulders. His eyes never left hers, however. "I'll tell you what you never did do...talk to me."

"Ben—"

"No conversation over dinner or on a walk. Not even a phone call. No warnings, no signs. After over a year of dating and two months of engagement — with me the happiest I'd been in a long, long time — you sent me a one-sentence text message to rip my heart out."

"I'm sorry."

"'I can't do this' it said. And I never heard from you again."

"I was ashamed."

"Try it from my vantage point."

"Ben...I'm sorry. I know it doesn't change it. But it's all I've got. I was so scared."

"You think I wasn't?"

"Things were happening...moving...so fast. They were great, but they were so fast. I needed some space. You were holding on so tight, it felt suffocating."

"Why didn't you just say that?"

"I was falling more in love with you every day, and it terrified me."

"Pull the car over."

"Ben, we need to talk about Knoble."

"Pull the damn car over now."

She took a deep breath and obliged, silently admitting that it was always easy to follow Ben. At first, it was because she was scared of what might happen if she didn't. But as they grew close, it was because she wanted to. Independent as she was, he made her feel protected.

She exited at Cermak Road and headed east, pulling over to the shoulder after a few hundred feet. There weren't any streetlights and at just before ten, only a few headlights far off in the distance. The air was dry; visibility was clear. The engine running, she unbuckled and hopped out of the crossover. When she reentered via the back door, she saw him up-close for what she hoped would be the last time.

Or the first of many more.

Ben scooted to the middle and she studied his unshaven face and faded blue jeans, both attractive complements to his familiar eyes and bulging forearms. This guy was still all man.

"What did you mean?" he asked.

"What?"

"You said you were terrified by how much you loved me."

"The last time I felt that way about someone he broke my heart."

"So you bolt on me because of your ex?"

She recalled their conversation at Irish Times Pub, when she poured her heart out over a warm fireplace and cold Guinness. With what Ben knew, he could've used very painful words — words like "cheating" and "already married" and others — but he didn't.

Even now, she knew he was protecting her.

"I'm not proud of what I did, Ben. You were special to me, and I cared about you so much. You have no idea how many times I stared at my cell phone and almost called you."

"I wish you would have."

He looked at her with a solemn, remorseful, and forgiving gaze that supported her fear she'd made a mistake. He didn't say anything, but this man — who she hated for killing Bill Knoble — was tugging at her heartstrings again.

"Ben, I can't walk away from the case."

She more announced it than said it, changing the subject rather than reinforcing a point.

"I want to give us another try, Nikki."

For a moment, she stopped breathing. She could've sworn her heart was going to explode it was thumping so fast.

"When this is over...when Joe is safe again...I want to be with you."

"Ben, I can't think about that right now," she answered, wiping the corners of her eyes.

"I know you think I'm a monster you don't even know now. I can't blame you. But one day you might not feel that way. And if so, I want you to know now I forgive you."

"Forgive me?" she squinted her face.

"I still want to be with you. To start over. A fresh beginning. Just you and me. I'll move anywhere you want. I just want you in my life."

"This is too much."

"I've never stopped thinking about you, Nikki. And the possibility of being with you is the only good thing I have left."

Then Ben did what Ben could always do.

Swept her off her feet.

The kiss was soft yet aggressive, gentle yet passionate. She felt his strong, steady hands take hold of her trembling shoulders. And she leaned closer, throwing her arms around his muscular neck and pushing her face deeper into his.

"No," she whispered, pulling away from the man she was convinced was her soul mate just a year ago.

And whom she still loved today.

"I can't—" Ben stopped her by placing two fingers over her lips.

"Don't answer now," he said with dreamy, almost boyish moist eyes. "We both know it can't happen now. But please, back off the case. Follow your own protocol. I'm not saying the FBI should drop it. Tell Stevens or whoever everything, including this conversation. What you think I've done, what you know about Joe, anything. Don't lie. And don't hold anything back."

He paused, but she didn't have the words.

"Tell Stevens to have the right FBI agents hunt me down. I'll turn myself in if I don't get caught first. I promise."

Ben wiped the tears from her cheek and continued in an even softer voice. "In thirty seconds I'm going to leave. I want you to drive far, far away. Leave me here and don't look back. But if your opinion of me should ever change, please give us another shot. Don't let a molehill from a year ago become a mountain today. To hell with the past."

He seemed so serious, yet so sincere. Open, vulnerable and honest.

When Ben opened the door she didn't say a word. She just watched him slide towards the passenger side before leaning back towards her. She didn't move. She couldn't move.

She let his tender lips kiss her tear-soaked cheek and stayed pressed to her face, his light stubble softly scratching her cheek. Second later, he withdrew and scooted away. She missed him the second he was gone. Yet, she couldn't reconcile the fact he'd just killed a man while trying to win her back.

As he exited the car, he looked straight at her and revealed tears of his own, uttering words she knew she'd never forget:

"I want to build a future with you."

36

The coward's voice slithered through his ears: "You'd better wise up."

Having been trapped in the closest thing to hell he could imagine for God only knows how long, Joe thought he'd take anything over the blackness. He'd welcome death or embrace any obstacle the light might bring.

He was wrong. This was far more horrifying than darkness.

"Tell me about Terrance Smith," the goon whispered with a calmness that sent a surge of panic through Joe's limbs, making his brain feel too big for his skull.

Empty, robbed of what little adolescence he had, Joe knew he'd never see Abigail again. His faith in mankind torpedoed by this chicken-shit six-foot fat ass hiding behind a mask, he forced his badly swollen right eye open but couldn't see anything clearly because of the tears and blood. Sitting in a wooden chair, he rotated his neck as far as it would go to see the other three. They were also in black and hid behind masks, hovering in the corner like a pack of lions watching the dominant male hunt.

The room was more or less as he pictured. Four walls of uneven, jagged stone with no windows. Cracked concrete floor. A large metal door with a deadbolt that operated like an emergency door in that it could only be opened from the other side. The room was taller than he'd guessed, maybe fifteen feet. The terrible heat had subsided and it didn't smell like shit anymore, but that could've been because his broken nose wasn't working.

"Arminius said you were to be provided for," the man continued. "That's why you got food."

Provided for?

"But he also told me to get answers. However I deem necessary. When he orders, I deliver. And I'm old school. My tactics work. And if it ain't broke, don't fix it. This won't stop until you talk."

Joe knew very little about the four captors. He could tell this guy, who appeared to be the leader and did most of the talking, was a white man. He could see the top of his chin through the mask's mouth cutout. And his voice was deeper than an average man's, yet carried a slight twang. A drawl of sorts. Not a thick southern accent like Alabama, but maybe Virginia? Aside from that — and the obvious fact the guy was heavyset — Joe had bupkiss.

He also wasn't sure how much he could trust his senses. He tried to keep count, and if he'd done so accurately, it'd been over an hour since he got stuck with the needle. The coward didn't say what clear liquid was, but he felt lightheaded a few minutes after. Then it got hard to concentrate; focusing took a monumental amount of effort.

Evidently, he still hadn't said what they wanted to hear. After the injections came the thigh slaps with ping-pong paddles, then punches to his stomach and face. They threw a bucket of ice water on him when the drugs started pulling him into a deeper haze than was desired.

"I told you," he gasped. "My dad never mentioned any Terrance Smith."

"Now you listen. If you don't speak up, we're gonna get everyone you love. Your little blonde girlfriend, your crazy pseudo-uncle and your big, bad stepdad."

The goon paused and turned his body towards the other three in the corner, as if seeking applause.

"We'll get every one of them."

Soaked with sweat, filled with hate, the room spinning like a merry-go-round, Joe lowered his head, reaching for the smallest measure of comfort. Just to have his chin touch the metal...

That's right...they took it. They took Mom's locket.

"Your stepfather's the reason you're here. Just remember that."

The three other goons in the corner snickered.

Don't believe his lies.

"You hear me? They're all going to suffer. Then they're all going to die. All because of Daddy."

"I don't know anything!" he shouted, eyes still shut.

"Unless you tell me what your dad told you about Terrance Smith."

It was Dad's...fault...?

"Every last detail, boy."

37

Administrative FBI positions were supposed to be nine-to-five gigs, but in the past two weeks he'd been called three times after hours. Ordinarily, that might've bothered him. But this was SAIC Robert Stevens calling, so Junior Agent Roy Dietrich didn't mind.

"This is Roy," he answered as his phone turned to 11:02 p.m.

"How does it feel being a GS-9?"

"Quite nice. Thank you again, sir."

"You earned it," Stevens replied. "Feel like earning more?"

He sat up on the couch and turned off the television. *Die Hard* could wait. He grabbed the notepad next to him and turned on the light.

"What can I do?"

"I just took a call from Special Agent Nikki Benton. She's in the cyber crime division. Do you know her?"

"No sir," he answered, grabbing his laptop from the coffee table. When the screen turned on, he opened up the internal directory.

"She was Ben Siebert's fiancé."

Roy paused his search. Not just because of the mystique surrounding Siebert and his two previous assignments, but because Stevens informed him yesterday that Siebert was likely responsible for the Knoble killing. He was getting pulled into the biggest story of the year.

"Benton told me she met with Siebert tonight."

"Tonight?" he quickly replied. Even to him, it sounded too excited.

"About two hours ago. Now listen closely, Roy. Benton's not involved with him anymore and I'm certain she's not a part of Knoble's murder, but Siebert still has feelings for her. He reached out to meet and we need take advantage of that. This could be the break we're looking for."

"What can I do?"

"They met at an O'Hare rental car facility and drove south on the Tri-State for about fifteen miles. The meeting lasted less than a half-hour, and then Siebert got out of the car and another one picked him up. Benton didn't follow it, and Siebert jammed her cell signal so she couldn't call. He can't be far. I just forwarded you the details."

When Benton's profile pulled up, he raised his eyebrows. She was beyond attractive. Chiseled face, soft lips, auburn hair and big hazel eyes.

"I want you to backtrack the shit out of their encounter," Stevens continued. "Head to the rental car facility and retrace every single one of their steps. Then get with Surveillance and find any street camera footage, highway images, O'Hare videos and anything else you can get your hands on. You get any pushback, send it to me. Compile everything and see if you can learn something."

"I'll go right now."

"Roy, you may get a call from a friend of mine at the CIA. Her name is Susan Reynolds. I'm going to call her as soon as we hang up."

"The CIA?"

"Give her whatever she wants. She might ask for pictures, videos, whatever. Give her full cooperation and keep me in the loop."

"Yes, sir."

"But outside of Reynolds, keep this to yourself. You hear me? Not a soul."

"Understood."

"I've already contacted your supervisor. As of now, you work directly for me on special assignment."

"Really?" he asked, excitement bubbling up like a volcano.

"I put you in a tough spot last time. Asking you not to log your work on The Lounge surveillance was wrong. You were right; it was outside process and didn't need to be. Now that you work for me, there's no grey matter. Your security clearance has already been elevated."

"I don't know what to say...thank you sir."

"Don't thank me. Get on this. Like white on rice. Report back to me ASAP. And remember, outside of Reynolds keep this on a need-to-know basis."

"I will sir," he responded, standing up he was so excited.

"Roy, I want to know everything. How close Benton and Siebert got, how long they talked, the split between drive time and parked time. Everything. I'll need a report by noon tomorrow the latest."

"You'll have it."

"Keep delivering and there's another promotion in your future, Roy. A big one."

38

"Susan Reynolds, please report to the front desk."

The high-pitched feminine voice on the intercom felt like a life alert response team, and she happily dismounted the stationary bike. Her quads felt like Jell-O and she was dizzy. After almost falling over, she hobbled towards the door and shot Peggy — her über ripped instructor with the body of a triathlete and intensity of a drill sergeant — a look that said she would've been happy to kick the six a.m. class's ass, but simply had to go. Peggy wasn't fooled. Susan's soaking wet T-shirt and blatant limp gave her away.

She belonged to three different gyms but only spent four hours a month working out. Every time she did, she felt rejuvenated and vowed to make it more of a habit, but work always found a way to intrude. She liked gyms because she remained anonymous. They offered recharge and reset without anyone knowing her business. Decades at the CIA had made her paranoid about her privacy.

When she arrived at the front desk, she froze.

He stood ten feet from the door wearing a pair of black Tearaways, gray pumas and a red polo. A face full of stubble and St. Louis Cardinals ball cap she was sure served to conceal his face, Ben Siebert flashed his empty hands and motioned with a sideways tilt of his head.

"Ben."

"Join me?" Ben raised his eyebrows while motioning towards an empty studio room used for Zumba and kickboxing classes.

As she followed Ben she couldn't help but think…why can't the CIA's mandatory retirement age be the same as the FBI's? Fifty-seven didn't seem that far away; sixty-five felt interminable. And she knew she wouldn't leave until they kicked her out.

When the door opened, lights automatically flickered on around the perimeter to reveal free weights and floor mats along the walls and an open wood-floor space in the center. She folded her arms and planned to go on the offensive right away.

"Little sweaty?" Ben's quip beat her to it.

"Rush Ride" was XSport Fitness's high-intensity bicycle riding class. It crammed hours' worth of cycling into one thirty-minute barrage of pain, grunting and sweat. She'd felt like death by minute fourteen.

"You've got a lot of nerve, Ben."

"I'd appreciate if you didn't use my name."

"I'd appreciate if you didn't murder people."

"Don't you dare."

"Excuse me?"

"Excuse you. You dragged me into this. And now my son's life is in danger. Take your condescension elsewhere."

"Give me one good reason I shouldn't haul your ass away."

"Give me one good reason I shouldn't hold you captive until I get my son back."

The threat wasn't genuine…she knew that. But Ben was daunting. He didn't flinch — not a single movement of his arms, hand, legs, nothing — and the intensity in his eyes was terrifying. In that moment, Ben Siebert appeared capable of just about anything.

"The terrorists are still out there."

"You gave them what they wanted. I can't believe that you, of all people, did that."

"You disappoint me, Susan."

"Call me Mrs. Reynolds. I like to keep it professional when talking to fugitives of the law."

"And I like not being pulled into situations that make me a fugitive of the law. The world's an imperfect place, *Susan.*"

"I didn't make you a fugitive. You did that all by yourself."

"With as much time as you've spent in the CIA studying terrorists, learning their ticks and tocks, what drives them and how they think, for you to assume the terrorists will just go away at this point is laughable."

"I didn't say…" she trailed off, thinking about her four decades with the CIA.

She'd seen and done many things she wished could be unsaid and undone. Witnessing children dying at the hands of terrorists because negotiation didn't work, forcing a president to make a decision with limited information, personally quantifying the value of a human life. It made for thankless days and sleepless nights.

The worst situations were exhausting and soul testing…and offered no happy ending. Her job in those cases was to identify the lesser of many evils and find a way to live with it. The specifics always varied, but they all shared one trait: when they were over, when she could finally breathe again, she could always trace the source of her involvement back to a single conversation. A conversation she never had to have, where she could've justifiably hung up the phone or walked away to pass on the assignment. The dominos fell from there and didn't stop until they were all a toppled mess surrounding her. She was never made as whole as she was before that initial conversation happened.

And she just knew this would be one of them.

"You're probably right. The terrorists aren't going away. What's your point?"

"That you need to help me prevent more innocent people from getting hurt."

"That's ironic, coming from you."

"Nikki Benton is going to contact you."

"What makes you say that?"

177

"Because I know her."

"Pretty thin." She smacked her lips.

"With people, it's always thin."

Just then someone at the desk must've accidentally cranked up the volume because Normani's "Motivation" started blasting from the speakers in the studio next to them so loud she could make out the words through the wall. It was quickly lowered, but the ephemeral clamor gave her a few seconds to regroup before Ben was staring her down for more answers.

"Why are you telling me this?"

"Make sure she stays away from this case."

"I didn't know she was involved."

"Don't ever lie to me again," Ben curtly replied. Those eyes. It was as if they never blinked...

"I meant I didn't know she was still involved."

"You and Robert tried to leverage my feelings for her to catch me."

"You disappeared. We needed to find you."

"Save it. We both know what you tried and we both know it failed. I understand, you've got the law to consider—"

"So do you," she interrupted him with her own flash of stern.

"Get Nikki out and we'll call it even."

"What's this all about?"

"I just told you."

"Oh yeah. Rambo wants to protect people now."

"Innocent people."

"I'm not in a position to help someone wanted for murder."

"So you know for a fact I killed Knoble, is that it?" Ben took a step towards her. His eyes were so intense she felt they were looking straight into her innermost thoughts.

"You're the suspect. You tell me."

"I don't have time for this."

"Then stop wasting mine. You're here to size me up. To see if I think you actually did it. To read my reaction like a book and know if I'm friend or foe."

"No offense, but that's not worth my time. Or the risk. Frankly, I couldn't care less what you think of me. All that matters is I get my son back and Nikki stays safe. This one's way over her head, and I can't protect her."

"Then why don't you tell her that?"

"I tried."

"You tried?" she raised her eyebrow.

"It didn't work."

"When did you see her?"

"She's going to come to you. When she does, you can ask her. But you also need to talk her off the ledge."

"How are you so sure?"

"I told you. I know her."

"Ben, I have a lot of respect for you. The things you're capable of, the information you obtain, the way you so quickly read a situation and people. Look at how you dissected the phone conversation with Robert and the terrorists. After hearing it once, you picked it apart like a junkyard owner finds the valuables in a lemon. Quite frankly, it scares me how shrewd you are. I wish you worked for the CIA."

"Why do I get the feeling this is a build up to you saying no?"

"I don't want to know if you killed Knoble. Because if I found out for a fact you did, I'd be finding out that I'm breaking the law by not apprehending you. But regardless of Knoble, you're asking me to aid and abet a fugitive of the law. I can't help you. My advice is to turn yourself in. Tell me what you know and let me help you."

"It's time for you to leave."

"Excuse me?"

"Get your backpack, get in your Nissan, and get out of here."

Before she could respond, Ben turned around and walked away, gently pushing through the glass door and heading towards the exit, leaving her stymied and confused.

She should have followed him. Or at the least, she should've called for backup and had him picked up. Even Ben couldn't elude the police if they knew exactly where he was. Her cell phone sat idle a mere hundred feet away, stashed in a locker, waiting for her to come get it and do just that. She stared into the full-length mirror bolted to the wall meant to make people feel good about themselves. It had the opposite effect on her.

She had no idea how much things were about to change.

39

Susan flung her backpack into the Nissan Armada's backseat and angrily slammed the door behind her without even noticing.

Frustrated with Ben and the mysterious crap that always came out of his mouth and second-guessing her decision not to call the cops, she gripped the beastly SUV's leather steering wheel until her knuckles cracked. Not even then did she see it. It was only when she pushed her head back into the headrest as hard as she could that her peripheral vision caught a glimpse of it out of the corner of her eye.

The legal-sized, nine-by-twelve-inch standard light-brown envelope sat innocuously on the front seat. Both sides were blank and its gum flap unsealed, but the small metal clasp at the top had been butterflied to enclose its contents. Something small and rectangular bulged from its center, and she opened up the envelope to discover it was a small black voice recorder. She put it aside and reviewed the plethora of documents attached to each other via paperclip.

There were several sheets of paper — a few typed on official letterhead of varying sources and one handwritten note on standard notebook paper. A handful of full-color, date-stamped photographs followed before finally, both the most straightforward and perplexing item emerged: the "Neighbor" section of yesterday's *Daily Herald* newspaper, with "Friday, May 14" in the upper right corner highlighted in yellow. The Chicago suburban newspaper didn't appear to have any other markings on it and no stories were circled, starred or otherwise marked.

It took her about ten minutes to peruse everything before she listened to the tape recorder. Then she listened again. And again. And then again. Each time, the two-minute message confirmed what she'd suspected all along, yet it still felt like a punch to the gut.

How is this possible?

She'd have the tape rigorously analyzed at the lab, of course. Audio authenticity and voice identification tests with percentage match analysis, digital forensic audio enhancement, the works. She'd have the handwritten note evaluated and crosschecked against the CIA and FBI databases, as well as an image analysis on each of the photographs. The other note, typed out and signed by Ben, had even suggested she do so in order to prove the authenticity of what she was seeing and hearing. To be certain, every single item from the light-brown envelope would be thoroughly evaluated with the most advanced technology there was.

But she knew it was legitimate. The pictures, documents and tape exposed how much she'd underestimated the situation, how far behind she really was. Ben had killed someone else in Bill Knoble's place, and no one noticed. As she contemplated how the hell he pulled it off, she felt like a kid thrust into a grown-up's game.

Just as she expected, her phone then began to ring. Caller ID matched the phone number written at the bottom of the handwritten note. She had no doubt it belonged to a prepaid cell phone that couldn't be traced. And she had no doubt who was calling.

"Now, do you understand?"

"Ben, why didn't you just tell me?"

"No time for that now. Do you now agree Nikki needs to stay out of this?" Ben asked.

"Yes, but we need to—"

"Then do what I asked."

"We have to talk about this. You can't just hand me this and then disappear again."

"Can't do it."

"Just tell me where you are. I can meet you. You can't be that far."

"You'd be surprised. Keep Nikki safe."

"I'll try."

"Don't try. Do. And get the Merriweather family to safety, too."

"The who?"

"Joe's girlfriend. Abigail Merriweather. Her family's being watched. Have Robert get them out of the house."

"Who's watching the family? I'll have Robert pick them up."

"Just get them out of the house."

"How do you know this?" she asked, wondering why Ben was withholding so much. Was it because he didn't trust her? Or was it because of something else?

"Either you do it your way, or I'll do it mine."

She had no idea what that meant, but the possibilities felt as dreadful as they did ambiguous.

"You're saying the Merriweather family is in danger?"

"Stop fumbling around like some shell-shocked rookie. Grab a pen."

"I'm not grabbing anything until we talk face to face."

"You just said ten minutes ago that you respect me. Now that you've seen what you've seen, it's time to either act like it or prove you're full of crap. Either way, you won't see me again until I get my boy back. Your call, Susan."

She pushed the cell phone into her chest and sighed deeply, staring at the Armada's wool-roof headlining, knowing this was another one of those conversations she was going to regret.

Fairly certain he was watching her, she leaned over to the glove compartment and grabbed her Uni-Ball and the small notepad that she used to track gas mileage.

"I'm listening."

"Soon, you're going to get a phone call from an acquaintance of mine."

183

"Who?"

"His name's David Keene. There's a personnel file in your glove compartment."

"How did you…" she stopped herself from asking the stupid question. *Of course this man can get into your car.*

"We'll get to his background. But first, we have to talk about something more important."

"Such as?"

"How you can find out that he's trustworthy."

"I'm not following."

"We're going to need him. You're going to need him. But you're not going to allow what needs to happen until you know you can trust him."

Oh, hell. She already regretted the conversation.

40

After driving her Armada around for a half-hour to clear her mind with the A/C on full-blast, Susan called Robert's cell and said she needed to talk. This was too important to not bring him in. He didn't object or ask questions, and she drove into the city to meet him at his condo.

Taking the long elevator ride up to the newly remodeled two-bedroom high-rise, she considered what Robert's reaction might be to the news that Ben had contacted her. As much as she respected Robert, she'd only been acquainted with him for a few years and she didn't really know him. Would he feel slighted in some way? Would he assume Ben trusted her more? She didn't know why she cared about his reaction, but she did.

Dressed in blue jeans and a tucked-in white golf shirt with loafers, Robert welcomed her in and offered fresh-squeezed lemonade. She accepted and took a seat on his brown latte fabric sofa in front of the fireplace. Robert sat in the recliner to her left; waiting to hear why this couldn't wait until Monday.

After she recapped her conversation with Ben, and Robert had reviewed the contents of the manila envelope, he looked up from the paperwork and sighed. Right foot on his left knee, he stared in her general direction but not straight into her eyes. Focused on what she guessed was the large American flag hanging above the mantle next to a grainy black and white picture of a young man in uniform, he cleared his throat before breaking the silence.

"What a surprise."

"I haven't confirmed it at the lab yet," she replied.

"But we both know what the results will be."

"Robert, we need to find Ben."

"If that wasn't Bill Knoble in that restaurant, then who the hell was it?" he demanded, plopping his glasses on the coffee table.

"I'm sure you'll find out. But in the meanwhile, what's the next move?"

"I'm the FBI Special Agent in Charge, and I'm getting this information secondhand from you."

To whom he was objecting, she wasn't sure. She chose to simply nod, as there wasn't much to say. The room suddenly felt warm, even hot. Her skin started to itch all over.

"Ben said they haven't contacted him yet?" Robert asked.

"Not a word. It's driving him nuts."

"How do you know that?"

"The way he talked about it. He's worried they might know Knoble isn't dead. Wouldn't you be freaked out? It's been three days."

Robert started chuckling, shaking his head and looking down towards the ground.

"What's so funny, Robert?"

"Nothing," Robert stopped laughing on a dime. "Not one damned thing about this is funny. Why did he contact you?"

"I don't know. Why did the terrorists contact you?"

"Easy. I'm not insinuating anything."

"No, more like outright suggesting it. I don't know why Ben approached me. Maybe because he knows telling you, the head of the unit charged with finding him, would put you in a comprising situation."

"Don't kid yourself, Susan. We're both compromised by this."

Now it was her turn to sigh. After she did, she stood up and walked to the window to take in the Chicago sights from the forty-third floor. Robert relocated from Phoenix a year ago, and she still saw unopened moving boxes on the floor. But the view was impeccable.

"Robert, what do we do now?"

"Nothing."

She turned to him and raised her voice. "Nothing?"

"What do you think we should do?"

"An APB seems more appropriate to me."

"If we do that, Ben will never contact you again."

Sounds good to me.

Robert continued, "Regardless of his reason for contacting you, he only would've done so if he trusted you. Since we're not having a lot of luck finding him, it seems counterproductive to squash the only viable connection we have."

"What are you suggesting?"

"We keep looking for him, but not via full scale APB. We hunt for the information and the lead we must be missing on the DL. If he contacts you again, let me know. I'll do the same. But we can't give up the only connection we have, even if it's on his terms."

There was an argument to be made they should exploit Ben's trust in her. But once again, it felt Robert was under-doing the next move, not being aggressive enough. That didn't work out with Ben's son's kidnapping or Knoble's disappearance, and she worried it wouldn't this time either. Her eyes gravitated towards the flag on the wall and framed picture of the young man in uniform below it.

"That's my grandfather," Robert said. "Served in World War II. Lied about his age to get into the service. He's only seventeen there. Looks just like my son..."

She turned towards him. "I didn't realize you had a son."

Robert paused for a moment before forcing a smile. "Lost him in Afghanistan a few years ago. IED. I can't look at him in uniform...but his grandfather's close enough."

"Oh, Robert. I'm sorry."

"About Ben," Robert quickly pivoted, approaching her with a limp that looked more severe than it did a week ago. "I realize I've made some poor judgment calls, so I'm going to think this over and consult some folks in the bureau. If you really think the best course of action is a full-scale manhunt, I'll push for it.

"My concern is we'd be giving up our only advantage. If Ben trusts you, he'll come to you again. Maybe we'll find out who took Knoble's place. Or better yet, maybe the terrorists will contact him again and we'll find out what they want. They're still out there, and I'm worried about what happens next."

She took a deep breath and exhaled loudly, uttering, "No, I think you're right. It's probably best to keep it on the DL. I'm just worried we'll find out too late what happens next."

Robert put his hand on her shoulder and offered a sympathetic frown, his eyes watery as they moved from the picture of his grandfather towards her.

"Me too, Susan."

41

Three days after his deadline to kill Bill Knoble or lose his son, there had still been no word from the terrorists. No phone call, message, or hint as to why. Frustrated and anxious, Ben sat on Glen Eagle Golf Club's gray flagstone patio Saturday morning, the setting he'd chosen for one of the most important conversations of his life.

The May weather was impeccable: a slight breeze from the east, the sun peeking in and out of soft, wispy clouds, and not a trace of humidity. Lush, dark-green grass and beds of colorful flowers ringed the outdoor dining area. Golfers were enjoying the course in full force, but the patio was wide open. He'd chosen a two-person table at the far edge of the balcony overlooking the ninth hole. Its spectacular view made it a logical choice, but its real appeal was that with binoculars one could easily watch it from afar unobstructed.

He tried not to think about Joe and the dried blood on the locket or Nikki and that magical kiss, but each kept circling back in his mind like a boomerang. Uncharacteristically second guessing decisions that couldn't be reversed, he tried to clear his mind of everything except the mission at hand. Easier said than done. After watching Tom devour his second hot dog, however, he realized his mentor didn't have the same concentration problems he did.

They'd practiced the conversation multiple times. Specific words, voice inflections, facial expressions and body language. Improv was taboo; everything was going to be interpreted, so it had to be choreographed. It was a lot of prep for a short conversation, but they only had one chance. And the stakes were high.

He had two phones with him. The first was his normal cell, with a number that, despite his insistence friends and family commit to memory rather than store, Joe's captors had most certainly obtained. Private as he was, he'd had the number for years and these people would find it. It sat on the table next to his iced tea in plain sight, with GPS, Phone Tracker and Find my iPhone all enabled.

The other, which not even Tom knew about, was vibrating like crazy in his pocket. It had no third party applications or downloaded apps. There weren't any pictures, web browsing or e-mail. Texts poured in from his sources, all using pseudonyms, with updates specifically worded to make sense to him but be gibberish to anyone else. He didn't motion towards the phone, but kept it on vibrate to know if information was coming. Taking a sip of iced tea to bring his arm towards his face, he checked his watch as the glass touched his lips.

It was 11:06, time to roll.

"Have you heard from them?" Tom asked on cue, his mouth stuffed with fries.

"Not a peep."

Scripted silence for a few seconds.

"Why do you think they haven't called?" he invoked the plural pronoun. "Why give a deadline and not respond after I meet it?"

"Who knows, Grasshopper," Tom replied once the waiter was out of earshot. That too was scripted. The people watching knew he and Tom wouldn't talk in front of anyone.

"There's no chance they missed it," Tom continued. "It's all over the news. I can't believe all the marches."

"Then why the waiting game?"

"Maybe to see if you get implicated. Did you talk to Nikki?"

"Yeah...I told her to stay the hell away."

"You sure that's the right move, Grasshopper? Maybe she can help."

"She never should've been involved," he said, shaking his head. "I can't believe you did that. Enough innocent people are in harm's way. At least she's out now."

"Doesn't seem to bother you that I'm in harm's way," Tom replied with the perfect mix of sarcasm and seriousness. "Lighten up."

"How am I supposed to lighten up? It's been three days and I haven't heard from them."

"Let them in your head now and it's over before it begins."

He sighed, "I guess you're right."

"I'm always right."

Ben started to respond and Tom cut him off, exactly as they'd rehearsed.

"Sorry, no more jokes. So Nikki bowed out? She actually listened to you?"

"It's not exactly a hard sell."

"I thought she'd push back."

"She doesn't want anything to do with me, Tom. Or this case. She's moved on, and she doesn't want to look back. She was pissed that you called her. You're not always right...you were way off on that one."

"I had to do something."

"She chases child predators. She doesn't have the skill set, jurisdiction or desire to help with this. She didn't get anywhere, and she isn't involved anymore. I'll never see her again, thanks to you."

"Don't you dare pin that on me. I didn't end your relationship then and I'm not stopping it now."

"It's over, Tom."

"No it isn't." Tom violently shook his head. In rehearsal, Ben worried Tom's body language was overstated, but it played well now. "You're just afraid of getting hurt again."

"She has a different life, a better life. New job, new people, new apartment. She's happy. And she deserves to be. She never wanted any part of the Hubley investigation; she was a programmer who got thrust into it. And now that she's out, she's out for good."

"Maybe that's for the best."

Ben kept his mind focused and acute. The objective of this conversation was to show the terrorists Nikki wasn't a threat, but he couldn't overdo it. Joe, and the fact they hadn't called, was what they'd expect to be on the forefront of his mind. And it was, but he had to segue the conversation. If he didn't, they'd catch on.

"Tom?" he asked as Tom started hot dog number four. "Do you think they'll hurt him? Or that they already did? I haven't wanted to ask that out loud."

"Grasshopper, I wish I could say no for sure. But I couldn't tell you."

"I did what they asked," he leaned forward, elbows on his knees.

"Shitheads like this aren't logical or predictable. You knew that going in."

"So, I'm just supposed to keep waiting?"

"What else can you do? Report it? Call the cops? Nah…if there's a next move they have to make it."

"I gotta go," he quickly replied, grabbing the phone from the table, hoping it'd ring. His tuna melt and fries untouched, he was already on the steps by the time Tom called after him. The conversation reminded him of how helpless he felt, how worried he was. The shenanigans notwithstanding, at the end of the day he was just waiting for bad things to happen.

42

"What flight?" Arminius asked skeptically.

"United Flight 219, departing O'Hare at 10:10 tomorrow morning. Returning on United Flight 218 at 3:55 p.m. Honolulu time Thursday the 27th, landing in Chicago at 5:08 local time the next morning."

"Just the three of them?"

"Yes," Rausch replied.

"Tickets confirmed?"

"First class both ways for everyone. Total airfare was just under thirteen grand."

"Booked today?"

"At just after one. The father's work schedule was cleared for the duration of the trip."

"But it wasn't clear yesterday?"

"It doesn't appear so."

Arminius deposited another "thinking tool" — a monster Kodiak Ice tobacco dip — into his mouth, tightly tucking it between his lower lip and gums. Careful to grab it and not the red cherry Skoal can, his third dip of the day burned so hard that it almost had him believing the fallacy the stuff contained fiberglass. But it was worth it. He'd learned in the military that the burning was an acceptable trade-off for the calming influence his thinking tool provided.

Certainly the parents could've decided their daughter needed a break from everything. And what better way to get one than Hawaii. Given the lack of progress on the Joe Leksa Missing Person Report, it made sense. The FBI hadn't contacted the Merriweather family since Benton's visit almost a week ago, and no news isn't good news when it comes to Missing Person investigations. A spontaneous trip to lift the girl's spirits was a plausible scenario.

But the timing didn't sit right with him. No one had mentioned it before today, either in the house or on the phone. And the father was a busy lawyer with a hectic schedule. To clear his calendar the day before an eleven-day trip didn't make sense. Unless he smelled danger.

"How did the girl react?"

"Like a distraught girlfriend."

"Details…"

"Said she didn't want to go," Rausch cleared his throat, "that she wanted to wait for Leksa to turn up. But the father told her it wasn't an option. She stormed off, put up a real fuss. But then she apologized a few hours later after the mom talked her off the ledge."

"Did anything unusual happen the past few days?"

"No, sir."

"Even unrelated to this vacation? New visitors? Phone calls that seemed cryptic, like someone might be trying to disguise a message? Unusual packages or boxes?"

"Nothing out of the ordinary. The father's mom did come to town a few days ago from Indianapolis to spend the day with the girl."

"What'd they do?"

"High tea and some shopping and lunch. The girl was reluctant and the grandmother dragged her the whole way. Grandma drove home the day before last. No visitors since."

"Has the family discussed the Leksa boy?"

"Not since Special Agent Benton's visit. The parents actually discussed not bringing it up to keep the girl's mind off it."

"When?"

"Three nights ago in bed, right before he had his way with that tasty woman."

"You sound like that filth Clay Braun. I won't have it."

"I'm sorry, Arminius," Rausch quickly responded in a jittery voice.

"Don't be sorry. Be professional. Braun may be yapping about it, but I know how you feel about the Merriweather woman. Keep it in your pants. We have work to do. If you perform, we'll discuss it."

"Yes, sir."

He spit another gargantuan amalgam of saliva into the soda can and some of the brown discharge dribbled its way down his chin. He shook his head. Braun and his fantasies…He understood people had fetishes. But being a pervert was one thing; letting it get in the way of the job was another. And that reflected more on Rausch than Rausch seemed to realize. It reaffirmed to him his decision to limit the information he shared.

"Have they made any plans for Hawaii?"

"Yes, sir. Snorkeling the day after they arrive and swimming with the dolphins. A couple days later they're riding bikes down a volcano. It looks to me like they're trying to escape, sir. You know, get away from things."

He wasn't interested in Rausch's theories. However, he couldn't argue with the conclusion.

"I have their hotel reservation as well. Four Seasons hotel in Maui."

I'll bet you do.

"Leave them for the time being. I have another assignment for you. If we need to get updates, there are other ways."

"Other ways?"

"Don't concern yourself with it."

"Yes, sir," Rausch dutifully replied.

"Is there anything else I need to know about this trip?"

"No sir."

"What about Benton? Have you seen her poking around?"

"Not recently."

"She hasn't interviewed anyone else?"

"Not since yesterday."

Benton's discussions with Peter Hubley's former work associates had Agricola concerned, as had her research on the late Dominick Riddle. Even though he'd assured his partner he had things under control — that she was merely following protocol — she was definitely tougher to shake than he'd expected.

"Anything else at all on her?"

"No sir. She's been relatively quiet the past few days."

He thought back to the conversation Siebert and Fedorak had at Glen Eagle Golf Course and spit into the soda can. The former Marine knew it was a mistake to bring Benton into it; that wasn't farfetched. The flow of the conversation made sense; Fedorak would get defensive and Siebert would argue what he knew was right. But something seemed off. Everything lined up a little too neatly for the real world. He certainly welcomed the dialogue...if Benton really was off the case. It would make things that much simpler. But it didn't sit right. Siebert was too clever to assume he didn't have something up his sleeve.

A few seconds was all it took to devise a plan. It materialized quickly and brought him relief the way a burst of rain does a desert.

The thinking tool strikes again.

"Stay on Benton. Start at her office Monday morning and track her movements. Constant surveillance. Who she talks to, what she does, where she goes, the ordinary and the suspicious. Report back to me no matter how mundane."

"Will do, sir. I'll be all over her."

I knew you wouldn't object, you sleazy pervert.

"If you do a thorough job tracking Benton, we can discuss your bonus."

43

The prospect of a reward involving the Merriweather ladies had Clay Braun giddy as a schoolboy.

FBI Special Agent Benton went to bed almost four hours ago, but even at this hour sleep wasn't in his immediate future. So with the Merriweather clan headed to Hawaii in eight hours and no other work to do per Mr. Rausch's orders, he took a joyride into the city. He hit up Pink Monkey and Gold Club and the strip clubs delivered as promised, priming the pump for his reward. Then he made his way to Rivers Casino in Des Plaines and sat at the blackjack table for a few hours, gawking at scantily clad waitresses and sucking down Bacardi and Cokes two at a time.

The combination of his sexual fantasy and the ice he was popping like aspirin would make tonight an all-nighter. He left the casino down two grand but was too high and too excited to care.

He needed that reward.

He felt like gambling some more, so he set out for Hollywood Casino in Aurora. Getting there would be a pain because Rausch insisted he pay cash at the tolls instead of I-PASS, but he had the time to burn and it was a hell of a night for a drive. No clouds, no humidity. The windows in his grey Lincoln MZK down, radio blasting, wind toying with the cloud of cigarette smoke from his fifth pack of Marlboros, he laughed out loud and sang along to the classics on 94.7 FM. The glint of gold fillings emerged in the rearview mirror as he blew himself a kiss, picturing Abigail Merriweather and her tight-ass mother.

He made it 25 miles before he had to use the can at around three-thirty. No surprise with all the drinking he'd done, not to mention that speed made him piss like a racehorse. He thought about pulling over and pissing on the shoulder, but I-88 was pretty well lit and he didn't want to get picked up for something stupid. Not with Ms. Benton waking up in a few hours. And the double "Merri" award he'd get soon after.

He got off the interstate at Route 59 and headed north for a mile to the Speedway at Butterfield Road, open twenty-four seven. At almost three in the morning, the gas station was empty. A dented Ford Contour was parked in one of the side spots but otherwise the lot was empty and there weren't any cars at the pump.

What sucked was the bathroom was in a remote building about a hundred feet behind the convenience store. Tucked away over by the air machines and diesel pump, it required a key. The walk to the cashier felt like a mile he had to piss so bad. The twenty-something-year-old punk working the register didn't even take out his earbuds when he asked for the key. He could hear rap music blasting when the punk grabbed a wooden backscratcher with a string and key tied to it. Why the hell was the key tied to a backscratcher? He almost asked just to make the kid take out the earbuds, but he really had to piss.

The unisex bathroom looked like a vanilla explosion. The tile walls and floor, ceiling, sink, hand dryer, toilet and soap dispenser were all white. Except for the light brown layer of grime that coated the entire space. Brown and yellow stains marred the seat. The toilet was leaking in the back, so a tiny puddle of water had collected against the wall. He decided to piss all over the seat and floor in protest. When the flow of relief began, it felt tremendous, gratifying, better than sex. *Almost.* He swirled his hips to make sure his light-yellow tinkle covered the entire surrounding area. He closed his eyes and started singing Sonny and Cher's "I Got You Babe" out loud.

Then he felt scorching pain.

Something pounded into his lower back, hard, from behind. His knees buckled and his upper body fell backwards, piss going everywhere. He overcompensated for his chest suddenly jerking backwards, and his whole body started to fall down. He clutched the grab bar mounted to the wall behind the toilet to break the fall, pissing all over himself.

Then he felt a hard snap in his left leg, right behind his knee. It was searing; it felt like a tendon had ruptured. Both his legs instantly dropped to the grimy floor, his knees soaking wet in front of the urine-stained crapper. He kept hold of the grab bar, arms fully extended. And before he had a chance to turn around, he felt cold steel wrap around one wrist and then the other. He knew that steel; it could only be one thing. Both sets of handcuffs were then locked around the grab bar. He tried to jerk his hands free but the bar wouldn't budge. When he tried to stand up for more leverage, the scorching pain in his leg wouldn't let him. He got about two inches and then collapsed onto the wet floor, his wrist skin pinching against the cuffs as his body thumped down. He couldn't break free. All he could do was turn his head to face his attacker.

"What the hell?"

The guy towering behind him reached back with his right hand and smacked his face so hard it felt like a wooden spoon had cracked across his cheek. The guy was wearing latex gloves, but it was the worst sting he'd ever felt. Pins and needles were all over, made worse by not being able to rub it. He turned away and stared towards the wet floor. The tears couldn't be stopped.

"Make one more sound...I guarantee you'll regret it for the rest of your life."

He said it in a calm voice, almost a whisper. He was tall, maybe six-and-a-half feet. Short, light-brown hair; stubble, scary-looking blue eyes, and he was strong. Big forearms; bulky chest. Jeans and a purple polo. He looked into the guy's eyes until they looked back. He didn't want to see that shit for one second longer than he had to.

"Who the hell are you?" he cried through the pain.

The man didn't respond. Instead, he turned around and pressed the hand dryer button. That thing was louder than it looked, and it was on a timer, not a sensor. That meant that when the freaky dude with his freaky eyes turned around with something shiny in his hand, it just kept blowing. The guy reared back and swung down like a tomahawk towards the grab iron.

He caught a glimpse of the butcher's knife right before it smashed into his right hand. Three of his fingers were immediately severed and blood squirted everywhere. The pinkie and ring fingers fell to the piss-stained floor and got swallowed up in puddles of grime. The middle finger sat atop the toilet. He howled in pain staring at his mangled hand and the river of blood flowing from the top of the crapper to the floor. Then he looked at the guy, just in time to see him swing a metal mallet — which he knew then was what hit his lower back a few seconds ago while pissing — down onto his right kneecap.

He felt bone shatter. Pain spread through his entire leg so fast it felt unbearable. He thought he was going to pass out, howling *why* to the freaky guy doing this to him. Again no answer.

He just pressed the hand dryer button again.

44

The rancid gas station bathroom would make a fitting tomb for Clay Braun.

Its soiled floors, cracked walls and overall aura of disgust properly symbolized the manner with which Braun led his life. There would be no cleansing tonight. Not for this room, and not for Braun.

The freelance informant turned his body to avoid putting weight on either knee, and to make that work Braun's entire left side hugged the toilet, his armpit pushing over the flush handle, legs rubbing the bowl. He sat on his bottom, his body twisted halfway between the toilet and sink. Arms bent at the elbow, pants covered in his own blood and urine, belly poking through the bottom of a soaking-wet T-shirt. His mangled knees bulged from loose-fitting jeans stretched tight by the twisting of his body. His dismembered hands trembled atop the toilet.

Ben gently placed the mallet in the sink and grabbed the butcher's knife, running it under water to wash the blood away and re-expose its shine.

"Try me again, Clay," he said in a voice just loud enough to be heard over the hand dryer. "See what else I'll chop off."

He tilted the butcher's knife towards the floor where Braun's pants were still unzipped and his penis partially exposed. Braun whimpered like a little girl.

"You're not so tough when you have to face someone. It's a little different than watching your monitors and driving around spying on women and children."

"What do you want?" Braun asked in a sheepish voice.

"This bad boy pumps out some air, doesn't it?" he replied, gently tapping the hand dryer with his gloved left hand. "I'd guess 200 cubic feet per minute...*plenty* to make sure no one hears you scream. We don't need it, we're pretty far away from the cashier and he was listening to music. But why not be thorough?"

"I'll pay whatever you want."

"See this knife? It's called a 'chopper cleaver.' Whatever that means. It's nice though. Seven-inch blade, stainless steel, ergonomic handle. It'll more than serve our purposes tonight."

Braun lowered his face towards his arm and blew his nose into his Cubital Fossa, the crevice near the forearm opposite the elbow.

"I didn't do anything -"

Very swiftly he swung the knife again, this time targeting Braun's left hand, resulting in more screams and tears. He pressed the dryer button to reset the thirty-second cycle.

"Don't you dare lie to me, Clay. I might be running out of fingers, but I've got plenty of other extremities to choose from. You want to minimize your pain? Tell the truth, the whole truth and nothing but the truth, so help you God. And you definitely need God's help tonight."

Ben gave the next thirty seconds over to silence as he slowly ran his index finger along the edge of the smooth side of the chopper cleaver. Then he looked at Braun and nodded. The dread in Braun's eyes indicated it was time.

"Why were you watching the Merriweather residence?"

No words. Still only tears. He lifted the knife into the air to get things moving.

"I don't know."

"That's cute. It won't be so cute trying to jerk off with no hands."

"It was just a job," Braun forced out over his sobs. "I don't know why."

"Speak up!" he yelled, grabbing Braun's shoulders and digging into the pressure point. "A job to watch the house?"

"The girl," Braun choked out.

"Abigail Merriweather?"

"Yes."

"Why?"

"I told you, man. I don't know. I just do the job."

"Who paid you?"

The look on Braun's face revealed he knew it was over, yet there was still resistance. Whoever was pulling the strings might've had something over Braun beyond even his life. Ben knew the most ruthless villains made it clear entire families would suffer if their employees ever squealed. He hoped that wasn't the case with Braun, but something told him it was.

"Who paid you?" he leaned in real close.

"I don't know his real name."

"Real name?"

"He calls himself Arminius," Braun said before closing his eyes.

"Arminius," Ben replied, combing his memory bank. "The German warrior?"

"I ain't no damn history professor."

Braun's answer was interrupted when Ben gently placed the butcher knife's blade on his left thumb and pushed down hard, feeling it grind into the white porcelain once the thumb was fully severed. Then he stomped on Braun's right kneecap with his foot.

"You're funny, and I usually like jokes," he yelled over Braun's whimpers. He pressed the button on the dryer to get a fresh thirty seconds. "But we should probably get serious."

"I told you, I don't know his name."

"How'd you find him?"

"He found me."

"How?"

"I've got a lot of feelers out there. Word of mouth, advertising, whatever it takes. Freelance surveillance, work for the highest bidder. People find me. Folks I did jobs for hook me up with others, Craigslist, whatever. I don't know how they found me."

"They?" Ben raised an eyebrow.

"One day this guy called me. Asked if I'd be interested in a surveillance job. Sounded all formal and technical and shit. Fancy words."

"What was his name?"

"Didn't say."

"How'd he get your number?"

"I told you man. I've got feelers out there. Same number in all the places. Said he got a referral but he didn't say who. Didn't buy it, but didn't care."

"Why?"

"These dudes are different from anyone I ever worked for. Real formal. Deep pockets."

"Then what happened?"

"He kind of interviewed me, it was weird. Asked me what technology I knew, the kinds of jobs I'd done, stuff like that. I thought the job was for him."

"But it wasn't?"

Braun shook his head. "He was just screening me. Never had that happen before."

"You never got screened before?"

"Usually I only talk to one dude for one job; ain't no middleman. I figured the extra layer meant whoever the job was really for was a rich son of a bitch, so I wanted to impress. I guess it worked. Guy called me three times to ask me about my past, said he did a full background check," Braun rolled his eyes while saying.

"Did he?"

"No idea. But after all those calls, I got an envelope with ten grand in it. Best day of my life. There was a cell phone too. Prepaid. The guy told me someone named Arminius would call."

"But you never got a name?"

"I swear, man. He said he worked for Arminius and wanted to see if I could do a job. With green like that I wasn't gonna ask questions."

He wasn't sure that was true. While Braun didn't have any trouble giving up this Arminius, it seemed unlikely he didn't have another name. He wondered if that person had the leverage and Arminius had the anonymity.

"What about the phone?"

"It's got an encryption system on it. Silent Circle. I'm supposed to use it when he calls."

"And Arminius wanted you to watch Abigail Merriweather?"

"Yeah."

"What else?"

When Braun didn't answer, Ben slapped him hard against the face. Braun started crying again and Ben leaned in close.

"What else," he grimly whispered.

"Some FBI Agent. Benton. I was supposed to keep tabs on her."

When he heard Nikki's name, he kicked Braun in the groin with all his might. Watching Braun clutch his nether region with a hand missing fingers, he lowered to within inches of Braun's face.

"What about Benton?"

"Nothing, man," Braun forced out with a wheeze, hogging air and lowering his head in pain.

"What did I say about lying to me?"

"I ain't lying, man. I swear! I asked…but all he wanted me to do was watch. Watch her and tell him who she talked to. Interviews and stuff; who she met with."

Ben paused to watch the worthless weasel bleed and fade. Much as he hated to admit it, Braun's story was plausible. Nikki had stirred some pots and they would want to watch her. The curious thing was that Arminius himself gave the direction. Probably because Arminius wanted to spread his risk over multiple people. Give a lot of people very little information to minimize his overall exposure. Rare, but very smart. Had Ben not set up a stakeout of the Merriweather residence, he wouldn't have found Clay Braun in the first place.

"Where's my son?"

"What?"

"Don't play games with me. Where's my boy?"

"Dude, I don't know anything about that."

He stared at Braun for a final time. His face said it all. He knew his life was over; he'd given up on the idea of walking out of the fetid restroom. The pain in his body had overcome the hope for life in his mind. Resistance had succumbed to reality.

Keeping Braun alive for days was of little value. Torture didn't work when the assholes didn't know anything, and Braun was a pawn. He knew that by how carless Braun was…driving around at two a.m., frequenting bars and strip clubs…a true professional would've been a ghost.

He'd get Braun's car, phone, ID, and anything else on him. Then run an exhaustive search to flesh out Braun's background. But even if a connection existed, he doubted he'd learn what he needed to know. Whoever Arminius was, he'd proven his intelligence and caution. It was highly unlikely there was anything else to get. Braun had no reason to lie, unless Arminius really did threaten a loved one. And if that were the case, this last resort was all Ben had.

It was now or never.

"Clay…here's the deal. You tell me everything you know about Arminius, I'll kill you quick," he snapped his fingers. "You don't deserve that, but you have my word."

"I already told you what I know," Braun choked out, horror in his eyes.

"If you don't, I chop off a few other things. Then I let you bleed a slow death on this piss-drenched bathroom floor."

45

The soft knocking awakened her.

"Genie," the voice whispered. Her jerky breathing either returned immediately or never stopped. Her heart was still sprinting and sweat had soaked through the blonde wig in her sleep. She'd worn it for 72 hours; naively telling herself it offered protection from Mr. Knoble's killer. Dried tears turned crusty and the skin under her nose was red and raw from all the blowing.

Frazzled and disoriented, she hopped out of bed and stood in the middle of the room like a cat burglar, both arms up, swiveling her head around. The alarm clock read 4:22 a.m. and she was pretty sure it was Sunday, but it took her a moment to orient herself. She'd come to define this paranoid, confused and exhausted state as normal. Not even late-night *Friends* repeats could lull her to sleep. Rest, like every other aspect of her life, had been completely decimated. She'd become a shadow. She hadn't said more than a few words to another human being since Mr. Knoble's death and was hunkered down in a cheap motel, burning through her savings. She didn't know what to do or who to turn to. And now, someone was knocking.

They were coming for her. She didn't know who they were, but she knew they'd find her. She was dead. Just like Mr. Knoble.

"Genie," the voice repeated. Then a few more gentle taps.

There were no other exits. She was done; caught; finished. She clutched the pillow from a bed that hadn't been made in days. She'd refused to let sleeping pills or booze help her cope. *You need to stay as sharp as you can*, she'd told herself. Her only indulgence was Edy's chocolate chip ice cream, but now even that was gone. The empty cartons lay hallowed out on their sides, melted white ooze dripping from the edges onto the dark carpet. Certain that doom was on the other side of #6's flimsy wooden door, she wished now she'd stoned herself. Why die sober? She hadn't lived long enough; hadn't experienced enough.

"Genie, I'm here to help. I know you're scared and I don't blame you, but please open the door," the man said. She didn't recognize the voice, but it had a certain genuineness to it. It sounded concerned. Yet obviously this person knew who she was and tracked her down. She couldn't let her delirium or desperation allow her to make a stupid decision.

As if she had many options.

She crawled on all fours like an animal to the window, which she'd blocked with the thick curtains she'd wedged together and held in place with the hotel Bible from the nightstand drawer. Flashing lights from *Married with Children* strobed like a disco ball behind her as she slowly pulled back the corner of the curtain, inch-by-inch.

The man was older than she expected, maybe in his sixties. He wore a pair of blue jeans with brown boots and a black shirt under a red flannel jacket. His rimmed glasses sat on a severely wrinkled face, and his light brown hair was combed straight back. He didn't have anything in his hands, but she felt certain he had a gun. Just because she couldn't see it didn't mean it wasn't there.

She closed her eyes and tried to think, but all she saw was Mr. Knoble.

Sitting at that table. Staring at her.

She began to sob, dislodging previous eye crusties with a river of fresh tears. With no means to protect herself, she grabbed the wooden leg from the chair she'd smashed against the ground last night and held it like a baseball bat. As if that could save her. Why didn't she get a gun? And why didn't she…what's the point? This was it; she was going to die.

"Genie, my name is Tom Fedorak. I'm a friend of Ben Siebert's. Please, open the door."

"What do you want!" she summoned the courage to howl, picturing Mr. Knoble getting into Ben Siebert's car.

"Genie, I'm not here to harm you. You're in danger. You can't stay here."

"Leave me alone! I don't know anything. I don't *want* to know anything." She threw her hands up, as if this Tom guy could see it.

"You can't stay here," the soft response came. "I'm sorry it's taken me so long to find you. Your efforts are admirable, but paying cash for a motel room doesn't help if you withdraw it from an ATM around the block. They'll find you if you don't let me help."

"They'll find me? How do I know you're not them?"

"Genie, look through the peephole. Stare at my face and decide for yourself if you want to stay here and wait for them or trust me. If you decide you'd rather wait, I'll leave. I'm not here to hurt you, but I'm not going to break down the door and drag you away. You decide."

Against every natural urge, she got up from the filthy matte carpet and looked through the peephole with her right eye, half expecting it to get shot out as she kept the left side of her body as far from the door as possible.

Rain poured down behind the man, his face illuminated by the outdoor light bulb. He had wide pupils and a furrowed brow. Sure, his eyes looked honest, but how could she trust him? He huddled under the balcony and looked back, as though he could see through the peephole.

"Okay, I looked. Now leave!"

She shouted it as loud as she could and stepped away from the door, still holding the chair leg. No matter how innocent he appeared, or how much she wanted to believe he was there to help, she wouldn't open the door. He could kick it in. He could shoot the lock and then shoot her. There was nothing she could do to stop that. But she sure as hell wasn't going to open the door to her own death.

"Okay Genie. You win. But indulge me one more time."

Here it comes.

She said a prayer asking God for forgiveness, salvation, and a quick death.

"I know you threw your phone away, which was smart. So before I leave, please look through the peephole one more time. After this, I'm gone if you want me gone"

Expecting to see the business end of a shotgun, she leaned forward and instead saw a black iPhone. The man inched it close to the peephole until it consumed her entire view. On display was a contact on the Favorites tab named "XX" with a mobile phone number she didn't recognize aside from its 312 Chicago area code. The man tapped "FaceTime" two lines below, initiating a conversation. The screen dimmed and a couple seconds later the connection was made. The screen revealed a ghost.

It can't be...

Mr. Knoble sat behind a brown table with a beige wall in the background and nothing else in sight. He wore a white polo and his gelled black hair was parted to the right. The dimples looked the same, and she knew the eyes were his.

"Genie," Mr. Knoble softly said, "I'm so sorry."

He paused as if he knew she was crying. As if he could hear her.

"You didn't deserve it. You should be relaxing, waiting for your exam results. I missed breakfast with you yesterday. I missed having food envy, and hearing about how I tip Cindy too much. I can't tell you how sorry I am, or how much I've worried about you.

"But I need you to listen. Mr. Siebert saved my life, Genie. I know it's a shock and the opposite of what you've been thinking, but it's true.

"It's a real son of a biscuit you saw what you saw. I'll explain everything. Mr. Fedorak is there to get you to safety. I can't come myself, and you'll understand why after I give you a ginormous hug."

Was this a dream? The FaceTime app looked legitimate. It was clear it wasn't a video, and the man looked exactly like Mr. Knoble. The data was also there: the reference to Cindy, biscuit instead of bitch, knowing about her law school, using ginormous. But she saw him die. She watched him get shot and keel over. The whole world knew William T. Knoble was dead.

"Genie, I know you're scared. I know you don't know what to believe. And I'm proud of you. I knew you wouldn't just take Tom at face value. I told him he'd have to use FaceTime to prove it to you. Remember when I told you that you reap what you sow in this life? I'll show you exactly what I meant, but first you've got to go with him.

"If you want, ask me anything. Things only I would know. Remember our motto, Genie? Test it. Prove it. Verify it. Make sure you do all of that before you trust this man. But once you do, you need to get moving. Fast."

Her knees failed her, and she turned around to inch down the door, her paisley shirt rising up her dewy back until she landed on the floor with a slight thud. And buried her face into trembling hands.

46

Arminius had been instructed to wait for a call. The request came at 10:50 a.m., about four hours ago, but by now he was used to playing the waiting game whenever he needed to speak to Agricola.

Any time they needed to have a conversation, there were several arrangements that Agricola insisted be made. An overabundance of caution in everything the man did, the preparations included but were not limited to: Agricola's private transportation to an undisclosed location, creation of a rock-solid alibi for his whereabouts, utilization of a secure telephone line outside of any potential FBI surveillance, careful monitoring of both vehicular and foot traffic to look for anything unusual, and the stern practice of constantly reassessing the situation's risk as the call time approached.

Twice before, Agricola had called a conversation off because something didn't feel quite right in the moments leading up to it. A meeting time was never scheduled far in advance because Agricola believed putting any unnecessary information out in the universe — private as they may've assumed it was — was an avoidable risk they couldn't afford to take. Arminius thought it was overkill, but he also understood. Agricola's experience had taught him that privacy was never certain, and there was obvious risk. That meant Arminius always had to wait by his prepaid cell phone until Agricola was good and ready.

The effort Agricola went though every time was one of the reasons he didn't like requesting a conversation, but it wasn't the most significant. "Partners" was a term they'd both used to describe their relationship — and one he liked to think was appropriate — but he knew Agricola was in charge. Agricola's access to information and people was vital to their objective.

Arminius knew he was in a supporting role. And he was fine with that. But it meant that whenever he needed to have a conversation, it felt like he was letting Agricola down.

But as he sat in his home office reviewing Susan Reynolds's confidential personnel file, he knew it was necessary. A thinking tool relaxed his mind, but the PDF contents reaffirmed that his decision to reach out to Agricola was appropriate.

He answered on the first ring, caller ID blocked as usual.

"What is it, my friend?" Agricola asked, straight to the point. He could hear a rumbling noise in the background, maybe a train. It sounded like Agricola was outside.

"I'm sorry to bother you," he answered with a soft but confident voice, telling himself that the need for a conversation wasn't a failure.

"You're never a bother, Arminius. We're both patriots doing what we can for our country. I hate that our talks must be so limited, but we need to continue exercising caution. Revealing too much puts American lives at risk."

"I understand and agree."

"So you think we need some extra surveillance on Mrs. Reynolds?"

"I do," he answered, spitting into a plastic cup. "As I've thought about it more, the fact and the way Siebert reached out to her tell me two things. First, he trusts her, and he may try to contact her again. Next, doing so at her gym means he didn't want others to know. If he does try to contact her again, he'll do so in a similar fashion. I think we need to be aware of any contact the two of them have ASAP."

"I agree. What'd you have in mind?"

It was obvious Agricola had already thought through the idea in advance. He wasn't one to make snap decisions, and his immediate agreement told Arminius they were fully aligned before the conversation began. A wave of relief swept across his insides.

"For starters, do you have any contacts at CIA Personnel?" he brought up the subject again. Agricola paused for a moment.

"I'll look into it. Is everything still on track for your conversation with Siebert?"

"Indeed it is, Agricola. The time has come for him to learn his true purpose."

"It'll feel out of the blue to him, but stay the course. He'll come around."

"I will."

"It appears your stall tactic worked. He's quite nervous he hasn't heard from you."

"Thank you, sir. We'll find out for sure tomorrow."

"Before we hang up, anything else on Benton?"

"Nothing we haven't already discussed, Agricola. She's still involved with the investigation, despite the warnings."

He waited through the awkward silence, trying to picture Agricola absorbing the news. He understood why Agricola felt the way he did, but Benton had disregarded both her friends' advice and her direction from the SAIC. The threat had to be acknowledged.

"Has she…learned anything?"

"Not yet, but…" he paused, considering if the time was right. "Sir, I know you don't want action taken, but—"

"She is not to be harmed."

"I understand, partner. But if she doesn't stop snooping around the Hubley case, we could have a real problem. She's diving in hard, and she's good at research. Smith covered his tracks, but no one's perfect. If she finds out —"

"Anything else?" Agricola interrupted.

"No sir," he responded. The tension in Agricola's voice was all he needed to hear. His partner knew he had a point. That was enough for now.

214

47

The call came on Sunday night at 11:42 p.m.

It had been nine days since Ben heard from them, and that felt like an eternity considering the deadline they'd given. Replaying the staged conversation he and Tom had yesterday, Ben still didn't know what to make of the delay. There was definitely a reason — these people seemed to have purpose behind everything they did — and he wanted to think it had nothing to do with Joe. But that was predicated on the assumption they believed Bill Knoble was dead. What if they knew he wasn't? What if the reason he hadn't heard from them was because Joe was already dead?

With no information, to keep his sanity he chose to assume there was some other reason. The office-turned-crash pad looked like a tornado had just spun its way through: papers scattered all over the desk and two conference tables in no discernible order; whiteboards lined the walls covered with multi-colored dry-erase scribble offering unconnected thoughts and off-the-wall theories that grew less plausible as time went on; random articles of clothing strewn across the floor and empty water bottles littering the space. The MR. COFFEE beeped in the background, its ninety-minute idle shut off warning.

Ben had drifted off on the loveseat — a two-person piece of furniture not fit for a child to sleep on much less a man his size. With a wadded up jacket for a pillow, it was very fitful rest, as were all of his short catnaps. But he was quickly alert when the phone started ringing, still holding the pen he was scribbling thoughts with before he finally nodded off. It wasn't the phone with disconnected Wi-Fi, a disabled MAC address and no data.

It was the one the world knew about.

He rolled off the loveseat and sprang upright, pulling his polo down over heavily wrinkled beige slacks. Caller ID was blocked. The hour was late and the call unplanned. He pressed START on the wireless tracer and RECORD on the phone.

"Siebert."

"Your reputation precedes you," the scrambled voice answered, as enraging as it was mysterious.

He wondered if it was Arminius; though confirming it wouldn't help him find the man.

"Where the hell have you been? It's been ten days."

"We operate on our timeline, not yours."

"Where's my son?" he replied.

"Convincing the world you've killed a man. That's a special kind of skill."

Is he fishing, or...?

"You've impressed us, my friend."

"Don't call me friend."

"Don't underestimate me."

"You told me if I eliminated Knoble, I'd get my son back."

"Indeed I did. Under the terms of our original understanding, that was the exchange."

"Original understanding?"

"I also told you we'd send your son back to you in pieces if William Knoble was not dead. Do you honestly want both parties to hold each other accountable to the terms of that agreement? Or would you, by chance, like to forge a new one?"

He didn't answer immediately, and Arminius — if that's who in fact it was — jumped on his hesitation.

"Our offer for a new understanding has an expiration clause, Mr. Siebert. Do you want to make a new deal? Right now. Yes or no?"

"If you hurt my boy, I'm going to -"

Arminius jumped in before he could finish. "It seems you prefer that both parties be held to the terms of the original agreement. That being the case, you can expect a package of particular importance to be delivered to you soon."

Ben paused. Responding to that offered little upside and a ton of risk.

"Mr. Siebert, do you want a new agreement?"

They clearly knew Knoble was alive. The whole world, including the woman who knew him best, thought he killed Knoble. But there was no mistake in Arminius's voice. This was no bluff. *How does he know?* Susan was the only person he'd told, and while part of him wished otherwise considering the alternative, she wouldn't betray his trust. *But that would mean...*

"Yes, I want a new agreement."

"That's good news, Mr. Siebert. Though I must warn you, the new agreement will be ironclad. It will be adhered to one way or the other. We'll forgive your breach of the original agreement on the basis of its surprise circumstances and the fact it was merely an understanding between two parties. But this new deal will be a contract. Contracts are enforced. So should you choose to violate it, or fail to uphold your end, there will be no more deals. There are no relief clauses, and there are no outs. The penalty will be enforced and you will lose your son in a most painful fashion. Am I being perfectly clear?"

"Yes." His heart was breaking, his voice stoic.

"Excellent. I'm recording this conversation, as I'm sure you are. It is not our desire to harm your son. But we, like you, are utilitarian. We understand 'casualties of war' isn't just some political term."

"You're causing this war all by yourself."

"We're recording this because if you force us to enact the contract's penalty clause, it will be much easier for us to do so after listening to you say you understand and accept its terms. And by the way, I think you'll find your trace attempt wildly unsuccessful."

"What do you want?"

"Are you familiar with the cardinal, Mr. Siebert?"

"The bird?"

"The cardinal isn't just a bird, Mr. Siebert. It's a symbol. One you have a great deal in common with."

"Okay…"

"In many ancient civilizations and modern Native American cultures, the cardinal's virtue is broken down into three primary characteristics. Loyalty, demonstrated by its monogamy and lack of migration. Importance, it sticks out because it's different and its bright red colors don't go unnoticed. And clarity, through its clear communication and beautiful voice, it speaks its mind. And when it does, people listen.

"Loyalty, importance and clarity. These are traits you embody in a way we've never seen, Mr. Siebert…from your time in the Marines to your willingness to help Robert Stevens and Susan Reynolds ten days ago. You're going to need all three."

"Stop comparing me to a damn bird and tell me what you want."

"Patience, Mr. Siebert. And please, no more profanity."

Ben looked at the ceiling in frustration at the power trip. Arminius continued on, possessing all the leverage.

"There are two separate yet equally important conditions. First, you must assassinate the President of the United States before Memorial Day is over."

Ben stared at the word "Arminius" on the whiteboard, with arrows radiating from its blue letters to subtopics such as "Clay Braun" and "military" and "Knoble" with question marks by all. Bullet points capturing the struggle to make a connection surrounded each link.

Yet now, it all seemed so impertinent; futile and misdirected.

The laughter that came through the scrambler sounded like a kid's toy with a failing battery. Its volume rose and then lowered, reverberating between high and low-pitched waves of inflection before coming to a gradual end.

"You're patience has returned," the voice turned serious. "The act cannot be tied back to you or us in any way. If it is, even posthumously, the contract will be deemed null and void and the penalty clause enacted."

"Where's this coming from? A week ago all that mattered was killing a lawyer few people knew. Now you want to kill the President? Why?"

"That is not your concern. As long as you complete the objective by the deadline and there is no connection back to you, you will have met the first condition. The second and final condition is that you give yourself up to us."

"That I what?"

"After you complete your mission, we will offer a trade. Your life for your son's."

"How do I know you'll honor your part?"

"Once the first condition has been met, you will be contacted regarding the second. It's almost midnight, Mr. Siebert. That means you have exactly two weeks to fulfill your end of the contract or we will be forced to fulfill ours. Contracts are binding."

Mysterious as the request was, it confirmed to Ben what he'd suspected: this was never about Bill. Bill was just a medium for Arminius to get to him so he could make his true request. And he couldn't dwell on the "why" right now. The only thing in his control was his reaction. He had to keep emotions at the door and control it.

"If you know me half as well as you pretend to, you know I won't do this."

"We disagree. We feel that by leaning on your loyalty, importance and clarity, you'll evoke the necessary resolve to do what must be done. And your background and military training will drive the task's success."

"An operation of this magnitude requires more than two weeks to plan."

"One warning. You can't fake your way through this, Mr. Siebert. If it didn't work with Mr. Knoble, it certainly won't work with your new target."

Ben stared at the whiteboard, unwilling to expose the chaos he felt.

"Mr. Siebert, there are always choices. If you choose to deny this request, you're choosing to accept the consequences. It certainly won't be easy. But for you to say anything is impossible is either a kneejerk reaction or outright lie. You're not one to give kneejerk reactions, so that narrows it down. Don't ever lie to me again. Do you have any further questions about the contract?"

"How do I know my son is safe?"

"You don't."

48

Pressing the phone into his temple with enough force that sweat formed in his elbow crease, Ben replayed the conversation in his mind. He needed to carefully consider what had already been said before saying something else. Remote as it felt, he had only one chance. And taking it would require both discipline and faith, as doubt was making an aggressive move towards his heart.

"I'm not doing anything until I have confirmation Joe's okay."

"Your choice, Mr. Siebert. Contracts are full of options, and noncompliance is one of them."

"Don't call it a contract. A contract has built-in protections for both sides and requires mutual acceptance based on its terms. This is blackmail and coercion, and I have no assurance that if I do my part, you'll do yours."

"If we really wanted to harm your son, he'd be dead already."

"That's not good enough. You've already changed the terms once, and you've more than upped the ante. I have no reason to believe you won't do it again."

"You're the one who changed the terms, Mr. Siebert. And as for the ante, you can always fold if you don't want to see our raise."

"I'm not carrying out any mission — especially one that involves the assassination of America's military leader — until I have proof my son is alive. I won't be strung along to do your dirty work only to find out you've already killed him." Saying the words out loud left a lump in his throat.

Arminius kept his response businesslike. "You're not in any position to make demands."

Ben shook his head, as if doing so would shake a new revelation loose. He needed to learn something from this conversation, and Arminius didn't take the military bait. An outburst, a laugh, even a pause would've revealed Arminius was put off by the reference and could've served as a hint. Instead, another one of his attempts to find the man's weakness resulted in another dead end.

"Furthermore, given your shortcomings relative to the original understanding, the fact we're even willing to reopen a discussion is quite generous of us."

"I'm not doing it, asshole," Ben replied in a deadpan voice.

"Then don't. And see what happens, Mr. Siebert."

"I need a picture or a video showing Joe is alive. And I need proof that it's current."

"There you go again, confusing needs with wants."

"If I don't get it, kiss your mission goodbye."

"That would be disappointing, but we will find another way."

"What, you don't want to send a photo? Worried I'll trace it back to you somehow?" Ben now tried to appear desperate, not that it was very difficult.

"We will not play your game, Mr. Siebert."

"This isn't a game. It's a contractual requirement. If you won't send a photo, just ask Joe the name of his and my rendezvous point if we ever get separated after a terrorist attack and the cell phone networks are down. Only he would know the answer to that."

"We have nothing else to discuss."

"I don't care what the proof is. But I need to know he's alive."

"Good evening, Mr. Siebert."

"Why me?" he snapped back, trying to keep the conversation alive. The fact Arminius hadn't already hung up was encouraging, but it wasn't enough. He needed Arminius to have at least some skin in the game for the long shot plan to work.

"Consider it flattery, Mr. Siebert."

"Says the guy who'll kill me in two weeks."

"Who said we would kill you?"

"Trade my life for my son's. Isn't that what you said?"

"Even if that was our intent, aren't there some sacrifices worth making?"

"Why are you doing this? Do you really think eliminating one person, even the president, is going to change whatever's up your ass? I don't know your beef with him, but your plan is an act of desperation."

"That is irrelevant to our contract."

"Is it?"

"Comprehension is not a prerequisite of cooperation. Furthermore — and this should go without saying, but we'll say it anyway — should you agree to it, the terms of this contract are not to be shared with Susan Reynolds of the CIA, Robert Stevens of the FBI, or any other government official in any other capacity whatsoever."

"You really are crazy if you think I'd agree to this."

"Why would we not permit you to share this, Mr. Siebert?" Ben considered a few different responses, but concluded that keeping the conversation alive was paramount.

"Because if they found out, they'd be obligated to share that information with their national offices."

"And if that happens, the Secret Service would go on High Alert. Then, even you wouldn't be able to fulfill the mission."

"Don't call it a mission."

"In more ways than you understand, that's precisely what it is. But that's equally beside the point. Call it whatever you like, Mr. Siebert. But for your son's benefit, keep this conversation and the contract on a strictly need-to-know basis."

"No deal without proof my son's alive."

"We don't think so, Mr. Siebert. You've demonstrated an exceptional and rare ability to fulfill difficult tasks. Recently, you even created the illusion of death. We feel we have the perfect man for the job, and we're confident you'll be motivated to do it."

Ben thought again about Arminius seeing through the Knoble plot and revisited the possibility that Susan spilled the beans to the CIA. Had she done so, the leak could've come from anywhere. But that didn't feel any more plausible the second time around. His once crazy theory now suddenly felt very real.

Please be something else...

"Your attempts at deception and misdirection have been noble...remaining hidden some of the time and purposely exposed others, creating a mirage of distance from certain individuals, maintaining calm demeanor here but acting like a flippant amateur there...it was all a splendid act. But it didn't work. You know that, even as we speak. And if you had the slightest clue who we were, you wouldn't have even tried."

"Enlighten me."

"Mr. Siebert, you know what you need to do to save your son. And you know you can do it. You epitomize loyalty, importance and clarity, and you'll need to work in secrecy. In that way, Mr. Siebert, you are the silent cardinal."

"Two weeks isn't enough time."

"We wish you well, silent cardinal, for your son's sake."

"OK," Ben shot back, knowing his time was winding down. "Let's cut the bullshit. You're right. I'm the guy to pull this off for you. I've got the training and the capability and the motivation. You're lying through your teeth when you say you can just find another option, and we both know it."

"This is unproductive."

"Without me, your mission won't be complete in two weeks. And something tells me there's a reason you have the deadline you do. I don't care what that reason is, but I'm the only one who can meet it. Proof that Joe's alive isn't asking much, considering what you're getting in return. It's nonnegotiable. Otherwise I have no choice but to assume Joe's already dead."

"We'll know in two weeks just how nonnegotiable it really is, won't we?"

Part III

49

Susan read the old-fashioned facsimile for a third time. Try as she might, she couldn't find any holes in his theory or come up with a better one. Desperate for an alternative explanation, she picked up the phone.

"I've been expecting your call."

"Robert," she said nervously, forcing herself to slow down. "This is a hell of a way to start my morning. Are you sure?"

"I wouldn't say that, but don't you agree the evidence is pretty convincing?" he replied calmly. "The kid working the register said the guy asked for the bathroom key a little after three-thirty in the morning. Said he was definitely drunk, probably high. He would know, too. When you work the graveyard shift at the only 24/7 gas station around, you see a lot of interesting stuff."

"What about surveillance?"

"Clean shot from the security camera over the register. He parked his Lincoln MZK and went straight for the bathroom. Didn't buy anything or spend any time at the counter. He also stumbled walking out, corroborating the clerk's guess he was inebriated."

"Then what?"

"After forty-five minutes, the clerk went to check on him. Poor kid expected to find him passed out on the floor. Instead, he saw that..."

Susan took a deep breath and flipped through the pictures again, nibbling her lip. The victim had been identified via DNA match as Clayton Braun, a forty-nine-year-old train wreck of a human with a professional background in commercial security systems. He hadn't held a job for more than three years and was fired from two of them for cause, but he clearly had some expertise. One doesn't become an installation manager at ADT without knowing a thing or two.

Braun's personal history was an ugly story. An unstable childhood led him to being a loner in adulthood. Three divorces, two of which involved allegations of abuse. No children. No jail time, despite being charged twice with assault and battery. Toxicology reports confirmed the clerk was right — Braun had a .36 BAC and benzoylecgonine levels over 500 nanograms per milliliter. The guy was drunk as a skunk and high as a kite on cocaine at the same time.

Before he died from a two-inch-thick knife wound that spanned the length of his gut, Mr. Braun sustained two broken knees and three severe lower back hemorrhages. A total of seven fingers had been severed between his two hands, and all the digits were lying on the filthy bathroom floor next to a bloody butcher's knife and metal mallet. Both weapons were void of fingerprints, and a pair of latex gloves was in the trashcan next to the door. Braun's wrists had been handcuffed to the toilet grab bar, and the tendons in both arms had been snapped as a result of blunt force trauma. The autopsy confirmed Braun died from bleeding out at about four in the morning. That meant that, even with the drugs and alcohol, the last half-hour of Clayton Braun's life qualified as the most painful she'd ever encountered in over three decades at the CIA.

Robert continued, "According to the DMV, Braun owned four vehicles. I had the Tollway Authority pull all the records for the past month to see if we'd get lucky."

She flipped to the next page. IPASS transponder payment receipts and a picture of Braun's red Chevy Tahoe going through the westbound tollbooth a few miles from Abigail Merriweather's house in South Barrington. The time stamp was just after one p.m. on Mother's Day, and the license plate matched the DMV records. There was no eastbound toll paid.

She leaned back in her desk chair, holding the phone to her ear, considering Robert's theory again.

"Toll records don't prove Braun was watching the house."

"No, but they sure as hell suggest it. There are no street cameras near the house, but considering Ben told you to get the Merriweather family out because someone was watching them, I think we need to start making some educated assumptions."

"What about outside surveillance?"

"Not much help," Robert continued, "but check out the last few pages. A car with no license plate parks next to the bathroom a few minutes after Braun enters, and the person who goes in is wearing a mask. The picture is very grainy though. Gas stations don't care so much about monitoring bathrooms, so they don't have a camera near the door. Even when you zoom in, there's not a clear shot."

"The person's height?"

"About six feet, four inches. Based on what little we have, it matches Ben's description."

"Okay, let's assume for the moment that Ben killed Clayton Braun. What's that mean?"

"Aside from what it makes Ben?"

She shrugged, as if Robert could see her do it.

"First, it reinforces what a poor decision I made to bring him into this. When you told me Knoble wasn't dead after your little powwow with Ben at the gym, I won't lie and say I wasn't relieved. But *someone* died that night, Susan. It's too bad we don't know who because the body is already cremated, but someone got shot and Ben is the person we think pulled the trigger. But now there's a definite corpse to add to the count."

"Yeah...the world lost a real saint," she hissed, knowing it was a mistake the moment she said it.

"We both know we don't get to pick and choose who deserves punishment and who doesn't. All that matters is Ben has killed at least two people…that we know about."

Robert was absolutely right. She silently chided herself for her tendency to support Ben. Why did she always look for ways to defend him or rationalize his behavior?

"Let's be clear," Robert continued, "I won't lose any sleep over Clay Braun. Maybe we can even use this to find out who these people are. Assuming there's a link between him and the terrorists who kidnapped Ben's son, we need to learn everything there is to know about him. I've got an iron in every fire you can imagine looking into his known associates. Maybe it'll get us a lead."

"I'll run it through the CIA database."

"Not worth your time. Braun was local. He hardly left the state, much less the country. No international travel in his travel records. If there's a connection, it's in the US."

"I'll still—"

"I also need a favor." Robert cut her off. It surprised her that he didn't want the CIA search, but he was probably right.

"I'm listening."

"Here's the thing. I was the one who asked Tom Fedorak to bring Nikki into all this. I thought her history with Ben could help, but it's spiraled out of control. I don't think Ben would hurt her…but after she told me about their little rendezvous at O'Hare, I'm worried I've put her in harm's way."

"You're her boss. Reassign her. If she was even assigned in the first place."

"I did. I told her this morning to back off, but I worry she's too personally invested. I could see her sticking around, even against my orders. I know that's not her MO, but she still loves the guy."

"What am I supposed to do about it, Robert?"

"She knows you, respects you, likes you even. Maybe you could give her a ring and—"

"Manage your own employee. I don't have time for this."

"What's up your ass?"

"Two dead bodies, terrorists we haven't found, a missing boy, an unidentified murder victim. Take your pick."

"Fair enough." Robert dismissed the idea as quickly as he brought it up. He was all over the map lately. *Did he even notice how mercurial he'd been acting*, she wondered.

Robert continued, "The truth is, even if Ben did do this, I'm still more worried about the folks who almost blew up Ogilvie than I am him. And I don't think a full-scale manhunt helps us find them. It could actually hurt, if it prevents Ben from contacting you again. But I've made some poor calls lately, so I've been second-guessing myself. I'd like your opinion."

Robert sure was wishy-washy on how to handle an investigation in his jurisdiction, but he had reason to be. A full-scale manhunt might find Ben, but would they ever learn more about the terrorists if it did? Was the world better off with Ben off the streets? After Ben proved to her that Bill Knoble was alive — absolutely stunning her — she didn't know what to think. Every assumption they made about him turned out to be wrong. Could this be wrong too?

"I agree with you, Robert. But the body count can't keep growing. One more alleged victim, and you've got to open the floodgates."

"We need to learn everything we can about Braun. We've got to find Ben and find him soon. The terrorists are out there, Susan. It's clear they want something. I'm worried that whatever it is, Ben just might give it to them."

50

Nikki sat in the waiting room like a junior high student summoned to the principal's office.

She was grateful for Susan Reynolds's unexpected check-in call, but the fact that it ended with her asking Susan for a meeting made her feel like a gazelle seeking the lion's help. She just didn't know what else to do. Joe deserved her best efforts no matter how idiotic, and doing the right thing had to count for something. Seeking Susan's guidance felt like the only option she had left. Still, she knew her involvement was unsanctioned. She was the kid who started the food fight, asked to talk to the principal and now had to answer for it.

But the worst part was that if she'd acted sooner, Bill Knoble might still be alive.

After she signed in, provided her credentials and obtained a visitor's badge, Nikki learned that the friendly receptionist was a temp named Marge who felt it was her duty to pass the time with aimless chatter and questions. The fifty-year-old chatty Cathy rambled on like Zeppelin as Nikki's anticipation of her meeting grew.

"Mrs. Reynolds will see you now," Marge finally announced.

The words jolted her out of confused musing just before four-thirty. She marched through the double-doors and was greeted by a massive office with floor-to-ceiling windows overlooking sunny downtown Chicago. Four bookshelves packed with hardcovers lined the remaining windowless wall, reminding her what business Susan Reynolds was in. The intelligence officer rose from a six-person table littered with file folders, notepads and pieces of paper.

"It's good to see you." Susan embraced her.

Susan hadn't changed much in two years. The dark circles beneath her eyes validated the wearing stress of her job. She wore a trim, dark pants suit and black flats. Her hair was still long and brown, and fell with a small wave just below her shoulders. She was thin, almost emaciated, with bony hands and sunken cheeks. In contrast to the conference table, Reynold's red maple desk was impeccably clean, not a single sheet of paper out of place. The calculator, telephone and printer were exactingly placed within its rectangular design, forming perfect right angles.

"Thanks for your call earlier," Nikki nearly whispered. "And thanks for seeing me on such short notice."

She mentally compared this Susan Reynolds to the Susan Reynolds she met as the undercover CIA Officer two years ago. That version, posing as Karen Hovey, secretary at Peter Hubley's investment firm, was a different human being altogether. Friendly to the point of flaky, generous, and innocent. Very unassuming. Even now, Nikki was astounded at how real that Susan Reynolds felt, how genuinely she came across. It reminded her that Susan Reynolds could be whoever she needed to be.

"How are you, Nikki?"

"I'm okay," she answered sinking into a plush leather chair, accepting a bottle of water.

"It didn't sound like it on the phone," Susan said, skipping the pleasantries.

"Well...it's been a short two years but a long twenty-four months."

"I know the feeling."

"There's some serious security here." Even with an appointment, she had to sign five forms and walk through two metal detectors. The guard patted her down at the entrance.

"We have to keep this place pretty secure. Some very convincing characters have tried to get in before. So what brings you here?" Susan asked.

"Well, I need your help."

"I'm all ears."

She put it out there and told Susan everything, from her conversation with Tom at Café Salsa to meeting Ben. It was surprisingly therapeutic to say it all out loud, uninterrupted.

Susan remained stoic, occasionally sipping her water or nodding her head, but not much else. No raised eyebrows, no gasps, no shaking of the head, no disbelief in her eyes. She'd most certainly heard far worse tales throughout her career. This was a nightmare to Nikki; it was child's play to this woman. When the recap was over, she learned Susan was the type who saved her questions for the end.

"So there's an unclaimed suitcase full of nice clothes at DFW?" Susan tried to ease the tension. Nikki forced out a smile before Susan turned serious. "You don't agree with Ben? That you should stay out of this?"

"Stay out of it? No, I don't agree. There's a dead man who would probably like some justice."

"I don't mean the FBI. I mean you. In fact, aren't you violating your jurisdiction by remaining a part of it?"

"Technically, I guess. It's just…"

"It's just what?" Susan asked, slightly raising both arms in a shrug.

"I know Ben. Personally. I know how he operates. I know how he thinks."

"I'm not sure anyone knows that."

Susan's raised eyebrows and continued arm flails came across as impatient to her, tense if not outright shaken. It seemed the very mention of Ben had kick-started an unplanned reaction. Susan quickly masked it with a fake smile, but Nikki saw what she saw.

"He murdered someone," she replied with a touch of sass, adding her own shrug. "If we want justice, I have insight no one else does."

"I seriously doubt that."

"Why?"

"Maybe that's what Ben wants you to think."

"What's that supposed to mean?" Nikki suddenly felt the urge to defend herself.

"Forget it."

Susan rapidly tapped her fingers on the desk a few times before leaning forward in the chair to rest her elbows on it. Now it was clear the CIA officer was losing her patience. Nikki still didn't know why.

"That's beside the point. The fact is, it's not your job. Why are you on the fence at all?"

"Ben acts like he's trying to protect me."

"And why would that put you on the fence?"

"What if it's his way of trying to protect himself?"

Susan put her index finger over her mouth and nodded skeptically. "Let me make sure I understand this. You think that Ben Siebert — a man who has proven he can elude authorities and find people not even the CIA can — is worried that your involvement will bring him down?"

Susan paused for a moment before concluding. "And your basis for that theory is that in a meeting he initiated and you didn't tell anyone about, he came across as trying to protect you?"

She absorbed the question as Susan exaggeratedly raised her eyebrows and bit her lower lip, a conspicuous smirk across her face.

"I think you need to reconsider your theory. Maybe Ben really is trying to protect you."

"How can you assume that?"

"I'm not assuming anything. I'm empathizing. He lost one woman he loved and his son is being held captive. You two were engaged; he loved you, probably still does. He already accidentally put you in danger two years ago. It doesn't seem far-fetched to me that he'd go out of his way to protect you today."

"A bit of a conflict of interest, don't you think?" Nikki answered, renewed vigor pumping through her veins. "He doesn't want to get caught, and he knows I might help catch him."

"I don't think he's worried about you catching him."

"Agree to disagree."

Susan raised an eyebrow ever so slightly. "You've got some conflict yourself, don't you?"

"What's that supposed to mean?"

"Listen, Nikki…I don't question your resolve or your intentions. But you obviously still have feelings for him. You're torn because you can't believe he'd kill Knoble, yet you know he did. And you feel guilty, as if you could've prevented it. Because you still love him."

"I do not love him."

"Are you sure you're thinking objectively?"

"I'm here, aren't I?"

"Please, don't get defensive. If all you really want is justice to be done, relaying what you know about Ben and any theories you have to the appropriate FBI Agent is the best way to get it. You can always be available to help upon request. That also happens to be the best of both worlds. You can do your part for justice and not ambush Ben."

"I'll ambush him if I have to."

"If this was anyone else, would you even hesitate on what to do next?"

Now she felt ambushed. Her mouth hung open, yet no words came. Susan wasn't empathizing or even considering her perspective…this felt more like an interrogation than a counsel.

"I'm surprised you'd side with the fugitive on this."

"I'm not siding with anyone. I'm being objective. You're emotionally involved and want confirmation you should do something the data clearly say you shouldn't. I can't offer you that."

"What if he kills again?"

"All the more reason to get debriefed ASAP. Pass on what you know to the people whose job it is to prevent that."

"Why is the CIA involved?" Nikki asked.

"You know better than to ask me that."

"Why? You know Ben too. We could compare notes; try to anticipate his next move." As she spoke, Nikki raised both hands in a sort of half shrug, pleading for Susan to get on board.

It didn't work.

"Let's be clear: I don't know him," Susan replied sternly. "I was forced to work with him on an unrelated case two years ago. It's not appropriate for me to comment on an investigation the CIA may or may not be involved with."

"Even to the FBI?"

"Except that I'm not really talking to the FBI right now, am I?"

Unable to restrain herself, Nikki sprang from the chair and walked to the window, shaking her head. Disbelief filling everything between her ears, she glared at Susan.

"That's it? 'No comment' is all you have to say?"

"What did you expect me? Are you listening to yourself? Do you really think I'd encourage you to stray from Robert's direction?"

Nikki's mouth hung open, shocked that Susan knew about her Sunday visit with Robert. She made it clear to him that their conversation was private. *Why did he tell her?*

"He gave you clear and sound direction. Listen to your chain of command."

She turned around to start walking towards the door as Susan added, "I'm not speaking to you as the CIA, Nikki. I'm speaking to you as a friend. Listen to me."

Nikki turned around and faced Susan, who took a deep breath and raised her arms to motion her to do the same, gently raising and lowering her fingertips.

"You're not thinking clearly, Nikki. Your hesitation is way too obvious if you're revealing it to me. You're questioning your own assumptions and looking to others to squelch your self-doubt. You've heard the same counsel from Robert and me, and you know deep down we're right. You know it's wrong to stay involved, but you're doing it anyway because you have a personal interest. That's the textbook definition of a conflict of interest. Two years ago you questioned why Ben never followed the rules. But now...it's you who's disregarding them."

"How can I just walk away?" she whispered.

"You came here seeking advice, and I can understand why. But the protocol is clear. And this is why protocols exist. Don't question it. Just do your job and follow it."

She just stared, Susan's words replaying in her head. The silence endured, ten, twenty, thirty seconds as they stared at each other. Susan's jitters were gone, replaced with stern posture and confident facial expression. Nikki, on the other hand, felt more uncertain than she did before she arrived.

"You need to extract yourself from this case, Nikki. Immediately. Let the system work. Sever your personal connection to it; be the team player you expect others to be. Take your slap on the wrist for not doing it sooner. I'm certain Robert will make sure it's nothing more than that. But get out. Now."

51

It didn't take long for Arminius's suspicion to be confirmed.

The cell phone he'd instructed her to call rang at just after eight on Monday evening, two hours after Chicago's not-secret-but-not-so-advertised CIA office closed for the day. The sun was near the end of its decent, and Arminius had just finished his medium rare filet. He rubbed his mustache and took a swig of Anti-Hero IPA to wash the last mouthful down before picking up.

"Yes?"

"Good evening, sir."

"Where are you?"

"My apartment, as you requested."

"No one is with you?"

"No, sir."

"You're certain you weren't followed? Your cover wasn't blown?"

"Not in the least."

"Excellent. What do you have for me?"

"I'm calling with an update. Your were right."

"Oh?"

"FBI Special Agent Benton paid a visit to Susan Reynolds late this afternoon."

The news actually did surprise him. Of course he'd speculated Benton wouldn't drop the case right away as Siebert had asked, but the extent of Benton's disobedience towards the former Marine, her ex-fiancé, was unexpected. She'd again completely disregarded his request, but thankfully she continued doing so in a clumsy and obvious manner.

"Are you certain?" he asked.

"Most definitely. I talked with her at Reception and got a good look for a long time. Full name is Nicole Angela Benton. Brown hair, average height, 130 pounds. She provided her FBI credentials as well as her driver's license when she signed in. She looked very nervous. And I could tell she didn't want to talk; that she was trying to concentrate on something."

"She signed in with her real name?"

"Yes."

"Was she with anyone?"

"No, she came alone."

Siebert was right; Benton had no business staying involved in this case.

"And she met with Reynolds directly?"

"Just the two of them. She made an appointment earlier in the day, but it must've come direct to Mrs. Reynolds because Benton wasn't on the pre-agenda. The slot was reserved though, for four o'clock."

"How long was the meeting?"

"They finished at five-thirty, so just under an hour. I was able to stall Reynolds for about forty minutes to do some digging while Benton waited. I would've called you sooner, but Reynolds asked me to stay after hours to file a few things."

"You did the right thing. Your behavior had to appear completely typical to Reynolds. Do you know what they discussed?"

"Unfortunately, no. All of Mrs. Reynolds's appointments are closed door. I tried to listen in, but it was too muffled. I'd also guess she's especially sensitive when there's a temp working the desk."

"And you're sure Reynolds didn't pick up on anything?"

"Yes, sir. I had all the proper credentials as usual, and I got cleared through the temporary staffing agency last night. I got my notification call within a few hours, and my background check came out clean as a whistle right away. The whole process was lighting-fast. You must have some serious connections."

"What makes you say that?"

"I've never seen a government assignment happen so quickly. Usually it takes weeks, maybe even months, for a temp agency to fill an assignment with a new placement once it's posted. There's a ton of background and scrutiny baked into the process. And for last minute needs like an illness or death in the family, there's usually a wait list of pre-qualified candidates ready to go. For me to get the call as soon as I did, especially for a CIA office, your connection must be pretty high up."

Agricola wasn't a connection; he was *the* connection. At first Arminius had hesitated asking for the favor to get "Marge" into Reception at the Chicago CIA office, worried that it might alarm his already-overcautious partner. But he decided in the end it was worth it. And Marge was right...as high up as Reynolds was, only a handful of people in the country could've made everything happen so fast. An hour after he spoke with Agricola, the regular secretary was reassigned to a satellite office for a temporary and highly confidential assignment. Marge was contacted the next day with instructions to report to the office the following morning, pending a successful background check.

"You said you talked to Benton?"

"I tried, but she wasn't very social. I used a few different approaches while she waited, but Benton didn't budge."

"You didn't overdo it, did you?"

"No, sir. Like you always taught me. Close enough to see, not to smell."

"Excellent."

Arminius knew he could trust her. In contrast to Rausch's hired hand Clay Braun, he knew her personally. Having a history had its downsides, and she knew more about him than he would've preferred, but his exposure was minimal and she was very reliable. If only she were a surveillance expert, too.

"Stellar work. The $20,000 will be delivered as per normal. Keep an eye on Reynolds. Let me know if anyone else of interest pays her a visit. Your fee will be doubled for any additional information."

"Always a pleasure doing business with you, sir."

Arminius hung up the phone and contemplated his next move. Agricola wanted Benton off the case, and everything suggested she should've been. Her background, decision-making patterns and profile all said so, but she had more grit than he anticipated. First Siebert couldn't talk her off the ledge; now the SAIC and her CIA acquaintance. Much as Agricola wouldn't like hearing it, she'd need to be dealt with another way.

However, first he had to call Rausch. If Clay Braun had been given any information, he had to assume Siebert got it out of him. He needed Rausch to confirm his poor judgment was limited to the poor hire. He knew Rausch would come clean if it wasn't. Military loyalty is in a league by itself. But he had to move quickly, and do so without alarming Agricola.

Then he'd deal with Benton.

52

David Keene stared at the computer holding a double chocolate donut, noting how sad it was that he ordered late-night office takeout often enough the delivery guy picked him up a Dunkin' on the way. He wore his standard after-hours attire: blue jeans, gym shoes and a half-zip. Questioning why he wasn't at Kraft trying to figure out new and creative ways to get kids hooked on ketchup and noodles, he rubbed tired eyes that couldn't see as well as they once did.

He hadn't slept much in five days, since receiving the package and mysterious letter from Siebert. Since then, zero word from his admirer. And the silence only added to the ambiguity he felt since passing on the job.

"Chicago Sun Times," he rudely answered the phone, annoyed at life.

"Good evening, David."

The voice was unmistakable and unforgettable. It would stay in his memory bank until the day he died.

"Is this...you?"

"I heard you passed on the Kraft gig. Forty grand has just been deposited into your TCF Checking Account. My way of saying thanks for the good faith gesture."

"I...um..."

"A Senior Reporter rendered speechless? This has to be a first."

"What can I do for you?"

"I've been following your work. Articles are still factual, sources still protected. Good man. Not happy with the job though, eh?"

243

"I don't know," he answered, his mind solely focused on what Siebert wanted. It sure wasn't to catch up, but it felt safer to stay there than wherever this conversation was headed.

"More success will come. You shouldn't quit the industry, but don't rush success either. If you do, you won't have anything to look forward to."

How the hell does this guy always know what I'm thinking?

"You're engaged, right? To that Julie girl?"

"That's the one."

"Congratulations, David. Treat your wife like a gift from God."

"I…will. So what can I do for you?"

"To be honest, your writing hasn't blown me away lately. But I think that's because you don't like the subjects much these days."

He didn't know how to answer that, partly because he agreed with Siebert and mostly because the guy scared the ever-loving shit out of him.

"Your research, on the other hand, has gotten even better. Very factual. I can tell…a lot of digging went into those articles. Do it all yourself?"

"I have a staff that helps."

"Three people under you. Moving up quick."

Not quick enough.

"I've got an assignment for you, assuming you're interested. But no farming it out to the underlings. This one's got to be just for you, and you'll have to keep it on the down-low."

"I'm listening…" he replied, probably with a little too much excitement. Whatever it was Siebert wanted, his guess was it was dangerous, maybe even illegal. It would've been better not to show his hand of excitement before knowing, but the prospect of another career game-changer was too exciting.

"This won't be like last time. I'm not spoon-feeding you a great story and waiting for you at the Pulitzers. You're going to have to bust your ass, and there's no guarantee of a return. In fact, you could get into trouble."

"What kind of trouble?"

"You'll also have to disappear and do more work in a week than most folks do in a month. Hardcore research, completely offline, independent of the *Times*. You'll be searching for a tiny needle in a huge, messy mountain of a haystack. You could very easily end up mining for ore that's just not there. Either way, you won't get any credit for the work you do and anything that makes the papers has to remain anonymous."

"You're really selling this."

"That's not even the catch."

"Okay..."

"If certain people were to find out what you're doing, you'd be in a great deal of danger. So you need to keep your mouth shut and buy yourself some time. Away from home and work. Tell Julie whatever you have to tell her, but don't endanger her by telling her about this conversation or me."

"Endanger her? What's this all about?"

"Wish I could tell you more, but that can't happen until I know you're in."

"Do I really have a choice?" he asked as nonchalantly as he could.

"Of course you do."

"Well..."

"Take your forty grand and head to Kraft now if you like. I'm not forcing you, David."

Not overly comforting, coming from you.

"Right now, yes or no? You've got all the background I can give. Need an answer."

There were a hundred things he should've asked and a hundred more he should've considered. But excitement trumped prudence. Partly because it was Siebert; mostly because he was hungry. And this felt like a giant plate of hot meat.

"I'm game."

"Get out of the building now. Set an Out of Office response to your e-mail and leave your computer. Dump your backpack in the trashcan at the corner and hail a cab to Morton's Steakhouse on Wacker Place. Wait outside the entrance in front of the revolving door. Get moving. Someone will be there to pick you up in exactly thirteen minutes."

53

"Why are you telling me this?" Nikki asked, her eyes not meeting Tom's.

It'd only been five days since she'd reconnected with Ben, and already she was an emotional mess. Her brain — unwilling to let her heart off the hook — kept the questions coming. *Are you really surprised? What do you expect? Why did you meet with him?*

"Because," Tom answered, "Ben wanted you to know. And it's time for you to start listening to people like Susan Reynolds."

"What?" she raised her eyebrow.

"Susan told me about your visit to her office. Why *don't* you want to back the hell off?"

They sat at a plastic two-person table in Yorktown shopping mall's food court during peak lunch hour, surrounded by what she'd always wanted. To her right, a mother and two children, maybe four and six, eating Mac & Cheese. Haphazardly coloring the way only children could, they laughed aloud while singing "Ring Around the Rosie" and made a mess of everything they touched. To her left, an elderly couple sat in a built-in wall booth, munching on salads. Newspapers pushed aside, the pair regarded the small children with warm and knowing smiles. Probably, she guessed, reminiscing about their earlier years.

"You're saying Bill Knoble is alive?" she asked skeptically.

"That's what I'm saying."

"Then let me talk to him."

"Can't happen."

"Why not?" she snapped, unwilling to allow herself to be manipulated.

"I'm not at liberty to discuss that."

"Then how do I know for sure?"

"So now you think I'm lying to you?" Tom asked, his face pointedly aimed at her.

She sighed in regret. *Rock and a hard place.*

"No, I don't think that."

"Have I ever lied to you?"

She lowered her voice to a near whisper. "No, you haven't."

"Then I think I deserve the benefit of the doubt."

Tom's reaction was fair; he'd always been honest and upfront with her, even when it was to his own detriment. And the news he'd shared, assuming it was true, certainly removed some of the mystery from Ben's comments in the rental car regarding how she might one day feel differently about him. But while Tom deserved better than for her to doubt him, this was too much leash and not nearly enough sidewalk. She needed more.

"Tom, I want this to be true. But if it is, why wouldn't Ben tell me?"

"I can understand your confusion with the timing," Tom answered, shrugging his shoulders and then dropping both hands to the table. "But don't forget this is about Joe. These jerk offs told Ben they'd kill his son if he didn't kill Knoble first. Think about that. Obviously, he's got to keep a lid on the fact that he didn't actually do it."

"He told you, didn't he?"

"I'm a lifelong friend who doesn't work for the FBI."

"And you weren't engaged to him."

"Nor did I try to alert the cops the moment I saw him."

She shook her head and looked down in some combination of defiance and defeat. She wasn't sure of the split.

"Nikki, you're running around telling Susan Reynolds, Robert Stevens and anyone who'll listen that Ben killed Knoble.

Not to mention interviewing Sally Hubley about her dead husband's coworkers and God only knows who else. And you're doing it to chase a case that's outside your wheelhouse. Let it go already."

"What does that have to do with anything?" she rolled her eyes. "And did you forget? You're the one who brought me into all this."

"That was a mistake."

She felt the sadness on her face that caused Tom to pause, but said nothing.

"I won't apologize — not to you and certainly not to Grasshopper — but it wasn't the right move. It seemed like a good idea at the time, but even I screw up every decade or two."

"Someone died that night, Tom." She forced her face stern, looking him in the eye, crossing her arms.

Tom's finger-to-the-lips motion wasn't necessary; she'd scanned the area on her own without his shushing. As she did, she was thankful the few other folks in the food court at eleven o'clock on a Wednesday morning seemed happily engrossed watching the rambunctious yet delightful game of tag that had unfolded between brother and sister.

"Can't deny that. Someone did die," Tom finally replied.

"Who was it?"

"Am I talking to FBI Special Agent Benton, or my friend Nikki?"

"That depends on what you tell me."

"That dog won't hunt."

"What do you want from me, Tom?"

"Have you been listening? This isn't me. It's Grasshopper. You think it was my idea to tell you this? Momma didn't raise no rat in a tin shithouse."

"Excuse me?"

"It's a big gamble to tell you this, with no measureable upside. And it sure wasn't my risk to take. Grasshopper's ass is on the line here, in case you forgot. The fewer people in on this, the better. Yet against his mentor's advice — his very wise mentor, I might add — he wanted you to know. I think that deserves a debt of gratitude."

"Gratitude? Are you kidding me?"

"Would you rather be confused and pissed, or in the dark?"

"Who died last week, Tom? It stays in this food court, but I need to know."

Tom smacked his lips and ran the top of his tongue along the bottom of his teeth, loud enough she could hear the scratching. After a long pause, he leaned in and said in a whisper:

"Now you've got me wondering if *I* can trust *you*."

54

Tom crumbled up his third hot dog's tin foil wrapper, drained half of his Coke with one massive gulp, and pushed the plastic tray aside. Then he eyed her through the same bug glasses that once made her laugh but now made her feel like she was in an intense staring contest.

"His given name was Christopher Janosch. People called him Tubes."

"Tubes?"

"Evidently, he gave up television for Lent one year as a kid. You know, back when TVs had cathode ray tubes. The nickname his third grade buddies gave him stuck for life."

"Who was he?"

"He used to be a Kentucky coal miner, but his COPD diagnosis eight years ago forced early retirement."

"Chronic Obstructive Pulmonary Disease," she whispered, biting her lip.

"COPD is some serious shit, Nikki. It's the third leading cause of death in the U.S. About a 150,000 people a year, and there's no cure in sight. You get a diagnosis, you get a death sentence. This guy had Grade 4, the final and most agonizing stage. He had less than thirty percent lung capacity for the last six months of his life. And that was on top of his chronic bronchitis. And emphysema."

"Oh my word."

Just then they were interrupted by what she guessed was a four-year-old boy with blonde-hair in blue overalls. The youngster was taking it upon himself to rearrange the chairs by dragging them from one children's table to the next. Pushing a tiny green seat with both arms extended, he trekked past them without care or notice, the chair's metal legs pressing into the tile floor. No one seemed to mind the racket, and Nikki actually welcomed the disruption.

"I can't begin to imagine how much it hurt Janosch to take a breath," Tom finally said. "Or maybe I just don't want to."

"How did Ben know this guy?"

"He didn't. They got connected through Chris's brother, Larry."

"How?"

"Ben reached out to his contact in Brazil."

"Sidarta Perdigao?" she asked, recalling surveilling Ben on his trip to Sao Paulo a few years ago when she was handed the Hubley case. She recalled the good-looking, forty-something-year-old Brazilian businessman who'd spent ten years in Fort Worth before moving back to Curitiba. He'd played a key role helping Ben track down Terrance Smith, the man who orchestrated the Peter Hubley smear campaign to keep the public's eye off the real reason he was killed. Sidarta was shrewd and honest. To think he had a hand in this was hard to swallow, but at this point she didn't put anything past anyone.

"Also against my advice, though I'll admit now it was the right move. Much as I hate to admit it, Sidarta knows his stuff. He did a good job."

"A good job doing what?"

"Finding a match. And being Grasshopper's middleman so there was no trace back to him."

"Match?"

"Ben needed someone with two very distinct characteristics. First, the guy had to physically look a lot like Knoble. Not freckle for freckle, but at least in overall body type and prominent physical traits. Close enough that some TLC on the details would sell the world at a glance he was Knoble."

"Go on."

"Ben didn't know anyone who fit that bill, so he asked Sidarta to comb his network for a match. He's very connected, and he did better than I expected. Janosch was about the same height, just an inch taller. After he lost seventy pounds from the chemo, he was also roughly the same weight. Fifty-one-years-old, no major skin problems or an oversized head or a prosthetic or anything else that distinguished him from Knoble. Overall, a very similar physique."

"What about those details?"

"A custom-built mask created with the world's best laser technology and specifically modeled around Knoble's face — down to the dimples, pores and skin pigment — took care of those."

"A mask?" she squinted her eyes.

"Skintight, ultra lightweight, perfectly conformed to Knoble's facial skeleton. I'm here to tell you it's pretty damn impressive. And when you combine it with some fine tuning of Janosch's accent, give him the right wardrobe, and teach him to use certain hand gestures and pantomimes, you've got a Bill Knoble replica."

"You're kidding me."

"It didn't have to be perfect. Just good enough for government work. Still pictures had to look like Knoble. People's general recollections had to align with his description, stuff like that. But it was way better than government work."

"That's why Ben kidnapped Knoble, isn't it? He needed to mold his face to make the mask."

"That, and the fact that Knoble can't exactly be seen walking around the streets now."

"So he makes a reservation under Knoble's name, uses the mask and dresses Janosch like Knoble, then lets people connect the dots."

"That alone probably would've done it. The best deception is simple deception; overcomplicating things usually leads to downfall. But you know Grasshopper…he's way more thorough than that."

She sighed, nodding. "What else?"

"They say the devil lives in the details. If that's true, Grasshopper was Lucifer's neighbor on this one. Townhouse wasn't just some random restaurant selected by chance. Everything about the setting, from the place to the table to the day to the minute, was carefully chosen for one purpose."

"To make the world think Bill Knoble got killed."

"Exactamundo."

"Tell me. Tell me every last detail."

"First, the lighting. It's real dim track lighting to begin with, and it gets turned down even lower after seven. That serves the ambiance the place is going for, along with the small candle on the tables that Janosch had not so coincidentally blown out. So right away, there's limited visibility for detailed observation.

"Go on."

"Then there's the table's orientation to the southern wall, where the bullets entered from the street and the plaza it's connected to. It's more or less at a forty-five degree angle, with limited views and broken lines of sight because of the pillars in front of the building. They must've designed it that way so people wouldn't see pedestrians on Wacker Drive while they're trying to have a romantic meal."

"Meaning?"

"Meaning that aside from one specific view from one specific orientation, you'd have a so-so cursory glance of the tables at best."

"Limiting exposure..." she said slowly, following along.

"To everything except that very specific vantage point."

"I'm guessing both advantages were utilized."

"He chose the table at the far end of the southern wall for two reasons. First, so that one and only vantage point would have a clear line of sight to someone getting shot. Second, to force the conclusion on who that someone was."

"Why?"

"Ben had reason to believe someone walking towards the restaurant was being watched."

"Who?"

"Not important. What is important is that this person's reaction to the gunshots had to be genuine."

"So...you're saying he pulled the trigger just as the person was approaching from that specific vantage point?"

"The best sales pitch is sheer honesty."

"Huh?"

"Think about it. This person didn't know the shots were coming and thought they saw Knoble — someone they knew personally — get murdered right in front of them. Their raw reaction would sell anyone watching that it really was him."

"That's awfully cold. Is he or she okay?"

"They're fine."

It was obvious to Nikki that Tom was going out of his way to conceal the gender of the person. Why would he do that? Was it someone she knew? The abundance of caution suggested the possibility. Almost as if Tom thought saying *he* or *she* specifically might tip her off. Nibbling on her fingernail, she racked her brain searching for the connection. *Think horses, not zebras.*

"The secretary," she excitedly replied. "That's it, isn't it? It was Knoble's secretary. She's been missing since either Wednesday night or Thursday morning. She wasn't at Knoble's office the day after the shoot -"

"Again, not important," Tom held up his hand in interruption. "The point, Nikki, is there weren't many people oriented such that they actually saw the shooting. And as soon as it did, they all ducked for cover. Remember, there was an element of surprise to everyone except Janosch. Folks went crazy tripping over each other to get out. Screaming, crying, running for the exits. It all happened so fast that the only thing people remembered was the victim was alone at the table, and talking on his cell phone. Maybe the most observant person, real close by, might recall he had dark hair and a jacket, but nothing more."

"The cell phone..." she whispered, the ah-ha moment popping into her head.

"Yes...?" Tom replied with a slight smirk.

"When the cops ran the transcript, there was mention of Knoble's twin nieces in the conversation. Lydia and Jessica were their names. They were threatened if he didn't give up Ben."

"Kind of ironic considering Ben was the one talking, eh?"

"The voice was scrambled..."

"It's pretty easy to get your hands on a scrambler. Since Grasshopper had heard the terrorists' he could pick one that sounded close enough. He also used a lot of formal vernacular like they do to convince authorities. Obviously, it worked."

"So," she sighed, "that whole conversation was just to reference Knoble?"

"Why do you think the cops got the transcript so easily? And did you think it was a coincidence the cell phone Janosch had was prepaid, with no recent calls or addresses stored?"

"Knoble's nieces were never in danger..." she whispered, more to herself than Tom.

"I'm sure the Portland police feel like heroes, but the girls would've been just fine without their protection."

She leaned back and shook her head. It was farfetched and believable at the same time. She never thought about the transcript being so readily available. The terrorists had already proven they were technologically savvy enough to block access, so why didn't they do so right before they killed a person? It was obvious now, but she'd failed to connect the dots before.

"Don't beat yourself up, Nikki. No one else caught it either. Even Robert heard the hoofs and thought horses. When the transcript shed so much light on the situation, why look for a zebra?"

"Right," Nikki replied. "And since it's too dark to get a good look, the only thing witnesses remembered was the guy who got shot was on his phone. Then the transcript points to Knoble, and the cops confirm the reservation was under his name."

"And since he looked like Knoble..." Tom paused for her to finish.

"They just assumed it was him."

"If it walks like a duck and quacks likes a duck..."

"I can't..." her voice trailed off in disbelief.

The conversation with Ben in the rental car, the way Knoble's secretary disappeared, the lack of details Ben offered. She didn't have evidence proving this, but she didn't need it. It added up, much more so than her Ben killing Knoble.

Wait, she chided herself. *Her Ben?*

"He still killed someone, Tom..."

"Hence the second distinct characteristic I mentioned earlier."

"Which is?"

"Ben needed a man who wanted to die."

"How is that any better than killing Knoble?" she asked.

"Did you really just ask me that?"

"It's still murder..."

Tom leaned in to again rest his elbows on the table. The levity once there was nowhere to be seen, and he lowered his voice another notch. "A year-and-a-half ago, Janosch moved to Mexico so he could die in the sun. But it didn't happen. Instead, each day got worse than the last with no immediate relief in sight. The best drugs in the world couldn't make the guy feel good and coherent at the same time. He had a constant migraine, a cough from hell, and a heart working overtime that ached with every beat."

"That doesn't make shooting him right."

"Spare me your idealistic bullshit. The man was tired of waiting for death," Tom hissed, though still in a whisper. His eyes turned angry and honed in on hers, the tension in his cheekbone consistent with teeth forcefully grinding against each other.

"His brother said Chris had considered swallowing a bunch of pills for about a month before we found him. And when he learned there was a way to go quick and save a young boy's life...all while making a ton of money for his brother...he jumped on it and didn't look back. Sidarta tried to talk him out of it three times — at Ben's request — but the guy was dead set."

"The paramedics didn't see the mask? And what about the autopsy? It confirmed that Bill Knoble was the victim."

"Both the paramedics and the coroner were aware of the situation."

"You've got to be kidding me."

"Nikki, I know it's a lot. And it's obviously a darker shade of gray than you'd prefer."

"You can say that again."

"But remember, Janosch wanted this. He wanted his pain to end, and to help his brother the only way he knew how...by letting him move on. No kids, no wife, no other extended family...and pain, literally every second of every day. You're telling me you wouldn't consider doing the same thing?"

As she pondered Tom's question, the irony wasn't lost on her. She was ten feet away from small children savoring the joy of life the way bees suck nectar from a flower, and they were talking about a man so desperate for relief from pain that he wanted to end his. The children's laughter was so antithetical to the sadness Janosch must've felt that she couldn't help but feel sorrow.

"You're telling me the coroner misidentified the deceased because he's buddies with Ben? He could go to jail if that ever came out."

"It goes a bit deeper than 'buddy' but for all practical purposes, yes. The paramedics and the coroner all knew the risks involved, but also what was at stake otherwise. They made their decisions of their own free will."

258

"What about…" her voice trialed off as she realized she didn't know what to say.

"Assisted suicide is legal in several states. Is this really all that different?"

"Yes, it is."

"I'll be the first to admit, I tried to talk Grasshopper out of it. So did Sidarta. But considering the circumstances, I understand it."

"Where's Knoble now?"

"In a safe location. Alive and well."

"You can't expect me to believe this at face value."

"Nikki, I'm not sure what I expect. But I know that you seeing Knoble is out of the question. As is providing you with any physical evidence that conclusively proves he's alive."

"Who has the trust issue now?"

"Like I said, I didn't even want to have this conversation. This is Grasshopper's move."

"Then why isn't he making it?"

"He's otherwise indisposed."

"But you're not going to tell me where, what or why?"

"You were always clever."

"Why are you doing this?" she asked the kneejerk and stupid question. As soon as the words came out, she waved them off. After a brief moment, she whispered, "I won't let Ben control me like this."

"The landscape has changed since you and I met at that Mexican joint. Do you know how many cars I switched between just to get here? Did you not take a hint when I made you assure me you'd do the same? Don't you see how cautious people like Ben and I are being?

"And by that, I mean people who have been in the military and know their share about covert ops and surveillance? We're taking every precaution we can to avoid being seen, and we know what the hell we're doing. You're a neophyte. You gallivant around in the same Chevy Malibu you've been driving for years, advertising to the world who you're seeing and why."

"Last time I checked, the law didn't need to cover its tracks."

"Then I suggest you remove the blinders and check again."

"Excuse me?"

"If you're hell-bent on staying involved, you need to be more careful."

She just watched Tom continue, feeling tightness in her chest.

"Grasshopper *and* Robert *and* Susan are right — get the hell away from this thing, as far and as fast as you can. I'm sure that's why Ben wanted you to know Knoble is alive — to give you a clear reason to get out. That, and the hope you'd think better of him. But you're a smart girl…so if you decide to keep sticking your nose where it doesn't belong, at the very least don't be so damn stupid about it."

She thought about all those people offering the same advice. Some of them had conflicts of interest, others had proven to be manipulative in the past, but she respected them all. Perhaps she should listen. She got involved to help find Joe, and remained involved to bring down Ben. Both now seemed out of reach. So maybe Tom was right. But she also knew there was more to this, and she was tired of being handled with kid gloves.

"What aren't you telling me?"

Tom didn't respond, and she persisted.

"If the terrorists think Knoble is dead, then Joe should be safe. If that were the case, Ben wouldn't still be playing renegade. What aren't you telling me?"

"I haven't been a great friend to you the past nine days. And I'm sorry about that. First I called you into this mess, only to tell you now you should get out of it. Then I encouraged you to reengage with Ben romantically."

"Now you don't think I should?"

"Not now. Maybe one day. You two really were great together. But Ben's in a different place right now...with different people. Where he's going, you can't follow. I wish I could tell you more."

"You can."

"No, I can't. For your sake."

"I hate it when people presume to know what's better for me than I do."

"And I hate it when my integrity is questioned."

She inched closer, her eyes focused on his. "Tom, bring me in. Tell me how I can help."

"The best thing you can do is stay away, from this case and Ben."

"*Damn it*, Tom."

"We won't see each other for a while, Nikki. But please give this some serious thought. And no matter what you do, be careful."

In contrast to his cocky strut and laid-back body language when Tom first arrived, he was now rigid and rough. Over the course of their conversation he'd transformed, and it scared her to see him that way. The levity and laughter were gone, vanquished to a distant memory; seriousness and sternness were all that remained. She wished she had something more profound to say when he got up and ambled towards the downward escalator.

But all she could think of was, "You too, Tom."

55

The silent cardinal answered the phone. "Siebert."

The voice sounded neither wide-awake nor half-asleep. It didn't crack or offer telling inflection. It was spoken at regular volume, neither whisper nor shout, with average tempo. At 11:35, Arminius was quite certain Siebert had been up for hours, but Siebert concealed his exhaustion well. A skill learned in the military, no doubt.

"How is your mission progressing?" Arminius asked.

"Since I don't know if there's any benefit to me completing it, I haven't started."

"Let's not begin this conversation that way."

"Let's not begin with one-sided questions. A contract has two parties last I checked."

"Straight to the point as usual. Fair enough. Should you ever become separated from your son after a terrorist attack on the United States and lose the ability to contact each other, your rendezvous point is an abandoned log cabin next to Mondoman Peak."

The silence on the other end was exactly what he wanted.

"Given your previous statement that only your son would know the answer to that question, my assumption is your request for proof of life has been satisfied. Is that a valid assumption?"

"It is."

"Good. Then listen, and listen well, Mr. Siebert. There will be no more information provided; and there will be no more phone calls. This is our final communication before Memorial Day, by which time you will have either saved your son's life or chosen to let him perish. Proof of life was unnecessary, but it was a goodwill gesture we offered to prove it's not our intent to harm the boy."

"If that's true, send me a picture of him."

"It was a one-time gift, Mr. Siebert. There will be nothing further."

Arminius severed the connection, self-affirming his decision once and for all.

Emotion rarely got the better of Ben Siebert, but requesting a photo was an act of anxiety. Anxiety that had almost certainly been amplified by Arminius's planned delay in contacting him after Knoble's supposed death. It was difficult to go dark for so long, but Arminius knew it would work...even on Ben Siebert. The lack of communication made the former Marine wonder and worry why. Siebert had no doubt questioned if son was already dead because his plan had failed. His mind had played out the worst-case scenario. It'd put the silent cardinal on edge and made him feel powerless. *Yes*, Arminius thought to himself, *it was worth the wait*. The stall tactic had worked perfectly. Siebert was desperate. It was a thing of beauty.

Siebert's plea for evidence the boy was alive during their last conversation was promising by itself, the follow-up request for a photo confirmed that Siebert felt the desired pressure. He knew how real and how high the stakes really were.

But Siebert was also right; he was necessary. The silent cardinal was the only man for the job. And though Arminius didn't want to potentially project weakness by satisfying the request, he decided it was a more than equitable trade.

After the boy told him, Arminius verified that Mondoman Peak was about ninety minutes south of Chicago, an appropriate distance for such a rendezvous point. It was also well within character for Siebert to plan ahead for such an event, as well as store nonperishables in advance. It served as final confirmation that proving the boy was alive was innocuous, as well as a small price to pay. It would keep Siebert hungry and focused, and allow Arminius to exploit the former recon's only weakness right up until mission completion.

The silent cardinal belonged to him.

56

After Arminius hung up, Ben swallowed hard and collected his thoughts. At this point every second mattered, so there wasn't time to waste. But there were so many moving parts — and so many directions — that he had to process it all holistically before taking the next step.

Measure twice, cut once.

He inhaled deeply through his nose and exhaled out his mouth. Both hands on either side of his face, he closed his eyes and cleared his mind of everything except what should happen next. Breathing one gigantic breath after another, he kept his eyes shut tight in the small, windowless room where he'd held Bill Knoble, forcing clarity into his brain.

The first phone call had to be to Xerox. Arminius had either already gone to the website or wouldn't do so at all, but either way he needed to let Xerox know what happened.

The next conversation would be with Sidarta, to verify that Larry Janosch was indeed off the grid for the foreseeable future. The transfer had gone through, but Ben needed to know Larry was safe. The rabbit hole Arminius was in ran much deeper than he first expected, and he owed it to Christopher Janosch to keep his brother safe.

Finally, he had to decide what to tell Susan. With Tom it was simple. Less was more. He wouldn't be able to help much at this point anyway, and that way he could be there for others if something happened to Ben. But Susan…she was more ambiguous, and the decision's stakes were higher. Telling her too much now would put her at risk, but keeping her out of the loop might set her up. It was clear she had no idea who Arminius was working with, but there was no playbook for deciding what to share and when. On top of that, he didn't have definitive proof. That would only complicate things if he told her now.

He stroked his chin and embraced the deep stare that followed, ultimately deciding that he had to trust a Senior Intelligence Officer in the CIA would know how watch her own back. Telling her now would only serve to put a target on her back too big to miss.

God, please let that be the right decision.

His final thoughts were of his son. The logistics of Xerox and Sidarta and Tom and Susan out of the way, he permitted his brain to give into his heart and think of Joe. Poor Joe. How alone he must feel, how scared he must be. He would've gladly given his own life to save Joe's, but he knew Arminius wouldn't allow that to happen. Indeed, as farfetched as his plan was, it was all he had.

He put the gun in his pocket and stood up to leave the room for the last time. But first, he forced himself to smile. Determined to exit with optimism and focus, he thought about the only bright spot of these two wretched weeks. How even with how scared and alone Joe felt, as young and innocent as he was, his son remembered. He didn't give up or give in. He didn't stop fighting. He did what he could with what he had; he remembered to breathe and pray and get back to the basics. Despite the hell he was going through, Joe remembered what Ben had always taught him. He couldn't be more proud of his son.

Or mad at himself.

57

Very few people knew his given name, but those he worked with him called him Xerox. In the sea of false identities, secondary profiles, and binders full of passports, birth certificates and social security cards that proved he was legally named this or that, Xerox was the one unique identifier that stood the test of time.

His voice-secured, end-to-end encrypted telephone rang just past midnight for the second night in a row. It was the same caller both times. Before picking up, he looked out the window into the star-filled sky, admiring Pike's Peak from forty miles away.

"I still don't have it, Ben."

"ETA?"

"I wish I could tell you. But the second I do, you'll hold me to it."

"When will you know?"

"Now you're asking for an ETA of my ETA?"

"It's been almost twenty-four hours."

"I know, Ben. But the site was accessed less than a day ago, and there are a lot of hoops to jump through to do this right. Don't forget...it's your specification that makes it so challenging. Like I told you before, I could be a lot more efficient if you let me access certain government networks and databases to gather the data."

"I can't risk it," Ben replied in a colorless voice. "I know you're good, the best even, but there's no way to be sure you wouldn't tip the feds off. And if you did, none of this would matter. It'd be game over."

"There actually is a way to be certain."

"What's that?"

"For you to give me the time I need. My specialty is accessing complicated and clandestine information so that I can provide qualified solutions to difficult problems, but only when I have the time I need to do both."

He was given the name Xerox in recognition of his ability to recreate highly technical, cyberspace scenarios as a way of conducting high-end computer surveillance analysis. By forcing himself to literally recreate, or copy, an entire system and meticulously look at every detail in that system, he afforded himself the chance to find its Achilles' heel. He used code — some original, some "borrowed" — to run millions of simulations per minute to ensure no stone was left unturned.

His basic goal was always the same: to grind out each and every possibility and utilize the process of elimination ad nauseam...on the most sophisticated systems ever created. Brute-force sequenced data analysis. It was somewhat simple to say, but extremely hard to do. It wasn't sexy, but it worked. He coined it "cyber-replication theory," though no trademark was pending. If even his made-up name for what he did were to be exposed, a lot of people would perish, and in all likelihood America would be at war.

Its only flaw was that it took time. Time Ben didn't have.

"Get what you can with the time you've got," Ben softly answered.

"In that case, my ETA is ASAP."

"Are street light cameras that hard to crack? Even without accessing government networks?"

"They are if you keep your tracks as covered as you say you want to, and if you don't know what or who you're actually looking for. It's easier when there's a specific target."

"But you have the website's time-stamp. Can't you just—"

"Ben, I know the urgency. And I know what's at stake."

"How do you know that?" Ben asked with inquisitiveness, not skepticism.

"Tom filled me in."

"Who the hell told him to do that?"

"Don't be mad. It helps to have the whole picture, and I know you don't have time to paint it for me. But you know you can trust me, and you know I care. Why do you think I'm working on this around the clock?"

"I know you're on it. And yes, I know how much you care."

"Then stop bothering me and let me do my work."

"That's not the only reason I called."

He waited a moment, but Ben didn't continue. An uneasy silence hung in the air as Xerox imagined what other challenges were about to be added.

"What is it, Ben?" he asked, unwilling to let the suspense persist.

"I have some bad news. I'm pretty sure he won't visit the site again. You've got all you're going to get."

Xerox muted the phone to let out a disappointed sigh. It was clear Ben knew how unfortunate this was, but there was no need to sigh to the father of a kidnapped child who it affected most.

His devout faith and 1 Timothy aside, he believed incomplete information — not money — was the true root of all evil. It'd been confirmed time and time again, most recently two weeks ago. Tom had sent him a smashed, water-soaked Motorola flip phone and asked if he could pull data from a SIM card and circuit board floating in a watery pool of their own hardware remains. He was good at his craft, perhaps exceptional if he dared use that word, but too often Ben and Tom confused him with God. His inability to help with that request only further motivated him now, but yet again lack of information posed a formidable challenge.

"All the more reason to leave me to my work. I'll get you reliable information as soon as I can. But if I send guesses that turn out to be wrong, it'll set you back even more."

"Thanks, Xerox. You know how grateful I am."

"I do, Ben. You have my word I'll do all I can."

"But…?"

Another brief mute, another deep sigh. Ben needed to hear this as much as he needed to say it.

"But your expectations have to be realistic. The site served its purpose. It provided what it was intended to, but the assumption when I created it for you was that the IP address alone would be sufficient. I can't make you any promises on the rest."

"It's the only chance my son has."

58

Friday, May 21

It'd only been three days since he took the call from Siebert.

Yet David Keene's entire world had changed since.

He couldn't blame himself for not knowing beforehand. Three nights ago, as he was scrutinizing his decision to pass on the Kraft job, there was no way he could've known where things would go. And it was Ben Siebert asking, so his decision was risky but justifiable.

Go big or go home.

He'd left his office in a tizzy and barely got to Morton's Steakhouse on time, only to end up in an old pickup truck driven by a guy in a checkered flannel shirt and brown fisherman's hat. Few words were spoken, but he did get a name: Tom Fedorak. Fifteen minutes of awkward silence later, he walked into a cookie cutter office building on Jackson Street in The Loop, then rode an elevator to the ninth floor. When he got off, he entered the room he'd been in ever since. For seventy-two hours.

What he'd learned in those three days was so mind-blowing and surreal that he felt stuck in a dream loop after one too many spy movies right before bed. After the shock that Bill Knoble was not only alive but also in this room set in, terror took over. What did he get himself into? Was there any realistic chance of getting out of it? Was he ever going to leave this room?

He took another long swig of Root Beer, hoping the carbonation's burning sensation would jolt him out of a nightmare. When it didn't, he asked Tom if he could give

Russell's Reserve a crack at it. A stern eyeballing later, he learned whiskey was out of the question.

He didn't regret telling Julie he was on a business trip one iota. White lies were very real. Even if he'd known the truth then, it would've been much less caring. No, the only thing he regretted couldn't be undone. As he considered what'd been asked of Ben, the realization he may never leave a confined room again — regardless of how this ended — felt more and more plausible if not inevitable.

There he sat, slouched over a large light-oak desk, arms fully extended, right cheek resting on his right bicep, staring sideways at a tiny piece of scratch paper. The area code, 312, was for Chicago. The rest of the phone number he didn't recognize. The traditional landline telephone just stared at him, judging his apprehension. Yes, it was his only way to fight the ambiguity. Yes, doing nothing only assured more unanswered questions and anguish. But the unknown felt immensely riskier. If he called, he was going to get answers…but did he really want to ask questions?

"Dial the damn number," Tom Fedorak yelled.

59

"First off, this conversation never happened."

"Then maybe we shouldn't have it," the voice on the other end of the phone replied.

"Mr. Keene," Susan began in a tone just above a whisper, "I'm going to give you the benefit of the doubt. Let's start again with introductions. I'm a Senior Officer in the CIA, charged with obtaining information vital to the safety of America and given full jurisdictional authority to do so. You are a newspaper reporter."

"What's that supposed to mean?"

"That not only did this conversation never happen, but the very notion someone in my position would even take your call is out of the question. And certainly shouldn't lead to me being referenced as a source for any article whatsoever, anonymous or otherwise."

"I never said I was writing a story."

"And should I ever learn you do," she continued on as though Keene hadn't said a word, "you may find yourself in a third-world country's tiny jail cell sucking brown water off a filthy floor, pondering if it was really worth it all those years ago. Am I being clear, or is this phone conversation over?"

"What phone conversation?"

"Good."

Susan hated resorting to threats, empty as they may be. But what Ben was asking — for her to consider granting a reporter she didn't know anonymous, unrestricted access to a number of highly classified government databases and files — was a tremendous risk by itself. For her to be in the dark as to why...that was over-the-top dangerous.

Ben's terms were very clear. If she wanted his help, working with Keene was the price. And she trusted Ben, maybe even too much. But that trust and her need for his help notwithstanding, there wasn't a chance in hell Keene was getting access to anything more than a visitor's badge until she knew more. A lot more.

She'd initially refused Ben's request altogether, while on the phone in the XSport parking lot. Then he assured her many more lives were at stake, right after proving how far ahead of the authorities he was.

She recalled the voice recording of Knoble divulging personal information that only he could know and reading a newspaper word-for-word dated two days after his supposed death. Since then, the voice analysts had confirmed it was Knoble to the tune of 97.9% accuracy. The date-stamped pictures of Knoble holding the newspaper were a nice touch, even though the lab couldn't confirm with as high of a degree of confidence it was him due to the graininess of the photo. She wasn't sure if carbon dating was accurate to the day, but Forensics confirmed the blood sample provided was Knoble's and, via Raman spectroscopy, that it was less than a few days old.

The death certificate, which her best analysts swore was legitimate, had since been confirmed as fake. Down to the State File Number, cause of death and burial location. The body had already been cremated, so she of course couldn't verify it. She was still waiting on the carbon dating, but she was pretty sure the corpse was not Knoble.

That's when she realized she had to at least vet Keene. No promises beyond that, and Ben agreed that was fair. Her intent was for this conversation with Keene to make it easy to tell Ben to piss off. That the risk wasn't worth even his help.

Scare them into submission she'd once taught a classroom full of budding officers at The Farm about how to control potential leaks in the field. Time to practice what she preached.

"I don't understand why I'm talking to you," she said into the receiver, flipping through Keene's dossier. "Late twenties, Columbia College undergrad. Journalism major. There's a shocker."

"Is there something wrong with journalism?"

"No, no. Art & Crafts is a fine way to go."

"What's your problem, lady?"

"No drugs, alcohol at least twice a week. And you do like your vaping. Not a porn addict but you don't shun the stuff. Member of a rock band, let's not go there, and you still call your parents once a week."

"This is bullshit."

Short temper. Easily agitated.

"Mr. Keene, I'm trying to understand what made our mutual acquaintance choose you for this. Of all the reporters at all the newspapers, he wanted you. And after spending an hour reviewing your file and talking with you for five minutes, the only evidence of intelligence I see is that you came to your senses about this conversation never happening."

C'mon kid…spill it. Make it easy for me to say no.

"It took you an hour to review my file?"

"Certainly not lacking in the sarcasm department are we, Mr. Keene."

"Nor in the condescension department, Mrs. Reynolds."

Confident. Stands his ground.

She jotted it down, then added a subsequent note.

In over his head & knows it. Trying to muscle his way out. That's stupidity, not bravado.

"Why don't you just ask him?" Keene shot back.

"Because I'm asking you."

"Feels more like an interrogation."

"Obviously you've never been interrogated."

"That's because I'm not a criminal. So stop treating me like one."

"It's nothing personal, Mr. Keene. At least not yet. I just don't see what stands out about you. Normal Chicago suburban upbringing, positive and loving childhood, mediocre college student while you were figuring things out, enthused employee, hard worker. Smart but not a genius. Noble but unremarkable. Engaged to a beautiful yet equally average nurse at Northwestern Memorial who wants four kids. Better get moving on that, by the way."

"Leave Julie out of this."

Overprotective of fiancé. Honorable, but also a vulnerability.

"And if I don't?"

"This isn't working for me. Just tell our mutual acquaintance to get someone else."

She paused to consider the good sign that he offered to walk away. But it wasn't enough. She needed to know if she could really believe him.

"Tell you what," she softened her tone. "Stop being such a hard ass, and I'll ease up a bit."

She guessed the long pause was because Keene wanted her to think he was contemplating an alternative.

"What do you want to know?" He raised his voice, agitated and not trying to hide it.

"You know what I want. Why does he trust you?"

"He said it was because he respected my approach to my craft. That I was honest in a dishonest profession. That my word meant something, and I didn't put personal advancement over professional integrity. I don't know if that's the real reason, but that's what he said."

"This is your last chance, David. Either tell me the truth, the whole truth, or suffer the consequences."

"I did," Keene replied without the least bit of hesitation.

After a few seconds of silence, Susan checked her watch and knew she had to make a decision. Keene was smart enough to know when he was out of his league, yet he didn't bite. Much as she would've preferred otherwise, he fit the bill.

Damn you, Ben.

"Okay, David."

"Okay what?"

"We both know you have the evidence to write a front-pager about how the CIA botched the Dominic Riddle operation two years ago, and that lives were compromised because of it. Even today, it'd be a groundbreaking story that would take your career to new heights. Then Ben arranged for you to be anonymously bribed for a source, as a test to see if your integrity or pocketbook came first. And even though you're frustrated enough with your career to quit your job, you haven't written the article and you didn't take the cash. You honored your promise to Ben, and you saved lives at your expense by not printing confidential information.

She didn't have to see Keene's face to know it was in shock.

"I told you I needed to know why Ben chose you. Why he trusted you. I didn't want to hear it...I wanted to see it. If you'd broken your confidence with him when I pushed you, this conversation would've been over. Yet even after I threatened you, you stood your ground. That doesn't mean I trust you yet — and *everything* I said about a third-world jail cell is true — but it's table stakes for this conversation. So, what've you got and how can I help?"

When the shell-shocked reporter didn't answer, she said, "Start talking before I change my mind, David."

60

"I thought I made myself clear."

The comment rang in his ears like nails on a chalkboard. Arminius closed his eyes and held the phone like an egg to control the tension pulsating to his fingers. Even the Kodiak Ice thinking tool didn't calm his nerves. He'd been speaking with Agricola for over twenty minutes, but this was the part he dreaded. Agricola needed to know.

"You did, sir. But as you know, optimal scenarios often don't play out in practice. It's no longer possible to put this off. Benton's close to finding the link to Smith, and we've waited long enough. We either act now or suffer the consequences of indecision."

"The consequences of indecision?" Agricola howled in frustration. "What are you, some kind of professor?"

"We need to deal with this now. I'm just being upfront."

"Don't tell me what we need to do. Not after our chat the other day."

He sighed in silence, knowing there was no upside to a response. Though it provided an explanation for the lack of communication, learning a few days ago that Rausch's surveillance expert, Clay Braun, had been tortured to death in a gas station bathroom made for a very unwelcome surprise. Even worse was the fact it seemed all but certain Ben Siebert was the culprit. Worst yet still: Agricola told him, not the other way around.

"Don't ever forget who you're talking to," Agricola shouted so loud that he had to move the phone from his ear.

He knew there was no getting out of the shit at this point. He could dance around any number of explanations, but the fact was it was unprofessional. He'd let Agricola down, and part of him expected to go to sleep one night and never wake up.

"I have no excuses, sir. It was an oversight, and it will not happen again."

"This is your last chance, Arminius."

"Understood." He swallowed his pride. "So I have your permission?"

"Do what's necessary to serve the mission. Stop disappointing me! I didn't want it to come to this, but your mismanagement of the operation has left me with no choice."

The notion of their "partnership" was gone, and Arminius didn't expect to hear the word again. The food chain went on full display when they "discussed" Braun's death a few days ago. His screw up — letting Rausch choose his own help outside the military — had cost him dearly.

But self-pity wasn't an option. There was only one appropriate response. He must exceed Agricola's expectations from here on out. He had to drive the mission's success beyond what even Agricola envisioned. It was time to play the trick he had up his sleeve since the beginning.

"It will be done, Agricola. The mission will prevail."

"You understand what I mean by last chance, don't you?"

"Yes sir. I do."

61

He was still recovering from his conversation with Susan Reynolds two hours ago. If the shock of Bill Knoble still being alive wasn't enough to drive a man to whiskey, that woman sure as hell was. David prayed he'd never have to meet her face-to-face.

"Grasshopper will be here soon."

Tom Fedorak made the announcement as though arranging a national press conference concerning an item of extreme importance. Not even the quirky fisherman's hat and bug-eye glasses took away from its seriousness. And David sensed things were only going to get even more interesting. Was it a good thing that Siebert was on his way? He wasn't so sure.

There were two other people in the room with him who appeared to receive Tom's comment the same way. He couldn't be sure, but the way they both held their breath and looked at one another indicated as much.

The first was Bill Knoble himself. The infamous thought-dead lawyer looked older than the pictures in the paper after his supposed shooting. His hair had either rapidly changed in those two weeks or he'd previously colored it black, because he now had far more salt atop his relatively small head than pepper. He stood six feet tall and weighed maybe 160 pounds. His baggy eyes, creased face and sluggish posture screamed heavy exhaustion.

Seeing Knoble in the flesh while simultaneously recalling his coworker's zest to be the first reporter on the scene of his death was a penetrating paradox to David. The kind of irony that could drive him insane if he thought about it too much. He decided three days ago when he first met Bill that he wouldn't allow that to happen, but it'd been harder in practice than he thought. He forced himself — mind over matter — to steer clear of the path of endless unanswered questions, primarily because there was no returning from that rabbit hole. But his innate reporter's curiosity was present every waking moment.

It further elucidated just how over his head this felt. And the fact it wasn't going to end well. He didn't feel in danger, per se, but trapped by things outside his control and understanding. The most terrifying thought was what would happen if he failed Siebert. He knew before leaving the office three nights ago that Siebert had a knack for acquiring intelligence, and the man knew things about him no one else did. But learning that he could somehow orchestrate a man's fake death the world totally bought took Ben's abilities — and David's concerns about letting him down — to a whole new level.

Bill sat on the black leather couch next to the other person in the room, his former secretary. Her name was Genie, or so she said. She was young, maybe late twenties. She hadn't smiled once since David had arrived, but he knew when she did it was the kind of smile that lit up a room. She had long brown hair and a very pretty face. Tiny nose. Smooth skin. Soft cheeks. She didn't say much, but he could tell she was smart. Bill said something about law school exams to her. Genie was still clutching the wooden leg she 'd taken from the hotel chair that she was holding when he first met her. He had no idea why, but figured now wasn't the time to ask.

The three of them stared with ambiguity at the flippant yet serious seventy-something Tom Fedorak. Fedorak mentioned earlier that what they knew was only the beginning, and the rest would be revealed when Ben arrived. He guessed that was supposed to pique their curiosities, but for him all it did was enhance his regret.

The room's accommodations were lavish. The spacious, almost ballroom-like open office space had a large chandelier hanging from a faux-golf plaster ceiling. Black leather and green velvet couches that converted to surprisingly comfortable sofa beds made a "U" around a glass-top coffee table with the same clawed feet as the adjoining bathroom's tub. Massive windows with waves of thick drapery would've revealed breathtaking, sweeping panoramas of the West Loop — had they not been covered with opaque whiteboards. The layout suggested that the room was designed to be some sort of executive penthouse.

If this was the ninth floor, David wondered what floors 10-15 looked like. It was well stocked with food and refreshments. Most anything they wanted was there, and he couldn't complain aside from the prohibition of alcohol.

There was also no shortage of professional materials: computers with high speed internet access, tablets, printers, faxes, papers, folders and anything else he might need to do his work. The whiteboards and sticky easel pads circumventing the room converted its feel from penthouse to war room.

"I have to use the bathroom," David said.

Tom turned towards him and withdrew a dull gold pocket watch. He held it in the air before letting it fall until the chain yanked it back.

"You've got three minutes."

"Forget it. I'll hold it."

Accommodations or no, this place was a prison.

And he was a prisoner.

Creature comforts were no match for freedom.

At present, he languished in the velvet sofa opposite Bill and Genie, utterly fatigued, nearly lulled to sleep by a man the world just knew was dead gently stroking his former secretary's hair. Not in a perverse manner, but rhythmically; the way a loving father would his daughter's.

He envied how content Bill and Genie seemed. They were already there when he arrived, and though he could tell Genie was just as surprised as he was if not more so that Knoble was alive, she still came across as more relaxed than he felt, even holding the wooden leg. That said, he couldn't deny it felt good to know he wasn't the only one stunned.

Tom stared at one of the nine whiteboards, his intense focus transforming blinking into a luxury that couldn't be afforded. Tom was munching on another hot dog, his third or fourth Oscar Mayer of the day and maybe his tenth since picking David up outside Morton's Steakhouse. But the man didn't even look down to take a bite.

The name "Clay Braun" was in the center of a brainstorming web with lines extending to words such as "military" and "Arminius" and a few others like "Merriweather" that David didn't recognize. Neither did Tom, evidently, because each connection had a question mark next to it and Tom had been staring at the same board for over an hour.

"Sorry to keep you waiting," Ben announced upon entering at nine p.m.

He instinctively straightened up and eyed Ben, scanning his person. Ben wore plain clothes: a pair of blue jeans, tucked-in green polo and brown loafers. His face was clean-shaven, in contrast to the heavy scruff when he first met him. His baggy, bloodshot eyes and missing five o'clock shadow didn't take away from Ben's commanding presence. His strong, confident posture and deep stare wouldn't allow it.

The man who'd transformed David's life two years ago — and he feared might end it soon should he fail whatever task he was about to receive — merely nodded in silent response to his gawking.

"Mr. Siebert," Genie abruptly snapped, "how long are you going to keep us here?"

"I know you've been through a lot. I wish I could let you go right now."

"Why can't you?"

"I trust everyone in this room, which is why I've shared what I have," Ben answered, motioning towards Bill. "I realize what I've put you through the past few days is no way to treat people you trust. But the circumstances didn't give me much choice, and I don't apologize for it. You're here for my son's safety."

David watched Genie's burst of furry fizzle away. Her eyes looked watery, but she kept them composed and pointed at Ben.

"I'm sorry you saw what you did, Genie, but at the time I was convinced they were watching every step you took. If you'd known what was coming, you would've given it away. I couldn't take that chance. I hope you find it in your heart to forgive me."

Genie just stared back, equally if not more surprised by Siebert's remorse than his candor. David noticed the water in her eyes began the transformation to actual tears.

"Let me answer your question. Today is Friday, May 21st. This will all be over no later than May 31st, Memorial Day."

"You said 'at the time'..." Genie ignored what David immediately thought: *ten days.* "So now you don't think anyone was watching me?"

"They might've been, but it's clear that killing Bill was never their primary objective."

"Then why did they insist it be done?" she asked.

"Bill's bounty was a red herring, scripted from the beginning to get me where they wanted me. Everything from the call to Robert Stevens to Joe's kidnapping."

"I thought you said the bombs at Ogilvie were real," Bill interjected.

"They were real. Very real. The terrorists needed Robert to know they could've done a lot of damage. The explosives established their credibility. But they never intended to detonate them."

"How do you know?" Genie replied, her squinty eyes projecting skepticism.

"Why do you think they led Robert right to them? And why were they so clear about deactivation? They went out of their way to make sure the bombs didn't go off."

"Yeah…because they're such nice guys," Bill shot back, rolling his eyes.

"No, because blowing up a train station would bring a lot of attention they don't want, considering they're trying to kill the President of the United States."

"Yet you're saying their whole point was to get the FBI's attention." Bill said.

"No, I said they wanted Robert's attention."

"But he did tell someone. He told Susan Reynolds." Just saying her name made David like her even less.

"Of course he did. And they knew he would," Ben responded.

"Is it just me or are we doing Abbott and Costello?" Genie asked.

"Robert didn't broadcast it to the FBI," Ben replied. "He called one person he trusted at the CIA. The bombs told him he needed all the trustworthy help he could get. This isn't some mass multijurisdictional case; it's a few individuals who trust one another. People who can work together but also keep a lid on it."

"And you're saying that was all so Robert would call you?"

"That's right."

Bill said, "How did they know he would?"

"We'll come back to that. First, the key question hasn't changed. It's the same question Susan and Robert were asking, and the same one I asked at the very beginning. Why would people capable of blowing up Ogilvie need help murdering one ordinary lawyer from Chicago? They could've easily killed you and made it look like a botched robbery or a car accident. Even a suicide. No offense," Siebert shrugged his shoulders at Bill, who merely nodded in agreement.

"The other important question," Tom added, "is why did they insist on it being so secret. That fits the terrorist mold about as well as a nun in a whorehouse."

"It didn't add up then, but it does now," Ben continued. "They never wanted Bill dead. They want…someone else dead."

"And getting bombs planted in Ogilvie might not be trivial, but it's a hell of a lot easier than killing the President of the United States," Tom concluded.

Bill shook his head and bit his lip as he brought up a counterpoint. "Getting the FBI involved seems like a lot of added risk on their part."

"The FBI's involvement was inevitable. Doing it this way allowed them to control how, when, and most importantly, why."

"How do you figure the FBI's involvement was inevitable?" Bill asked.

"What do the terrorists want? They want me to assassinate one of the most popular and protected individuals in the world. Right?"

"Right," Bill answered, sounding skeptical.

"And to get me to do it, they knew they would have to incentivize me."

"Enter your son."

"Correct. But if all they do is kidnap Joe, they expose themselves."

"How so?" David heard himself skeptically blurt out. All four of them turned in unison and stared at him. Listening to Bill and Genie go back and forth with Ben and Tom for a few minutes not only had his head spinning, but also wondering what value he brought. He had to get at least one question in edgewise.

"The authorities are aware of Joe's kidnapping, right? FBI, CPD, even the CIA?"

"Yes."

"So like I said, the FBI's involvement was inevitable. You can't kidnap a college kid in this country without the authorities getting involved."

286

"I'll give you that," Bill continued. "But at the end of the day, they still have your son and you still know what they want. How did the Ogilvie threat help them?"

"Ogilvie provided a reason for me to be involved. Because Robert and Susan brought me into the Ogilvie situation, the terrorists could put Bill's death on me. As far as the FBI and CIA are concerned, that was my only goal. My motive was clear."

The room felt silent for a few seconds as he, Bill and Genie considered Ben's theory. No one said a word, and Ben continued.

"It's actually quite clever. They created a diversion, a perfectly logical rationale for Joe's kidnapping that has nothing to do with the president."

"So that no one knows what they really want..." Genie said.

"Think about it," Tom added. "The feds catch one whiff of this and it goes straight to the Secret Service. If that happens, they'll have the president hunkered down in some underground bomb shelter before you can flick your hair."

"Hmm..." whispered Bill, nodding his head as if it all suddenly made perfect sense.

"It also keeps the authorities working on the wrong things," Ben continued.

"What do you mean by that?" he asked, feeling like the only one not following.

"Look at what's happening," Tom jumped in. "Even now, nine days after Bill is supposedly dead and gone, everyone...FBI, CIA...all of the authorities are looking for the connection between the terrorists and Bill. And, they're hunting Grasshopper down because he supposedly killed him. You know what no one is looking at? Any other possible motives these people might've had for kidnapping Joe. The authorities are focused on what the terrorists want them focused on and nothing else."

"And who could blame them," added Ben. "They're all being led down the primrose path, and it makes too much sense to look elsewhere."

"What about your son?" Genie asked. "Aren't they looking for him?"

"Yes, but not half as hard as they're looking for me."

The candor in Ben's response actually made David feel guilty for his self-pity. Here he was objecting to his confinement to a well-stocked room, while Ben's son was in grave danger. Truth was, he couldn't blame Ben for doing everything he could to save him.

"Why do they want you for the assassination?" he asked.

"Whatever the reason, I'm not flattered. Regardless, there's no doubt it was the plan from the beginning. The first time I spoke to them on the phone, they mentioned how I wasn't invited to the discussion with Robert in the first place and implied they weren't happy I'd become a part of it. The fact is, that's what they wanted from day one."

"This is incredible," Genie said loudly.

Silence and stillness swallowed the room like a python, slowly and with suffocating force. But the true source of the nervousness stemmed from the realization that he — and it seemed Genie and Bill as well — was coming to independently: the explanation made sense. The perfect diversion had been concocted and enacted. Everything had gone exactly the way the perps wanted it to, and Siebert was the only one smart enough to figure it out.

"Nikki was right all along," Tom finally broke the silence.

"Who?" David asked.

"Never mind," Ben snapped, eyeing Tom.

"Can we take a step back for second?" Bill asked

"Yes?"

"This whole…killing the President of the United States…I mean, you're not seriously planning to go through with it, are you?"

Ben and Tom looked at each other the way two friends would after one of them told the other he'd been given a terminal diagnoses. It was clear the question had been asked — and answered — between them already. But now, reticence hung in the air like the stench of rotting food in an open trash can.

David focused on Tom. Ben was so indomitable that trying to read him felt like a waste of time, whereas Tom either didn't have a poker face or simply chose not to wear it. Tom's look throughout the conversation had projected confidence in the assessment of where they were and how they got there. But his lip biting, raised eyebrows, and shifting weight now indicated he was far from sold on where they were headed. He motioned for Ben to answer, further reaffirming to David that the two of them disagreed on what the next steps should be.

Ben looked at Bill before answering the dead man's question.

"I'm going to do whatever's necessary to save my boy. And I need your help."

62

When it first dawned on Bill Knoble that if he actually survived this fiasco he'd not only need a new identity but a completely new life, it didn't feel possible. When the world thinks you're dead, how do you find your place in it? His kneejerk reaction was that it seemed too daunting to contemplate, let alone live out in reality.

Yet one-by-one things fell into place, and before long the idea became logistically feasible. He'd never practice law again, of course, but Ben had already more than taken care of the financial side and he sure as hell wouldn't miss the profession. He wasn't famous or memorable, and old clients wanted nothing to do with him, so the chances of someone recognizing him years later were very slim. He had no lifelong friends and had fallen out of touch with most of his acquaintances over time, mostly the result of his own drunken stupidity. Flawlessly fabricating new medical records, a professional background and other information critical to a person's existence out of thin air seemed implausible to him, but Ben assured him it had been done before and could be done again.

There were still unknowns. What about when he wanted to visit his nieces, Lydia and Jessica? What would he tell them? Or his siblings for that matter? What if he met someone and she asked about his past? He wasn't signing up for a witness protection type deal. That would mean a total break from his current life, and he wasn't game. He wanted to see Lydia and Jessica and on some level have a relationship with them. So how would he explain his staged death? What could possibly do so, even to an adult, let alone a kid? He didn't have answers, but unanswered questions had become the norm.

He decided to take things one day at a time and cross each bridge as he came to it. Of course, right now those unanswered questions seemed inconsequential anyway, considering he had no idea what the country would look like in eleven days and the fact he didn't expect to get out of this alive.

He rubbed the small scar below his right cheekbone where Ben had taken the sample of his flesh. It'd been the only painful part of his entire two weeks of capture, and the final thing Ben did while trying to determine if he was involved with the terrorists.

This is going to hurt, he repeated Ben's words in his mind.

Finally, Ben finally concluded there was nothing to learn from him. Ben told him what'd happened and from that point on treated him more than fair, even generously, especially considering Ben's son was still missing and these people had offered to trade Joe's life for his.

He couldn't really blame Ben for doubting him at first. Some of the decisions he'd made before meeting Ben were shady at best, and it certainly wasn't a stretch to think he'd inadvertently brought this upon himself. Strangely enough, the entire experience brought the two of them together in a peculiar sort of way. Despite the circumstances, an even stronger bond had formed. But what Ben was asking now would've felt unreasonable no matter how strong their friendship was.

He sunk deep into the leather couch and smiled at Genie next to him. She was still shell-shocked and it pained him she got dragged into this. Genie was a tough young woman and would get past it, but watching her go through pain he had a hand in administering — directly or otherwise — made him feel remorseful and sad.

He eyed the news reporter on the opposite couch. David Keene struck him as a sharp kid, but in way over his head. He didn't say much and was evidently just as surprised as Genie about the staged murder. David was also young...so young that he couldn't see him as anything other than naive and inexperienced. Ben had insisted for two weeks David was a diamond in the millennial rough, but all he saw was a scared shitless kid. Could this whippersnapper of a reporter really do what Ben needed him to do? The plan felt farfetched even before meeting David. But after watching him over past few days, he honestly didn't think the plan had a snowball's chance in hell.

"So what exactly do you want us to do?" David bluntly asked.

"What I want is to find these people. What I'm prepared to do is to save my son however necessary." Ben's answers were so void of sentiment they came across as rehearsed and robotic; just words off a page spoken by a narrator, with no emotional connection to their meaning.

"Okay..." Genie's response trailed off, her raised eyebrows and glossy lips hanging wide open for all to see.

The truth was, Bill hadn't really thought about how Genie would fit into his new life, assuming he got the chance to live it. That too made him feel guilty, but he decided he had to focus on one regret at a time. He'd cross the "what-about-Genie" bridge when he got to it. Plus, who's to say she'd even want him in her life after this...

"You're all here for different reasons," Ben continued. "And this is highly confidential information I can't afford to have you running around with it." Ben turned to the news reporter's couch first.

"David, you're one of the best investigative journalists in the city, and now you have access to presidential files, databases and data repositories that no other private citizen does. Anything else you need, the CIA can help you get. You must've impressed Susan Reynolds, because she told me that herself."

"Does she know what they want you to do?" David asked softly.

"No, and she can't find out."

"Why?"

"Telling Susan would create a major conflict of interest for her. And I know she'd do the right thing."

"Which is?"

"Alert the Secret Service," Ben answered. "Immediately."

"What if she asks? You want me to lie to *that* woman?" David's words got caught in his throat.

"She won't ask."

"How do you know that?" Bill noticed David was literally holding his breath. It was clear the seasoned CIA officer had put the fear of God into the kid.

"Let's just say she and I have an understanding. The fewer questions she asks, the better. You'll get whatever access or files you need. And I've already prepared the legal documentation that indemnifies and absolves you of all wrongdoing should you need it."

"On what basis?"

"That you were coerced and acted under duress because I threatened to harm Julie if you didn't. I had a lawyer review it to confirm it satisfied the legal requirement," Ben concluded before nodding towards Bill.

He nodded at David, affirming that Ben was right. He was impressed that the kid got to that as soon as he did. Maybe he was smarter than he looked.

"You'll be protected. But I'm going to need every ounce of talent you've got, and I'm going to need it now."

David just stared, biting his lip.

"Bill," Ben said, turning to him. "As we discussed, you might not have been the primary target, but it wasn't a coincidence they chose you either. You're not a pure red herring, and I need to know why."

"I've been looking through all my old cases for weeks. I can't find anything," he said.

"Look harder and faster," Ben answered. "There's something there."

He started to protest but Ben cut him off before he got out another word.

"You've got a world-class researcher sitting next to you and the best assistant I've ever met. Use their help."

Even with David and Genie's assistance, this was going to be like finding a needle in a haystack dangerous enough to be on fire. He tested the waters before agreeing.

"What makes you so sure about this, Ben?"

"Everything they've done has been efficient. No waste. Every action and every word has served a purpose. There's a reason they want you out of the picture."

"I'll keep looking, but don't hold your breath…"

"Genie…" Ben cut him off before turning to her, frowning.

Bill knew Ben always had a soft spot for Genie, and Genie had always been openly fond of "Mr. Siebert." She assumed Ben was too busy to notice her, that he saw it as Bill running the show with her deep in the background merely along for the ride. But Bill knew otherwise. He knew Ben saw a lot of his late wife, Anna, in her. That was partly why Ben paid for her law school despite insisting that he take credit for it.

"You truly are a casualty of the situation."

"Textbook definition," Tom commented.

"And I'm very sorry for that, Genie. I know I can't buy your forgiveness, nor would I want to, but please know that you won't be harmed in any way. You're only here because you're in danger. And because you're a threat to my son."

"How am I either of those things?" Genie asked with a toughness that flashed signs of her old self.

"If I'm right, if they chose Bill for a reason, they'll want to eliminate any connection back to him that could present a threat to them. How do they know he didn't tell you something they want kept quiet? How can they be sure whatever threat he posed, you don't still present?"

"He didn't tell me anything."

"We both know these people aren't going to assume that."

She gave a deep sigh and stared at Ben with pointy eyes that he knew were meant to be defiant. Instead, they announced to the room: *I know you have a point, but I'll be damned if I give you the satisfaction of saying it.*

He felt for Genie, but Ben was right. It was possible, maybe even likely, that she was in danger. And for that reason alone she couldn't leave.

"Fine, you want to lock me up because of some connection you haven't found that Mr. Knoble doesn't think is real, I can't stop you. But don't tell me I'm a threat to your son."

"You are."

"How?" Genie roared.

Ben took a deep breath and lowered his voice even more.

"Genie, at your insistence you now know what these people want. You know what this is all about. If I let you go and you tell the cops, I won't be able to save my son."

"I won't tell the cops."

"I can't risk it," Ben replied calmly, shaking his head.

"Mr. Siebert!"

"You'll be safe here. You can have whatever you want. If you feel inclined to help Bill and David, I'm sure they could use a top-notch law student's assistance. But I'm not asking you to do anything."

"Or letting me leave."

"Consider it a well-paid two-week work trip."

"You can't buy me."

"Of course not. But you're staying here regardless. I hope you find it in your heart to forgive me one day."

The room fell quiet until David cleared his throat. "Not to interrupt…"

"What's on your mind, David?" Ben answered.

"I understand the part about you wanting me to get access to the president's daily schedule. So I can…you know…be an accessory to murder and treason at the same time…even though I have a special note from you that'll supposedly spare me from lethal injection..."

"Go on," Ben said without pause or reaction to the quip.

"But just how in the hell are we supposed to help you find these people? So you...you know...don't actually have to assassinate the president."

"Genie was on the right track earlier."

Bill could sense a slight quiver in Genie when she heard her name.

"You need to start by looking at the one mistake they made..."

"What mistake?" Genie asked. "I didn't say they made any mistakes. I don't even know—"

"Their plan was perfectly executed. From calling Robert to Joe's kidnapping, the whole thing was very well done. Everything lines up, but there's an inherent flaw."

"Do tell," David said.

"The only way they could know Robert would contact me — whether they anticipated him calling Susan or not — was if they knew about our connection."

Genie perked up, her eyes revealing that she recalled the same thing he did. Her question: *How did they know Robert would call you?*

"Holy crap," David replied. "How did that get overlooked?"

"Because," Tom Fedorak butted in, "no one's looking for the connection back to Grasshopper, remember? Robert called him on his own to help with a situation; a situation that was put in play precisely so he *would* call. And because it was, there was no reason for the FBI or the CIA to wonder how the terrorists knew that Robert knew Grasshopper."

"That's the other reason the Ogilvie plot was so important. If all they did was kidnap Joe, everyone would know it was to get to me."

Bill could tell from their slight nods and wide eyes that Ben's earlier comment was now making more sense to both Genie and David. He had, of course, heard it before and made the connection. But watching David and Genie process it for the first time revealed just how clever the plan was. And, it made him worry that the people who'd concocted and implemented it wouldn't be outsmarted by a whippersnapper news reporter, terrified law student and over-the-hill burnout attorney who was supposed to be dead.

"You never met Robert or Susan before the Peter Hubley case?" David asked.

That didn't take long, Bill thought. *Maybe Ben was right about the kid after all.*

"No."

"So these people have some connection back to it," Genie said.

"There are a lot of possibilities. But any way you slice it, it's the best place to start. You two need to work together," Ben pointed to David and him.

"We'll try," he answered, shrugging his shoulders.

"Compare notes, dig up histories, map everything out. If Genie is willing to help, take it. Bill's already started, but Plan A depends on you guys finding it."

"Plan A?"

Just then Ben's cell phone started ringing and he walked away to answer it. When he opened the door and exited, the rest of them stared, wondering if he'd be back. Bill had learned that mysterious phone calls were never-ending with Ben, just another part of his daily routine that added to his mystique.

He thought he heard Ben say "xerox" but couldn't be sure. Tom reassumed his leadership position and asked if there were any remaining questions.

David asked what everyone was thinking.

"Mr....uh, Mr. Fedorak?"

"Spit it out, kid."

"If we don't...I mean, if we can't..."

"For shit's sake boy. Are you trying to ask me if Grasshopper is really prepared to kill the President to save his son if we can't find out who these people are?"

"Uh…yeah."

"I'd like to think not, but he's already surprised me and I sure as hell don't want to find out."

Part IV

63

Ben sat alone in the dark and dingy lounge of what used to be a thriving downtown hotel. Its owners either unwilling or unable to continuously reinvest in the business, the once top-shelf décor and posh atmosphere it was known for became cheap and outdated over the years. The fact the original green and yellow paisley carpets had faded to a muted brown and that visible cracks scurried up and down the walls like trails of disoriented ants on their way to the popcorn ceilings didn't help matters. In addition, the staff's ubiquitous lack of courtesy caused guests to ask on Yelp and TripAdvisor if this was intended to be the Ed Debevic's of the hotel industry, the retro-themed Chicago diner known for its overly sarcastic servers and intentionally rude customer experience.

On a good night, occupancy was at forty percent. Even so, the rates weren't competitive with several adjacent hotels. The perks were nonexistent: no free breakfast, parking, spa, gym or complimentary newspapers. In spite of it all, people still had to wait extended periods of time for the staff to pick up the phone or address requests. The owners were as transparent as they were aggressive regarding their search for a buyer, and Ben theorized that if they didn't find one in six months, the doors would be closing.

It was as good a place as any to conduct his business alone.

"Talk to me, Xerox," he answered his private cell phone while opening a can of Coke, yearning for the caffeine.

"All the images have been sent. E-mail address you provided."

"You son of a gun…" he omitted the profanity out of respect for Xerox, "you did it."

"I know it took longer than you wanted, and it's definitely not the slam dunk you were hoping for. But yes…they're all there. Triangulated street view shots walking into and out of the library between ten and eleven a.m. on Wednesday, May 19th."

"No video?" Ben asked.

"Not possible."

"You didn't need to access the government networks?"

"Why do you think it took so long?"

"Touché. So we're clean?"

"You bet."

"One hundred percent?"

"I work in discrete signals," Xerox answered. "Clean is clean, dirty is anything not 100 percent clean."

He was always thankful the world's grayness never penetrated Xerox's life. The man lived in black and white, right or wrong, go or no go. Ben had experienced too much gray, both in the Marines and outside of it, to have such an outlook. But though he personally abandoned the concept of absolutes, he envied and appreciated that Xerox had not.

"How many individuals are we talking about?"

"That's where it's not a slam dunk. Quite a few potentials. It's a pretty popular place."

"How many who fit the profile?"

"Since I don't really know the profile, I'd rather not answer that. But everything is in your INBOX. Very clear images of each and every candidate."

"Thank you, my friend."

"Anytime, Ben. I'll be in touch on the rest. But remember…that part won't be easy at all…"

"I know. This was top priority. Thanks. Over."

Finally some news that wasn't bad. It was too early to tell if it was good yet, but at least it wasn't bad. He had his own cameras planted five days ago, and the live feed was still coming. It'd be plenty of data to crosscheck with Xerox's photos and compare to the timeline. Tom was right: it was dangerously thin. And Xerox was right that it probably wouldn't work. But it was also still the only prayer he had. He drained his Coke and dialed the number.

"Pictures are in. Time to go to work."

64

If there was one thing Joe learned for himself during his time as a prisoner, it was a lesson he'd heard from others many times before: there's no escaping death.

No tricking her. No avoiding her. She can't be reasoned with. She can't be bargained with. She has no limits. She finds everyone and everything she seeks. And when she does, she gets what she wants.

If you do this, she's coming for you.

Joe tried to ignore his intuition's warnings, but disobeying one of Dad's strongest rules proved very difficult. He'd been taught for years to rely on his instincts, not disregard them. But a plan that purposely shined a light on his insubordination was a tough one to try the concept out on.

He hadn't seen the leader of the four — the tall, fat man with the southern drawl — for some time. Two days by his count. Leading up to the leader's abrupt disappearance, twice someone important named Arminius called; he could tell because the leader's voice turned serious before he hurriedly stepped out of the room.

The other three captors came in and out of the room sporadically. They wore identical black clothes and ski masks, so he labeled them the three stooges to differentiate. Moe was medium height and short-fused; probably the smartest of the stooges. Curly was short and plump, without a doubt the dumbest of the three. He was usually on his phone, watching some YouTube video. Twice the other two stooges had told Curly to shut up. Larry was tall and the quietest of the three. Not as dominant as Moe, not as clumsy as Curly.

They usually entered the room one at a time. What they did when they weren't interrogating him, he didn't know. But each would come in and quickly lock the door behind him. Then they'd try their hand at beating information out of him that he didn't have. He thought about lying just to stop the abuse. But that would only lead to more questions and more whipping.

When he first conceived of the plan he was contemplating, he wasn't sure he could muster up the courage to try it. It more or less centered on him sticking out like a sore thumb and hoping they didn't kill him when he was done. It was a poor plan and, perhaps, he thought, he could just wait it out.

Then Moe showed him the picture.

"You think you gettin' outta here alive without talkin'? Think again, white boy," the raspy-voiced thug shouted at him.

Moe's accent sounded like a black man's, and the white boy reference suggested it, but he couldn't know for sure. Maybe Moe did it on purpose to throw him off? He spoke through a mask with no mouth cutout, so his voice was muffled. Drugs worn off or not, it was hard to be sure without hearing a clear voice. But when Moe held a cell phone up to his face, he stopped caring about that.

It wasn't the clearest photograph and the screen was small, but he could tell right away it was Abigail's house. Completely engulfed in flames. Red and orange filled the colonial home's windows, and its shape had begun to deform. A large chunk of the roof was missing, a hole in its place, and huge clouds of black smoke formed across the top.

"See what happens when you don't talk, punk. Your little bitch. She gooone."

A burning rage Joe didn't know was in him ignited. He felt an overwhelming urge to grab the thug by his throat and squeeze. He always wondered if he'd have the mental fortitude to take a life should his family's safety depend on it. Tonight, he got his answer. He imagined ripping that mask off and watching the stooge suffocate one second at a time, clutching even harder when Moe started to twitch and plead for life.

But that was in Joe's mind. In the real world, he had to remain calm. He needed Moe to walk away. He had one chance, and he couldn't waste it on a bad temper.

Moe laughed in his face, up close and personal.

"You a real pussy, boy. Someone tells me they capped my bitch, I do something 'bout it."

Then Moe hocked a loogie and spat it into his food before dropping the plastic tray from a few feet above the ground. White liquid splattered onto the floor, and Moe belly laughed.

"We'll be back. Yo ass better be talkin'. Or Daddy's next."

Joe wanted to lash out and enact his fantasy, but he focused on his opportunity instead. Moe exited the room singing while Joe tried to focus. He was definitely a black guy. Despite the gloves, the voice and laugh gave it away. Moe wasn't exactly trying to conceal it either. Moe knocked on the door and one of the other stooges opened it from the outside. When it slammed shut and he was alone again, he closed his eyes and prayed for strength. Trying to put the burning house out of his mind, to focus on what needed to be done, he thought first of the timeline.

The Photos app on Moe's phone was in Browse Mode, and the header above the picture read:

Monday
10:54 PM

There was no location, which confirmed Moe didn't take the picture with that phone. It must've been sent to him. Maybe that's where the fat leader went, he considered. But really it didn't matter. What mattered was that Moe's phone could receive texts. If it could receive…

He couldn't be certain how long he'd been in this hellhole, but he had an educated guess. Despite being on and off powerful drugs, he harbored enough coherency to know they brought him food twice a day. Always mushy, liquid crap. He stared at it with disgust. It looked like a bowl of snot. Yet he was so hungry that until now he'd eaten every drop like it was delicious clam chowder.

Whichever stooge brought the food always left the room afterwards. He didn't know why, but the privacy allowed him to break off a tiny piece of stone from the jagged walls every other meal. The rocks were uneven and very brittle, so it wasn't hard to snap a tiny fragment off as he walked around the room to give his legs some exercise.

The collection of small stones in the far corner had grown to nineteen pieces. Almost three weeks. It felt like three years, but when he rubbed what he could legitimately call a beard, it confirmed the guess. A few years ago, he'd gone to Jamaica with his best friend for a couple weeks. Neither of them shaved the entire trip and his facial hair's length was close enough to tell him three weeks was about right.

He walked through the information in his mind, gently whispering to himself to keep focused. *I was kidnapped on Abigail's birthday, May 6th. It was a Thursday. The photo's label just said "Monday" as opposed to a specific date, so the picture was taken less than a week ago. If my nineteen stones are right, the picture was taken the Monday before the third week, which would be the 24th. But it didn't say "Yesterday" either, so today had to be the 26th give or take.*

While the timeline was fuzzy, one thing was very clear after seeing the picture. It wasn't in the plan for him to get out alive. No matter what happened to Abigail or Dad or anyone else, they had no intention of letting him leave breathing. His previously hesitant conscience now told him something different:

If you do nothing, you will die.

That's what he needed. A long shot plan was better than none. A few days ago he was momentarily encouraged when the leader asked him about the rendezvous point with Dad if the cell phone networks went down, but that felt like decades ago and nothing happened since. But now…desperation replaced hope. He didn't have a choice. His time was running out.

Curly was the target.

He instructed himself. No matter what, when that door opened, if Curly walked through it alone, this was happening. Regardless of any apprehension he felt, no matter how scared he got, he had to do it. And do it now.

The locking mechanism cranked open and, lo and behold, Curly entered alone. Knowing the door could only be opened from the other side, the sound of Curly slamming it shut filled him with trepidation. And seeing Curly didn't make him feel grateful. Rather, it felt like God was calling his bluff. Dread instantly consumed him. He couldn't breathe.

Then he thought of the picture…

Just as Curly approached, he swung the tray upward as he sprang from the chair, striking Curly across the right side of the face. When Curly swore and instinctively moved both hands to his face, he kicked Curly's testicles as hard as he could with his left leg. Curly did what any man would do, instantly dropping to his knees in agony. Both hands over his nuts, exposing his face. Joe revved up and swung his dominant right leg directly under Curly's chin, landing solid contact beneath the jaw and sending Curly tumbling. Curly lay on his back, still, eyes closed.

He had *seconds*.

He reached into Curly's back pocket, where he'd seen the stooge put his phone time and time again but still feared it wouldn't be. When he felt the bulge, he let out his first sigh of relief. Next came his concern that the phone would have a Passcode, but thankfully Curly's did not. He sighed again and quickly did what little he could.

When it was over, the rage was gone and only fear remained. Curly still unconscious, he scooted away from the stooge on his bottom, across the dirty floor towards the corner of the room. Tears started pouring out seconds before he heard the door unlatch.

This was it. He was exposed and helpless. From Moe's perspective, he was already insubordinate and unhelpful; now he was violent too. There was nothing left to do except wait for the vicious beating he was sure to receive. Then meet death. Moe would barge through the door and beat and kill him on the spot. All for the tiniest sliver of hope that felt pretty damn hopeless.

65

Thursday, May 27

"Where the hell did you get this?"

Ben didn't respond to the whispered question and Tom's eyes turned to saucers, indicative of the fact they were looking at one of the most confidential documents the United States had to offer. It was a little after two a.m. the Thursday before Memorial Day, and Bill and Genie were snoozing on the couch under blankets. David was still at the desk, ghostlike, surrounded by a tree's worth of paper and seven empty Red Bull cans, the printer still running.

"This information comprises the President's Daily Brief..." Tom's voice trailed off.

"Some of it," he whispered.

"How did David get this?"

"It's not a single document from a single source. It's a scattering of several reports that may or may not end up in the PDB."

"I don't care if it's the beer-soaked corner of a bar napkin," Tom replied. "We're talking about the President of the United States' Daily Brief. How the hell did David get this stuff?"

"Are you worried it's not accurate?"

"That's the farthest thing from my mind right now."

"The PDB is a group effort. The Director of National Intelligence owns it, but he collaborates with The Defense Intelligence Agency, NSA, FBI and -"

Tom put his hand up in interruption. "Let me guess. The CIA."

"That's right. In fact, if anything, it's the biggest contributor."

"What makes you say that?"

"The PDB contains the latest intelligence updates on CIA missions around the globe. Current information from agents, updates from the field, confidential codes, the works. It's meant to paint a very candid picture at a specific point in time of things in constant motion."

"Hence the need for a daily update."

"Correct. And most of those pictures have the CIA's brushstrokes on them."

"So you're saying David got this from Susan?"

"Not exactly."

"I'm not getting any younger here, Grasshopper."

"Susan provided David access to several confidential databases. He could piece a lot of this together if he read every single one of them cover-to-cover. In fact, I need to be able to prove he could."

"But?"

"But there's nothing in the files about the president's schedule, and there's way too much information for one person to sift through. You could read at the speed of light 24/7 for a year and still not make a dent in it. If you don't know exactly what you're looking for and where to find it, the odds of pulling this information together would be close to impossible."

"Why do you need to be able to prove there's a slight chance? To cover your ass?"

"To cover David's."

"So if he didn't get it from the databases, where'd he get it?"

"He got some of it from there."

"And the rest?"

Ben didn't answer, and Tom stared back, biting his cheek in stern disapproval. He understood Tom's frustration. Unspoken communication had been both friend and foe in their relationship the past twenty years, but Tom knew he was being kept in the dark. Tom knew Ben was doing it to protect him, but that didn't mean he liked it.

"That's why you need to prove it could come from the databases," Tom slowly nodded. "Not to cover David, but to keep the spotlight off your other source."

"Let's not go there."

"You can't even tell me?"

"It would incriminate you."

"I'm pretty sure we're past that point."

"You might be right. But if I told you how I got this, in a court of law they could prove you had all the pieces of the puzzle before Memorial Day. I can't let that happen."

"You honestly think that makes a hootenanny's worth of difference now?"

"Tom," he put his hand on his mentor's shoulder. "When this is over, they're going to hold someone accountable. And that person will go down. Hard. So let me be clear. I'm the only one who can know everything, including all the sources."

"You already said Xerox was having a hard time with this part."

"Please Tom," he said, before mouthing, "drop it." Tom stared back and he replied, "It's the only way, and you know it."

"You're really prepared to do this, aren't you?" Tom asked, wide-eyed.

"I already lost Anna. I'm not losing Joe."

"Ben," Tom shook his head and sighed, looking at the whiteboard. "I'm with you one hundred percent, but I've got to know everything."

"My offer still stands. Any time you want out, just say the word."

"What does David know?"

"Pretty much everything except the other sources. I steered him in certain directions once he got access to the databases, then filled in some of the gaps. He took it from there. He's even sharper than I thought."

"Is he committing a felony?"

"He knows enough to be dangerous but not enough to be convicted. There's enough plausible doubt."

"And coercion."

"That's been the plan all along."

"Duress by threats isn't surefire. You realize that, right?" Tom smacked his lips. "You could be setting the kid up for decades in the can."

"It worked before. I'll make sure it works again."

"How?"

"By leaving enough proof behind to make it clear it wasn't his choice."

"He left the office and got in the truck all by himself."

"He wouldn't have even answered the phone if he knew where this was headed. I had Xerox send a few pre-dated e-mails to his personal account with pictures of his fiancé walking home from work. The wording in the message is more than suggestive. If David didn't do what I asked, her life was at risk."

Tom exhaled a massive amount of air through his nearly closed lips, creating a loud blowing sound through the small hole.

"You can't protect everyone, Grasshopper."

"Someone has to."

"How noble do you think Susan is going to think you are when you point the finger at her after it's all said and done?"

"I'm not pointing any fingers."

Tom held up both hands in protest. "She granted David access to the databases you're going to suggest hold the roadmap to assassinating the president. At your request, while you were wanted for Knoble's murder. How is that not finger-pointing?"

"By making her the only person who can bring me down."

"Immunity?" Tom shook his head and laughed. "You think they'll grant immunity to a conspirator to the president's assassination?"

"To be able to conclusively prove I acted alone? In a heartbeat they will."

"I'm not so sure about that."

"Susan doesn't even know the databases have all this information, and that'll be apparent in the investigation. As will the fact she had evidence I didn't kill Bill. Once they rule out intent and consider her background, they'll let her off with a silent slap on the wrist if she can give them a way to tell the world I acted alone. What they'll want is to shut the case as soon as it's opened. Nobody wants another JFK conspiracy. She'll have to retire. That's it."

"What do you means she doesn't know what's in the databases?"

"Remember, Tom, these documents are revised every single day with inputs from hundreds of people around the globe. There's far too much information for one person to know it all."

"That's why they're confidential, Grasshopper."

"More than thirty people in the White House get their hands on the final draft of the PDB before it's dropped on the president's desk. It's not out of the question she wouldn't know all the specifics."

"No wonder you were so insistent Susan not find out what the terrorists want." Tom aggressively shook while saying, "I can't believe what I'm hearing. These pages detail the president's Memorial Day schedule, and you're acting like it's okay because there are other words around it."

"It's subject to change at any minute."

"It's the *President's* schedule!" Tom flailed his arms.

"Even the public knows that presidents visit Arlington on Memorial Day."

"Sure, for a few minutes. But this shows the details. What time, what transportation route, what happens before, after, everything. Even having this is against the law. And you think you're protecting me by not telling me where you got it?

"Like I said, any time you want out, just say the word."

"Grasshopper, take a breath for a second and -"

Just then, Tom's phone beeped. Ben was thankful for the interruption…until Tom looked down to check the message. When he did, his jaw hung open. His eyes didn't blink.

"What is it?"

"Grasshopper," he turned the phone.

Chocolate malt

"Oh my God."

"Is this what I think it is?"

"Yes," Ben answered. "Get a pinpoint on the source," he sprang from the chair.

"I'll get it to Xerox right away."

"Tell him to use Braun's phone for the security. I need a location."

"I'm on it."

"Third degree, Tom. We won't get another shot."

"I hear you Grassho—"

Ben cut him off and shouted, "Find it, Tom."

"Where are you going?" Tom asked as Ben exited the room. Fearing the worst, Tom stared at the two-word text and prayed for favor.

He knew he wouldn't see Ben until after Memorial Day.

66

His third thinking tool of the day clarified the necessary next steps.

Rausch may have been a good soldier, but on the outside he'd proven unreliable and careless. More of a liability than an asset. The man's poor taste in hiring Clay Braun already jeopardized the mission, and Arminius wasn't about to ask Agricola for more support. Getting the assistant in Susan Reynolds's office was enough. He let the Kodiak Ice smolder in his lips while Rausch finished relaying the unfortunate news over the phone.

"He was just sitting in the corner, crying?" Arminius asked when the recap was complete.

"Yes, sir."

"Why take such a big risk to sit in a corner?"

"He said he was trying to escape."

"But the door can't be opened from the inside?"

"No sir."

"And it was latched?"

"Yes, sir. No way to get out."

"Doesn't make sense," he replied suspiciously. "This is Siebert's boy. He's smarter than that. There's something else."

"He was crying like a baby and—"

"You should've installed cameras. Nothing is missing from the room?"

"There's nothing even in the room, aside from a tray of food."

"And your goon?"

"He's okay."

"I don't care about his well-being. Is anything missing from his person?"

315

"Such as what, sir?"

"How should I know?" he hollered, shaking his head and looking up at the ceiling. "His wallet, his Moron's Incorporated gold membership card, his lucky charm, whatever!"

"No sir. Nothing is missing."

"I can't believe they didn't bind the boy's hands."

"Sir, he's in an enclosed room with a deadbolt and—"

"What kind of idiot gets manhandled by a boy? Even Siebert's boy. I knew I should've chosen your team myself. Did he at least follow the rules and leave his phone outside?"

"Yes sir," the response came, a hair too quick.

"He needs to be eliminated."

There was no response.

"Don't question my orders, Rausch. You've never had the authority to do so, and you sure as hell don't now."

"Of course not, sir."

"Do you have any comprehension how embarrassing this is?"

"I'm sorry, sir."

No, you don't have a clue. And you're not as sorry as you will be.

"Nothing has been lost, sir. The boy is still under control, still in the same place he was before it happened."

You're not talking your way out of this.

"Has he revealed anything?"

"About Mr. Smith? No sir. Quiet as a mouse. We even showed him the pictures of his girlfriend's house as you suggested. Still said he doesn't know anything. At this point, I tend to believe him."

"And I tend to believe you haven't properly motivated him."

"I know you want to make absolute certain, Arminius…"

"But?"

"But even you said, when we first spoke that Smith, that it was a long shot. That the boy probably didn't know anything."

"Your point?"

"The boy has endured quite a bit of pain, and his story hasn't changed. Maybe you were right all along. Maybe there's nothing to get."

There was no need to tell Rausch the arson wasn't his doing. It had to be Siebert's — another clever move by the former Marine — intended to keep the Merriweather family out of Illinois even longer. He thought if the boy saw the house in flames, he might open up in his helplessness. Turns out that even with adopted children, the apple doesn't fall far from the tree.

"Eliminate your goon. Immediately. Discussion over. I won't have his carelessness as a liability to the operation any longer."

This conversation confirmed it: his history with Rausch wasn't enough to change his mind. He wouldn't tolerate incompetence. Not from the idiot Siebert's boy knocked unconscious, and not from Rausch himself. When Siebert fulfilled his mission on Memorial Day, all liabilities would be removed.

"It will be done," Rausch said.

"Do it in front of the boy. Leave the body in the room."

"Sir?"

"Make him watch. Let him witness death and smell its rotting flesh. Remind him both are in his future unless he starts talking."

"Will do, Arminius."

"Between now and mission completion, we are to have minimal communication."

"Sir?"

"The end is near, my friend. Per our plan all along, we need to be overcautious. In case Siebert has any tricks up his sleeve, we must limit our exposure from here on out."

My exposure.

"Yes, sir," Rausch dutifully replied.

"Call if you must. Otherwise, you know what you need to do. I'm trusting you'll do it."

"I won't let you down."

"We'll rendezvous on Tuesday as planned. Same time, same place. But in a much stronger nation. Don't be late." He had Rausch right where he wanted him.

"Ten four."

"One more thing. You mustn't leave the room anymore until the mission is complete. I need to know there won't be any more surprises, and you're the only one I trust. The responsibility is yours."

Arminius hung up the phone and reconsidered the situation. The minor setback with the boy aside, the plan was indeed still on track. That was paramount. He'd update Agricola on that and omit the rest.

With regards to Rausch, he thought of his favorite line from his favorite movie, *The Godfather Part II*. It echoed in his mind and soothed him like a nursery rhyme does a baby:

Keep your friends close, but your enemies closer.

67

Friday, May 28

I want to build a future with you.

Ben's words reverberated in Nikki's mind like strings on a guitar, a soothing and welcoming melody for her brain. She'd been sitting on the park bench for over an hour, replaying them over and over, an ear-to-ear grin across her face. She pictured Ben through the car window at O'Hare, exactly two weeks ago tonight, and decided to finally stop pretending.

It was same bench she used to sit on to think, to lose herself in KenKen puzzles and crosswords. Cozily nestled in the southern tip of Navy Pier, it was her lonely yet secure refuge from the world. It felt like it'd been built just for her, right down to the expanded metal mesh backrest. It'd been perfect for a confused middle-aged woman trying to find herself after life's curve balls made her feel like a perpetual strikeout. And until Ben Siebert entered her life, it was the only comfort she had.

A little after eight o'clock, it was a perfect Friday night in May. Such weather in Chicago was ephemeral — wedged between brutal winters and muggy summers — so she made the most of it, delighting in her very own super-secret squirrel bench, a rare corner of privacy in a big city. Admiring a clear view of Lake Michigan to the east and the magnificent skyline to the west, she sat amongst the greenery mesmerized by the sky's chandelier of stars.

She thought back to college — and simpler times — twenty-some years ago. She'd gone about her days convinced there was no gray in a simple black and white world. She was ignorant, uncultured and lacked perspective. She was also blissfully happy.

Then she lost her fiancé to cheating, her parents to 9/11 and almost her life to stupidity. She still dreamed about the day she stopped feeling sorry for herself. That was her last pillar day, the term she coined years ago to signify an important foundational time in her life.

Twelve years later, she was right back where she started: alone, brokenhearted, and diffident. Her relationships were shattered and her career unstable. She needed a new pillar day. And she decided she was going to make it happen, rather than wait for it. It was time to turn things around and get her life back in order. It happened once and, by God, it was going to happen again.

Today.

She would run to Ben. Run to her man. With renewed confidence and vigor, she sprung from her bench and its view of the relatively new Centennial Wheel, which replaced the city's iconic 148-foot Ferris wheel. She darted past the Wave Wall and its steel louvers that transformed into curved, wooden steps. She quickened her pace, reaffirming her decision along the way.

Ben told her to stay away from him. Robert told her to stay away. Susan told her to stay away. Tom told her to stay away. Even her own brain told her to stay away.

But her heart had other plans.

She loved him — no matter what he did or didn't do — she loved Ben Siebert. And she was going to get her man back.

A huge smile broke out across her face as she ran west towards Lake Shore Drive. When she saw a family walking out of Jimmy Buffet's Margaritaville, it reminded her of the last conversation they had before she foolishly broke up with him. He was right then…there were lots of kids in the world that needed good homes and good parents. And he was right now…there still are. She wasn't too old to be a mom. Fear of failure wasn't an excuse to run away from her dream. She'd have a partner to help her through the tough days. Someone to hold her hand and travel the world with. To be there forever, and never make her worry otherwise.

Life was short. It was time to stop fearing loss and start seeking gain.

She bubbled with excitement. She could've kept running — the train station was only a few miles away — but she wanted to get to Ben as soon as possible. She felt like a kid again. Giddy. Unbridled. She cut north to Grand Avenue and, lo and behold, a taxi was sitting there all by its lonesome. As if it was waiting just for her on her special night. The stars were aligning to get her to her man. This was happening.

Today is your pillar day.

She climbed in euphoric, unwilling to let her brain interrupt. "Ogilvie, please," she said to the middle-aged driver in a White Sox hat, who clicked on the meter.

She was surprised he didn't take Wacker but didn't think much of it. Then he turned south onto Franklin Street. Binny's was on the left and a vacant parking lot was on the right, next to the Assumption Catholic Church. The brown line's tracks rattled as the CTA train passed over them. And by the time the car came to a complete stop, the driver had already turned around and pointed the silenced nine millimeter at her.

The first shot was so shocking it didn't seem real at first. The stomach pain that followed told her it was no dream. The second struck her just above the heart. Too stunned to speak, she quietly covered her chest with both blood-soaked hands. Despite the urge, she didn't look up. She didn't want her killer to be the last thing her eyes saw.

Instead, she saw Ben and a two-year-old girl with pigtails. All three of them were walking on a quiet neighborhood street amongst falling autumn leaves. She and the little girl wore matching yellow sundresses. Ben was in tan slacks and a light blue button down, sleeves rolled up to combat the early fall heat that still hung in the air. Everyone was laughing as Mommy and Daddy lifted up their little girl by the arms and swung her in the air between them, her giggling warming both their hearts.

The little girl's smile was all she needed to know that heaven was real.

68

The pounding on her front door yanked Susan from fitful rest on a stormy night the way a bungee jumper gets jerked back when the cord goes taut. Her heart was thumping through her chest, and she widened her eyes to force her pupils into action. She cursed under her breath after checking the clock on her nightstand and seeing 2:41 a.m.

Tiptoeing out of bed to let Phil continue the snore-laden rest she so envied, she grabbed her robe and hustled to the foyer. Through the peephole she saw Robert Stevens, standing on her front porch in front of the pouring rain. He wore blue jeans and gym shoes with an untucked green golf shirt that was soaking wet. Tears were in his eyes.

"Robert, do you know what time it is?" she gave into her frustration, certain a phone call would've sufficed.

"It's Nikki..." Robert choked out. She waited for more words, but none came.

"What about her?" she fearfully asked.

"She's...she's dead, Susan."

A wave of emotions began to flood her heart like a river through a busted damn. Shock, confusion, and sadness led the rush. Her mouth hung open as Robert sobbed loudly on her doorstep, his head down and head buried in both hands.

"What? How?"

"Shot," he answered through his sobs. "Her body was in an alley in Logan Square."

Before she could respond, Robert yelled so loud she worried he might wake the neighbors.

"I knew she was in danger!" Robert cried, stepping backwards and then forwards, his arms shaking. "I knew it...and I didn't stop it!" Just then a clamor of thunder hurled itself towards the house and she jumped. Robert didn't flinch, his head still aimed straight down; almost as if he was encouraging God to strike him down right there on her porch.

"Robert, come inside."

"It's my fault, Susan. All of it. I'm the reason she's not with us anymore."

"Robert, stop that. You didn't—"

"I'm done, Susan. I'm done with this shit, and I'm done with these people. She's the last person I'll let down."

Susan crossed her arms and offered a sympathetic frown that Robert didn't see. Then she stepped towards him, but he shot up his hand and took a huge step back. He kept retreating, looking at her as he did, until he was no longer under the roof. The heavy rain danced on his balding head and dripped down his cheeks, mixing with the tears.

"Robert, please come inside."

"I'm leaving. I just wanted you to hear it from me. I'm sorry I didn't listen to you, Susan. I'll never forgive myself."

Robert turned around and plodded towards his car, hunched over in visible depression. When he finally got there, dripping from head to toe, he didn't look back before getting in and backing out of the driveway.

She remained still, remembering that Robert had moved from Arizona in part because of Nikki. Thinking of Nikki and her visit earlier in the week, the troubled young lady's face implanted itself in her mind's eye. Her knees buckled as she thought of the tragic loss of life. And the fact she worried Robert might take his own.

69

Ben sat in the basement's janitorial closet next to the boiler, unbeknownst to the building's staff or anyone else in the world. The tiny space he'd converted to an artillery asylum was cramped, hot and suffocating. He preferred it that way. He was certain Joe was in an even harsher environment, and the discomfort helped him relate to his boy.

Surrounded by over twenty guns alongside several knives, grenades and other various weapons, he was as prepared as he could be but had nowhere to go. He felt like a hunter with no prey, a pilot with no flight plan, a captain with no compass. But above all, he was a very worried father. He clutched the M240 machine gun and closed his eyes, trying not to picture his son getting tortured, or worse. In the military, he always hated it when the missions came down to the waiting stage. The ones where the prep, planning and setup were complete but he was still at the mercy of others, awaiting the right timing or go ahead. That was brutal; this was much worse.

When his cell phone finally vibrated at 3:49 a.m. he tried not to get his hopes up.

"Tell me you got it."

"Got it, Grasshopper. Texting it as we speak."

"For real?"

"Braun's cell phone helped Xerox decipher the Silent Circle source code; he took it from there. Don't ask me how, but he did it."

Still holding his breath, Ben whispered, "That encryption software is top of the line. I was worried I didn't get enough from Braun…"

"You got what was necessary. There was nothing else to get from that slime, Grasshopper. If Braun had any songs to sing, he would've turned into a canary the second he saw the knife."

"Were you able to learn anything else?" he asked before wiping his sweaty forehead again.

"No dice. I'm surprised we got what we got."

"I can't tell you how much I appreciate this, Tom."

"Ben…" Tom's voice softened. "There's something else."

"What is it?"

Tom didn't answer. Ordinarily he would've paid much more attention to the uncharacteristic silence, but he was already looking for the text and reaching into his jam-packed duffle bag.

"Nothing, Grasshopper."

"Tom…?"

"We'll talk later. You stay focused right now." Tom's face was deadpan.

"I can handle it. What are you not telling me?"

"It can wait, Ben. Focus on what you're doing. The place is bound to be crawling with hazards you don't know about and won't be able to see. You've done zero prep work, and you're walking into a ton of unknowns."

"Every minute I spend prepping is another sixty seconds Joe could die."

"I understand that. But if you die trying to fulfill this mission because you were unprepared, you'll be guaranteeing it. They don't have any use for him without you."

"I'm not sitting around strategizing while they torture my son."

"All I'm saying is this is very risky. Doing it this way, going in so cold. And alone. You sure you don't want me to come along?"

"I appreciate the offer. But you've got to stay on Bill and David. Not for long, one way or the other, but we can't take any risks until it's over."

"You mean any *more* risks."

He didn't respond.

"When you get there," Tom continued, "you call me if anything necessitates a change to the plan."

"I'm not aborting this mission."

"Ten four. But remember, the ability to adapt is what separates the men from the boys. Don't turn this into a suicide mission to save a few hours of planning."

"Thanks for everything, Tom."

Tom released another long sigh that Ben knew wasn't premeditated. Something wasn't right. And it wasn't the emotion of the situation, or the risk of the mission. They'd been on too many life-threatening operations together for Ben to believe that. Something else was off with his mentor. Something different, something deeper. But Tom was usually spot-on when it came to timing, and he was right — the mission was very risky. He did need to focus. And if Tom thought it best to put off, he was probably right about that too.

"You be careful out there, Grasshopper."

"Will do. Remember the plan. Anything happens to me, you know what to do."

"Roger.

"Out."

70

Joe lay spread-eagle on the grimy, wet floor; both eyes bruised shut, left leg broken in two places. Hours earlier, the bandage had been so brutally yanked off his hand with a vise-grip that it still throbbed. Particles of salt remained stuck to his bloody skin, remnants of the handfuls they'd pressed into his re-exposed wounds. He kept his left arm as extended as he could, for it was now handcuffed to a headless corpse.

The three of them, the leader and the other two stooges, had marched a sobbing Curly — handcuffed behind his back, mask removed — into the room solemnly. Curly's face was bloated and both sides were covered with acne and tears. No facial hair. Short buzz cut. And it didn't take long to learn why Curly's mask had been removed. While Moe and Larry held Joe down, the leader brought Curly to his knees with a powerful kick, then held the double barrel shotgun inches from the back of Curly's head. Joe stared into Curly's almost pitiful face for a few seconds before the leader pulled the trigger. The bulbous head disappeared in an instant, and he was suddenly covered with chunks of brain and blood. The river of red formed immediately and made its way to him in less than a minute. He felt a large pool collect around him, his already-filthy clothes now soaking wet as well.

He had no idea if they knew about the text. He sent it and deleted it…and no one mentioned anything…but at this point he didn't care. What did it matter? Abigail was dead, Dad was probably dead, Tom was probably dead, and he just wanted it to be over. After the beatings and the threats and the yelling and the killing, he just wanted to die. He wanted to close his eyes and never wake up, to reunite with Mom and Abigail in Heaven and have no memory of this Hell.

Through all his pain and in all his helplessness, only one thing still haunted him. Everything else he'd submitted to the raw nakedness of the situation, the harsh cruelty of the world he was certain he'd soon depart. But one unanswered question lingered in his mind, alongside his unwillingness to answer it:

Was this really...Dad's fault?

He closed his eyes against the horrible notion, knowing he'd never find out and would soon be awakened to more pain and death. But the drugs must've been making him hallucinate, because he stirred to a loud pop and then what he thought were screams. They sounded like loud shouts; howls of what he could only guess was excruciating pain. He didn't move a muscle. He didn't look up, shift his arms, or try to reach for anything. Nothing. He was imagining things. In reality, he was a goner, handcuffed to a large pile of smelly death rotting inches away, knowing he'd be there soon himself. It was utterly helpless, no matter what he thought he heard.

The cries stopped, as he knew they would. Eyes still shut, he listened for footsteps or any other sound. But it went from raucous to silent. *There, proof.* He was dreaming, hallucinating, imagining, whatever. He probably still was. He just lay there, waiting for his own screams, which would be very real.

Then he heard the latch.

Against all physical will, he forced his blackened eyes open and turned his neck towards the door. The tall figure walked in holding a large gun in each hand, dressed in black from head-to-toe. But the outfit was different from what the stooges wore. It was tighter to the skin and full of pockets, all around the torso and down each leg. There was a black mask covering the mouth and nose, and it sat underneath a hard black helmet with goggles attached. When the figure moved the goggles aside, the revealed blue eyes looked oddly familiar. His vision was far from clear, but he could've sworn it was Dad, staring at him lying on the floor. Not a word was said. Shortly after he thought he saw those blue eyes, the figure faded into the darkness that overtook him.

71

"Deadline" had taken on a whole new meaning to everyone in the room.

Despite his initial doubts, Bill Knoble couldn't deny that he'd come to respect David Keene over the past week-and-a-half. Aside from the brief conversations David had with his fiancé each day, closely supervised by Tom Fedorak, the reporter had done nothing but put his head down and work. The results showed. Equally impressive was the way the go-getter had convinced Tom it would arouse suspicion for him *not* to touch base with his fiancé while on a two-week business trip. Ben was right: David was intelligent, persistent and adaptable.

And at the moment, very pissed.

"I get that," David said. "But it's ten in the morning...we've known for four hours that Ben's son is safe. Why the hell are we still here?"

It was clear David was more than a little stir crazy, and he could tell Genie felt the same. But in stark contrast to David — who paced the room flailing his arms like a shipwrecked passenger stuck on a desert island — she sat calmly under a blanket, cradling a cup of apple cinnamon tea to counter the brisk sixty-six-degree temperature David preferred. Keeping quiet for the most part but certainly not aloof, she showed particular interest in David's latest round of blunt outbursts objecting to why it wasn't all over. It was interesting to watch. It was as though David was reading Genie's mind and speaking for both of them.

"Memorial Day isn't moving, David," Bill replied.

"That's not my point. Ben's son is safe. They can't exactly kill him now if Ben doesn't go through with the assassination. There's nothing they can do anymore."

"Think about that for a minute."

David glared at him in response. He could almost feel the reporter's beams of anger and frustration crashing into his body. His breathing was loud, wheezing in exasperation.

"I understand your frustration. But these people, this guy Arminius…he'll find another way to get what he wants. He obviously doesn't use carrots, so he'll grab another stick and it'll be rinse and repeat at some point in the future."

"What does that have to do with us?"

"Maybe nothing. For you specifically, most certainly nothing. Unless of course he finds out you're involved. But is that all you're concerned about? Getting yourself out of this mess?"

"We spent the past ten days trying to figure out where the President is going to be so Ben can kill him. Just saying it, I feel like a wack job. But outside the absurdity of that statement alone…now, thanks to last night's rescue we don't have to anymore. We shouldn't be trying to figure out who these guys are."

"David, you tell me. What should we be doing?" he asked calmly.

"Are you kidding me? We should be destroying every piece of paper in this Godforsaken room and praying it never turns up again. We should walk away and hope to never see each other for the rest of our lives. And we should notify the feds…you know, the people who are *supposed* to be finding these people, and stay the hell out of it. Yet for some reason, not a single sheet of paper has been shredded and we're still here!"

"Arminius has been a step ahead of the feds from the get-go. You have to assume he's got a contingency. It might stall things for a bit, but walking away is only going to bring more death into the world," he replied, holding up the pre-released Sunday newspaper.

The article was a half-page long with no pictures. Entitled "Sad Times At The FBI," it summarized the unplanned and unfortunate departures of two prominent members of the FBI, both on one tragic early Saturday morning. Special Agent Nicole "Nikki" Benton, forty-two, ten-year veteran of the FBI, was tragically killed in what appeared to be a mugging gone awry. Her body was found in an alley outside Logan Square at approximately 12:30 a.m. There was no indication why the cyber crime specialist was more than ten miles from her Chicago apartment. The autopsy would be performed over the weekend, but the gunshot wounds to the stomach and chest left little ambiguity regarding cause of death. The patrolman who found her body was quoted as saying, "the victim's missing purse, her torn shirt and the position of her body suggest a struggle consistent with attempted robbery, but an investigation needs to be conducted." No sexual assault was suspected. But suffice it to say, the morning of Saturday, May 29th was a truly devastating one for the FBI.

Then, the article continued, "insult was added to injury" when, upon hearing the news of Benton's death, fifty-six-year old veteran and recently appointed Special Agent in Charge (SAIC) Robert Stevens tendered his resignation after more than thirty years of service. The article concluded that Stevens's replacement, as well as more details surrounding the circumstances of Special Agent Benton's death, would be released as soon as possible.

"Mr. Knoble?" Genie whispered.

"Yes, Genie."

"Have you talked to Mr. Siebert?"

"Not since Tom told him the news."

"Is he going to be…okay?"

He wished he could say yes without hesitation, but the truth was Bill had no idea. Tom held off on breaking the news to Ben until his son's rescue was complete, which was a good move. Ben called a little after six to confirm Joe was safe and in a secure location, receiving the medical care he needed. Tom didn't elaborate, but it was clear the poor kid had been through a horrendous ordeal and suffered extensive physical trauma.

But still, Joe was alive, which should've put Ben in a positive state. Ben returned around seven-thirty, and Tom pulled him aside within minutes of his arrival. He remembered the sick feeling in his stomach as he watched the two of them walk towards the corner of the room. Tom's cocky demeanor had vanished, replaced with an inconspicuous yet clear trepidation. There was no smiling. There were no jokes. He couldn't hear Tom's whispers, nor did he want to.

He expected Ben to go on a rampage — screaming, punching walls, smashing computers, that sort of thing. He recalled Ben telling him once that his reaction to his wife's death years ago was a dangerous combination of alcoholism and anger. Which, when combined with Ben's fierce intensity and determination, made rage a logical assumption for Ben's immediate reaction.

Instead, the former Marine remained silent. Eerily silent. He looked down at the floor, solemn, then back up at Tom briefly before disappearing through the door without saying a word. Best Bill could tell, no questions were asked, no clarifications requested. There was just ghostly silence, followed by vanishment.

That was fifteen hours ago. No one had heard from Ben since.

"I honestly can't say, Genie. I know he loved her very much."

"That guy is gonna bring down the China wall," David replied. "He's a one-man wrecking crew now."

"Let's not concern ourselves with things that don't concern themselves with us."

"This concerns us," David shot back. "What is he gonna do if we can't find these people?"

"Thank you for proving my point."

"What point is that, Bill?" David's eyes narrowed, frustration oozing out of his skin like alcohol the night after a binge.

"The President needs us, whether he knows it or not."

"What's that supposed to mean?" Genie asked. Her watery eyes and sad face were filled with confusion and disappointment.

"Don't you two get it? Arminius will just find the next target. We don't know who it'll be, but we do know things will be right back to where they are now. Except more death will have occurred you won't be able to deny is in part on our hands."

David replied, "On our hands my ass."

"If you can pretend otherwise, go right ahead. Whatever helps you sleep at night, kid. But the fact is if we don't carry out Arminius's request, more people are going to die. And then either we or someone else will have the same ultimatum again down the road. You want to live with that?"

"I sure as hell prefer it to Ben killing the president!"

"I couldn't agree more. Which is precisely why we need to figure out who the hell these people are," he snapped, holding up the pocket reader.

The advanced prototype mobile biometric device he held came from Crossmatch, a company he'd never heard of. Connected via USB to an iPhone, it was roughly the size of a small radar detector. Its blue landing lights and thin design reminded him of the ancient palm pilots, but the technology itself was night and day.

Ben had delivered it with four index fingerprints preloaded in its database, labeled A, B, C and D. Tom instructed David to use the CIA databases to try to match four corresponding names to the prints. The technology was slick, transferring the image from the device to the phone and then to the computer to access the files.

Tom had also told him — unbeknownst to Genie and David — that Ben had three sets of molars in case the fingerprints didn't suffice. The teeth were already at a lab for analysis. Bill wasn't sure why Tom shared all of that with him, and he definitely didn't want to know why there wasn't a fourth set. Fortunately, the fingerprints worked. David navigated the system well and they got four names. Now it was a matter of using those names and the cell phones to try to find out what they really needed to know, who Arminius was. That objective, unfortunately, proved far more challenging than he'd expected.

"We need to crosscheck military records, personal histories and anything else we can get our hands on."

"We've been doing that," David yelled.

"And the Hubley Case. Ben still thinks this has something to do with it."

"You think we don't know that?" David's tantrum ramped up like a toddler's. Bill was sure stomping would follow.

"We have limited time, David. So why are you complaining instead of working?"

"Mr. Knoble," Genie said from the couch. "If we can't find...I mean if we aren't able to..."

"Spit it out, Genie."

"Do you really think Mr. Siebert will do it?"

"I think Ben Siebert is capable of just about anything right now."

"So he's really flying to DC tomorrow?"

"As far as I know."

"Killing the president is what Arminius wants," David said. "Why on earth would he do that?"

"The quick answer I've already told you, to save lives in the long run. This problem isn't going away."

"And the long answer?" Genie asked.

"The long answer is that David's question is a very logical one for what I'm afraid might not be a logical situation."

Just then Tom Fedorak reentered the room, holding a 64-ounce plastic cup and brown lunch bag, its bottom soaked with what he guessed was grease.

"I picked up some hot dogs. It's gonna be a long night."
Everyone went back to work.

72

Sunday, May 30

Xerox was an honorary title, a sort of unofficial military call sign given to him despite the fact his less than 20/20 vision precluded him from flying jets two decades ago. The irony was that that fact, while devastating at the time, turned out to be a blessing in disguise. Had he not been told flying was out of the question, he wouldn't have enrolled in Computer Science at the United States Air Force Academy. If that hadn't happened, he wouldn't have joined the computer programming team, where he met Brandi and got the job that changed his life. He didn't know it then, but being told his dream of flying jets would never happen was the first step of a long, winding staircase that ended at his destiny.

He'd been stuck in the same second-story office for the better part of two weeks. On the clear-sky days, the office's freshly cleaned floor-to-ceiling windows offered an impeccable view of Pike's Peak, and allowed sunlight to stream in warmth onto his pale face. He closed his eyes against the harsh blue light of the four computer screens in front of him — which had been on since he arrived — and imagined he was on a catamaran in the South Pacific. He opened his eyes briefly to watch the wind playfully wrestle with the needles of the evergreens outside, then squeeze them shut and pretend he could feel that same breeze as he sailed on indigo waters.

He opened his eyes with reluctance and checked the phone again. Nothing.

He did everything he could, and he hoped it helped. There were some clear wins: the website data and resulting images, the text message's source location ID, the comprehensive Timothy Rausch acquaintance analysis. The list was not unimpressive.

But neither was it complete. He didn't get much with the cell phones, and he couldn't get the classified information Ben requested...not without accessing government networks. He worried the defeats outweighed the successes, that overall he failed one of the only people in the world he could call a friend. Ben hadn't said as much, or even implied it, but his worrying personality assumed it to be the case. Ben's deadline was now one minute past and his three phone calls weren't returned.

So when the phone finally did start to ring, it was almost as if it was doing so because he willed it to happen.

"Ben," he answered.

"Thanks for everything you did."

"I'm sorry I couldn't get the last part."

"No need to apologize. You did more than was fair for me to ask."

Ben's voice was noticeably sober. Subdued. Gone was the confident, directive, instructing tone of a leader. In its place, a timid, soft-spoken, wounded tenor.

"Are you okay?" he asked in a soft tone to underline concern.

"I'm fine. I called for two reasons. The first is to ask a final favor."

"Anything."

"Check your e-mail."

"Now?"

"Now."

He quickly accessed Monitor Two and opened the secured message, sent just a minute earlier. There was no written content, but the attached JPEG jerked him into a state of mixed emotions he'd never felt before.

His kneejerk reaction was to smile for the first time in fifteen days. It was clearly Joe Leksa and he was clearly safe, cradled in

Tom's arms like a baby, eyes closed. Tom looked down on him the way a loving father would his own son.

But upon closer inspection, he frowned and felt tears begin to form. Joe's face was badly injured. Black and blue all over the forehead and cheeks, numerous red cuts under the eyes and on the neck, mangled nose with a white bandage over it, and noticeable bumps and bruises from one ear to the other. He now understood why the 22-year-old was sucking his thumb.

"You...you saved him. I'm so happy about that, Ben."

"I wouldn't have without you."

"Is he going to be okay...?"

"The doctor said it would take some time, and his nose might not ever look the same. But there's no physical damage that won't heal with enough medicine and rest. It's his mental state I'm worried about."

"I'm so sorry this happened."

"Xerox," Ben whispered, "I sent you the picture instead of just telling you for a reason."

"Why is that?" He asked the question that had entered his mind the moment he saw the image.

"I wanted you to see firsthand that they were going to kill him. Without your help, they would have. You saved my boy, Xerox. At eight tomorrow a deposit will be made into one of your alias accounts, but—"

He quickly interrupted, overcome with emotion. "Please don't. That's totally unnecessary after all you've done for me,"

"I'll never be able repay you. Never. But I had to tell you how thankful I am, and the picture shows why. You're the reason my son is alive today."

"I don't, I don't know what to say."

"No response necessary. I just wanted you to know before..."

An awkward silence ensued.

"Before what, Ben?"

"That's the other reason I called."

"What is it?"

"We won't talk for a while, my friend. If ever…"

"What's that supposed to mean?" he asked, panic rushing his brain and body.

"I don't have time to explain. Soon enough you'll understand. But before you do, I wanted to say good-bye. And that no matter what happens, I'm forever grateful for what you did."

"You're really freaking me out here, Ben."

"Over, friend."

He sat motionless for nearly a half-hour, his mouth open and eyes fixated on the picture of Joe. His mind desperately — and unsuccessfully — trying to figure out what Ben was about to do…

Part V

73

Memorial Day

Monday, May 31

Breakfast on Memorial Day began at six o'clock sharp. It consisted of hot coffee, three eggs over easy, shredded hash browns and sourdough toast with whipped butter. Arminius wore a pair of dark-wash blue jeans, a white polo under a blue blazer and penny loafers. He wore the same style of shoes for years. When one pair wore out, he simply ordered another. He handled his employees the same way. His neatly trimmed mustache on an otherwise clean-shaven face twitched slightly as he walked west towards the restaurant, the sun rising behind him. He felt a hint of nervousness, butterflies of jubilation on this fine national holiday.

The local diner was void of other patrons, and he sipped the heavily creamed coffee musing about what the day would bring. Starting it off with a hearty breakfast and finishing it to the recap of the president's assassination on the evening news would make it the best Memorial Day of his life.

Rausch had followed orders and ceased communication with him. He was hopeful that Siebert's son would reveal whatever he had to reveal, but the possibility the kid really didn't knowing anything felt more and more plausible. It would fit Siebert's character to withhold information about his affairs from the boy, to keep him protected if nothing else. And if there was nothing to get, he was fine by that.

Nevertheless, even that seemed inconsequential today. He'd deal with Rausch and the boy tomorrow. Ties would be cut clean, and he would be on to bigger and better things with

Agricola mapping out a new future for a new nation. Today was about watching Siebert pull off what he knew could be done. He wasn't going to let small potatoes interfere with the big picture.

Back in his home office, reclining in his leather desk chair, all six televisions were turned on to the major networks. CNN, Fox News, ABC, NBC, CSPAN and PBS gave him the best coverage a citizen could get, and he felt giddy guessing when it was going to happen. Would he actually get to see it? Would it happen live? He was recording them all just in case. He'd want to watch it over and over.

It could happen during the prelude at ten-thirty, or perhaps the wreath-laying ceremony, maybe the grand finale to the president's final speech...Or, it could be some other time altogether. En route to Arlington Cemetery, or on the return trip to the White House? Was Siebert able to get the motorcade information? Did the silent cardinal know which car the president would be in and what route would be taken? Could he find a good spot for the sniper rifle approach? There were so many possibilities. Siebert had all day, and not knowing the plan made it even more exciting to him, if that was possible.

Siebert's itinerary from yesterday had been confirmed. American Airlines flight 3397 departed O'Hare at 8:45 a.m. and landed in Washington eight minutes past noon local time. Plenty of time to get set up and prepare. He half-expected Siebert to do it yesterday, utilizing the element of surprise the day before such a formal event, but this way was better. Siebert checked into the hotel and paid with a credit card, and he assumed the former Marine took cabs and paid with cash because no rental car was on file. The bottom line was Siebert was in Washington, complying with his request. A father's love for his son knows no bounds.

He spoke with Agricola just before four to verify there had been no change in plans. Agricola didn't reveal as much excitement as he would've liked, but that was the man's style.

Analytical and cautious, Agricola always remained levelheaded until there was something to celebrate. He respected that. It showed self-control and intelligence.

After today, the slight blemish on his otherwise pristine record would be wiped clean. Agricola would forget all about Clay Braun once the president was dead.

He opened the drawer and eyed the Kodiak Ice. He didn't need a thinking tool just yet, but he craved the relaxation and morning buzz. Everything was where it should be; no more prep could be done. There was nothing to do except wait for the good news. Excitement filled the air like the pleasant aroma of a perfumed woman strolling by.

He took off his reading glasses and strongly rubbed his eyes, digging his fingers into the corners. As he did, he thought he heard something from behind. He put his glasses back on and spun the chair around, seeing the bifold closet door was cracked slightly open. He didn't recall leaving it that way, but he must've just not closed it tight. The room's door was still shut and the office empty.

Maybe it was the ceiling fan. It hummed gently above, creating just enough breeze to make it pleasant but not so much as to stir the papers that covered his desk. Satisfied the sound was nothing, he turned back to watch the six TVs and prepare to insert his morning dip.

That's when he heard the second sound.

A second too late.

Behind him and to his right, adjacent to the closet but closer to him, the unmistakable sound of a gun being cocked echoed through the room. By the time he snapped his head around he knew it was too late.

"We meet at last," the voice whispered.

74

Arminius absorbed the shock of his sneak attack without revealing any emotion whatsoever. No open mouth gasps or confused wide-eyed stares, no alarm in his eyes or trepidation in his body. The perfect poker face. Ben expected no less.

The man he was staring at — whom Xerox identified as Hector Byrd — had been trained by the best in the world: the United States military. The Army taught a young Hector Byrd how to read people and mask his emotions. The ability to manipulate the mind to maintain a psychological advantage was surely second nature to him by now. Arminius understood the human psyche in a way most therapists could only dream, and the man would never give his opponent the satisfaction of surprise.

Arminius hadn't changed much physically from the last photo of Hector Byrd that Ben had, dated six years earlier. About 6'4", slender and toned, almost a runner's body; very short black hair with salt and pepper sideburns, thick, neatly-trimmed mustache and an otherwise straight and narrow looking face. He projected the image of a good ol' boy, but his knowledge of violence was vast and his expertise unparalleled.

"Well, well, well," Arminius answered, smiling. His grin looked neither counterfeit nor contrived.

"Hi, Arminius."

"Ben Siebert...I am impressed. Your reputation precedes you indeed. You really are the silent cardinal."

"I never liked that title."

"Under different circumstances, I'd say the pleasure of meeting you is all mine."

"You'd be right about that."

"How did you find me?" Arminius asked with a minor smirk.

"Your power lay in secrecy, not autonomy. Living off the grid wouldn't permit you to run this kind of operation."

"Indeed. And yet finding me is still no small feat," Arminius forced out a chuckle, his eye keenly focused on Ben. Ben remained straight-faced, staring at his enemy...also unwilling to give him the satisfaction of a response.

"If you say so."

"So you're not even going to tell me how you found me?"

"That is irrelevant to our discussion."

"That does sound familiar."

"Once I identified Timothy Rausch as your right-hand man, there was a trail back to you. Faint, but existent."

"Ah, my trusted Major."

"Six years as an O-4 Field Officer, fifteen in the service before that. And you turned him into a criminal."

"I knew from the beginning that Major Rausch could be a problem," Arminius replied, more to himself than to Ben.

"How is that?"

"He was a fine soldier. I'd go into battle with him without thinking twice, but he was far from a stellar employee."

"If you say so."

"There's more to it than that, silent cardinal."

"Oh?"

"Major Rausch was under my employ, but he didn't know anything of true value, certainly not my whereabouts. As with Clay Braun, the pig that Rausch hired, only the truly necessary information was given to him, one piece at a time. Ignorance is the only surefire way to limit exposure."

"So that's why Rausch was so steadfast in not giving up your location, just like Braun didn't give up Rausch's. I knew it wasn't out of loyalty...Braun sang your code name 'Arminius' like a canary as soon as the molar extraction process began. But he never gave up your location, and I couldn't figure out why.

But now I see. It wasn't that he gave a damn about you, he just didn't know."

"As I said, Rausch and his hiring was a liability from the start."

"I want you to know something, Arminius," Ben said, raising his eyebrows with a touch of sternness, "With Rausch, interrogation was necessary. Something I had to do to obtain information. With you...I'm actually going to enjoy it."

"Major Rausch's phone was deactivated for potential triangulation, so while you might've been able to connect him to me, the question remains: how did you find me?"

"You'll never know."

After a few seconds, Arminius started shaking his head and offered a conspicuous smile. It turned into an outright laugh and heavy cough. Arminius covered his mouth but kept laughing loud enough for Ben to hear through the hand, looking down and then up at Ben.

"It's that damn rendezvous point, isn't it? You son of a bitch."

"If you say so."

"You asked for a picture of the boy to distract me. Made it seem like you'd accept the answer to a harmless question if it was all you could get, but that's what you really wanted all along. You even sounded panicked, desperate, which I knew was uncharacteristic but didn't think was unreasonable given the circumstances. Even for you, silent cardinal. But it was all part of a plan, wasn't it? You slippery little shit."

"It's time to talk about the future."

"That website isn't real, is it? Even the place isn't real. *Mondoman Peak*. I thought it sounded bizarre, but that's because you needed it to, isn't it? You needed something obscure, something no one would find without specifically searching for it, and it had to make me curious enough to check it out myself. You tricky bastard."

"You fell for it like an amateur."

"The website isn't real," Arminius carried on, nodding to himself more than to Ben. "It's a trap designed to reveal the location of whoever accesses it, right? You had it built long before your son disappeared, and always told him to have that answer ready just in case."

"I'm going to enjoy extracting every single piece of information there is from that smart little brain of yours," he replied straight-faced.

"But I accessed it from the library. So how did you find me here? Wait, I see…once you had the location, you could obtain pictures of people going in and then cross-reference them to me once Rausch gave you my name. You are good, silent cardinal. You were calm under pressure when you needed to be, threatening to walk away with your son's life on the line like that. You didn't flinch.

"Then you took it a step further, just to throw me off the scent, when you asked for a picture the second time *after* I'd accessed the site and answered your question. You had what you wanted already, but you needed to make sure I didn't know it. You needed me to think you wanted more. I'm impressed."

"I'm not. You've gone downhill since the Army. How does that happen?"

"I don't see it as going downhill," Arminius said plainly, shaking his head.

"To go from a respected Colonel to a kidnapper who tortures children? And drags his Major into his ugliness? How can you rationalize that?"

"No persuasion was necessary for Major Rausch. He was as committed as I to improving America. Just not as competent."

"I guess he's a little less skilled at killing innocent people than you are. I'm sure there's an equally patriotic explanation for your connection to Terrance Smith, too."

"Well," Arminius whispered, "you are quite resourceful, aren't you?"

"My boy didn't know anything about Smith. How dare you do what you did," Ben spewed at Arminius. He took a step closer, gun in hand. Arminius didn't budge.

"My dealings with Mr. Smith could've exposed things that can't be exposed. As difficult as the decision was, I had to make certain that didn't happen."

That confirms it. Now to find out about his partner.

"I'm going to break you, you filthy traitor. And by 'things' that can't be exposed…do you mean 'people,' like Agricola?" he asked, pantomiming the quotation marks.

Arminius didn't respond, but Ben could tell by watching his chest expand and contract that he momentarily held his breath. It was the first time Arminius had revealed even a hint of surprise, and there was no hiding it. Subtle as it was, it was there.

It made waiting in the closet for eight hours feel even more worth it to Ben. The snooping around the desk, looking through drawers, eavesdropping on the phone conversation Arminius had with Agricola at four that morning, it all paid off when he saw Arminius's chest move up and down. Clearly, Arminius didn't expect Ben to know the name Agricola.

Or want him to.

"I'm impressed," was all Arminius said, quickly putting his poker face back on.

"He must be important, with how far your head is shoved up his ass."

"I can't speak to that. But as for Ms. Benton…you must feel terrible."

"Your mind games won't work on me, traitor." He repeated the term he thought Arminius would find most insulting.

"For a man so skilled at doing what needs to be done, you sure did let her down."

The change of subject sent a clear message. He considered the information before him now very carefully. No matter how crazy it might be, in Arminius's head, protecting Agricola —

whoever he was — was more important than protecting himself.

Agricola is the key.

"What would young Hector Byrd think of what you've become, Arminius?"

"Ah," Arminius smiled, "young Hector Byrd believed to his core that when he was in the Army, he was fighting for a country that would protect its citizens and support its veterans no matter what. First and foremost, and without compromise. Not a country that sacrifices both to appease politicians and liberal groups that couldn't care less about preserving real freedom."

"Oh, is that it? You're worried about the Millennials and their laziness and the younger generations ruining this great country you spent decades defending? And you think you can fix it by assassinating the president? How idealistic. Pretty unoriginal, too. Generations before you had the same concerns. They became traitors too."

"Don't you dare call me that again!" Arminius snapped, breathing heavily and loudly through his nose.

"What's that, Benedict Arnold?"

"Can't you see where this country is headed, boy?"

"Don't call me boy," Ben snapped his wrist, pistol-whipping Arminius across the face.

"You'll have to control that temper to fulfill your mission."

"There is no mission anymore."

"Oh, yes there is."

"And sure, I get it. You have a problem with a few of the nation's trends…so why not hatch a scheme to assassinate the president? Makes sense. Why not become a traitor? Why not go against everything you swore to serve. Do you really think killing the president is going to solve your problem? Are you out of your damn mind, or are you really that stupid?"

"It's a start, not an end."

"You really are batshit crazy, aren't you?"

Arminius chuckled, his eyes scanning the room, clearly in search of a way out. He moved his hands from his thighs to his stomach and then interlocked his fingers. Ben saw his trepidation even though Arminius was trying to backpedal via the tough guy routine. Too little, too late. Ben saw what he needed to see.

"From where I sit," Ben continued, "all you've done is trade a thirty-year military career worthy of a medal for thirty days of crime punishable by death."

"America used to be the best in the world. Now we tell young people it's OK to be second, or third, or tenth. You know why? Because it doesn't matter. There's no scoreboard. You're a winner just for showing up. Get the participation trophies, kids. Everyone's a winner today. Except America is losing!"

"How profound."

"I know I've crossed lines that can't be uncrossed. But this is about a country that encourages people to seek handouts and wants kids to feel entitled to success instead of working for it."

"Now you sound like a bitter old man."

"And it's about the rest of us, damn it, who see where America is headed and do nothing. We sit idle and watch our nation lose."

Arminius rose from the chair with excitement, his arm extended towards Ben, finger pointing. "Well I'm not going to stand for it! Agricola's not going to stand for it!" Arminius said, squeezing his fist. "The fact is, Mr. Siebert, Arminius is more of a patriot than Hector Byrd ever dreamed of being."

"I can't believe you've fooled yourself into believing that. Now get your ass back in that seat before I put my foot in it."

"I will defend America at any cost, Mr. Siebert."

Ben snapped his backhand across Arminius's face and sent him tumbling into the seat so hard the chair made a popping sound. Arminius rubbed his cheek and looked at Ben, the chair's backrest now bent at an angle.

"Hector Byrd was the true patriot," Ben whispered. "A warrior. A man who put it all on the line for the rest of us. Arminius is just a coward. A worthless traitor who preys on the weak. He's the one who gave up on America and let his country down. Talk about giving the armed forces a bad name. Military man to military man, I'm ashamed."

"I unapologetically do what needs to be done. Just like you."

"I'm nothing like you."

"History will be my judge."

"You didn't have to kill her, you son of a bitch," he snapped, no longer concerned with concealing the rise Arminius got out of him. He towered over the old man without regard for anything aside from revenge for Nikki. He gritted his teeth and slowly shook his head, eyes glued on Arminius.

"I am sorry you let Ms. Benton down, and that had to happen as a result. Even you nudged her, yet she refused to step away despite several warnings. I couldn't allow her to interfere with the operation and had to make a difficult decision. We both know casualties are an unfortunate consequence of war."

"I'm going to find every single person who was involved, from Agricola to the man who pulled the trigger. They're going to suffer in ways they can't even imagine. They'll beg for death before I'm finished with them, Arminius. So will you, you filthy, pathetic traitor.

"Nikki wasn't fighting a war. She was an innocent citizen. The kind you swore to protect when you put on the uniform you've now disgraced. You didn't need to kill her, and doing so was an act of cowardice. Ultimately, it'll result in your failure. How does that make you feel, Arminius? To know you failed Agricola. That you failed your mission?"

Arminius smiled yet again. "Ms. Benton was indeed fighting a war. As we all are. Some of us are just more willing to admit it than others. But as for the mission, it's far from over. You've postponed it at best, Mr. Siebert. But rest assured, it will outlast me and it will outlast you. It's ironic my chapter will end at the hand of a military man. Do you know why?"

Ben just looked at him, the anger building as he continued gritting his teeth.

"Arminius, the German chieftain, was killed by his people. His own tribe stabbed him to death, fearing he'd gained too much power. Just like, my fellow serviceman, you're going to do now."

"I want you to know something, Arminius," Ben whispered, leaning to within inches from his face. "I'm going to burn your mission to the ground. I've already destroyed the old bomb shelter you dragged my son to, and I'm going to kill every other person that's involved with your crazy plan. Anyone who played a part in your sick little game — no matter how small — will burn here before they burn in Hell. Your entire plan is going up in flames. If it's the last thing I do, I'll make it happen. Before you take your last pain-free breath, I wanted you to know that. You've taken my world from me. Now I'm going to take yours. Let's get started."

Ben didn't wait for Arminius to respond. He grabbed Arminius's right hand and jerked the thumb downwards, snapping the bone like a twig before moving to the index finger to do the same, leaving them both at a ninety-degree angle. Arminius howled in agony as he grabbed his mangled right hand with his shaking left.

"Clay Braun didn't know your plans," Ben said in a soft voice, unmoved by the wails. "So I got what I could from his phone and put an end to his pathetic life pretty quick. But you...you have answers, my friend. I'm going to keep you alive as long as it takes. I'm going to learn everything I need to know. You think you're committed to the mission? Get ready to prove it, you son of a bitch. I'm going to draw it out of you name...by...name," Ben said with deliberate pause. "You're going to tell me your whole plan, then you're going to die an excruciating death knowing I'm going to bring it down. Maybe the Devil will let you watch. And I'm starting with Agricola."

Arminius didn't respond, other than to stare back at him while gripping his hand. Silence hung in the air for a moment as Ben inched the revolver towards Arminius's leg.

"I've always liked revolvers. A bit loud, but we're all alone here. They're just so reliable. They never jam," he said, the gun aimed at Arminius's right quadriceps. "Tell me about Braun."

"I can't," Arminius said with a whimper.

"Oh, you're going to, Hector," Ben replied, gently rubbing the revolver. "You're going to tell me everything."

Arminius sighed loudly, staring at him with eyes meant to look pitiful that weren't anything but dark to Ben. He began to speak but had to stop twice due to choking.

"Given the road I have ahead of me, any objection to a final guilty pleasure for an old veteran?" Arminius asked, slowly picking up a cherry Skoal tobacco dip can with his left hand and tilting it towards him.

Consumed with anger and grief, Ben's focus only toggled back and forth to Agricola as opposed to staying on him. Arminius was no pawn, but it was clear Agricola was the head of the snake. And Ben was too grief-stricken over Nikki to catch his mistake before he made it.

"Make it quick," he snapped.

Arminius grabbed a massive pinch of tobacco and wedged it into his mouth, a coy smile pasted across his face as his entire lower lip bulged outward. Ben stared him down, dreaming about how he was going to break him. Even the toughest men in the world had breaking points, and Arminius had to know Ben would find his.

"Mr. Siebert," Arminius finally spoke. Tobacco particles pushed up onto his teeth, and he forced them back down with his tongue and smiled.

"Yes?"

Arminius's eyes grew extremely dilated. It looked like his face was twitching, too. Slightly at first, but then more pronounced.

He continued, "I hope you join the cause one day, Mr. Siebert. For your own reasons. But regardless…you're not bringing anything down."

Before Ben could respond, Arminius grabbed his own right arm and gripped it tight, his fingernails turning white. His breathing was clearly off, and a slight trembling emerged from his bicep. The smile on his face turned to distress as he clutched his arm even tighter. Then the muscle spasms increased tenfold. By the time Ben realized what was happening, Arminius resembled a man holding his breath for an extended period of time. His chest puffed out, eyes looked like they might pop out of the sockets, cheeks grew bloated with inflation and face turned redder by the second.

Arminius started drooling and convulsing as the powerful neurotoxin prevented his nervous system from sending messages between his brain and muscles, initially merely impairing his motor skills but soon after aggressively attacking his respiratory system. Respiratory failure set in seconds later as Arminius's lungs became unable to function, and his mouth hung open like a fish trapped on land. The spasms become violent as he grasped the chair. Arminius was suffocating. Right in front of him.

And there was nothing he could do about it.

75

Tuesday, June 1

Susan arrived at Saints Peter & Paul Cemetery in Naperville a few minutes early just to be sure.

The first day of June didn't bring the weather it typically did. At just before eleven, the temperature lingered at a pleasant seventy-eight degrees and the humidity that typically accompanied the first month of summer was conspicuously absent. Combined with a gentle breeze and ample morning sunshine, it felt like San Diego. She was in her work clothes, watching him from afar.

Wearing new blue jeans, a tucked-in, short-sleeved button down and freshly polished loafers — as dressed up as the man got — Tom Fedorak appeared to carefully walk on only the grass between the memorials, perhaps out of respect for the deceased. He kept his head down and didn't reciprocate her waves of hello.

She remained still, staring at the modest rectangular tombstone roughly two feet by one foot in size. It lay flat in the ground, and the grass around its perimeter had been impeccably manicured. She thought it must have been trimmed with scissors or some other hand tool. A fresh bouquet of red roses and white lilies from Ray's Florist had been placed on top, along with a handwritten note the CIA and FBI would soon confiscate for their investigations.

"How are you, Mr. Fedorak?" she asked softly when he got there.

"Call me Tom, please."

"Tom."

"You strike me as a peach and a half, Susan. Why is it that we always meet under these types of circumstances?"

"You read my mind," she replied, offering a fake, forced smile. She then looked back down at the headstone:

Anna Blair Siebert

"She must've been quite a woman."

"Oh, she was. One of the classiest and toughest women I've ever met."

"Sounds like the perfect match for Ben."

"It broke Grasshopper's heart when she died."

"She still gets lilies and roses every week?"

"Like clockwork."

"I was hoping Ben would personally deliver them." She couldn't help but smirk.

"Now, Susan…When your best friend asks you to deliver flowers and a love note to his late wife's gravestone because he's sure the FBI and CIA will be waiting for him there, what are you supposed to say?"

"How about 'why don't you turn yourself in?'"

"You know Grasshopper, right?"

"I do indeed."

"Then you should know how pointless that conversation would be."

She offered the only appropriate response: a slight nod and even slighter smile.

"Any word on the analysis of that Skoal tobacco dip can?" Tom asked.

Susan wasn't surprised when Ben called her as opposed to the FBI after Hector Byrd died from asphyxiation on his home office floor. He didn't know anyone at the FBI since Robert retired following Nikki's death, and he trusted her. She got boots on the ground to the location he provided in less than fifteen minutes, but it was already too late. Too late to learn anything meaningful and certainly too late to get anything out of Byrd. She flew down that afternoon on the private jet to see Byrd's mangled hand and corpse for herself, piecing together her best guess as to what happened.

The tobacco residue on Byrd's left hand confirmed he was either forced to put the tobacco dip into his mouth or committed suicide by doing so. Regardless of which, based on the time of death and the fact Ben called her about thirty minutes later, Byrd presumably died in front of him. Ben's fingerprints were on Byrd's mangled right hand as well as all over the office, almost as if he wanted them to be found. After studying the scene for over an hour, her guess was that after Ben broke his fingers, Byrd committed suicide to prevent further torture. The odds were pretty good that Ben was interrogating Byrd, trying to learn something from him. Assuming that was true, the suicide theory made sense, and Ben probably didn't want Byrd to perish...at least not so soon. Something told her Byrd was headed to the morgue regardless, but simply took the easy way out.

Byrd's office was clearly rummaged through, and the computer was missing from its docking station. The filing cabinet's drawers were only half full and the desk picked apart piece by piece. Though she had no idea what Ben had taken, one thing was certain:

Ben wasn't done hunting for something — or someone — just yet.

"The tobacco strands had significant amounts of Botulinum, both liquid and solid forms," she answered.

"Solid?"

"Small chunks of spore mixed in with the tobacco. Extremely toxic."

"Damn," Tom shook his head.

"Type H. The most lethal kind."

"The stuff works fast, that's for sure."

"It's the deadliest known substance in the world, Tom. Trace amounts of it inhibit neurotransmitter release and disable the central nervous system. Less than one microgram can kill a man."

"Did you say microgram?" Tom asked with a look of disbelief, his squinty eyes complementing raised eyebrows.

"That's right. One millionth of a gram."

"Mercy me."

"Kind of scary that it's used in Botox, no?"

"Crazy world we live in."

"How's Joe?" she asked in a softer voice.

"About as good as you could expect. Banged up, but healing. The kid went through a lot. Broken hand, broken arm, more bruises than you'd want to know about. He misses Grasshopper a ton, but having his girlfriend back has been helpful."

"I'm surprised her parents are okay with her..." her voiced trailed off.

"They probably tried to stop her, but let me tell you, there's no stopping that young woman. I like her. She reminds me of Anna. That girl would hitchhike from Hawaii on a paddleboat commandeered by pirates if she had to. She was going to get back to Joe. Her dad made the right move by letting her. At least this way her folks can keep an eye on her."

"Fair point, I guess."

"Of course it's a fair point. But it's not like I need to tell you that."

"Huh?"

"Why'd you even ask about Joe? We both know you have constant surveillance on my house, the townhome the Merriweathers are renting while their home gets rebuilt, and pretty much any other place the poor kid might go. You know exactly how he's doing."

"Standard operating procedure."

Tom held up his hand while he violently shook his head, saying, "My ass. There's nothing about this screwed up situation that's standard."

"If Ben tries to make contact, we have to be ready."

"Grasshopper's not that stupid."

"We still have to watch his son," she replied, shaking her head.

"Not exactly the way I'd expect a trusted friend of the CIA to be treated."

"Trusted friend?"

"Did I stutter?"

"It's not like Ben is giving me much choice. We may have worked together in the past, but —"

"You did more than that."

"Excuse me?"

"I don't think I will. We both know you're the one who fed him the confidential information about the president's Memorial Day schedule. If that ain't trust, I don't know what is."

"How did you know that?" she whispered before involuntarily looking over her shoulder as a gentle gust of wind from the east sent chills down her spine.

"Grasshopper didn't say it was you. You know why? Because that would expose you."

Susan didn't respond because Tom was absolutely right. Giving Ben that information should've been one of the most difficult decisions of her career, yet she trusted him so much that it didn't even feel hard.

But that didn't mean she didn't regret it now.

"You're the glue that held the possibility of an assassination together, and Ben still wouldn't give you up," Tom said, smacking his lips. "Then it doesn't happen because he calls it off. And this is how you repay him?"

"It's not that simple."

"You know he's not going after anyone who doesn't deserve it."

"How he got his information aside, he's a fugitive of the law."

"Administering justice you people can't."

"That doesn't give him the right to go around killing people."

"I guess that's a matter of perspective, isn't it?" Tom answered with a wink.

She sighed deeply in frustration. Not with Tom, with the facts.

Two people had perished since Arminius committed suicide and Ben disappeared to become a fugitive of the law. She knew it was beyond coincidental both had a connection back to Nikki Benton's death, but Tom's smirk solidified her theory.

The first victim was a fifty-two-year-old white man found three days ago in the same Chicago alley that Benton's body was discovered. The body had a katana sword pushed through its stomach and out the back. In addition, a large scar on the victim's right cheek had been created with what was presumed to be a pocketknife...*prior* to the man's death, at least according to the forensics report and autopsy. Inside the victim's White Sox baseball hat was a folded up sheet of paper identifying him via fingerprint readout. When she ran the name through an FBI database, she learned about his connection to Major Timothy Rausch in the Army. From there, a preliminary investigation had called into question his whereabouts the night Benton was killed, and yesterday he was posthumously named the prime suspect in Benton's "mugging" turned murder. Hired help from Arminius.

The second victim was a white woman whose official credentials identified her as "Marge Zriebec" when she showed up for work at Susan's Chicago CIA office. She recalled the day well, for it was only three weeks ago tomorrow. She didn't think anything of the new face at the time. Temps were normal, in and out. There was a rigorous screening process for all government workers, and she didn't give it a second thought on a busy Monday. The woman was a bit long-winded but otherwise relatively pleasant and organized. When her body was discovered Friday night in her downtown apartment, it turned out that her actual name was Erika Bushoven. A brown envelope — identical in size, shape and color to the one that was in Susan's car after she left XSport Fitness the day Ben interrupted her cycling class — was sitting on Zriebec's kitchen countertop with her name written across the center. It contained proof of Bushoven's extensive history with one Hector Byrd, also known as Arminius.

"Tom?"

"Susan?"

"What's he going to do?"

"All I can say with absolute certainty is that whoever Agricola is, he'd better watch his six. Grasshopper's coming for him."

"Doesn't Ben know the CIA is already looking for Agricola based on the information he provided through you?"

"I'm sure he does."

"Then why not let us take it from here?"

"Be real, Susan."

"What's that supposed to mean?"

"It means whoever Agricola is, the one thing that seems certain is that he *is* government, and high up in it. Someone who would benefit from the president's assassination and knew Arminius — a twenty-year plus military man — pretty damn well."

"So?"

"So leaving it to the authorities to find one of their own isn't Grasshopper's style."

"That's not fair."

"Whether it's fair or not, as far as Grasshopper's concerned it's a race between the good government guys and him. Whoever finds Agricola first, wins."

"Something tells me Agricola better hope it's us."

"Can't argue with you there."

Just then a hummingbird made its way into her line of sight. She followed its magnificent, blue body and rapid wings, watching it float in the air like a feather before abruptly disappearing behind a tree. Its hasty wings and sudden vanishment reminded her of Ben.

Then suddenly, she shivered.

"You know we have to go after him, right? I may personally believe he'll only do bad things to bad people. I may even secretly be rooting for him. But even after what happened to his son and Nikki, the CIA and FBI can't just let a maverick run loose."

"I know. And Grasshopper knows. I tried to talk him out of it, but once that guy has his mind made up..."

She let that sit as Tom pulled out a ROMEO Y JULIETA CIGARROS and removed its 1875-branded red, white and gold label, crumpling and stuffing it into his pocket. When he retrieved a Zippo lighter to ignite the cigar, she asked what it seemed he already knew was on her mind.

"Should I be worried, Tom?"

At that precise moment, she regretted more than ever having that conversation with Ben at XSport Fitness. She had her chance then. All she had to do was walk away. Tell him she wasn't the right person.

And yet...

"You mean, personally?" Tom replied.

"He told me to keep Nikki safe."

Ben's words echoed in her mind: *Don't try. Do.*

They haunted her every single day. They hadn't stopped replaying.

"You're safe, Susan. Grasshopper's one of the good guys. Call him whatever you want to call him — fugitive, criminal, whatever. Hunt him like one. But at the end of the day, you know who you're dealing with and what side of right and wrong he's on."

She breathed a sigh of relief, believing it to be true.

But still...

"We should all be worried, shouldn't we?"

Tom puffed the cigar rapidly to ensure it got lit, then blew a thick cloud of smoke into the air.

"Yup."

She nodded her head and turned around, slowly walking away. She knew Tom wouldn't impede her investigation, or do anything that could be reasonably construed as an obstruction of justice. Ben needed Tom squeaky clean to watch over Joe. He needed someone he could trust would always be there for his son. And with Nikki gone, Tom was it.

But he wasn't going to help her or the FBI find Ben, either. Tom was not their ally. He was Ben's.

The former recon was out there. An expert, a sleeper, a hunter hunting someone within her government, and she had none of his allies to help her. As she climbed in her car, she saw Tom whispering to the headstone. Somehow, it was clear to her that Tom was speaking to Anna Siebert on Ben's behalf. Keeping her apprised of the events, informing her of all that happened...

And asking for forgiveness in advance.

Epilogue

The view from his Mediterranean style mountaintop home in Scottsdale couldn't be topped. Smooth, freshly blacktopped winding roads cut through the vast desert and weeping honey Mesquite trees that lined both sides of it like something out of a postcard. The early morning sky was still full of stars before the sun made her first appearance and drowned them out. Five-foot-tall cacti sprouted up in every direction of the open desert as far as the eye could see, offering an impeccable combination of brown and green landscape below an orange-pink sunrise that demanded admiration.

And every morning, after his two-mile stroll on a recovering knee that felt stronger by the day at five o'clock sharp, Robert Stevens spent time doing just that. Life was much simpler these days. Taking in the view with nothing but the chirps of the birds to interfere, he occasionally closed his eyes to enjoy the gentle cross breeze across his face from the comfort of his family room. The windows would stay open until the heat picked up around nine-thirty, and he oriented the Chaviano sofas to face east so he could watch the rising sun illuminate the desert, a cup of morning tea in his hands.

When he heard the front door slam behind him, he jolted and turned his neck around before fully twisting his upper body.

He couldn't believe what he saw.

"What the..."

"Save it, Agricola," the voice said.

Ben Siebert stood before him in khaki pants and a teal Desert Mountain polo, clean-shaven, sunglasses resting on his head and fierceness in his blue eyes. His white gym shoes were covered with traces of brown dirt, and the look on the man's face told Robert his sins had finally caught up with him. Aside from the terrifying eyes, Siebert's face remained deadpan as he withdrew a silenced pistol from his pocket.

"Did you really think you were going to get away with it?"

He didn't verbally respond, but he knew his face said plenty. He didn't try to stop it. Defeat was in the air. Fear instantaneously penetrated every synapse of his nervous system.

"I've never been a fan of nine millimeters," Ben announced. "They're easy to conceal, and I like the fifteen rounds in a magazine. But they jam too easily for me. But do you know what the significance of this particular one is?"

Ben focused his eyes on the nine millimeter and tilted his head ever so slightly. "It's the gun that killed Nikki. I had a ballistics report run just to make sure…right after I shoved a katana through its owner's stomach and watched him breathe his last breath. Just like I'll watch you breath yours."

After pausing a few seconds, Ben continued. "But first, let's chat."

"Ben, please -"

His backpedalling was interrupted by the remarkably quiet sound of a bullet exiting the weapon's chamber and entering his right kneecap. Howling in abrupt agony, he clutched the bloody joint with both hands, leaning forward to get a better grip on what was left of it.

Ben walked around him to each of the windows and turned the hand crank, slowly locking in his screams. When they were shut tight, he pulled the leather footrest towards the couch and sat down a foot from him. His face revealed no anger whatsoever.

"You were her mentor, Robert. She looked up to you. From Phoenix until the day she died a horrible death, you were her role model. And you took her from me."

Filled with tears, he looked up at Ben with pleading eyes. He was sure he looked pathetic, but his throbbing knee made him apathetic to that.

"Ben, I tried to…"

Ben whipped the gun around and spun it upside down in one swift motion, driving its handle into the hand cradling his knee, instantly breaking three fingers and grinding into his flesh. He groaned, pain radiating from his hand and knee. Gently holding his quivering wrist, his fingers dismembered and bent in all the wrong ways, he didn't look up when Ben continued in an eerie whisper.

"Go ahead, Robert. Play that card again. See what happens."

"Yes," he forced out between stuttering and breaths that were far too short. "I am Agricola."

He took a few small breaths and looked up at Ben. "This nation is on a downward spiral, and I wanted to do something about it. My son lost his life in Afghanistan fighting for a country that doesn't respect the military anymore. I'm not proud of what happened, but I stand by the mission."

"Don't give me that. You killed her because she was getting too close to Terrance Smith's connection to Arminius. Before Smith died, they worked together. You knew if Nikki found that out, it could lead back to you. That's why when she started diving into the Hubley case, you got so concerned. And why your thugs interrogated my son."

"I never wanted to hurt her. I never even wanted her involved after—"

"You brought her in, Robert. After you kidnapped Joe and pulled me into your pathetic scheme." Ben paused briefly before leaning in even closer. "You tortured an innocent boy and killed your biggest admirer to cover your ass."

The whispers were neither stern nor caustic. Rather, the silent cardinal spoke with no inflection whatsoever in his voice. Ben slowly inched the weapon towards his other kneecap and held it there for a moment before pulling the trigger again.

Searing pain spread from both knees to every corner of his body. He thought he was going to pass out it was so excruciating.

"Why did you bring Nikki in at all, Robert?"

He choked between pitiful weeps, losing his breath and spitting up. Just as he looked up, the front door opened and another voice emerged.

"I've heard enough, Ben."

The voice belonged CIA Intelligence Officer Susan Reynolds, who marched into the family room wearing blue jeans, a white blouse and brown open toe sandals with heels, holding a black UHF receiver that looked like a walkie-talkie. Her eyes were on him the whole time.

"It was because you needed it to look like you were doing all you could to stop the terrorists," she yelled. "Wasn't it, Robert? You knew that would sell me your story!"

Ben withdrew a miniature blue transmitter from his pants pocket.

"It's a micro transmitter with an external microphone. Not exactly top of the line, but good enough for Susan to hear you admit to being the head of this wretched snake."

Then Ben rose again and walked towards the window, looking out at the horizon. He whimpered in pain, shifting his eyes between Ben and Susan.

"Susan didn't believe me," Ben continued, looking back at Susan, whose teeth were grinding, her pointy face red with anger. "She thought for sure I was off base...because the idea of you being Agricola was so reprehensible. She was right about that part."

"You son of a bitch," Susan scathed, watching him grasp his knees. "It was all fake. That whole production about not wanting the full-scale manhunt on Ben after Joe was kidnapped or after Knoble disappeared...freaking out when I had Nikki tailed...acting like you made so many mistakes handling the case and caused so many problems...even your pleas to bring

Ben in for help after your buddy Arminius called you on your cell phone to start the whole thing. It was all a smokescreen.

"Some stuff you brought me in on, like Clayton Braun's murder and Ben getting contacted at the golf course. The intelligence on Knoble, the dead ends looking for a possible motive...but they were all things you knew I'd find out anyway. You wanted to give the impression you were being a team player, so you told me first to make it seem like I was in the inner circle. But other things, like the night Ben called you from the city, the fact you knew what Arminius wanted him to do...you kept those to your filthy, lying self. You snake! The whole time you were making calculated decisions, knowing I'd give you the benefit of the doubt."

He looked through Susan's rage and straight into Ben's eyes. The silent cardinal didn't budge one iota. Susan lowered herself down and spat in his face. That's when it dawned on him: she wasn't here as a CIA officer, that would be outside of her jurisdiction anyway. She was here to see him one last time before the silent cardinal dealt with him...

"Answer me, you pig. You cried like a baby on my doorstep when you told me about Nikki. Put on a real show. You're nothing but a terrorist in a suit."

When he didn't respond, Ben calmly whispered, "Robert, it's not nice to ignore a lady." The silent cardinal pulled the trigger again, and the bullet ripped through his shoe and wedged itself into the top of his foot like a ditch digger driving into the ground. The pain was even worse than either knee or his hand, and he bent over in agony, wailing.

"I said answer me! Or I'll ask Ben to incentivize you again!"

Susan walked closer to him and pressed her wooden heel straight onto his wounded foot. The pointed pressure forced both pain and adrenaline through his body, and he barked what he knew would be his final bark.

"That's right, you bitch," he shouted with what little breath he had, slapping her foot away before she side kicked his arm with the other leg.

The unexpected blow knocked him off the sofa, and he landed on his mangled hand. When his knee hit the ground he shouted out in agony, then forced himself up and collapsed back into the vinyl. A dark red circle the size of half a kneecap remained imprinted on the carpet, but he did the best he could to avoid giving her the satisfaction.

"You did exactly as I knew you would. You, Mrs. Reynolds, were under control the whole time. Like a mouse in a maze."

He stared at her with venomous eyes before continuing, "But Nikki...I never wanted to harm her. I was devastated when I learned what had to happen. She was the only part of the plan that wasn't under control. Those tears weren't fake."

"Save it, Agricola," Ben said. "You don't get to play the victim."

"It was always about the mission. She was the only one who didn't do as we thought she would. Her involvement was necessary at first, but I wanted her out of it right after and she didn't leave. She kept digging into the Hubley file, putting the mission in jeopardy. Everyone else told her to get out, but she never did."

"So you killed her," Ben concluded, moving the pistol towards his head.

"I suffered another casualty of war, as I've done many times before. And make no mistake, we are at war."

"Then you had the audacity to say the grief from her death forced you to retire," Susan replied. "A nice little exit strategy. How pathetic are you?"

He spit on the floor and looked at Ben. "How did you know?"

Ben rose from the footrest and eyed him coolly.

"Everyone thought the terrorists were always a step ahead because they were smart. That they were visionary enough to know you would contact me because of our history. But it dawned on me that the best way to beat an opponent is to think like him. I never did buy that the FBI would consult me in the first place, despite my connection to Knoble. It didn't make sense, but it wasn't enough to suspect this. That is, until I started to consider that it gave you, the terrorist, a reason to do so that no one would question. I was also surprised you didn't put out an APB on me after Knoble disappeared. But even that wasn't enough."

"What was? What finally confirmed it for you?"

"Knoble."

He looked at Ben inquisitively. *Knoble?*

"The operation at the restaurant was thoroughly planned, and only a few people knew the victim wasn't Knoble. So there weren't too many other explanations for Arminius to know that Knoble wasn't dead…"

"Unless he learned it from the inside. But you told Susan about Knoble…"

"If I'd told you directly, you would've known it was a trap. You knew I was watching The Lounge Tavern that night. Why do you think I stood outside on a street corner for all the cameras to see? I knew you'd check the surveillance videos and see me there, and that your takeaway would be I knew you didn't trust me."

"So that's why you weren't in disguise," he said while shaking his head. "You wanted me to see you watching, pretending to see if I'd come after you. The truth was, you knew I would. That was insignificant. What mattered was that I believed you didn't trust me because I was with the FBI."

"Because the FBI should be the good guys," Susan shouted in his face, six inches away.

Ben said, "When I told Susan that Bill was still alive, I knew she'd tell you but keep it a secret otherwise. So when Arminius knew so soon after, I knew the sad truth."

Susan lurched forward and slapped him hard across the right cheek, urging him to involuntarily move his blood-soaked hand from his knee to his face. He felt the blood smear and trickle down his skin. She leaned down again to whisper to him.

"Before you meet the Devil, there's something I want you to know. Ben being cast as an American traitor…that was for your benefit. After he killed your puppet Arminius, he called and told me everything. We worked out our own little plan to make him a nationwide fugitive of the law just so you'd never suspect he was onto you. I even played it up to Tom Fedorak in case you had spies watching.

"When this is over, Robert, the whole world will know what a scumbag you were, how you betrayed your country. And Ben here…I'm going to make it my mission to get him the Presidential Metal of Freedom for bringing you down."

Her face grew to an even darker shade of red, and he swallowed in silence as she clenched her fists.

"Ben was right, by the way. Even after Arminius croaked like the coward he was, and Ben called me with his theory and evidence, I still didn't believe it. Not until today, you bastard, did I know the real reason you wanted the Clayton Braun homicide investigation limited was to control what information was discovered. Not until today did I know why you called him 'Clay' instead of "Clayton" when you told me about his murder. Not until today did I know you were using Roy Dietrich to stay ahead of the good guys. Not until today did it make sense for you to chuckle when I told you the terrorists' delay was wearing on Ben, or did I honestly believe you'd stoop so low as to kidnapping and murdering to turn on your country."

He began to respond but Ben cut him off. "You're wasting your breath, Susan. He did what he did because he thought it was right. He'd do it again. There's no fixing this man. You never believe me when I tell you — even with over thirty years in the CIA — but some people in this world are just evil. Sick, twisted, all sorts of other things…but ultimately, evil. Beyond repair. Robert sure wasn't born that way, but he's never going back."

Robert watched as Susan looked at Ben — the only one smart enough to figure this out — and frowned. Then, without warning, tears emerged from her eyes. Robert had never seen her cry before, and he knew they were tears of deep regret for trusting him.

"Ben, change of plans. Give me the gun. I'm ending this."

Ben looked at her and slightly shook his head. Bleeding out, he watched the silent cardinal, knowing what was going to be said.

"You don't want to do that, Susan. You've had a stellar career, and this isn't the way to end it. I needed you here, to see and hear for yourself what Robert did. But you don't want any part of what happens next."

"Ben, I..." Susan's voice trailed off.

As Susan Reynolds uncharacteristically burst into tears and embraced Ben, the pool of blood around his feet continued to spread towards the coffee table. It merged with the semi-circular stain on the rug to form a larger blob. Both knees and his right foot throbbed in unbearable pain, and he started feeling lightheaded. Soon, he found it even harder to breathe.

Ben walked Susan to the front door and gave her a hug. He heard Ben say he'd call her, but the rest of the conversation was too soft. Moments, which felt like hours, passed as he watched Ben stare out the dining room window. He saw a brief flash of light, the reflective glare of Susan's car backing out of his driveway. A minute later Ben walked towards him, standing a few feet away from the growing puddle of blood.

Ben didn't say anything...he just stared. The piercing gaze felt like the sun's direct rays beaming straight into his pupils. It wasn't anger, and it wasn't venomous like Susan's. It was disappointment. Disgust. Ben shook his head and actually frowned for the first time. Then, the silent cardinal lifted the nine millimeter towards the center of his forehead.

The barrel's steel — which had cooled from the three shots already fired — pressed against his skin. It wasn't hard contact, but firm enough that he felt its entire circular shape on his temple. Weightlessness consumed his body, the anticipation of what was coming swallowing up everything, even the pain. He felt warm urine leave his bladder and make its way down his leg. Then Ben moved the gun towards his chest, right over his heart.

Agricola knew why.

He was going to die the same way Ben's love died. The silent cardinal was going to show him what Nikki Benton went through. He would know it was over before it began. Then he was going to watch it happen and see the blood cover his chest. And he was going to wait for his final breath. No more non-lethal wounds were coming. No more torture. There would be only one more gunshot. He looked at the silent cardinal and his fierce blue eyes, watching in horror. Waiting. Waiting for the moment.

"This is for Nikki."